THE CURSE OF DEAD HORSE CANYON

Cheyenne Spirits

Marcha Fox
&
Pete Risingsun

Kalliope Rising Press
Burnet, Texas

Publisher's Note: This is a work of fiction. Characters, names, places, and situations are products of the authors's imagination or used fictitiously and are not to be construed as real. Any resemblance to actual events, situations, locales, companies, events, institutions, persons, or entities living or dead is entirely coincidental. Quote attributions and historical references (other than those fabricated strictly for the story), however, are real.

Kalliope Rising Press
P.O. Box 23
Burnet, Texas 78611

Copyright © 2020 by Marcha Fox and Pete Risingsun

KalliopeRisingPress.com

First Printing 2020

ISBN-13: 978-1-7334186-0-7

Library of Congress Control Number: 2020914097

Cover and interior design by the author

Front Cover: Pikes Peak Highway photo by Mike Goad, Pixabay. Native American, 123RF, copyright Jozef Klopacka, 123RF.com license
Back Cover: Free-photos, Pixabay

BISAC: FIC059000, FIC024000, FIC039000

DEDICATIONS

This book is dedicated to the Indigenous Americans whom I've had the privilege of knowing during my lifetime.
First, to my Navajo (Diné) foster daughter, Becky, who joined our family for a school year back in 1980-1981.
Next, to the Indigenous Americans who assisted NASA in the field work required to recover debris left by the break-up on entry of the space shuttle, Columbia in the spring of 2003.
As a NASA worker, I had the honor of working with these amazing men and women.
Thank you for touching my life.

—Marcha Fox

I dedicate my life long spiritual journey to write in the spirit of truth my Northern Cheyenne Way Of Life to my very special grandson, Skyler S. Magee, to co-author this story, The Curse of Dead Horse Canyon.

—Pete Risingsun

DRAMATIS PERSONAE

*Bryan Reynolds - Systems Administrator, Denver City and
County Employees Federal Credit Union
Sara Reynolds - Bryan's wife
Charlie Littlewolf - Bryan's closest friend
Will Montgomery - Sara's father
Connie Montgomery - Will's wife, Sara's step-mother
Bernard Keller - CEO, BK Security Services
Eddie Johannsen - BKSS Task Force Lead
Eaglefeathers - Charlie's paternal grandfather
Liz Hudson - Sara's neighbor
Jim Hudson - Liz's husband, Col., U.S.A.F., ret.
Angela Bentley - Sara's neighbor
Bob Bentley - Angela's husband; U.S. Fed. Dist. Judge
Gerald Bentley - Bob's brother; CEO, Lone Star Operations
(LSO)
Phil Stafford, PhD - LSO petro-geologist
Ida Schwartz - Sara's neighbor, RV Park & Marina owner
Rhonda Wheeler - Sara's neighbor
Mike Fernandez - Falcon Ridge P.D.
Kyle Bishop, M.D. - Belton Reg. Med. Ctr.
Virgil Steinbrenner - EMPI Program Manager
Steve Urbanowsky - Captain, Falcon Ridge P.D.
David Tompkins - Manager, Denver Employees FCU
Patrice Renard - Proprietor, Cosmic Portals
Dick Duncan - LSO Toolpusher
Trey Maguire - LSO General Manager*

White men had found gold in the mountains around the land of winding water. They stole a great many horses from us and we could not get them back because we were Indians. The white men told lies for each other. They drove off a great many of our cattle. Some white men branded our young cattle so they could claim them.
—Young Joseph "Chief Joseph", 1879

BOOK ONE

What is life? It is the flash of a firefly in the night. It is the breath of a buffalo in the wintertime. It is the little shadow which runs across the grass and loses itself in the sunset.
—Blackfoot saying

PROLOGUE

COLORADO ROCKIES
April 17, Tuesday
4:17 p.m.

Breathtaking drops along the road that rimmed Colorado's Dead Horse Canyon terrified Sara Reynolds from the start. Cliffs and gorges stretched on and off for miles, few protected by guardrails.

"Too expensive," Bryan explained. "Not a priority for lean county budgets."

His advice for dealing with roadway-induced acrophobia was simple:

"Keep your eyes on the center line. Concentrate on the road. Whatever you do, never, ever look down!"

His words sprang from memory, recommendations moot. Ignoring the threat didn't make it go away. Especially when someone T-boned your truck on a blind curve.

Their mangled Silverado teetered on a ledge twenty feet below. She stared, incredulous, as steam twisted upward from its crumpled hood in a sultry, hypnotic dance. Vapors crawled along the shattered windshield, then teased the heart-shaped leaves of a young quaking aspen—the truck's only ally against a sheer drop of several hundred feet.

The realization she'd been the truck's passenger only moments before sizzled through her like lightning. Why was she weightless, brunette tendrils floating about her shoulders like a storm cloud? Her horrified gaze shifted to her husband, likewise weightless and wearing his signature crooked grin.

"What happened?" Her words were soundless, thought rather than speech.

"We're dead."

"What? Dead? What do you mean we're dead?"

He pointed to their truck. She gasped. Their lifeless bodies were clearly visible through the cab's passenger side window.

He was right—they were dead.

The tender expression in his hazel eyes embraced her heart as affection flowed between them. An unexpected sense of peace defied what lay below. Time froze, the forest hushed and serene as a leafy chorus offered a requiem in the spring breeze.

What seemed an eternity later, sirens screamed through the canyon. His demeanor shifted.

"I'm sorry, Sara. That didn't exactly work out as planned. I know—I should have listened to you. I love you, sweetheart."

Renewed panic surged. *"What are you saying, Bryan?"*

"You must go back. Promise me. Don't let them get away with this. Please."

He blew her a kiss, then his personage retreated, fading into a swirling vortex of unearthly light.

"No! Wait. Don't leave me! Bryan, please. Don't go!"

He didn't stop, her plea denied, his only response a wave of farewell as he vanished into the light.

She awoke to mind-numbing pain. Her shoulder, neck, and hip screamed, spasms twisting every muscle as if some wild beast had torn them apart. There'd been an ear-splitting crash, a brilliant flash of light. . .

Where was Bryan? Where was she?

Unless someone knew otherwise, surely it was hell.

Somewhere far away a muffled siren wailed. Fear of the truth conspired with her blood-crusted lashes not to open her eyes. Pain vetoed the refusal. Her eyelids trembled open.

A sandy haired, broad-shouldered man in a blue EMS uniform sat beside her, attention fixed on a beeping vital signs monitor. A metallic taste filled her mouth, lips swollen and heavy, her attempt to speak a scratchy whisper.

"What. . .happened? Wh-where's Bryan? Is he h-here?"

The man turned her way, regarding her with dark, concerned eyes.

"It's okay, ma'am. Don't try to talk." He placed a gentle hand on her shoulder. "We're getting you to help as fast as we can."

Her breathing quickened, ravaged muscles and nerves on fire, but the agony consuming her heart eclipsed it all. A sob caught in her throat, words an articulated whimper.

"H-he left me. Here...."

"Just relax." He emptied a syringe into the port of the IV line embedded in her arm.

The pain ebbed. Again nothing. Only darkness.

BELTON REGIONAL MEDICAL CENTER
April 17, Tuesday
5:37 p.m.

The sensation of motion breached the persistent fog. Her eyes cracked open as the gurney rumbled through a portal into blinding light. Electronic chirping, then muted voices, the smell of antiseptics.

She forced her query out from somewhere in her chest. "W-what h-happened?"

The pretty black nurse hanging a unit of blood looked her way. "You were in a bad wreck, darlin'. Just rest now. You're in good hands. You're awake and that's a really good sign."

"But my husband—"

"I know, darlin'. Don't worry about him. He's in a better place."

Tears flowed unbidden. It had to be a nightmare. Willing herself awake, however, failed. Abandonment and confusion in the grip of agonizing pain remained.

Our first teacher is our own heart.
—Cheyenne saying

1. GOING HOME

BRYAN & SARA'S CABIN
RURAL FALCON RIDGE, COLORADO
April 17, Tuesday
7:23 p.m.

Charlie Littlewolf regarded Bryan's timbered A-frame through narrowed eyes. Something wasn't right. A few hours earlier a dark, heavy void had crumpled his chest in a suffocating wave. His white brother's truck was still gone. No one answered the door or their phones. He and Sara were supposed to be there all week for spring break. Bryan was the most dependable person he'd ever known—always where he said, when he said. Charlie was the one who operated on "Indian Time."

Where was he?

He never left without saying goodbye. Or more accurately, *Ne' Stae va' hose vooma'tse.* Cheyenne for "I will see you again."

Never the finality of "Goodbye."

The rearview mirror of his old pickup framed the sun as it sank toward the Rockies, slivered moon in close pursuit. Maybe something came up back in Denver and they had to leave.

No—he would have called. At least texted.

A week before when Bryan messaged they were coming up, he mentioned he and Sara were going skiing. If so, they should be back by now.

He stiffened. Maybe one of them got hurt. Perhaps they were at the hospital.

He turned the key in the ignition and the old engine sputtered to life. Rear tires spun in slushy spring snow as the truck swung around, then squawked through bumps and washouts troubling the unpaved road. He continued past the turnoff to his own cabin, then turned left at the two-lane highway to Belton.

When he got to Belton Regional he drove around back to the emergency room entrance, then cruised the parking lot, looking for Bryan's Silverado.

Not there.

Nonetheless, the sick feeling in his gut persisted.

He parked and got out. His worn flannel shirt failed to shield him from the chill as twilight conceded to night. The ER's double doors loomed ahead. The smell of antiseptics, disinfectants, and alcohol wipes assaulted him as he went inside. To his left, a local policeman conversed with two ambulance attendants.

"Bad situation all around," the cop was saying. "Think she'll make it?"

"Hard to say," one of the EMTs replied, expression grim. "We had to resuscitate her twice. She's in pretty bad shape."

Charlie swallowed hard, their words impaling his heart like daggers. Heavy feet headed in their direction. The conversation halted.

"Excuse me, officer. Was there an accident?"

The cop's expression clouded as wary eyes met his own. "Yeah. Wreck out one of the canyons. Truck went over the side."

His heart hammered like a ceremonial drum. "Can you tell me who it was?" The cops brows lowered, expression conflicted. "Was their name Reynolds?"

The policeman worked his jaw, then nodded. "Yes, actually, it was. Who are you?"

He introduced himself and the two men shook hands. "Are you a friend of theirs?"

Charlie's eyes closed involuntarily. "Y-Yes."

The man's look softened. "I'm sorry."

Charlie blinked and glanced away, mustering control. "Where?"

"That big canyon out Highway 17. A few miles north of Falcon Ridge. One of those blind turns."

The familiar location appeared in his mind. "Are they both..." The man hesitated. "No. The woman's alive. So far. Her injuries are extensive, though."

"But her husband's—gone?"

"I'm afraid so. I hate to ask, but do you suppose—"

Intuition's stealthy whisper finished the sentence. Charlie turned and strode away without looking back. He pushed his way through the door, then held it open for a distraught couple carrying a toddler to rush inside. Back in his truck, he clenched the top of the steering wheel and rested his head on his fists, breathing hard.

Which was more cowardly? Refuse to identify the body? Or cry? He sniffed hard to restrain the tears, forbidding their bid for freedom.

He didn't remember driving home. Only that his heart had become an icy stone, like those tossed aside by the snowplow's unfeeling blade.

A sleepless night followed.

When dawn's grey light tinted his cabin window he got up, slipped on his denim jacket, and drove north on the two-lane highway. Several miles later, his headlights fell upon orange traffic cones strung with yellow police tape.

An indentation in the canyon wall yielded enough space to park a short distance away. He crossed the road, then sat cross-legged between the markers a few feet from the precipice's edge. Blackness filled the gorge beyond, ground beneath him chilled by morning dew.

The location's sordid history gave him chills. Now it had claimed another. Someone he cared about. The turbulence and unrest of the spirits brought hackles to the back of his neck.

Those who died there over a century before had suffered a bad death. They returned to *Seana*, the world of spirits, by the short fork of the Milky Way. A place from which some returned to cause trouble. Having a violent death, Bryan could be among them.

He remained until the rising sun's rays skimmed the pines, then worked their way into the ravine. At last he arose and stepped to the edge, hoping not to see what was surely there. He gripped the aspen beside the road as he leaned over the edge.

The familiar tan pickup lay on its side several hundred feet below, partially submerged in the icy waters of Tomahawk Creek. The undeniable evidence expanded the cavernous gap deep inside his chest. His eyes shifted skyward, fists clenched at his side, no longer able to restrain a primal scream. Keening mingled with a plea for answers reverberated from the canyon walls.

"Why my brother? Everyone has been taken. Everyone! My father. My grandfather. Even my wife, taken by another man!"

Another prolonged wail exploded from his throat. It faded to a growl, grief overruled by anger. "Why are you doing this to me?" he snarled. "What have I done to deserve this?"

Rage spent, but still defiant, he folded his arms and dropped back to the ground. His petitions continued, some aloud, others silent, but always demanding, angry, and bitter.

Cars and trucks whizzed by, some slowing, some not. Sunset came, answers didn't. When darkness fell, he trudged back to his truck. As he drove home a realization struck with the ferocity of a spring thunderstorm. That bad feeling the day before—he should have known.

His brother *did* tell him he was going home.

CHARLIE'S CABIN
RURAL FALCON RIDGE
April 19, Thursday
6:19 p.m.

The log cabin was a vestige from another time. Within its rustic interior, Charlie sat in a sagging garage sale recliner, mulling over the past two days. Like his thoughts, the room was dark, the only light admitted by two opposing windows. His gut ached, but not from hunger. The few bites of dried venison and an apple had failed to take it away.

Earlier that day he'd gone by the hospital to check on Sara. She remained in intensive care, visitors restricted to family. He spoke briefly with her father and his wife, who'd taken his number and promised to stay in touch.

Why? Why was his brother taken?

He and Bryan were both thirty-six. Men in their prime. Something felt wrong.

Very wrong.

He needed the truth, whatever it might be.

He cringed as shades of guilt crushed him in a strangle hold. Such knowledge resided in the world of spirits. Something he'd shunned for over two decades.

Perhaps this was one of those hard lessons his grandfather had warned him about.

Eaglefeathers tried desperately to convince him to embrace the Cheyenne way of life. He loved and respected the old man. Thus, he listened to his teachings and attended various ceremonies on the Northern Cheyenne reservation in southeastern Montana.

Accepting any of it to heart, however, stumbled over scars left by his Navajo mother's harsh criticism of such beliefs. His ears, mind, and heart closed, acceptance impossible.

He knew deep inside his grandfather could have explained this. A true holy man, patient and wise, who always knew the answers. He could have told him why fate left him forsaken and alone.

The Creator's mind is unlike that of man. His ways are not understood by two-leggeds. You were given this life because you are strong enough to live it.

His head bowed beneath the weight of self-recrimination. His childish behavior the day before was disrespectful and offensive. His throat burned as his anger at the Great Spirit rebounded back where it belonged.

No wonder he was being punished. He'd taken it for granted that he could ignore Eaglefeathers's teachings according to his own selfish timetable without consequence.

Teachings he needed now as never before.

If you follow the way of Maheo, *as I have taught you, then you will never be alone. He will always walk with you and be with you.*

He winced as fear and embarrassment shadowed him with shame. He'd ignored *Maheo* for years. Would the Great Spirit reject him now as well?

Desperation raged.

Was Bryan's death an accident?

Or deliberate?

The sun hung low in the west as he retrieved a pouch of tobacco and a box of matches from the rough-hewn mantle and went outside. The stone-lined pit in front of the cabin was overgrown with weeds. He yanked them out and tossed them aside, then gathered pine needles, small twigs, and a few branches to start a fire.

He arranged the wood upright, struck a match, and held it to the kindling. The needles sparked, smoldered, then a small flame emerged. His need for answers prevailed, subduing what little remained of his pride. He clenched his jaw, ready to accept his punishment, whatever it might be.

He scooped up a handful of soil, pondered it a moment, then proceeded as he'd been taught years before. He rubbed his palms together, the dirt's gritty texture a reminder of life's irritations. He spread it on his arms and face to honor the Earth Mother, then thanked her for the water of life.

The fire's crackle grew steady, its breath warm against his face. He opened the pouch and took out a pinch of tobacco, then tried to recall the proper way to make an acceptable offering.

He closed his eyes, seeking divine direction for the first time in his life.

Moments later, it felt as if a hidden force raised his hand toward the east. It lowered to the ground, then repeated the motion to the other cardinal directions. The prompting continued. He lifted it above his head, then down in four steps, when his hand touched the ground. The tobacco sifted through his fingers to the Earth.

Heart and mind focused on the world of spirits, he implored them to accept his offering and carry forth his request. He pleaded for forgiveness and that he might yet attain the qualities he'd been taught.

Strength—to shun past unhealthy behaviors he'd fallen prey to in difficult times and endure the hardships required to prove his worthiness and intent as a Cheyenne man.

Protection—from evil forces that may have taken his brother's life.

Wisdom and courage—to discover what happened and why.

He inhaled deeply, mind open to answers.

None came.

Silence stretched.

His heart fell.

Of course. He didn't deserve a reply.

Yet still he waited. Being impatient with *Maheo* was as wrong as ignoring him or his counsel.

What seemed a long time later, he realized why no response had come—he already knew the answer. Eaglefeathers taught him what to do, years before.

His forehead wrinkled with thought. Did *Maheo* ever respond directly? Or was prayer no more than finding answers within?

Did it really matter?

He blessed himself again with the Earth, then stared into the dying flames until only embers remained.

A few handfuls of earth put them to sleep.

The white man will never be alone. Let him be just and deal kindly with my
people, for the dead are not altogether powerless.
—Seath'tl "Seattle", 1854

2. RETURNING

HIGHWAY 17
RURAL FALCON RIDGE
FASTING VIGIL DAY 1
April 20, Friday
5:55 a.m.

It was still dark when Charlie sat before the fire pit the next morning. He made an offering, then began a ceremonial fast. The last time was under Eaglefeathers's direction, prior to leaving for college. It was difficult. He didn't make it through the entire four days, even with his grandfather's encouragement. He berated himself for being young, weak, and foolish.

Upon dousing the fire, he climbed into his pickup to return to the accident site. The headlights swept the road ahead, beams vanishing as they probed empty space beyond sheer drops. Their lethal potential blared through him as never before, fingers tightening their grip on the steering wheel.

When he arrived the traffic cones were gone. It looked the same as always. Vain hopes flared. Was it only a nightmare?

A cliff face loomed skyward beside the cutout as he pulled in, killed the lights, then the ignition. Darkness consumed the cab. He got out and closed the door. Its report rebounded as his rantings had two days before.

There was no moon, dawn's light occulted by towering rock. Walking blindly bordered on insanity, yet using the truck's emergency flashers or his flashlight felt wrong. Inability to see the dangers ahead fit why he was there.

His footsteps crunched along the pebble-strewn shoulder as he felt his way to the tailgate. Metal screeched as he pulled it open and sat down to wait for his eyes to adjust.

Stars appeared, starting with the brightest. Jupiter lingered toward the west, Mars and Saturn overhead, flanking the Milky Way. Shadows took shape where the celestial dome ended beyond distant trees. It seemed impossible that starlight alone could light the way, yet it did.

He slid from his perch, crossed the road, and resumed the same position as the day before. The leaves of the aspen to his right sang in the morning breeze.

Jupiter faded as the sky greyed with first light.

Like his anger at *Maheo*.

Grief, however, remained, his gut eviscerated.

His mind shifted to Bryan. He couldn't remember a time when he wasn't in his life. Even when life placed them on opposite sides of the globe.

As adolescents they discovered they had the same birthday and declared themselves twins. They shared youthful adventures, the pains of growing up. Teen crushes, and heartbreak. They encouraged each other through hard times, even when geographically separated. Their ability to sense each other's distress was uncanny, this time no different.

Except this time Bryan couldn't tell him what was wrong.

There was something he should do.

But what?

Why did the accident occur here? Spirits of all kinds occupied the area. Eaglefeathers made sure he knew its history.

Many years before the government forced their people to leave the land where they were born—land that *Maheo* gave to them. Rather than go to Indian Territory in Oklahoma or other remote reservations, a small band slipped away and came there.

A few years later white men lusting after silver and gold arrived. Conflicts arose that resulted in them forcing innocent people as well as a small herd of horses to perish in that canyon.

Their medicine man, Black Cloud, blessed the area with protection from further exploitation by the white man. Should any attempt to do so, he would not prosper.

Did Bryan stumble onto the curse? If so, how? He never thought of him as white, yet he was. Had he discovered something? His white brother, like himself, was driven by curiosity and clever at unearthing secrets.

His thoughts halted at the sound of a vehicle approaching on the other side of the road. The coming weekend brought increased traffic. He stood when the driver of a white SUV full of kids stopped and rolled down his window.

"Do you need help?" he asked. "Did your truck break down?"

Charlie forced a smile. If only it were that simple. "No. I'm okay. Thank you."

The man waved, rolled up his window and drove away, expression puzzled.

He sat back down and contemplated how Bryan and his grandfather had affected his life while the sun crawled across the cloud-strewn sky. At times it felt as if they were standing beside him, that he could see them if he were to open his eyes. Any comfort it wrought, however, quickly collapsed to another onslaught of soul-crushing anguish.

His thoughts stalled at the sound of another car, this time on his side of the road. He got up when it came to a stop and the motorist, an older gentleman, rolled down the passenger side window. The man's grey eyes were kind and sympathetic.

"Did you know them?" he asked.

Touched by the simple words of understanding, Charlie nodded, any response stuck behind the lump in his throat. The man offered him a bottle of water. It was rude to refuse a gift, so he accepted it and whispered thanks.

He no sooner got settled when another vehicle came along, this time a pickup. It didn't slow down, much less stop. The dust it left behind invaded his parched throat and triggered a coughing fit. He eyed the water bottle.

No food, no water.

He toughed it out, grateful it was only the first day of his fast.

The sun crept westward, dropping toward the mountain tops beyond the yawning canyon. Eaglefeathers's absence as well as Bryan's loomed as the night.

The day felt wasted. He knew no more now than when it began.

As he prayed to close the day's efforts, lamenting the loss of his grandfather's guidance, an impression struck at the speed of thought.

Why did you not bring him with you?

He stiffened at the ridiculous thought. *How?* His grandfather had crossed over years before—

—but still lived in the world of spirits.

Of course. How could he be so dense?

His teachings lived on as well.

As he considered the source of the mysterious words, a vision appeared in his mind. The old man had given him many things over the years whenever he and his father, Frank Littlebear, traveled to the reservation to attend a ceremonial sweat, a sun dance, sacred buffalo hat, the sacred arrow, or fasting at *Novavose,* their name for the Sacred Mountain.

He remembered showing them to Bryan, who compared them to Boy Scout Merit Badges he received as he worked toward the rank of Eagle Scout. Charlie didn't argue, but knew his were different. They were sacred. Blessed by his grandfather, a strong and worthy medicine man. Each item retained a measure of his essence. Others were handed down, like his medicine bundle.

All were stored in the chest he and Bryan built from local cedar. He bowed his head, ashamed he'd further ignored his teachings. Again it made sense no answers had come. He imagined the old man's piercing look, awed when rather than scolding peace surrounded him like a blanket in the cool of night.

Return tomorrow with the sacred items. Do that which you were taught and you will receive answers.

His head bowed in humble thanks. Venus winked as a beacon on a far mountain top, waxing crescent moon trailing in her wake.

BELTON REGIONAL MEDICAL CENTER
April 20, Friday
5:40 p.m.

Sara drifted in and out, days measured by diurnal light and nursing shift changes. Even through the deepest of drug-induced fogs, she knew. The unthinkable had happened.

Bryan was dead.

Gone from her life. *Forever.*

Her heart ached with abandonment, emptiness she'd never known. Sometimes in the dark of night he stood beside her bed. Told her he loved her, that everything would be okay. The comfort it wrought was real, even if his presence wasn't. He expected her to do something.

But what?

Why or how she'd arrived in this ethereal prison was unclear. A vague realization persisted that her father and his wife, Connie, were often there, holding her hand or stroking her face and hair.

The soft murmur of voices breached her consciousness. Again, the ugly truth blared.

He's dead.

Semi-reclined in a hospital bed amidst the chirp of monitors, heavy eyelids opened on a tangle of IVs.

Physical pain trailed increased wakefulness. Fiery daggers that mocked the futile yearning in her soul. Tears flowed, as if originating from her empty heart. Her trembling hand wiped them away.

She froze.

An entourage in green scrubs stood at the foot of her bed. A stocky uniformed Hispanic policeman with a Poncho Villa mustache was among them.

Confusion resumed.

"How are you feeling, Mrs. Reynolds?"

The speaker held a clipboard, probably a doctor, judging by the stethoscope around his neck. Of medium build with curly, brownish-red hair and a nicely trimmed beard, he appeared a decade or so older than she was, probably mid-forties.

Her reply was raspy and lagged her mind like an echo. "Awful. S-someone, please. Tell me. W-why am I here? W-what happened?"

The cop stepped forward, his round face solemn. The doctor waved him off.

"N-no. Please," she pleaded. "I want. . .*need* to know." The doctor's lips tightened, but he stepped aside, arms folded.

"Hello, Mrs. Reynolds. I'm Mike Fernandez, Falcon Ridge PD. I'm investigating your accident. I hope you remember enough to help. After the EMTs rescued you and removed your husband's body, we went back with the equipment to recover your truck. Unfortunately, it had fallen from that shelf into the canyon."

Her eyes widened. "Our truck fell into a canyon?"

Dark eyes searched her face. "Yes. You're lucky to be alive."

She stared back, speechless, the cardiac monitor's lazy beat shifting to staccato.

A tall nurse with a straight blond ponytail stepped over and took her hand. "We'll take care of you, Mrs. Reynolds. You'll get through this."

"Do you remember anything about the accident?" Fernandez reiterated.

"No. Only that Bryan left me—here."

The cop exhaled hard. "I'm sorry, ma'am. We're trying to figure out what happened. If you remember anything, let us know. I'm sorry we couldn't recover any of your personal effects. Any evidence of how the wreck occurred is also gone. Maybe you swerved to miss a deer, or someone ran you off the road. On a blind turn like that there are several possibilities."

Her heart raced, fear ripping through her. Something deep inside stirred, but her mind shoved it away. "I'm s-sorry. I have no idea what happened."

"Do you remember where you were going? Or coming from?"

She closed her eyes, trying to think. The time prior to Bryan's departure and everything since was blank. Only that blinding light that stole the love of her life.

"No. Nothing. I'm sorry."

Her eyelids drooped, the maelstrom inside her head eliminating lucid thought.

"You're the only clue we have." He placed his card on the tray table. "Call if you remember anything. Even something you think is insignificant could be important. Again, I'm sorry for your loss." He patted her hand, nodded at the medical personnel, and left.

The doctor stepped to the foot of the bed, rehung the clipboard, then came around beside her. "Good evening, Mrs. Reynolds. I'm Kyle Bishop, your attending physician. On a scale of one to ten, how would you rate your discomfort?"

Her eyes closed, then inched open a crack. Every nerve screeched with pain. "A lot," she whispered. "It's r-really bad. Can't you g-give me something?"

"Yes, of course. I needed you to regain consciousness, however, to assess your concussion. Once you stabilized from surgery, we cut back the sedation." He motioned to a nurse, who opened the valve on one of the IVs. "Do you mind if I call you Sara?"

She started to shake her head, but it hurt to move. "No. H-how hurt am I? Is it as b-bad as I feel?"

"You've been severely injured. If you feel as if you've been shoved through a meat grinder, you're not far from the truth. It's a wonder you're alive, Sara."

She groaned, wishing otherwise, though the worst of the pain had started to ebb.

"You sustained multiple injuries including abrasions, bruises, and several severe lacerations," he explained. "You've lost a fair amount of blood and may need another transfusion, depending on if we find any additional internal injuries."

"It feels a lot worse."

A crease formed between his brows. "It is. You didn't let me finish. You have a concussion, broken hip, and fractured collar bone. You're young enough we pinned them both. If you were ten or fifteen years older, we would have given you a new hip. Besides numerous stitches, there's a lot of soft-tissue damage. You suffered a severe whiplash from the impact as well. Impacts, actually. Your injuries indicate there were at least two, one from the side and another head-on."

She shifted in the bed, hand on her chest. Her fingers traced the incision from the collar bone repair. Something sensitive lower on her chest drew her attention.

"What's this?"

"Let me see. It might be from the airbag. They're known to cause various injuries." He lifted the neck of her hospital gown. "Oh. No, that's a burn. From the defibrillator. The EMTs brought you back, you know."

Moisture flooded her eyes. "I didn't want to come back. I wanted to go with my husband."

He placed his hand on her arm. "Now, now. That's not how it works. Tell me—what do you do for a living, Sara?"

"I'm a PT."

"Ah. Interesting." His amber-flecked brown eyes met hers. "Then you understand the importance and benefits of physical therapy. It'll take a while to get over the concussion, possibly as long as the other injuries. Expect dizzy spells, possible black-outs, nausea, and memory loss. But you're young and in otherwise good health. I'm confident you'll get through this."

His eyes were steady and honest. True, some of her accident patients suffered amnesia, then eventually recalled what happened.

Fear's shadow chilled her heart at the thought.

CHARLIE'S CABIN
RURAL FALCON RIDGE
April 20, Friday
7:50 p.m.

When Charlie arrived home that evening he turned on the single lightbulb slung from the rafters, then knelt before the chest at the foot of his bed and lifted the lid. A whiff of cedar and tobacco greeted him, triggering a host of memories. Snuggled beneath a blanket reposed his grandfather's medicine bundle, wrapped in a buffalo calf hide.

Many years had passed since he'd so much as touched sacred things. As his hand rested upon it, an admonition shot through him like an arrow. Ignoring spiritual matters had failed to make the void inside his heart go away. His hands trembled as he lifted out the bundle and hugged it to his chest.

Time exists only for those tied to Earth. For eternal matters it is never too late.

He paused as his psyche absorbed the impression.

It felt right.

It was time to humble himself and connect with the Spirits. Where Eaglefeathers, Bryan, his father, and answers resided.

He got up and sat on his bed where he untied the sinew, then unfolded it beside him, revealing several buckskin pouches. One of the larger ones contained offering tobacco. In addition he found red, blue, black, white, and yellow earth paints, prayer cloths in seven colors, sun dance medicine pouches, and big medicine.

All played important roles in sacred ceremonies. He held each for a moment to recall its purpose. Such were able to release the truth.

Truth.

The Cheyenne, known in their own language as the *Tseteshestahese,* had a specific way to attain it. His eyes shifted to the pipe bag hanging above the fireplace. His grandfather called it the sacred red pipe and promised it would carry his prayers to the Creator, who spoke only truth and would not deceive.

Grandson, life has hardships. You must turn to Maheo *for guidance in your everyday life. You will become a pipe keeper. It will lead your life and bless you with wisdom from* Maheo.

The words carried import he'd previously resisted. He retrieved the bag and opened it, releasing more memory-stirring scents— burnt tobacco, seared wood, and leather. The bowl and stem, an ash tree branch to clean it, and another tobacco pouch were inside.

While the Great Spirit heard all sincere prayers, some answers came more easily than others. Spirit animals, totems, and even plants delivered inspiration to find answers from within.

More serious inquiries that required deeper insights or specific direction demanded such supplications be performed with ritual and ceremony.

Maheo was bound to respond to such requests.

He set the pipe bag down with the bundle and other items, then returned to the chest. A smile formed unbidden when he spotted the red cloth roll that contained his badger hide.

Badger was a revered spirit animal who lived underground and granted special access to *Novavose*, the Sacred Mountain. To summon his help, he would need it, too. He unrolled it enough to caress its fur, then rolled it back up and set it aside with the pipe.

The prompting at the site had been clear.

Eaglefeathers handed down his pipe to him, and the badger hide was a gift to commemorate the first time he attended a sun dance. He placed them on the kitchen table, then returned the other items to the bundle and put it back in the chest.

The tobacco pouch on the mantle issued another reminder. He picked it up and went outside to make an offering with his evening prayers.

3. FASTING

HIGHWAY 17
RURAL FALCON RIDGE
FASTING VIGIL DAY 2
April 21, Saturday
9:10 a.m.

To show additional respect, Charlie wore traditional buckskin instead of his usual jeans and flannel shirt. Dead Horse Canyon yawned before him, spirits taunting his desperation to know the truth.

His badger hide lay on the ground before him, pipe bag nestled in its fur. Connecting with *Maheo* was done in a specific way. He'd attended sweats and other ceremonies where the pipe was used, but only as a helper. Since his arrival before dawn, his prayers and meditation scoured his memory for how to proceed.

It served him right for being a young and arrogant fool. Now he was on his own and had to get it right. Otherwise he'd never find out what happened to Bryan.

Divine petitions were more powerful with others present. Songs and dances enhanced the effects, but that couldn't be helped. His grandfather's promise about "never being alone" rendered a glimmer of hope. The words of the Grandfather Honor Song teased his mind. At first he hummed it, then found himself singing as a show of penance and for help remembering.

When he finished, consumed by peace and gratitude, his chest still ached. He blessed himself with the Earth and made a tobacco offering. A deep, determined breath escaped as he removed the

23

bowl and stem from the bag, then set them on the hide with the tobacco and matches. His grandfather's essence settled around him as he pondered the many times he'd seen him use the sacred red pipe to communicate with the Creator.

In his mind's eye he watched the old man pick up the pipe and hold it aloft, then offer it to *Maheo* and the circle of life. To summon his spirit helpers, especially Badger, Eaglefeathers then passed it from his left shoulder over his head to his right. After that, he cradled the stem in his left arm and connected the bowl.

From that point on, it was not to be set down until the ceremony was complete. Bowl in hand, his grandfather proceeded to load it with tobacco, lit it with a single match, then puffed slowly four times, blessing the pipe with the smoke.

Charlie whispered, *Nia see, namésémé* to thank the spirits, then followed the promptings of the vision. Lighting it presented a challenge. The persistent canyon breeze extinguished match after match before the tobacco finally ignited. He puffed slowly four times to bless the pipe. Smoke ascended in a steady stream. After that, he puffed only enough to keep it burning, without inhaling.

Prayers flowed from his mind and heart while pungent vapors carried them aloft. He asked forgiveness for his foolishness and gave thanks again for his grandfather's teachings. He poured out his heartbreak at the loss of his brother. Beseeched *Maheo* for understanding of what had happened, why, and for wisdom and direction regarding what he should do. Gratitude swelled in his breast for each and every thing, large and small, the old man and Bryan had done for him.

As the tobacco burned low, he added more and kept praying. Random traffic passed, some slowing, others not. He remained focused, their presence outside his awareness. Each time the pipe's embers waned, he refilled and lit it again. Eventually it only took one match, his cupped hands shielding it effectively from the wind.

As he set the match box aside, movement caught the corner of his eye. A bald eagle soared high above, identity confirmed by its white head and tail. The majestic birds migrated south in the fall when local lakes froze, then returned in spring, usually early

March. He watched, transfixed by its grace and power, then resumed his petition.

It startled him when the bird swooped past his line of sight, diving toward the stream below. His back straightened and brow creased at the feat's absurdity. No fish or game were found in Tomahawk Creek. Mine leachings polluted the water over a century before.

Was the bird daft, seeking prey where none existed?

He continued praying, refilling the pipe as necessary. In late afternoon, as the sun drooped toward the horizon, the eagle dove past again, this time so closely he could count the feathers in its wings and tail. When it didn't reappear he got up to see where it had gone.

The bird's mighty talons clung to the broken trunk of the young aspen on the ledge where the truck first landed.

Sharp eyes met his.

As meaning burst upon him he could almost hear Bryan comparing him to "a chicken watching a card trick."

He, not the bird, was the one who was daft.

Eagles represented a person's grandfather, his own even more so, considering his name.

The bird cocked its majestic head, then launched from the mutilated tree, flew across the canyon on mighty wings, and disappeared.

Charlie's hopes likewise took off.

His prayers had been heard.

BELTON REGIONAL MEDICAL CENTER
April 21, Saturday
8:14 p.m.

Sara awoke with a start as a maelstrom of panic exploded in her chest. Bryan was dead. That she knew. She saw him depart. He was gone. But what about his body? What happened to it? Did she miss his funeral? Where did they bury him?

Her father, Will Montgomery, got up from the chair across the room, blue eyes saturated with concern. He stepped to her bedside, Connie close behind.

"What's the matter, Kitten? Does something hurt? Should I call the nurse?"

She gripped the bed rails, eyes frantic. "What happened to Bryan?"

He winced as if struck in the face. "He's dead, Sara."

She hung her head. "No, Dad. No. I know. That's not what I meant. What happened to him? To his body. Did I miss his funeral?"

His hand raked through thinning brown hair, then came to rest on top of hers. "No, no. You didn't miss anything. His body's still at the coroner's. I, uh, identified it for them. The day after the wreck. They just finished the autopsy yesterday. He needs to know what you want to do. Then he can finish filling out the death certificate."

She frowned, confused. "Do? What do you mean, *do?*"

He took off his glasses and pinched the bridge of his nose. "Whether you want to bury or cremate him. The medical examiner's office wanted to finish up the paperwork before the weekend, but I've been stalling. Until I found out what you want. If he had a preference."

Even though they were only in their thirties, they'd had that conversation. When Bryan was in the Air Force overseas on TDY, she lived in fear that something horrible might happened to him. Once he was discharged and came home to stay, that worry dissolved into the expectation of a long and happy life together. They'd barely begun to talk about starting a family someday.

Her best efforts failed to restrain the sob. She wiped her eyes with the sheet before Connie could hand her a tissue. "H-he wanted to be c-cremated. Then he wanted his ashes scattered. Out by our cabin. The place he loved. More than anywhere else on earth."

When her voice broke again, he squeezed her hand. "Okay. I'll tell them. Is there anyone we should notify?"

"No. His parents died years ago. He was an only child."

"What about life insurance? Did he have any?"

"I think so. Through his work, if nowhere else."

"Okay. Do you want me to get that started, too, now that we'll have the death certificate?"

She blew her nose and nodded. "Yes. Please. That would be a big help. Thanks, Dad. The information's in a file cabinet at the condo. Upstairs, in our office."

"Okay. Don't worry. I'll take care of it."

"Do you need the key?"

"We already have one, Sara. You gave us one years ago."

Panic released with a sigh. She closed her eyes and lay back against the pillow. Connie's hand, a lighter touch than her father's, brushed the hair from her face.

HIGHWAY 17
RURAL FALCON RIDGE
FASTING VIGIL DAY 3
April 22, Sunday
6:40 a.m.

Charlie's gaze lingered on the forested peaks as he awaited day's first light. The medicine bundle and sacred red pipe rested on the badger hide.

Eaglefeathers explained the purpose of fasting years before. Sacrificing what sustained life demonstrated a person's intent in a tangible way. The discomforts were a reminder of his dependence on the Earth, which invited humility. Then he could approach *Maheo* with the proper level of respect. Denying physical demands strengthened his spirit and made it more receptive.

He thought back to his failed attempt to complete a ceremonial fast after he graduated high school. By the afternoon of the second day he'd refused to continue. He was starving and the paint on his body itched. His grandfather assured him he could do it and offered what he referred to as Big Medicine, a medicinal herb used in all Cheyenne ceremonies. He promised it would carry him through.

At the time the only thing he believed could carry him through was a hamburger, fries, and an extra-large Coke. He never forgot his grandfather's pained look when he insisted he was done and wanted to go home.

This time his motivation was sufficient to persevere. Hunger fled, though his mouth was uncomfortably dry. His energy level dropped more each day and he felt increasingly light-headed. Thus, his thoughts turned to the Big Medicine he'd been offered when his will faltered two decades before.

He removed the medicine bag from the larger bundle and took out the pouches it contained. He remembered its unique shape, which resembled a man's hand. He untied the first pouch, finding big root medicine. The next three held bear root, bitter root, and mint tea, respectively.

He spotted something slightly larger secured within a square of cloth with its corners tied together. He picked it up and felt through the fabric. Its hand-like shape revealed what he was looking for. He untied the corners, took it out. Used his pocket knife to cut off one of the root's fingers and strip its outer skin. He placed it beneath his tongue and closed his eyes.

Before long his eyes flew open as saliva returned to his mouth. All this time he'd believed the old man was trying to stall, trick or deceive him.

The simple token of relief reassured him he could do this. He vowed that some day he would return to Eagles Peak, to the place his grandfather designated back then and complete the entire ritual.

Physical discomforts momentarily relieved, he lit the pipe and prepared to send his request skyward. He closed his eyes, contemplating why he was there. Since his grandfather's death, Bryan was the one person he could count on. He trusted him implicitly. Now he, too, was gone, his life stolen. Again, he was alone.

Admonitions arose from within his soul. Indulging in self-pity was cowardly. This wasn't about him. It was about Bryan. If his death was wrong, he needed to know.

As his thoughts turned to his brother, it dawned on him that five days had passed since his death. Four marked the time when the deceased departed for the land of spirits. He started to sing the Cheyenne Journey Song to help him on his way.

The words stuck in his throat.

Was it too late?

Or too early?

Gooseflesh crept along his arms and neck. The same feeling that alerted him to his death. Was he lingering until his remains were scattered?

Sara's father texted the night before that they would do that after she was released from the hospital. Until then, maybe Bryan was watching over her.

Or could it relate to how he died? Suddenly and unexpectedly, leaving him lost and trying to find his body?

Being caught between worlds was something he understood. The conflict between his parents's cultures was bad enough, to say nothing of the white man's encroaching on both. He'd spent most his life not knowing who or what he was or where he belonged.

Bryan helped him navigate the modern world, but now that anchor was gone.

His Cheyenne roots were all he had left. No wonder he was drawn to them like never before. Yet, his connection with Bryan was what brought him there.

Where was his brother?

Whether he remained on the Earth plane or had already gone home, the fact remained that his brother was the only one who could tell him what happened and why.

Dark suspicions surrounded his loss.

Finding those answers was why he was there.

He cradled the pipe in the crook of his arm and sang the Grandfather Song in tribute, as he had the day before. Then, once again he prayed with a fervency born from the assurance he was being heard.

It concerned him when tears fell, not wanting to appear weak. Words of comfort settled as dew on his troubled mind:

When water flows from your eyes, it cleanses your spirit. No prayer is more sincere or pleasing to Maheo *than one that comes from your heart.*

He waited. At length, another impression came.

Your prayer was heard and accepted. Return tomorrow and your request will be granted.

The sun's rays splintered behind the pines in an explosion of color, then disappeared, ending the third day.

It was not so much hope as certainty that the next day answers would come.

HIGHWAY 17
RURAL FALCON RIDGE
FASTING VIGIL, DAY 4
April 23, Monday
6:28 a.m.

Charlie settled into his usual position overlooking Dead Horse Canyon. He lit the pipe, the ceremony now comfortable and familiar as he repeated his request.

The sun crawled across the sky as his petitions continued. When the westering sun touched the distant peaks, still no answer had come. Disappointment burned behind his eyes. Until now, his prayers, other than the songs, were in English, the language with which he was most familiar.

This time he found himself speaking directly from his heart, aloud in fluent *Tseteshestahese.*

"I have done as I was instructed," he said. "I have prayed and fasted four days. I beg forgiveness for any mistakes in my asking. Once again I ask in all humility. I ask humbly for knowledge of my brother's fate. Please tell me, *Maheo*—was it his time, his death intended? Or was the accident a deliberate act that stole his life?"

He focused on listening, all senses poised for an answer. The previous impressions had been whispered, words soft but discernible. Whether they came from within his psyche or without wasn't clear.

A truck roared by, breaking his concentration. Its wake peppered him with coarse dirt and a cloud of dust that triggered a coughing fit. Nearly blinded, he fumbled in the bundle for the Big Medicine. He cut off a piece, stripped its skin by feel, and placed it in his mouth, willing it to bring relief. It helped a little, but not as effectively as before.

Settled again, he uttered another plea from the depths of his soul. He bolted to attention, mouth agape, when the answer slammed into his mind. The voice was unfamiliar, certainly not his own. It surged through him, body trembling in response to its authority and power.

The accident that stole your white brother was the work of evil men. Their hearts are cold and cruel. They think only of their own fortunes, dominion, and control. Their minds are as those who tried to destroy our people. They would have succeeded, were it not for the journey of our Father, Morning Star. Listen to your heart, Okohomoxhaahketa. With your spirit guides it will lead you on the path to retribution.

At last the dark, oppressive weight he'd carried since that fateful day made sense. As he suspected all along, Bryan's death was not an accident.

Dishonorable men murdered his brother.

Okohomoxhaahketa, Littlewolf in English, was the name his grandfather gave him when he was six years old. His ancestor, Chief Littlewolf, was one of the most revered chiefs in Cheyenne history.

His Diné mother refused to accept, much less use it, however. Her culture's naming conventions were matrilineal, which dictated that his surname be the same as hers. As it turned out, the naming ceremony had been what lit the fuse on his parent's cultural differences.

Differences that tore him apart as well, driving him from both indigenous traditions into a barren no-man's land.

He meditated on the response until Venus appeared above the jagged peaks, the words indelibly etched in his heart. At last he stood, knees weak. The shattered vehicle below was barely visible in the quarter moon's silver light. Reflections danced off the stream's sullied waters like the new barrage of questions trampling his mind.

Why?

An airy, breathless sense of purpose surrounded him as he walked the canyon's edge toward his truck. As he prepared to cross the pavement a vehicle approached, its headlights blinding. Unsteady on his feet, his hand grasped the aspen until the truck sped past.

The light searing his eyes delivered another impression, that of a blazing dawn.

Bryan's death was not an ending.

It was a beginning.

Its scope, vast and incomprehensible, thundered through him as bison crossing the plains two centuries before.

4. MESSAGES

BELTON REGIONAL MEDICAL CENTER
April 25, Wednesday
1:23 p.m.

Now that Sara was awake and past the critical stage she felt guilty keeping Will and Connie away from their home in Boulder. They'd been staying at the cabin and claimed they preferred it to being a hundred-plus miles away. Job duties at Hewitt Satellite Imaging required Will to drive back and forth a few times, but he insisted he didn't mind.

Nonetheless, Sara insisted they return home, reminding them she was on a first-name basis with the nursing staff and slept most the time, anyway. They finally agreed when she asked them to help in other ways, such as picking up Bryan's cremated remains, notifying their places of employment, and taking care of the insurance claim for the truck.

Connie leaned over the bed to kiss the top of her head, mid-length auburn hair brushing her cheek. "I'll text you every day. I won't call, in case you're asleep. Call whenever you feel up to it."

She managed a weak smile for the woman she considered her second mom. "Okay. I will. Before you go, would you mind getting my purse from the nurse's station?"

"Of course," she agreed. She returned moments later empty-handed. "Nothing was there. They said you didn't have any personal effects when you came in."

Sara moaned with a different brand of discomfort. The wreck had stolen more than her husband. Her phone, credit cards, driver's license, tablet, car keys, house keys. . .

Overwhelmed by the thought of replacing everything, her face contorted.

Where would she even start?

Always sensitive to a damsel in distress, Will came forward. "Don't worry, Sara. We've got this. Who's your phone provider? We'll give them a call and get you a new one."

It was more complicated than expected. Establishing her identity wasn't easy without her driver's license, much less any memory of her pin or Social Security number. Fortunately, once they got past that, he drove to the AT&T store a few blocks away and picked up a new phone. Relief at being connected again was realized when, thanks to its Cloud backup, everything was restored.

When at last Will and Connie departed for home she decided to check her phone mail. Two were dated the day of the accident. The number was unfamiliar, which wasn't surprising given she couldn't even remember her own. Her heart raced as she tapped the icon to listen.

It was Charlie.

"Hey, Sara. Bryan's not answering. Where are you guys? I thought we were having supper together tonight. Is everything okay?"

She swallowed hard. If there was anyone who'd miss Bryan as much as she did, it would be him. Her father mentioned he'd come by while she was in ICU and that they'd texted him updates. At least he knew. She couldn't imagine being the one to tell him.

How *did* he find out?

The next message, left an hour later, was him as well.

"Sara? Hey. I'm really worried. This isn't like you two. Please let me know if you're okay, no matter how late it is."

The desperation in his voice tore at her heart. Bryan would want her to call. But what would she say?

"Hello, Sara. How are you doing?"

She jolted from her reverie, startled half to death to see him standing in the doorway.

"Oh! Charlie! I just got my phone replaced and was listening to your messages."

He came the rest of the way into the room and stood beside her bed. "Yeah. I was pretty worried. Obviously for good reason. I'm so sorry, Sara."

His dark eyes met hers, the pain behind them triggering a fresh wall of tears. She grabbed a tissue from the bed tray and dabbed them away. "What are we going to do without him, Charlie?"

"I don't know."

She blew her nose and sniffed back a sob. "I don't know, either."

He cleared his throat, then asked, "What happened? Who did this?"

The question made her head hurt. "I, uh, I don't know. It's all a blank. I don't remember anything. Nothing about that day, or even coming out from Denver. I guess it was just an accident. I don't know. The cops have been asking the same thing."

His eyes narrowed, something about their gleam suggesting he knew something she didn't.

"What?" she prompted. "Did he tell you anything before the wreck? Do you know what happened?"

He exhaled through his nose, mouth a hard line. "No. Not really. I just know that something isn't right. If it's the last thing I do, they won't get away with this."

The hair stood up on the back of her neck.

"Did Bryan tell you that?" she gasped. "That's the last thing he said when he died—not to let them get away with it."

His smile was sad, angry, and somehow saturated with irony. "I'm his red twin brother, Sara. We always thought alike. Constantly. We finished each other's sentences, got the same crazy ideas for our adventures. It is right that I finish this for him as well."

He didn't stay long after that. Once he was gone, she couldn't get it out of her mind how weird it was that he showed up when he did and then repeated Bryan's last words. On one hand, it felt good to know she wasn't alone. On the other, the sinister implications were terrifying.

The strange visit faded from memory as the days passed amidst a continuous medley of medications, x-rays, and CAT scans. At a certain point she wondered if seeing Charlies was another one of those strange dreams she was having, day and night.

Pain killers kept her only marginally aware, but it got better when she started physical therapy. Her own advice to patients came to mind: Measure progress weekly, not daily. The human contact felt good, providing more meaningful conversations than the nursing staff had time to provide. Sharing a profession offered plenty to chat about.

Her PT was a man in his late twenties named Deven. His unruly blond hair and easy manner reminded her of a friend at work. One morning as she shuffled along with a walker, they got into a conversation about natural remedies.

"A few things are good for inflammation," she commented.

His expression brightened. "Seriously? I'd love to know what. Some of my patients don't tolerate muscle relaxers well. I knew one woman who thought she'd come down with colitis. She went through an entire GI series only to find out it was the side effects of a muscle relaxer her doctor prescribed."

One hand pressed to her forehead she tried to think. Her mind was blank, other than the seemingly unrelated impression of a pineapple. "I can't think of them offhand, Deven. After I get back to my room, I'll check the internet."

When her session was over, he helped her climb back in bed. Her thoughts turned to her tablet. Then she remembered. Only her phone had been replaced.

Determined to deal with it, she got out her phone, went to Amazon, and ordered what she needed. With everything in her shopping cart, she realized she didn't have her credit cards, either. At one time she'd memorized her Discover card's number, but that had deserted her brain along with everything else. Furthermore, its loss needed to be reported, too.

This definitely called for a gripe session with her step-mom.

Sometimes she still thought of her as Auntie Connie, having known her since she was a child. She'd been her mom's best friend and roommate at college. It seemed weird to think of her married to her father, but not in a bad way. It always felt as if her mom could walk through the door at any moment. It was nice that they could sit around and reminisce comfortably, which wouldn't have been possible with anyone else.

It hadn't been her intent, but she didn't refuse the woman's offer to help. Again, it wasn't simple. Nonetheless, her father pulled it off when she signed a power of attorney, he got a copy of her birth certificate from the condo, and the doctor provided a statement describing her situation.

Meanwhile, Connie ordered her a purse even nicer than her old one, a wallet, and a new tablet. They were sent directly to the hospital so Sara received them three days later. Over the next week, duplicates of her credit cards and driver's license rolled in as well.

Once she had the tablet in hand she felt alive again. On Facebook she found dozens of condolences and expressions of sympathy. She wasn't a huge fan of social media, yet seeing how many people cared touched her deeply. So deeply, it meant more renegade tears.

What was the matter with her? She'd never been such a cry baby before.

She continued to text Connie and her father along with a few friends from work and check for updates on Facebook, Instagram, and sometimes Twitter. Such mindless activities masqueraded as normal, but that empty place in her heart refused to close.

BK SECURITY SERVICES (BKSS) LLC
ALBUQUERQUE, NEW MEXICO
May 1, Tuesday
10:32 a.m.

"Hey, boss. This just in. We've got problems."

Taskforce commander, Bernard Keller, gripped his phone and exhaled hard.

"I'm listening."

"The guy's wife survived. She just reactivated her phone."

"What?" His free hand raked his greying buzz-cut. "You're shittin' me, right? How the hell could anyone survive that wreck?"

"Damned if I know, boss. She must be one tough broad. No telling, but she did. The sniffer picked up phone activity. Plus she's texting and going out on Facebook."

Keller groaned. "Terrific. How long ago did this happen?"

"The phone was activated just under a week ago."

"Almost a week? What the hell, Johannsen? You're just noticing this now?"

"Yeah. Report just came in. I guess we're not exactly at the top of the NSA's priorities. Right, boss? Actually, it's lucky they hadn't cut the trace. We were about to have them ax it, then they sent this."

Keller muttered his pet profanity through clenched teeth. "Listen, Johannsen. If there's any luck involved, it sure as hell ain't yours. Why didn't we know she was alive?" Seconds ticked by. "Johannsen? You still there?"

"Yeah, boss. I guess she, uh, looked dead. When they got her out of the truck."

"So, you *assumed* she was dead."

"Uh, yeah. They bagged the dude and had one ready for her. She was covered with blood, unconscious, and looked it. I've seen dead people, boss. She looked dead. Real dead. D-E-A-D. "

"You know the definition of *assume*, right?"

"Huh?"

"When you assume you make an ass outa you and me. Get it, numbnuts?"

"Heh, heh. Yeah, I get it. You know, boss, if the goddamn ambulance hadn't gotten there so fast, she would've been dead. I guarantee it."

"So, tell me. What did that teach you?" More silence. "Well?"

"Uhhh. I guess we, uh, shoulda disconnected the telematics. When we installed the tracker."

"Details, Johannsen. You can't pee like a puppy if you want to run with the big dogs. If you'd done it right she would've been dead and you would've been outa there. Truck in the ravine, plus no dealing with the stupid cops." He expelled an impatient breath. "What phone activity has there been? Who's she called?"

"Just family. She calls her father. Either that, or he or his wife call her, at least once a day, usually more. But there's some good news."

"You can't be serious. *Hmmph.* Like what?"

"Well, from the transcripts, it sounds like she doesn't remember a damn thing. We might be okay."

"Huh. Do you believe in Santa Claus and the Easter Bunny, too?"

"Yeah, boss. Right. Hahaha. Don't worry, we'll keep monitoring the situation and see if we need to take any further action."

Keller rolled his eyes. "Uh, actually, you do. A lot. This is a huge complication. With the chick alive, you need a comprehensive background check on them both. Wire that address in Denver, the one on their truck registration. Have you checked their place for evidence?"

"No, not yet. With the guy dead, we didn't figure there was any hurry."

"Uh, it's been over two weeks. If they were both dead, as you *assumed*, it could have been cleaned out by now. Get your ass over there. Remember what I taught you about hidey holes. But don't make a big freakin' mess, understand? Be subtle. She can't know she's being watched. We absolutely need to know if their trespassing was a dumbass mistake or intentional. Maybe they actually *were* cross-country skiing and missed the lethal force posting. It could've been covered with snow. But their being there could've been deliberate. We need to know. Understand? It matters. A lot. If so, we have even bigger problems."

He ground his teeth, not wanting to think about where this was going.

"Depending on what we find, we may need to take her out," he went on. "But carefully. Make it look like complications from her injuries or something. Is she still in the hospital?"

"Yeah."

"Good. Easy hit. Check out her family. See if there's any concern with them if she remembers anything. At most, she's probably only an accessory, unless there's evidence indicating foreknowledge. We just need to be sure. Can I *assume* that's a no-brainer?"

"Roger that, boss. I'll keep you posted."

"Yeah. You do that."

Keller ended the call, face frozen with disgust. This wasn't the first time he'd questioned putting together a team to bid this job. He heard about it from his mother-in-law, which should have told him something right there.

The main problem was their collective lack of real-life experience. It would help if they had more of their own surveillance equipment, too. Except then he would have been forced to demand a whole lot more money and probably not gotten the contract.

As a disabled veteran with PTSD, a prosthetic leg, and an opiate problem, he hadn't worked in over a year and his wife was ready to throw him out. With a background in special ops, this sounded like a simple perimeter security job out in the boonies. Thus, he recruited some fellow vets and trained them the best he could in the time available.

Johannsen seemed comfortable with their type of work, or so he claimed. He shared some stories his great-uncle Gustav told of his Gestapo service back in Nazi Germany. They made Keller's skin crawl, yet Johannsen found them amusing. He believed the big kraut was as smart as he was cruel.

Apparently not.

He glared out the dust-laden window to the Albuquerque airport. Beyond that, the Sandia Military Reservation stretched for miles, still reeking radiation from nuclear testing decades before. An official business address was required, thus he maintained a tiny office in an aging, mostly unoccupied commercial building. The rent was cheap, so it was good enough.

But was his team?

If they didn't shape up fast he was screwed.

The wreck was only supposed to be a warning. Even though lethal force was authorized for trespassing, it was literally overkill for what appeared to be a couple of cross-country skiers. If their presence at the PURF site was deliberate, however, it would justify their action and save his sorry ass, should any family members make a fuss and find out his team was responsible.

Johannsen wouldn't admit it, but Keller knew damn well what happened. After months of mind-numbing boredom, the team got all hyped up when a chance came along to "do their thing." They were out for blood, justified or not.

He opened his top desk drawer and took out a prescription bottle, noting there were only five pills left. He shook one out, washed it down with the rest of his coffee, then set his good leg up on his desk and exhaled hard.

His service dog, Terminator, raised his massive head from his usual spot under the desk and favored him with a sympathetic look. He reached down and scratched the Rottweiler behind the ears.

It was what it was. Hopefully the chick wouldn't be a problem and there wouldn't be any more unpleasant surprises.

He shook his head and spit out another expletive.

Believing that was right up there with Santa Claus, the Easter Bunny, and the Tooth Fairy, too.

5. INTENTIONS

BELTON REGIONAL MEDICAL CENTER
May 4, Friday
1:23 p.m.

Sara lifted her face to the sun as her favorite nurse wheeled her outside. After spending over three weeks in the hospital the mountain air smelled fabulous. The woman helped her into her father's Mercedes and wished her well, blowing her a kiss as she closed the door.

Sara adjusted the seat, grateful she could do so on the door panel, and reclined enough not to cramp her middle. Not much could be done about the headrest bumping the cervical collar.

Will reached over and patted her hand. "All set?"

"Yes, Dad. Let's go."

The car eased out of the loading area, Connie following in Sara's Honda. A few turns later they were on the state highway heading north to Falcon Ridge. Familiar mountain terrain swept past, snow line receding with the onset of spring.

The last time she was on that road was in an ambulance.

"You doing okay, Sara?"

She closed her eyes, energy already spent. "I guess."

"I still don't understand why you insist on being out here. You need to stay with us. At least until you're fully recovered."

She ground her teeth.

Not this again.

"I know, Dad. I appreciate it. But this is where I need to be."

The past few days they'd pleaded with her, over and over, to recuperate at their place. One thing he couldn't argue was the need to scatter Bryan's ashes, which reposed in a container in the back seat. Her desire to surround herself with pine-scented air and good memories was likewise hard to dispute, though neither he nor Connie seemed convinced the quiet serenity would be better therapy than their doting care.

How could it be when Bryan's heart and soul resided out there? In more ways than she could count, the cabin *was* Bryan. His plea and accident aside, as a grieving widow why would she want to be anywhere else? Besides the time they enjoyed as a couple, he'd spent nearly all his summers there as a youth. Eventually he inherited the property with its ancient miner's cabin from his grandfather.

That building was old and primitive, but held so many fond recollections his eyes teared up when she asked if he intended to tear it down. Over the years he enclosed it within a spacious modified A-frame with exposed wood inside and a central rock fireplace, preserving the original structure as a cozy guest room.

Their bedroom comprised a loft with a panoramic view of the surrounding Rockies. His last improvement encircled it all with a deck, where they spent as much time as inside. A well provided running water and solar panels, electricity. It was rustic and off the grid, yet equipped with modern conveniences, the best of both worlds.

When she felt better, she could enjoy hiking and photography. What could be better therapy than that? She'd be on short-term disability for a month or so, after which she had to return to her job. With luck, that would be long enough for her memory to return.

Until it did, how could she keep anyone from "getting away with it," whatever *it* was?

She hadn't shared his last request with her father, much less her dead husband's multiple appearances at her bedside. No telling how Connie would react, but she knew exactly how he would. Mentioning anything outside the realm of cold, hard, verifiable facts would tell him she had brain damage, for sure.

Furthermore, whenever she lamented her memory loss he insisted she concentrate on getting well. He was downright adamant that some things were best left alone.

Was it possible the accident *was* unintended and Bryan was just being vengeful?

No.

That wasn't like him at all.

"I mailed the insurance claim yesterday," Will stated, interrupting her reverie. "They said you should have a certified check within two weeks. Were you aware it had an accidental death clause?"

"It did? No. I had no idea."

"He added it about six weeks ago. So you don't know how much is coming, do you?

"No. Doesn't matter. I don't care. I'm fine. My job pays enough for me to keep the condo and the cabin, which is paid for. We weren't spendthrifts, Dad. We wanted to retire by the time we were fifty, if we'd saved enough."

His quiet chuckle prompted her to study his face. His eyes were fixed on the road, but he was definitely smiling. No— *grinning*. Like he did when she was a kid and he brought her a surprise.

"What's so funny?" she asked.

"It's a good thing you're sitting down, Sara. You'll be able to retire quite awhile before that. Bryan's policy was worth over three-million dollars."

He burst out laughing at her startled response—until she started choking and grabbed her side, crying out with pain. Once composed, she stared at him, eyes wide. "Did you say three-million dollars?"

"Yup. As I recall, three-million, two-hundred-fifteen thousand, four-hundred-eighty dollars, and thirty-two cents."

"Wow." She exhaled sharply. "I had no idea. None."

"You're now a wealthy woman. I'll be happy to help you invest it. Or recommend an advisor, if you prefer."

She stared out the windshield while *three-million dollars* reverberated through her brain.

Her eyes teared up—that was their financial goal for when they'd retire.

COLORADO ROCKIES
EAGLES PEAK
May 5, Saturday
4:19 p.m.

Since his visit with Sara in the hospital over a week before, Charlie spent every day on an extended hike. The exertion felt good and hopefully the crisp air would clear his head. This particular day he headed for Eagles Peak. It wasn't one of Colorado's "fourteeners," but reigned over the region as last to lose its crown of snow when summer arrived. Most had melted at lower elevations, except patches that lingered in shade. A brief winter refrain could still show up until the end of the month.

The evergreen-shaded incline and snow's depth both increased beneath his feet, indicating he was nearing his destination. With every step he obsessed on what he needed to do.

As if in a crucible, the cold stone of grief transmuted to a seething mass of molten rage. It crept through every limb, even more so since seeing Sara struggling to overcome injuries inflicted by the same despicable individuals who stole his brother's life.

Finding out what Bryan said as he crossed over provided further confirmation of what *Maheo* revealed.

The truth he had wasn't enough. Why Bryan? Who would do such a thing? Did Sara know before the accident?

Maybe, maybe not.

Her injuries explained memory loss, but maybe Bryan hadn't told her. Having been involved with classified work in the Air Force—none of which he ever so much as hinted at to Charlie—Bryan knew how to keep a secret.

He also had an uncanny knack for finding them, the dirtier the better. If the situation were reversed, he would have identified the killer in no time at all.

What did he do?

His white brother never did anything halfway. His determination and perseverance were unmatched, the only possible exception Eaglefeathers—who never gave up on him, even in death.

And without whose help he'd never find out what his white brother had done that was deserving of death.

Increased brightness up ahead revealed he was approaching the treeline. A few steps later an expanse of white softened the crags and shelves of the rocky terrain. He brushed the snow off a large boulder and sat down to stretch his legs, relishing the magnificent vista that stretched to the horizon.

The lyrics of "God's Country" came to mind. One of Bryan's favorites.

His thoughts shifted to his fasting episode. No wonder his grandfather wanted him to have such an experience. He smiled that the answer came at the very end of the fourth day. As if *Maheo* were waiting for time to run out.

Or had a sense of humor.

Repressed anger at the answer he received, however, had prevented him from praying for days. Offending *Maheo* with another vicious rant was the last thing he wanted to do. Venting, however, was something else, the tension in his chest demanding release. It still ached, but fury smoldered within the grief-induced void.

He surveyed the terrain once more with different eyes. Somewhere out there was the person or persons responsible for murdering his brother.

But where?

He stood and closed his eyes, sensing which direction to face to unleash his wrath. Intuition nudged him from southeast toward due south. He sucked in a deep breath, filling his lungs.

"You will not get away with this!" he bellowed, voice amplified by crusted snow. "I will hunt you down and I will find you. And when I do, you will pay!"

COLORADO ROCKIES
SARA'S CABIN
May 12, Saturday
1:30 p.m.

Over a week had passed since Sara left the hospital. Most her waking hours were spent in a Danish style armchair staring out the A-frame's towering windows, trying to remember. Will sat at the breakfast bar with his laptop, telecommuting. Connie was in the kitchen, preparing lunch. Whatever it was, it smelled good.

While she was in the hospital they'd stayed there, at the cabin. Since she now occupied the guest room to avoid the loft, they spent each night in an RV rental at a local park. No doubt they were assessing her progress to determine whether she should be out there alone.

Their care was half endearing, half annoying. Having them around to fix meals and keep her from feeling too isolated was comfortable. Conversely, it felt intrusive.

Like today.

Whenever she drifted into a melancholy mood, one of them, usually Will, found an excuse to pull her back to the present. How could she remember what happened if she didn't ponder the past?

A past her father said she should leave alone.

Even as a child she hated being told what she *had* to do.

Like when EMTs yanked her back to life.

Her determination to recall what she was supposed to do initially displaced much of the raw grief. When nothing came back, however, emptiness and a heavy, downhearted feeling filled the void.

What if she failed to do the one and only thing Bryan ever asked of her?

"Lunch is ready," Connie announced.

Sara got up stiffly and shuffled over to sit on a stool next to Will. Everyone helped themselves to a plate of steaming calzones.

Her stepmom smiled at her across the breakfast bar. "Any progress remembering today, Sara?"

She shook her head, grateful the mouthful of food gave her an excuse not to speak. Sooner or later they'd go home and she'd be alone.

Or would she?

There were times when it felt as if Bryan were still there. He'd always referred to it as his heaven on earth. Did he plan to spend eternity in that very spot? Or perhaps it related to his cremated remains parked on the mantle.

"I'm feeling better these days," she asserted between bites. "I think it's time to scatter Bryan's ashes. I'm sure he doesn't appreciate being stuck in that urn."

Will scowled over the top of his glasses. "C'mon, Sara. Do you actually believe that?"

"You know what, Dad?" she retorted. "I do. It feels as if he's here."

"Sounds like a grief-induced illusion to me."

Her eyes met Connie's, which rolled in synch with her own. "When do you want to do it, Sara?" she asked. "It's a beautiful day."

"Let me text Charlie and see if he can make it. If not, then tomorrow."

COLORADO ROCKIES
SARA'S CABIN
May 13, Sunday
2:18 p.m.

Sara sat still as Charlie placed a small, woven bag around her neck, then guided its cord beneath the neck brace. Its earthy scent was pleasant, a mixture of lavender and other unfamiliar herbs.

"Smells good," she said, sniffing it. "Thank you. What is it?"

"A medicine bundle. Herbs to help you heal."

She pressed it to her heart, hoping it would work for that as well.

"Ready?" Connie asked.

Everyone agreed so they paraded out the back door. Will carried Bryan's ashes while Charlie led the way. His expression was stoic, but his dark eyes were clouded. Probably grief, Sara thought, though a certain hardness was there, too.

Holding Connie's hand, she made it about twenty yards. Once the trail started to ascend her hip screamed in violent protest. The others stopped while she leaned against a maple to catch her breath.

"No hurry. Take your time," Will said.

She sat on a nearby boulder. The landscape blurred and circled around her. "No, it's okay. You go ahead. This is it for me. I can't go any farther."

"We can do it another time. It doesn't have to be today."

"No, Dad, it's time. Please. I'll wait here."

Connie offered to stay behind to keep her company. Sara forced a smile and waved them on.

Charlie continued in the lead, posture slumped, single braid trailing down his back from beneath a black hat she hadn't seen before. The trio meandered up the incline behind the cabin, eventually disappearing among the trees.

Another dizzy spell dimmed her vision, stomach inching up her throat. She bowed her head and gritted her teeth, chin bumping the neck brace, which sent a fiery jolt into her shoulder. She lifted her head slightly and inhaled as deeply as she dared.

The balmy May afternoon required only a sweater. Springtime hailed from the mountain's shrinking snowcaps, billowing clouds frolicking like lambs amid a cerulean sky.

Perfect for a hike.

Or a day of remembrance.

Her eyes shifted to the dandelions, glacier lilies, and an occasional patch of purple and blue wildflowers. No need to send flowers to this funeral—nature did a spectacular job.

She knew all by name and photographed every kind at one time or another. Dozens of framed prints adorned the cabin's walls, second only to the many snapshots of her and Bryan on their various adventures.

Gradually she relaxed enough to bask in the idyllic view. She should have brought her camera. A perfect Facebook cover, representing her new life. She vowed to come back and capture it in its full, sixteen-megapixel glory.

Her Olympus SLR camera was the last thing Bryan had given her, endowing it with heaps of sentimental value. It had a multitude of features—*bells and whistles,* he called them. She hadn't even had a chance to explore them all. Being more tech-savvy, he fiddled with it quite a bit. As they sat beneath their Christmas tree the year before, she teased him about whether he got it for her or himself. His sheepish *Busted!* look flashed through her mind.

The same one he wore when he died.

She swallowed hard. What if she never remembered what he wanted her to do?

A clump of Alpine Forget-Me-Nots at her feet offered a whimsical reply, petals matching the sky, yellow centers like miniature suns. Her favorite wildflower. That spring two years ago, before his last deployment, Bryan gave her a bouquet as a token. Its portrait hung in their bedroom.

Don't worry, Bryan. I'll never forget you.

I know, sweetheart.

She blinked hard at the impression, punctuated by a flash of annoyance at her father's skepticism the day before.

A patch of pink Pasque flowers, which bloomed around Easter, drew her attention. Their official portrait graced their Denver condo's dining room. More than just another flower, they personified the Greek tale of Aphrodite turning Adonis' blood into a fragile anemone. A bloom so delicate it was destroyed by the wind, symbolizing the temporary nature of love.

Its leaves were poisonous, yet she'd read Native Americans used them to treat bruises, arthritis, and sore muscles. Maybe she'd give such a concoction a try. Perhaps someday, now that she didn't have to work, she'd become an herbalist. Her options were vast, at least once she fulfilled Bryan's last request.

Somewhere up ahead a small poof of grey rode a gust of mountain air. Her throat ached as the small cloud dissipated.

Now he was free.

Sometimes it felt as if he were on TDY, that they'd be able to Skype in a few days. Then she'd remember and wonder why their dreams were so brutally ripped to shreds.

At least she'd seen him depart. But why she was left behind still troubled her. The hospital staff claimed it was a miracle she survived.

Why?

If only his final words made more sense.

When the trio returned from their melancholy task she struggled to her feet, stabilized by one hand on the boulder. No one said anything, just fell into a group hug, then strolled back toward the cabin, the others adjusting their pace to match her faltering steps.

Will handed the empty urn to Connie and offered his arm, which she leaned on gratefully. His hair seemed greyer and thinner, his shoulders bowed and expression drawn.

Her heart sank. Between her mom and Bryan, she'd already been forced to say goodbye to two people she loved. Even though there were times he drove her crazy, the thought of losing him, too, was more than she could bear.

"Are you okay, Dad?"

His eyes met hers, brimming with concern, but sincere. "I'm fine. Just worried. About you."

Connie opened the back door and they filed inside. She looked tired, too, eyelids drooping against the laugh lines that usually resided there. Her auburn hair was fading with a few strands of grey, but still attractive in its medium bob.

The woman held out her arms. "Come here, honey." She held her close while Will got a bottle of champagne out of the refrigerator. The cork let go with the expected *pop*. It ricocheted off a cabinet and the stone chimney before coming to rest on the floor. Charlie picked it up while Sara went to the cupboard to get glasses. She grimaced, arms aloft, pain on a slalom run down her neck and shoulders.

Photos—she wanted photos.

The previous Kodak moment has passed, but she wasn't about to miss this one. Her mother's words resounded from memory, always met with a chorus of protests when they'd been forced to stop opening birthday or Christmas presents.

"If you don't think photos are important, wait until they're all you have left."

She got down the glasses. Will finished filling them and handed them around. "Wait," she said, raising her hand. "I want a picture. It's been a sad day, but a good one. It means a lot to me you're all here."

Her father's eyes grew distant. "I know this drill."

Selfie mode on her phone was simpler than setting up the tripod and messing with the camera's timer, plus it would be easier to upload and share.

"Want some help taking off that neck brace?" Connie offered.

"No, but thanks. It's part of the moment."

The four mourners huddled together in front of the picture window, held their glasses aloft and the moment was captured before a background of mountains shedding their winter cloak.

They toasted Bryan, then Charlie set his glass on the counter and excused himself, saying he had something to do. He nodded to each of them, solemn expression accentuating his high cheekbones and aquiline nose as he grabbed his hat from the counter.

"Would you like to join us for dinner?" Will asked. "We have plenty."

He hesitated at the door. "Thank you. I appreciate it. But I need to head out. Thanks for including me, Sara. If you need anything, just let me know."

"Okay. Thanks for being here."

As soon as he was out the door, Connie's look turned pensive. "He sure was quiet. He and Bryan were friends for a long time?"

Sara nodded. "Since they were teenagers, maybe even before. At least twenty years. They considered themselves brothers."

"That's what I thought," she replied. "While we scattered Bryan's ashes, your dad and I were both crying, but he didn't shed a tear. Instead, it was like this black cloud hung over him. He looked so morose. My heart went out to him. It was obvious he'd lost his best friend."

Will grunted. "True. But his body language added something else."

"What?" Sara asked.

"That he was extremely pissed off."

The ashes of our ancestors are sacred and their final resting place is hallowed ground, while you wander away from the tombs of your fathers seemingly without regret.
—Seath'tl "Seattle", 1854

6. THE ASPEN

COLORADO ROCKIES
RURAL FALCON RIDGE
May 13, Sunday
4:29 p.m.

Charlie tromped down escarpments strewn with rocks, boots crunching through patches of snow that persisted beneath the pines. The way was familiar, allowing his mind to ponder the day's events.

Memories of family members he'd lost besieged him. Their bodies were wrapped, then placed on high scaffolding to prevent them from being ravaged by wild animals. When sufficiently decomposed and dried, the remains were buried or, in some cases, burned. Burial sites were sacred ground, where one's ancestors dwelt. Now his brother would dwell forever along that trail.

Once *omotome*, the breath of life, ended and *mahta'sooma* returned to the Great Spirit, the person was gone. The Cheyenne, referred to death as simply "going home." So many died too soon: his father, his grandfather, and now his white brother. Yet, he knew they were only in another place.

When he reached his cabin, he gathered up the badger hide and sacred red pipe, then got into the Ford Ranger Bryan sold him a decade ago for fifty bucks. He drove to the accident site where slow, thoughtful steps took him to his former spot. Once again his arm hooked the aspen by the side of the road as he peered over the edge.

As expected, the wreckage still lay far below, battered and abandoned. Since the revelation three weeks earlier of evil design, no further information had come. During his fast he didn't think to ask for further instructions. He pictured Eaglefeathers shaking his head, wondering if he'd learned anything or not.

Thus, he'd fasted the day before as well as this one, not sure that would be enough. If no answers came, he'd continue to do so, though he didn't look forward to the rigors required.

He got settled on the ground, badger hide with the pipe and tobacco pouch spread out before him. After making an offering, he lit the pipe. Its smoke rose and blessed the leaves of the lone tree beside him, then continued heavenward.

Forgive my ignorance, he prayed in Cheyenne. *I am but a lowly human asking humbly for truth and direction. If I am to avenge my brother's death, please guide me. I know not what it is I am supposed to do.*

Eyes closed, he continued to pray and meditate for over an hour.

As always, the tail end of the weekend brought a steady flow of traffic. Before long, the bombardment of pebbles each time a vehicle passed brought too much distraction. At that point he no longer replenished the tobacco and allowed it to burn out. Disappointed, he packed everything up and prepared to leave.

Again gripping the tree, he stood at the precipice's edge. The knot in his gut winched up to his throat as he contemplated what lay below. The breeze carried a chill, western horizon marred by dark clouds.

Leaves overhead sang, their inflection sad. A few shriveled catkins still clung to its branches and littered the ground, indicating the tree was female. He regarded the tree with a speculative frown. As a witness to the sordid event, what might she tell him if she could talk?

Gentle hands caressed her smooth white bark slashed with black. Aspens exemplified beauty in multiple ways. Their noble appearance and musical leaves bespoke clarity. Determination. Overcoming one's fears and doubts.

His eyes shifted to the ledge where the truck initially landed. The young aspen's splintered trunk evoked another strong impression.

His fingers tightened. She, too, was mourning, having lost a daring child living on the edge. Empathy poured from his heart to another living thing who'd suffered from the vile deed.

Words flowed into his mind.

Answers lie below in your brother's truck.

A gust of wind pushed him forward as if to punctuate the statement. He staggered back, startled, then gripped the trunk again as he took another look at the decimated vehicle.

Swirling eddies of sinister intent swarmed the truck's body as vermin. Hackles rose on the back of his neck. He blinked hard, thinking it a side effect of fasting. He glanced around. His own truck across the road and the vista beyond were still and clear. Looking back to the wreckage, the aura persisted, but nowhere else. His heart swelled with the stamp of truth.

His mind, however, raced.

What was down there?

HIGHWAY 17
NORTH OF FALCON RIDGE
May 13, Sunday
6:15 p.m.

Will drove in silence for several minutes after leaving the cabin. He needed to be at the office the next day, so had no choice but to head back. His employer had been more than generous allowing him to telecommute as long as he had. A big meeting with one of his major clients was scheduled that he couldn't miss. They left early to get beyond the treacherous mountain passes before dark, but it felt wrong leaving Sara behind.

They tried one more time to get her to go home with them. Much to their dismay, again she refused. She thanked them for all they'd done and promised to call if she got lonely, depressed, needed help, or changed her mind.

"I'm worried about her," he said grimly. "She should have come with us."

Connie reached over and patted his arm. "Sara's a grown woman, Will. And quite competent. I'm sure she can take care of herself."

"I know. And stubborn."

"Ha! I wonder where she got that?"

He scoffed. "Actually, she's doing remarkably well. I'm proud of her. But it's more than that."

Her squinty-eyed look suggested she knew more than paternal instincts precipitated the comment. "Oh? Then what?"

"Now that she's out of the woods, I've had time to think about that accident. I can't get it out of my head. Something about it isn't right. When I was at the Bureau, we saw this sort of thing a lot. I think someone wanted Bryan, maybe both of them, dead."

Her gasp didn't surprise him, but its reasoning did. "I know. I felt the same thing. I just didn't want to say anything and sound crazy."

He glanced her way. "Okay, woman. What exactly does your female intuition tell you?"

"Well, that's all it is, intuition. Like something lurking in the air. Tension, darkness, as if facts are being suppressed or covered up. I even feel there's something she's not telling us. It almost felt as if she wanted us to leave."

"I agree. It's rather odd Bryan added that accidental death clause so recently. Maybe it was coincidence, but I doubt it. Do you mind if we turn around and backtrack a bit? I want to take a look at the accident site."

"No, not at all."

As soon as they reached a straight stretch of road with enough shoulder, he pulled in and cranked the steering wheel hard left, grateful for the Benz's tight turning radius. He thought about going by the site earlier, but couldn't bring himself to do so. Now that Sara was on the mend, it was less terrifying.

A short time later the car's data screen indicated they were approaching the location. With no one behind him, he slowed as the blind switchback turn came into view. Tires hugged the pavement's edge, inches from sheer rock looming hundreds of feet above. Gratefully, the drop-off of similar depth was on the opposite side, the road a mere notch in the canyon wall.

The car inched toward the accident site. He checked the rearview mirror, then stopped. The hood lined up perfectly with where the pickup tumbled over the cliff. A lone aspen, proudly clothed in its Dalmatian-spotted bark, stood as sentry nearby.

His chin rested on the steering wheel while a hollow feeling sucked the life from his gut. Connie's audible breathing suggested a similar reaction.

"Something coming from this direction could've hit them broadside," she said. "Drunk driver, maybe."

"Exactly. It's criminal they don't have guardrails on sections like this. Can you imagine driving this road in icy weather?"

"I don't even like it now."

"Me, either. There was snow on the ground when it happened. The roads were probably clear, though. Any ice usually melts by afternoon. That shoulder is only a few inches wide. It wouldn't take much—a blowout, perhaps—to lose control and go over the edge. Or something could have hit them. Spring thaws are notorious for rock slides and loose boulders."

He felt Connie's questioning look without turning to face her. "Seriously, Will? I suppose either of those things is possible. But if it was a simple accident, then why do we both have such a dark feeling?"

His stomach lurched. The site's sheer brutality demanded denial. A deliberate wreck, especially with his daughter a target, was too much to bear. While suspicions teased him all along, the logistics supported hostile action all too well. He drew a slow, even breath, mustering courage to face the truth.

"You're right. It's just too—too horrifying to imagine. No wonder she doesn't remember. Who'd want to? Let's find some place to park. I want a closer look."

The cutout a short distance away was barely wide enough, but served the purpose. Unable to open her door, Connie crawled across the console and driver's seat to get out. They walked in silence until they came to a section of marred shoulder. He stooped over to examine it, finding remnants of rubber along its edge. He stood up, rubbing it between his thumb and forefinger.

The sheer drop loomed before him. His heart floated toward his throat. The inside wall was invisible from his vantage point, the gorge's opposite side covered by a medley of evergreens and deciduous trees united by brush.

He edged forward until the ledge where the pickup initially landed came into view. The small tree that held it in place dangled precariously, trunk severed and bent as if pointing to what lay below.

Without it Sara would have died, too.

He took another cautious step. The crumpled vehicle looked like a toy, its chassis partially inundated by some random mountain stream.

Connie raised a hand to wipe her eyes. "Oh, Will. Who would do such a horrible thing?"

Too troubled to answer at first, he took her hand. "I don't know," he replied at last. "But I'm sure as hell going to find out."

He captured a few photos with his phone, noting there were no skid marks from either direction. After one final look at the wreckage, he draped his arm around her shoulders and returned to the car.

He was so worried about Sara that he hadn't paid that much attention to the wreck or its cause. Losing one woman he loved was bad enough. Now that he'd acknowledged his suspicions, further reinforced by his wife, it was time to see the accident report. He set his jaw, mad at himself for not doing so weeks before.

When they got to Falcon Ridge it didn't take long to find the police station in what was best described as a one-horse town. The greying desk sergeant beyond the wooden barrier looked up as they entered, his unmasked scrutiny broadcasting suspicion. He straightened in his chair.

"Can I help you?"

"I hope so. I'm William Montgomery, Sara Reynolds's father. I wondered if I could get a copy of the police report from her accident?"

"Hold on. I'll see if the officer in charge is still here." He picked up the phone and rang someone in the next room. "Hey, is Fernandez still around? Someone's here asking about the Reynolds case." The man nodded and motioned to the chairs against the wall. "He'll be here shortly. Just came in from his shift."

"Thanks."

Minutes later, a stocky, dark-haired cop with a heavy mustache appeared, opened the gate, and beckoned them through.

The man held out his hand. "Mike Fernandez."

"Will Montgomery, and my wife, Connie." He returned his firm handshake, then followed to a cramped glass-walled office.

They sat on metal folding chairs while the cop closed the door, then sat down behind a timeworn desk. He opened a drawer and removed a digital recorder. "Do you mind if I record our conversation?"

Will and Connie exchanged a look. "No, not at all," he said.

The cop turned on the device, stated the case number, date, and time, then placed it on the desk between them. "So you're related to the survivor?"

"Yes. She's my daughter. I was wondering what you can tell me about the accident. What were the results of your investigation?"

"No-can-do. That case is still open."

Will straightened in the chair, suspicions affirmed. "Why? Do you suspect foul play?"

"We haven't ruled it out."

His jaw tensed, feelings mixed that his and Connie's instincts were spot-on. "Can you tell me if you've made any progress? Or what you're looking for?"

"No. That's all confidential."

"Can you at least tell me who found the wreck? Who reported it and when? Were there any witnesses?"

"No witnesses, at least that we know of. Their truck was equipped with one of those automatic notification systems. When the airbags deployed, it summoned their dispatch center, which notified us, based on their GPS coordinates. That was how we found out." He retrieved a file folder from a drawer, then picked through its contents. "The notification came in at 16:17 on 17 April. No telling how long it would have taken otherwise."

"Oh. Thank God they had that."

"Yeah. Your daughter would have bled to death if we'd gotten there any later."

Will closed his eyes and shuddered.

"So, were your daughter and her husband getting along okay? Any marital issues?" the cop went on.

Hardly the question he expected. "No, not at all. They were very happy. He came back from Afghanistan less than a year ago. He served over there in the Air Force. After his discharge, they were just getting back into a normal life."

"You're sure of that?"

"Yes! Quite. Why?"

"Single vehicle accidents like that are often suicides. Harder to prove as such. So, your son-in-law was a veteran. Did he have PTSD?"

"No. Fortunately, he was mostly behind the scenes over there. Communications guy. He was glad to be home, but no problems, other than the usual for someone who's been in a warzone. I think he had some nightmares at first. That's about it, as far as I know."

"I understand he had a big insurance policy."

"What does that have to do with anything?"

"Possibly a lot. Who's the beneficiary?"

"My daughter."

"Any secondaries?"

"I have no idea." Will seethed, irritated by the implications. Until he realized that he *did* know, having filed the claim. "No, wait. Actually, I do. It was a friend of theirs, Charles Littlewolf."

"Is that the Indian around here who's a hiking and fishing guide?"

"Probably. He helped scatter Bryan's ashes. They were close friends for years."

"Does Littlewolf have family in this area?"

"I don't think so. I'm sure Bryan knew, maybe my daughter does. He doesn't talk much."

Fernandez's smile was grim. "Indians seldom do. Do you know if your daughter or son-in-law have any enemies? Anyone who'd want either or both of them dead?"

His heart sank as the same ominous feeling struck again. He looked the other man square in the eye. "No, I don't. But I have to tell you, there's something very suspicious going on. I don't like it and I expect you to find out what."

"We're doing all we can to close the case. If you don't mind, I'd like to add your contact information to the file."

Will pulled out his wallet, extracted a business card, and handed it over. "Do you have any objections to me seeing what I can find out? Possibly putting a PI on the case?"

"We don't have the authority to tell you not to. Besides, we've got limited staff around here and can always use additional help. We'd appreciate it, in the event you do engage a PI, if he'd check in with us, though. Here's my card."

"Thanks."

The two men shook hands again, after which he and Connie returned to the car. He sat there a moment, thinking, uneasy feeling lingering on.

"They know something," he declared, meeting her emerald-eyed gaze. He pressed the ignition button. "And I'd sure like to know what."

Everybody sooner or later sits down to a banquet of circumstances.
—Robert Louis Stevenson

7. NEIGHBORS

BKSS LLC
ALBUQUERQUE, NM
May 14, Monday
9:03 a.m.

"Hey, boss. This just in on the Reynolds job."

Keller set down his coffee and muted the morning news. "Go ahead, Johannsen."

"Their being there at the site definitely looks intentional. We recovered some interesting evidence in Denver, including, uh, well, a couple of rather nice pieces."

"Okay. Good. Except now we need to figure out his source. Did the background checks come in?"

"Yeah. They should be in your inbox. He's former Air Force. IT guy. She works at some physical therapy place. No police record for either."

"Any trouble getting into their house?"

He laughed, hard. "No. We have a key, remember? Besides, the place is deserted. We watched it a while and its clear she's not staying in Denver."

"No? Then where?"

"Well, we, uh, figured she went home from the hospital with her family. She, uh, well, she, uh, didn't."

"Another assumption, right?"

"Uh, yeah. I guess. Phone records just came in. You know how they're delayed. Not our fault. Anyway, cell tower data indicates she's in a rural area out in Belton County. We checked it out. Turns out they have a second home. A cabin. Stone's throw from the work site."

Bernie barked out an expletive. "Let me guess. This cabin of theirs. It hasn't been secured."

"Correct."

He blew out a breath, put him on speaker and got a bottle of hydrocodone out of his desk. He bumped out a tablet, made it two, then washed them down with a gulp of tepid black coffee.

"Also, the local cops called," Johannsen went on. "Her old man stopped by asking questions. Lots of questions. Contact information he gave matches what we already had. Name's Montgomery. William Montgomery."

Johannsen's tone suggested there was more and it wasn't good. "And?"

"He's former FBI."

The throbbing in his temples defied the opiates and exploded into a blinding headache. "Great. Just what we need. Operative?"

"No. Analyst."

"No better, possibly worse."

He spit out another expletive, head spinning. Why couldn't the guy manage a grocery store or something? Messing with a former spook was probably the stupidest thing they could possibly do.

Except for hurting the guy's little girl, an even worse move.

"So what do we do, boss?"

"Just sit tight for now. Keep watching. All of 'em. See what happens. He knows how this works. If he figures it out, he may be smart enough to leave it alone."

"And if he doesn't?"

"Then we scare the piss out of all of them. Get a tracker on her car. Sweep and wire the goddamn cabin. As covertly as possible. She's got to leave sometime. No drama. *Capiche?* Until you get inside, put a boom mic outside somewhere. I'm sure she opens the windows this time of year. Daddy's place, too. Think you can handle that?"

"Yeah, boss. Roger that."

Bernie hung up, heart racing. His fist slammed the desk. Terminator scrambled to all fours and nudged his arm. He rubbed the dog's head, convinced the Rottie had more brains than his entire freakin' team.

If he could be there to supervise none of this crap would have happened. What should have constituted a no-brainer obviously didn't to them. He had to tell them virtually everything in advance, step by freakin' step. If real-time contingencies came up, which was sure to happen in that line of work, things went straight to hell.

His shoulders sagged beneath the weight of truth—they were stark amateurs and lousy ones at that.

Unfortunately, his last arrest resulted in terms that bound him to New Mexico. Leaving represented too much risk, especially considering the nature of the work.

His parole officer would not be amused.

His career aspirations faded more each time they screwed up something else. Contract mercenary teams made obscene amounts of money as security forces overseas. Oil companies in particular paid incomprehensible seven and eight-figure fees for such services in Third World countries run by corrupt dictators.

He didn't know if the job's drilling contractor had any foreign interests, but they'd have connections within the oil and gas industry. However, if his team couldn't handle a job as simple as this one, the chances of landing anything more lucrative overseas were right up there with the proverbial snowball in hell.

Hopefully that Reynolds woman would leave it alone. Her father, too. If they didn't, it would mean a helluva lot more trouble for all concerned.

SARA'S CABIN
RURAL FALCON RIDGE
May 16, Wednesday
10:05 a.m.

Sara pedaled away on her stationary bike, staring out the window to a flawless blanket of white. A day or so after scattering Bryan's ashes a spring storm came through, bringing the snow line below the cabin. It was starting to melt, though what replaced it was a soggy, muddy mess.

Nearly a week had passed since she was on her own. Bryan's plea haunted her continually. Still nothing came back, as if her memory were secured in a vault. Before the accident she must have known. All she could do was be patient and give her poor, injured brain a chance to recover.

Patience, however, was not her forté. What if her memory never returned? Or her brain, for that matter. Several times a day she'd go into a room for something, then have no idea for what or why. This had to be what it felt like to be really old.

So far, she hadn't gone anywhere. Will and Connie stocked up the fridge and freezer, but supplies were dwindling. She needed to do some shopping and pick up her mail, but dreaded it. Especially in such sloppy weather.

She got off her bike, stretched, then admonished herself for being a wimp. Determined to just be done with it, she put on a sweater, slipped on her boots, then grabbed her purse from the back of a kitchen chair. Out on the deck, she locked the deadbolt with the spare key they loaned to guests, since hers was lost. The neck brace and sundry other discomforts made their presence known as she gripped the handrail and crept down the stairs, one at a time.

At ground level she stopped, looking for the best route around the slushy mess. Fortunately, the driveway was mostly gravel, minimizing the mud, but slippery. She made it to her car and eased inside, accompanied by sundry aches and pains. Her eyes traced the way back up the steps to the deck.

What would it be like hauling groceries?

Ugh! What was the matter with her? For heaven sake, what did she tell her PT patients all the time? *Look for ways to make your life easier.*

The back deck was level with the ground. Parking up there, then using the back door would eliminate the stairs.

Duh. What an idiot.

She swung around and backed up until the tires churned vainly in the slush. She gritted her teeth, hoping she wasn't stuck, relieved when the car moved forward, then sloshed and slid down the half mile or so to the main road.

She hadn't been by the wreck site since. Her heart and mind raced, consumed by panic at the thought. Fortunately, her mailbox was only a mile away in the opposite direction. She used to enjoy a brisk walk or jog to pick it up.

There wouldn't be much, if any, mail. Bills for their condo were all on autopay. When she got there, she found nothing but ads. What mail was in Denver? Fortunately, they'd opted for one of the larger boxes to accommodate Bryan's online shopping habit.

One errand down, she continued toward Falcon Ridge's Grocery Pantry. Driving wasn't difficult or uncomfortable, the worst part getting in and out of the car.

While passing one of many unprotected drop-offs, an oncoming Dodge pickup came toward her, slightly over the center line. Electrified with fear, she gripped the steering wheel with white-knuckled hands, then edged over as far as she dared, hugging the narrow shoulder as the truck whizzed past. The only thing between her and the cliff was an aging wall of dirty snow.

The road's two lanes were separated by a double yellow line, but few understood the concept. Speed limits weren't posted, much less enforced. Area ranchers drove over-sized trucks, often pulling trailers, that crept unbidden into oncoming lane. Traffic was sparse, but treacherous, especially the high number of cement and dump trucks lured by increasing development.

Her hands trembled as she eased back onto the roadway. Squealing brakes punctuated with a blast of a horn came from behind. She jumped, startled, then floored the accelerator as she lifted her arm in an apologetic wave.

Her nerves gradually settled as she wound through mountain passes toward her destination, fifteen miles away. Her neck and shoulder muscles remained tense until she came around the last bend within sight of the small shopping center.

Originally a village that supported both summer and winter recreation areas, it had grown into a small town of just over a thousand people. A vacation/retirement community about a half-mile away was gaining popularity. Many were retirees from New Mexico, Texas, and a few from Arizona, who spent summers there. Their enthusiasm at escaping their heat-infested southern homes was contagious. More cars than usual crowded the parking lot indicating the migratory snowbirds had arrived.

Any designated handicapped spots were hidden by slush, her temporary tag dangling from the mirror in meaningless futility. She grimaced when the only space was several yards away, between an Expedition and a flat-bed farm truck. The Honda eased between them, surrounded by mud-encrusted wheel-wells. More than ever she missed their Silverado, though it never would have fit. Climbing into its cab wouldn't be easy, either.

She stepped gingerly through the icy slop and hobbled to the store's entrance just as one of the year-round couples came out. Jim Hudson was a retired Air Force colonel who'd fallen in love with the area, thanks to Bryan, when they'd both been stationed in Colorado Springs. His wife, Liz, was slightly less enthusiastic, missing her socialite friends and metropolitan lifestyle, but nonetheless friendly. The woman spotted her and headed her way.

"Oh, my goodness! How are you, dear?" She dodged the neck brace to give her a cautious hug. As always, her dyed red hair was groomed to perfection, likewise her fire engine red nails. "We were so sorry to hear about your horrible accident. I must say I'm surprised you're still here." She giggled. "Oh—I mean *here*, not just alive. Of course, you're alive!"

Sara shifted her weight to favor her bad hip. "Thank you. Actually, being here was more comfortable. Our Denver condo has two stories. At the cabin I can stay in the guest room on the main floor until I'm ready for stairs."

The woman tilted her head. "Do you need any help? Can I bring you a meal or anything? Does someone help with your housework?"

Her heart warmed at the kind offer. "No, I'm fine. Thanks for offering, though." She could tell the woman was hungry for conversation while her husband's eyes were glazing over. "Anything new down your way in Lakeview Manor?"

"Well, Edna Parker's not feeling well, so we're taking her into the clinic in Belton later this afternoon."

"I hope it's nothing serious." Edna was a widow in her late sixties who stayed mostly to herself. Back when Sara would take her morning jog she often saw her working in her garden. She said hello once or twice, but that was it.

"Bob and Angela Bentley arrived a little over a week ago," Mrs. Hudson went on. "She's gradually getting used to the altitude. When she's up to it, I'll get the usual Mah Jongg group together. I hope Edna will be able to join us again. Angela doesn't want Rhonda to come, if she can avoid it. Would you be interested, dear?"

With some effort, she recalled the Bentleys were Texans and he was a semi-retired federal judge. Rhonda was a year-round resident in her fifties on disability.

"Thanks for the invitation. I'll think about it, Mrs. Hudson."

"Oh, please! Call me Liz. Listen, we'd love to have you. Then we'll have our foursome." She leaned closer and lowered her voice. "I'd rather not have to ask Ida, either." The woman rolled her eyes.

Ida Schwartz and her husband, Sam, ran the RV park on Lake Wilson where Will and Connie had stayed. There was something a little off about them, too.

Liz gave her a concerned look and patted her arm. "I'll let you go, dear. You look as if you're hurting. Call or text about Mah Jongg, okay? You have my number, right?"

"Yes, I sure do."

Liz gave her a careful hug, then they went their respective ways. Sara's mind cycled, mostly blank, as she proceeded into the store, trying to remember how to play Mah Jongg.

CHARLIE'S CABIN
RURAL FALCON RIDGE
May 18, Friday
2:32 p.m.

Charlie's canoe slouched against the north side of his cabin, beneath a tarp and a foot of snow. The compulsion to get down to Bryan's truck nagged him for days. Then a storm blew in. Digging out the craft, much less dragging it down slippery, snow-encrusted banks to the creek quickly doused his intent.

Impatience raged. Until the weather cooperated, however, it would have to wait. At least the sun was out. Snow would start to melt and, with luck, be gone in a few days. A week at most.

Unless another storm blew in.

His brow crinkled. Snow on that side of his house lingered far longer. That also applied to the banks of the creek. At this rate, it might be June.

Would any evidence be gone by then?

He slipped his denim jacket over his flannel shirt, pulled on his gloves, and went outside to check for winter or animal damage. If he found any, he could get it repaired and ready to go.

The snow was halfway to his knees as he trudged around to the side of the house. He brushed off the tarp, then yanked it off. No obvious problems, so he grabbed the craft by the gunwales, pulled it over, and inspected the inside.

A memory jumped out of when he and Bryan had built it.

As boys, they wanted an authentic dug-out canoe. It didn't take long to realize that was far more ambitious than expected. Bryan's grandfather offered to buy them an aluminum one. In response, he and Bryan exchanged a look, both wearing sour faces. Finally, old man Reynolds agreed to buy them a kit to build a wooden one, which they'd assembled together, with a little help.

A wistful smile claimed his expression as he recalled their adventures exploring local streams and fishing on Lake Wilson.

Not seeing any damage, he tilted it back up against the wall and replaced the tarp. Back inside, he shed his jacket and dropped into his chair, pondering the multitude of spring-fed tributaries to the Colorado River. He knew exactly how to reach the accident site, even though he hadn't been there for years. With no fish there was no reason to.

Leaching from abandoned mines polluted multiple streams, causing fish and aquatic life to die. Wildlife populations plummeted, some poisoned, survivors leaving the area. Anger festered. The white man not only invaded their territory, but destroyed it.

Given to his people by *Maheo*, stolen by palefaces, partially returned, then taken back yet again when gold was found. Indian givers, indeed. They extracted everything of value, polluting the land in the process. Living in harmony with the Earth was inherent to his culture. Such destructive ways were inexcusable, in some cases even punishable.

Money didn't represent value—resources did. Bryan and Sara understood. But too many didn't care. Profits came first. The earth, wildlife, and even humans dismissed as chaff before the wind.

The 2015 Gold King Mine disaster in the southern part of the state caused catastrophic economic impact to his mother's people in the Navajo Nation. Anger stirred as he recalled what her letter revealed versus what the news media reported.

The EPA miscalculated the amount of acid mine drainage they were charged to remove and failed to contain it. As a result, millions of gallons of tainted water flowed downstream. It began in a tributary to the Animas River near Silverton, eventually reaching the San Juan River, which approximately two thousand of his people depended upon for crop irrigation, home gardens, and livestock.

Ironically, the few crops that survived were later shunned at market for fear they were contaminated, further contributing to financial disaster. Compensation from the government was minimal and far from adequate, often never delivered at all.

Broken government promises spanned hundreds of years.

We will be known forever by the tracks we leave.
—Plains Indian Proverb

8. LEAKS

SARA'S CABIN
RURAL FALCON RIDGE
May 21, Monday
10:17 a.m.

Every morning Sara checked her tablet for the local scuttlebutt on *myneighbors.com*. The first item was a funeral notice for Edna Parker. Several neighbors had posted tearful emojis and expressions of sympathy to her family.

A more practical comment noted that Edna's house was already snatched up by an anonymous commercial buyer. Since the area was growing, it had good investment potential, and her heirs, who were all out of state, were apparently relieved to dispense with it through minimal effort.

Sara's mind raced with suspicions. How could they have known so quickly that the property was available?

Furthermore, it took months to settle an estate. Even her mother's took time. She had a will and left everything to her father—except she'd owned real estate before they got married, making it more complicated. Based on what Edna's house was worth, it would need to go through probate.

Did someone have enough clout to get it expedited? Apparently so.

No one knew the cause of death. Medical records were confidential, so being unknown wasn't a surprise. The only possible source was the Hudsons, who'd taken the woman to the doctor.

She picked up her phone to call Liz. If anyone would know, it would be her.

"Hi, Liz. Hey. I just saw Edna passed away. That's awful! And no one seems to know why or how."

"I know. I don't, either. We took her to the doctor but never saw her again. They called an ambulance that took her to the hospital. She must have been really sick."

"True. Did she say anything about how she felt?"

"She said she ached all over, had a hard time breathing, and was dizzy. That sounded like it could have been the flu. But it could have also been pneumonia, a heart attack, or even a stroke."

"Right. Those symptoms are pretty generic."

Breathing problems at high altitudes were pervasive among retired folks. Seeing them toting around portable oxygen bottles was common. Edna lived there all her life, however, and until recently was active, working in her yard and taking regular walks.

What happened to Edna? She and Liz agreed they'd probably never know.

"By the way," Liz said. "I saw your Indian friend out by the accident site. He was just sitting there staring off into space."

"Was it a week ago? On Sunday?"

"Yes, I think so."

Sara stared pensively out the kitchen window. "That was the day we scattered Bryan's ashes. They were close friends. He hasn't said much, but I can tell he's pretty upset."

"It looked like he was doing some sort of ritual or something. He was smoking one of those long, peace-pipe things with other stuff spread out on what looked like an animal skin."

"Probably his way of saying goodbye."

ELITE MANAGEMENT PARTNERS INC. (EMPI)
DENVER
May 21, Monday
9:00 a.m.

Virgil Steinbrenner's engineering team wore a variety of expressions as they came online for his weekly status meeting. He eyed his montage of worker bees on his monitor, convinced video conferencing was the greatest management tool ever invented. No need to travel, much less dress up or interact in person. Just report and get back to work, giving him more time to play the stock market.

The drilling contractor was the only one in a white shirt and tie. Those on the legal team and the government overseer wore polos, probably on their way to the golf course as soon as the meeting adjourned. Keller was decked out in his usual camo. Those on the construction team wore parkas, their underground work site no doubt clammy and frigid.

Certainly not an issue in his high-rise corner office in scenic downtown Denver.

As project manager at the apex of the org chart, Virgil issued edicts like a medieval task master. Conversely, his minions labored at his beck and call, responsible for maintaining their schedule on the PERT, visible on a second monitor to his right.

The Program Evaluation Review Technique resembled a genealogical pedigree chart, except each box represented a task. Connections mapped their relationships in the completion sequence. Some ran parallel, others serial.

Important milestones upon which the finish date depended constituted the almighty Critical Path. Anyone who clogged it by failing to stay on-schedule affected those downstream.

An absolutely horrifying and punishable cardinal sin.

He listened to each of their weekly reports while his secretary sat beside him and entered the results into the software real-time.

He really needed her to get a quieter keyboard. That *tap-tap-tap* was downright irritating.

When the last person finished and her fingers grew still, he leaned back in his high-back leather chair wearing his sternest authoritarian expression.

"Overall, the project is progressing well. I'm proud of the teamwork and professionalism you display in executing your tasks," he said. "Our customer is satisfied, provided we stay on schedule. I cannot emphasize this strongly enough. It's essential that Phase One be completed before the next budget cycle. Is that clear?"

A chorus of affirmative utterances and nods responded.

"Any questions or comments?"

He smirked when the previous affirmative response reversed without hesitation.

"Need I remind you that bonuses are calculated using a point system. Timeliness and budget compliance minus any screw-ups. It's possible to have a negative score, which will have contractually defined consequences. If you wish to know where you stand in this regard, contact me privately."

Some appeared hopeful, others skeptical, a few morose.

No different than when the meeting began.

Without further ado, he terminated the vidcon with a single click, his mountain vista screensaver reclaiming his screen.

He set his reading glasses on his desk, waved his secretary back to her own office, and swiveled around to savor his view of the skyline. Heels on the windowsill, he clasped his hands behind his head, not quite covering the fading dark fringe that rimmed his naked pate.

So far, things were going well. All things considered, of course. Phase One was nearing completion and ahead of schedule by several weeks. The more money he saved beating deadlines, the bigger his award fee. A small percentage of which was allocated for said bonuses.

One who was barely hanging on was Keller's security team. They'd already messed up once. It wasn't so much that they impacted the critical path so much as the budget, when intervention and additional resources became necessary.

This was Virgil's first Top Secret job. He'd never dealt with all that security crap before. BKSS came highly recommended. Which translated to being related to someone in the customer's inner circle. Keller sounded confident in his WAR, the apropos acronym for Weekly Activity Report. He claimed everything was under control and promised no more screw ups.

If they did, *hasta la vista,* baby.

Ridiculous quantities of cement were required for the overall infrastructure. They cut corners as much as they dared. He'd expected his biggest headache would be finding a subcontractor to install the geothermal energy system.

Another inner circle recommendation, they, too, were hanging by a thread. They seemed great at the onset, then ran into trouble. They blamed the budget and the ensuing compromises. Fortunately, Virgil's connections helped navigate the rough water.

He grinned at his unintentional, albeit brilliant, pun—*rough water*, indeed.

Slickwater, actually, the popular term for fracking fluid.

Lone Star Operations, a.k.a. LSO, started strong by killing two birds with one stone. Unfortunately, a few months in, they nearly landed him in hot water.

Another grin. Sometimes he amazed even himself.

Creating a geothermal well employed a process similar to hydraulic fracturing, which required obscene amounts of water. The initial expectation was that they'd have to pay dearly for it, which was included in their segment's budget. Millions of gallons were needed, which could be missed from the local supply. Even more so since the past several years were unusually dry.

They would have been totally screwed if the request had been denied, in which case they'd have to truck it in.

But there was a caveat that LSO exploited—the water didn't need to be clean. Which was where the area's history came into play.

Abandoned mines, many from the 19th Century, were everywhere in Colorado, sometimes estimated to be as many as twenty-three thousand. Extracting silver, gold, lead, or uranium via leaching and other processes involved chemicals. Nasty ones, such as arsenic, cadmium, mercury, and manganese.

All that crap was left behind in an era when outhouses were the norm and pollution unheard of amid the euphoric frenzy that propelled the industrial revolution.

In time, however, rain water and snow melt filled the excavated cavities. Minerals, along with all the toxic extraction substances that remained, then dissolved. They seeped into waterways, including streams, lakes, rivers, and aquifers.

A century or more later, enter EPA Superfunds, charged with the clean-up. The process was expensive, tricky, and at times made matters worse.

Water was water, however, as far as fracking was concerned. Thus, LSO cut a multi-million-dollar deal with the EPA to get rid of the area's tainted water. That saved a huge chunk of change, to say nothing of the hassle of obtaining water through other channels.

Right: *channels*—was The Virg in true form today or what?

To further sweeten the deal, he stepped in and agreed to backfill the mines to eliminate future drainage problems. How they were going to do that was deemed "proprietary" and accomplished in a way no one would ever suspect.

Proprietary, hell—it was Top Secret.

If all went according to plan, the cavity would no long exist as such and no one would ever know.

A classic win-win.

Needless to say, LSO's flowback was more contaminated than the acid mine drainage, or AMD. It was tainted enough already, but the fracking process added chloride, sodium, barium, glycol compounds, and strontium, to name a few. Such waste water was typically injected into disposal wells, deep underground.

Up until that point, LSO's innovation made them bonus material. But that was where things went to hell.

Tricky geology contributed to a miscalculation for the injection well's location. As a result, hundreds of thousands of gallons of AMD, further contaminated with fracking chemicals, found its way into a local aquifer.

Oops.

From what he heard, one hospitalization and one death had resulted.

Fortunately, with the help of a few confidential resources, one of Virgil's business partners managed to contact the deceased's executor to register an as-is offer to acquire the real property, assuring no snooping into the well's condition would occur.

The out-of-state heirs, not realizing the home's current value, happily agreed to a rock-bottom price, meaning they could flip it for a tidy profit.

All it had to do was get through probate. And a connection was on-hand for that, as well.

The small privately-owned water utility company it affected didn't flinch at the instructions, though the pay-off did have noticeable budget impact.

Actually, since the work site didn't officially exist, liability didn't, either. Furthermore, LSO's attorney stated that underground injection fluids were exempt from the Clean Water Act, as long as they weren't using diesel fuel. Since correcting their initial miscalculation, the new disposal location was working just fine.

He laughed. The whole scheme worked to their advantage, the company's *faux pas* buried as deeply as the well itself.

Construction of the power plant was nearly done. The only work that remained was to connect it to the energy source upon completion of the geothermal well.

The U.S. Army Corps of Engineers would get their boring machine out of there the following week, completing that phase. Infrastructure installation, including water and electricity, were in progress, then the final finish work.

So far it looked as if they'd all be welcoming the new fiscal year with a huge bang.

Virgil's grin stretched.

Life was good.

Your dead cease to love you and the homes of their nativity as soon as they pass the portals of the tomb. They wander far off behind the stars, are soon forgotten and never return.
—Seath'tl "Seattle", 1854

9. TWINGES

SARA'S CABIN
RURAL FALCON RIDGE
May 26, Saturday
9:18 a.m.

After checking for any new posts of interest on *myneighbors.com*, Sara lowered her tablet to the breakfast bar. Beyond towering glass cumulus clouds teased a vibrant blue sky, a color seen only at high elevations free of urban pollution. A breeze wafted through open windows, warm and inviting.

Six weeks had passed since the accident. Little by little, she was getting used to the twinges, though a symphony of random aches and pains persisted. Crying spells still besieged her from time to time, but both Liz and Connie repeatedly reassured her that her heart would heal at its own pace.

Her phone chirped—Connie's daily text.

How are you doing today, honey?

Pretty good. Sure is a pretty day.

Same here. You should get out for some fresh air.

Maybe I will. What are you doing today?

Dragging your dad out shopping.

LOL. Same old, same old, eh?

;-) Updating the kitchen. Sale at Home Depot.

Have fun.

U2. Promise to get some sun. OK?

OK.

Say it.

I promise. :-p

Later. xxxxoooo

Liz, too, provided some form of daily contact. Sometimes she called, others simply dropped by, usually when she'd done some baking. Her mouth watered just thinking about the lasagne she brought by.

She extended her arms overhead, wincing at the chorus of muscular complaints, but generally feeling better, energy level improving. Her heart's emptiness persisted as a hallow ache, but she was doing her best to manage that pain as well.

Forgetfulness hadn't improved much. Was she doomed to be an airhead for the rest of her life? What if she never remembered what happened?

Maybe more exercise would help.

She shed the cervical collar, then strolled to the back door and gazed up the path. A new color-filled wave of wildflowers had joined those in bloom when they'd scattered Bryan's ashes. The hillside's vibrant green and deciduous trees were leafed out and presented an inviting picture.

Literally.

When the hills were parched with summer heat she'd be sorry if she didn't take some photos now. Spring flowers weren't always so profuse, but varied year to year. Furthermore, Connie would expect a report. What better evidence than photographic?

She held her chin, trying to remember where her camera was. It was usually on the kitchen counter where she could grab it to capture a glorious sunset or an elk grazing out back.

A cursory search of the ground floor proved futile.

Upon getting home from the hospital, sleeping in the guest room was justified. The stairs were bare wood and steep, the climb hard on her hip. Furthermore, the risk of falling was unacceptable.

Enough time had passed, however, for her convenient excuse to expire. It was time to face that forbidden territory.

The burning throat and eyes that presaged another meltdown closed around her. She bit her lip and sniffed it back.

No. Stop that.

She'd chosen to be there. Closer to Bryan. To help her remember.

Where were they ever closer than up there?

She gripped the railing and plodded up a few stairs, pausing halfway to catch her breath.

The scariest thing she'd done since. . .since when?

Huh.

Probably opening her eyes in that ambulance.

Since when was she such a coward?

While growing up she was a daddy's girl. She even aspired to be an FBI agent. Her father ate it up. Having a gutsy, tomgirl for a daughter was as good or better than having a son. He taught her to shoot from an early age and told intriguing stories about his work.

The aspiration lasted until her sophomore year in college. That was when her mom got sick. Her father backed off, nudging her toward a safer profession. She felt betrayed, but obediently gravitated toward one to help people.

Like those who'd been so compassionate with her mom.

It took years to understand his motives.

Her eyes misted.

Now she did.

A few steps later she halted again. Six years ago she and Bryan spent their honeymoon there, every trip since a glorious rerun. Like every couple, they had their differences, but were so much in love they always worked things out. The corners of her mouth shifted upward—making up was always so much fun.

By the time she reached the top, her mind swam with a medley of melancholy memories. She stared at the door, paralyzed. Held her breath, turned the knob, and pushed.

The room was stuffy, dust afloat in sunlight streaming through the triangular windows. She switched on the ceiling fan. Dust succumbed to the ensuing chaos.

She walked around to his side of the bed, pulled back the spread, and picked up his pillow. She hugged it to her chest, then buried her face in it, savoring the faint scent of aftershave.

Determined not to indulge in another weepy pity party she put the pillow back and exhaled hard.

What was she doing up there, anyway?

Right—her camera.

When it wasn't downstairs it was usually on the dresser. Its black bag with a multitude of zippered compartments was right there.

The camera wasn't.

She checked the walk-in closet, dresser drawers, even the hall closet where they kept ski equipment and bunny suits.

After an exhaustive search, the conclusion was unavoidable.

It had been in the truck.

The worst part was its sentimental value. Bryan would expect her to replace it. It would still be part of him, regardless.

She looked around one more time, debating. Should she start sleeping up there again?

Maybe, maybe not.

Before the simmering sentimentality boiled over she left the room, closed the door behind her, then slowly made her way down the stairs to get her tablet and order a new one.

There was one exactly like it on Amazon. The picture brought back another onslaught of fond memories. He'd paid over nine-hundred dollars for it? Wow!

That was Bryan, alright. Only the best would do.

Her smile trembled a moment, then she clicked "Buy Now." It wasn't like she couldn't afford it.

She'd already owned one, so didn't bother to read the description. If Bryan bought it, she had no doubts it was the best one out there.

An eerie sense of déjà-vu flashed.

Wherever they were that day, she must have taken photos.

Perhaps physically holding the camera would bring something back.

It is no measure of health to be well-adjusted to a profoundly sick society.
— *Jiddu Krisnamurti*

10. IMPRESSIONS

SARA'S CABIN
RURAL FALCON RIDGE
May 30, Wednesday
9:18 a.m.

The camera turned out to be the extra boost Sara needed. She spent every morning photographing wildflowers and anything else that caught her eye.

The exercise it offered was a bonus as well. Tears still came, but with less melancholy. With her flexibility and energy level improved, she spread out her yoga mat by the front window and eased into her old routine.

Within a few days, disconnected thoughts appeared. Elusive, like shooting stars—there one moment, gone the next—but something about them tweaked her psyche.

Delusions caused by the concussion?

Severe, irreversible brain damage?

Or facts bubbling up from her subconscious?

The unmistakable impression came that Edna's death was not natural. When she rationalized it away, another impression directed her to insist upon an autopsy.

Since when was that her call?

If Edna's physician thought something was amiss, that was up to him. Her medical knowledge was certainly insufficient to question a doctor.

The thought refused to go away. Perhaps more information had surfaced. Secrets didn't survive in small communities. Especially with the likes of Liz Hudson around.

At her usual time, a few minutes past noon, Liz called.

"How are you doing today, neighbor?" she asked.

"Really well. I got some spectacular shots of columbines this morning. How about you?"

"I can't wait to see them! I'm doing great, too. Game night tomorrow. I don't suppose..."

The words spilled out unbidden. "You know what, Liz? Yes. Count me in."

Liz's momentary silence spoke volumes.

"That's fabulous!" she gushed at last. "I kept telling them not to invite Rhonda. I knew you'd join us eventually."

"How often and where do you meet?"

"Alternate Thursdays at seven-thirty. We rotate houses. Whoever's hosting serves a few *hors d'oeuvres* and a bottle or two of sweet wine. Tomorrow's my turn."

"That sounds great. How about you let me do the honors this week?"

"Fantastic! I'll let everyone know. Would you like me to bring anything?"

"No. I got this."

She smiled as set down her phone. The decision lifted her spirits, confirming it was the right thing to do. If nothing else, relearning the game would be good mental exercise.

The next day found her thoroughly enjoying herself as she prepared a cheese platter, veggie tray, little sandwiches, and homemade chocolate chip cookies. A large bottle of Sangria and the nice glasses, rather than the Lexan ones she and Bryan normally used, finished the spread.

That evening she and the other women sat around her kitchen table getting into the game when the conversation shifted to Edna. The woman was a regular in the group for a long time and Angela mentioned how strange it felt with her gone.

"I'm sure she's here in spirit," Liz remarked.

Angela nodded agreement, blue eyes peering out from a dyed blond mound of Texas big hair. "That would be just like her, wouldn't it? By the way, I found out why she died—kidney failure."

Ida looked up from arranging her tiles, grey-streaked, frizzy mane protesting the headband's restraint. "Kidney failure? Where'd you hear that?"

Angela straightened in her chair. "A friend in the county clerk's office. She heard it from Edna's daughter when she notarized the property transfer documents."

Sara stiffened, startled by the impression that someone should check Edna's well, but remained silent.

Ida's piercing, grey eyes met hers, then those of the other women. "I think someone oughta check her well. Somethin's not right. I can feel it."

Sara's mouth fell open. "I was just thinking the same thing! How weird is that?"

"Well, I think the whole thing's not only weird, but suspicious," Ida went on. "There's been a lot of dead fish washin' up onshore lately. Stinks horrible. Fishin's bad, too. Anyone who catches any says they taste funny. Not good for business."

Liz looked up from checking one of her nails. "Wouldn't we all be affected?"

"Not necessarily," Angela volunteered. "The Brown-Sinclair water system, which most of y'all are probably on, comes from a local spring. One of many that feeds the lake. Since they have several customers, the EPA tests it. If it doesn't meet their standards, they have to say so. At least quarterly. Don't y'all have purification systems, anyway?"

Everyone nodded.

Liz looked pensive. "Where could we get it tested? The hospital in Belton?"

Angela shook her head. "Probably the EPA."

Sara leaned over to retrieve her tablet from the counter to check their website. "No, it says here they don't care about private wells. Some state agency here in Colorado does that." She tapped through a few links, finding the Colorado Department of Public Health and Environment.

"Okay. Here we go, ladies. According to this, we should test for metals and pH. *Huh.* If we're worried about fracking, then we also need to check for chloride, sodium, barium, and strontium. *Hmmm.* Does anyone know if any of that's going on around here?"

Everyone exchanged a blank look except Angela, whose attention was fixed on her tiles.

Sara found a list of certified labs with instructions and selected the nearest one. "Oh. This isn't free and we need to pay up front."

Ida's heavy brows bristled as they collided in the middle. "Oh, yeah? How much?"

"Hold on. Alright. It depends on what we want. Wow. There's a huge list. Great! They have a metals panel that covers several. Adding in the others comes to around $250."

"That's a lot of dough just to satisfy our curiosity."

"True. But maybe it's more than that. It's odd we both had the same impression. Those of us with wells should definitely get them tested. With Bryan gone, I need to get used to taking care of all these maintenance issues, anyway. It says to do it at least once a year."

Ida snorted. "Yeah. So they can make more money. I pass."

"Me, too," said Liz. "We're on the Brown-Sinclair system, and I trust them to notify us if there are any problems. Besides, we have a whole-house filtration system."

"We have a purification system on our well, too," Angela stated.

"Well, I'm going to do it, anyway," Sara said.

When the game concluded, Angela the happy winner, everyone finished off the cookies and left. While it was fresh on her mind, she decided to find the file box in the guest room's storage bench where Bryan kept information pertaining to the cabin.

She tossed aside the throw pillows that disguised it as no more than a built-in bench seat and lifted the lid, releasing the smell of old wood and wool fabric. A few old blankets went on the bed behind her, then an old short-handled pick, a bone-handled hunting knife, and something that looked like a surveyor's tool.

The remaining space was filled with boxes. Some wood, some cardboard, others plastic, the different materials, shapes, and sizes suggesting their age and contents.

A file box beckoned, which she carried to the kitchen table. When she opened it she was grateful Bryan was so organized, each category in its own accordion folder.

One pertained to the property itself and its transfer upon his grandfather's death. Curious, she pulled out the deed, noting that besides the cabin, over five hundred acres were included. She was unaware they owned that much, surprised as she examined the survey of its boundaries. Next she found a quit-claim deed from when Bryan gave Charlie his cabin and fifty acres of surrounding property.

The original cabin's age teased her mind. Was Bryan's grandfather its first owner? Someday she needed to explore what might be lurking in those old wooden boxes.

Focusing back on her intent, she dug some more. The next document was one she'd never seen before—a land patent. Anything below ground was theirs as well, *i.e.,* mineral rights were included. She never thought about such things, always assuming that conventional land ownership went beyond the surface.

At last she found the well schematic. The paper was yellowed with age, folds fragile, some torn. The driller's name, his certification number, and location were barely legible. The Denver address lacked a zip code and the telephone number was a mere seven digits. The engineer's signature was unreadable, the date either the 15th or 19th of August 1952.

Surely it had been upgraded since then.

That folder contained no further information, so she grabbed another with construction records from when Bryan expanded the cabin. It was loaded. Sales and warranty information, financial records, credit card statements, and canceled checks.

At last she found the manual for the water softener. A reverse osmosis system that removed a long list of contaminants.

The system diagram identified the valves for testing incoming and outgoing water. A single sheet stapled to the back showed the test results from when the system was installed five years before. She dug through the file some more, finding similar analyses for every year since, little difference between them—perfect for a baseline.

In the morning she'd collect a sample and send it off.

She put everything back, wondering again at the strange prompting to do so.

The very dust under your feet responds more lovingly to our footsteps than to yours, because it is the ashes of our ancestors, and our bare feet are conscious of the sympathetic touch, for the soil is rich with the life of our kindred.
—Seath'tl "Seattle", 1854

11. THE CURSE

SARA'S CABIN
RURAL FALCON RIDGE
June 3, Sunday
9:42 a.m.

Various twinges persisted, but were diminishing enough that Sara ventured a bit farther with each hike, especially since the snow had melted. Camera over her shoulder, she strolled along her favorite trail. As was recently her habit, she was thinking out loud, half to herself, half to Bryan, this time about the land records.

A bend flanked by a stand of pines brought her face to face with Charlie. She blushed as she met his questioning look.

"Don't mind me. With Bryan's ashes out here, sometimes I talk to him. I know it's a little crazy."

His nod was solemn. "I understand." He tilted his hat to shade his eyes. "I do the same. You seem to be doing well."

"Yes, much better. I'm sure the medicine bundle you gave me helped. I still wear it, see?" She pulled it out from under her sweater to show him. "But I was wondering. Do you know how to make that sore muscle remedy from Pasque flower leaves?"

His response was a quizzical look. Had she somehow offended him? "I, uh, read about it a while back. In a book about natural remedies," she explained.

"Actually, I do. Why do you know of such things?"

"I love wildflowers. Plus I'm interested in herbal medicine. Can you teach me how to do that?"

His mien grew wistful. "I haven't done that in many years, but I think I can remember. My grandfather will be smiling. He made some for me one time when I was a kid. I fell and twisted my ankle chasing a rabbit."

"Is he the one who taught you?"

"Yes. That and many other things." The distance in his eyes deepened with some unfamiliar emotion.

"Was he a medicine man?"

Their eyes reconnected. "Yes. A great one. He was much revered by my people. I miss him. I'd be honored to make you some." He licked his lips. "Did they ever find out what happened? Who or what caused the accident?"

A memory flash of their crumpled Chevy pickup brought a shudder. "No. They couldn't without recovering our truck. Even if they had, how could they tell the difference between accident damage versus when it fell in that ravine? I think they closed it by speculating Bryan swerved to miss a deer or maybe a boulder released from the thaw cycle."

He shook his head. "It wasn't a deer. Wildlife avoids that area. Too steep and rocky. A chunk of rock, I doubt it. That cliff face doesn't show any signs of that. Did you know that ravine has a name?"

"Not that I recall. But remembering isn't exactly my strong suit these days. What is it?"

"Dead Horse Canyon."

Her nose wrinkled. "*Ewww.* Far from pleasant. But sadly I can relate. And it fits, in an eerie sort of way. Bryan always called the Silverado his 'trusty steed.' Is there a story behind the morbid name?"

"Actually, yes. That canyon and surrounding area is under an old Cheyenne curse."

"Wow. I wonder if Bryan knew?"

"Probably. I'm sure we talked about it when we were young."

"What was it about?"

"It goes back to the gold and silver rush in the 1860s. A group of miners raided our village while the men were off hunting buffalo. The youngest son of the chief, who wasn't old enough to go with them, got on his pony along with one of his brothers to get help. The miners caught up with them and ran them off that cliff. All the horses left behind, too. Then they murdered all the women, children, and old people in the village and burned it to the ground."

"That's horrible!"

"Yes. But typical. When the men returned from the hunt, their medicine man, Black Cloud, put a curse on the area. That no white man would ever prosper here and would pay for his evil ways. Less than a year later, that mine collapsed, killing the men who ravaged our village. Soon the other settlers left, too. It's only in the past seventy-five years or so that people have returned."

"Interesting. That must be when Bryan's grandfather came here. I'm surprised there wasn't some sort of historical marker."

"There was." Mischief sparkled in his eyes.

"History always makes us the bad guys. The marker declared it a victory for the miners. Every time I saw it my anger grew until I finally dug it up and threw it over the side. We're tired of being the bad guys. My people have been here for thirteen-thousand years. Then the white man came and stole it. Was it wrong to defend land the Great Spirit gave to us?"

"Absolutely not! I'm so sorry. I mean it. Good for you."

"Thank you. You and Bryan are different. You understand."

"I don't like anyone or anything being treated unfairly. But it looks like the curse isn't working. A lot of people are prospering in this area now, it seems."

"It will in time. Curses are patient."

"I wonder if the curse has anything to do with Bryan dying there?"

"I doubt it. He was a good man. Like those of my people who died there. Their blood calls for justice. It will come."

"I hope so. By the way, a friend of mine saw you out there the day we scattered Bryan's ashes."

His expression clouded. "Yes. I was telling him goodbye. In the Cheyenne way."

"Is that your native language?"

"No. My first language was Diné. You probably know it as Navajo. My mother's language. But my father insisted I learn Cheyenne. When I went to live with him as a young man, that's the only language he would speak. It's dying out, which is sad. The average age for those who speak it today is sixties or older. Much of who we are will die with it."

"I get that. The cultural implications would be lost as well. That would be a great loss to your people. So, you're trilingual. That's impressive. Which language do you think in?"

He smiled. "Actually, I speak some Spanish, too. I guess my thoughts include a little of each. If I spoke like I think, no one could understand me."

"I can imagine."

Silence stretched between them, attention waning as each got lost in their own thoughts. Moments later he caught her eye again.

"Have you remembered anything about the wreck?" he asked, cycling back to an earlier subject.

"No, not really. Just a bad feeling. But having a good feeling wouldn't make much sense."

"I have a bad feeling, too. There's something, well, uh, strange, even sinister, about it." The searching look that followed gave her the impression he wanted to ask her something.

"There's a lot that doesn't make sense," she said. "I hope when I remember it clears things up. Then maybe I'll understand why I have this creepy feeling that's entirely separate from losing Bryan."

He looked away and gnawed his lip before resuming eye contact. "I, uh, didn't want to upset you or cause more worry. You already have enough on your mind, besides your injuries. But I agree. Something about it is very wrong."

She paused, struck again by what he said in the hospital, but hesitant to bring it up. With all the pain meds she'd been on, maybe it wasn't even real.

"It makes me feel better to know I'm not alone," she replied. "If I remember anything, I'll let you know."

"Please do. If you need anything, let me know, too." His eyes lingered a few seconds longer, radiating an emotion she couldn't quite read.

"Thanks. You're probably the one person who misses Bryan as much as I do."

"I miss him a lot. I can't remember when he wasn't in my life." His shoulders slumped, sadness apparent. "Take care, Sara. Don't push yourself too hard." He nodded farewell, then continued down the path. She watched until he disappeared around a bend.

So he felt it too.

COLORADO ROCKIES
June 3, Sunday
10:05 a.m.

Charlie's continued down the rock-strewn path, chanting a Diné song from his childhood. He wanted to tell Sara what *Maheo* told him, but wasn't sure if she'd believe him, plus he didn't want to alarm her.

However, he could tell she suspected something, too, and there was a chance her life was in danger. That made it more urgent, giving him even more reason to get down to the wreck.

He checked the best access point every few days. Crusty snow and too much mud still infested the area. Even if he could get down the steep bank with his canoe, his truck would get stuck. He really needed to add a winch, just didn't have the funds. Actually, he hadn't felt much like doing anything lately, whether or not it involved money.

His thoughts slipped back to how he and Bryan met, then wandered the Rockies together. Much of what his brother knew of the area he'd taught him, sometimes contradicting what his grandfather said.

The sense of recognition at their first meeting startled them both. Like most Indigenous people, he distrusted whites. Yet with

Bryan he never felt that way. He showed him where to hunt, which mountain streams still contained trout, and shared his knowledge of medicinal plants. While many white men would have shown no interest, he welcomed the information with interest and respect. He felt more like his brother than the one he had, from whom he'd been estranged for years.

When Bryan told him he was getting married, he worried their relationship would suffer. It didn't. Rather, Sara was an easy addition, another kindred spirit. As his brother's widow, it was his duty to protect her. He tried to remember if there was a specific season or manner to harvest the leaves for the remedy she asked about.

It had to mean something that he and Bryan shared the same birthday. As if they entered mortality together, then connected across miles and opposing cultures. How many people had a cosmic twin? They speculated that perhaps they'd die the same day, too, possibly during one of their reckless teenage excursions.

His breath caught in his chest.

Could his time be coming, too?

If so, was he ready? What about Bryan? Was he expecting it? His brow crumpled into a frown. No, he would have said something.

Or would he?

A breeze threatened to steal his hat, bringing him back to the present. He snatched it from the air, as he'd done many times before. It's wide brim made it easy prey to the wind, yet he never failed to save it.

It showed its age, faded and a little moth-eaten from the years he'd forgotten to protect it with sprigs of fresh rosemary. The juniper branch he placed in the band to beckon protection along with its now ever-present rosemary were secure, untroubled by its unscheduled flight.

Its band was a colorful mosaic of tiny beads, woven in the nested diamond pattern known as the "Eye of the Medicine Man." Its function went beyond decoration, representing his grandfather's position in the tribe. He could still picture Eaglefeathers wearing it. He continued down the path, wondering what it might say if it could talk.

Would it comfort him?

Or flog him for his foolishness?

Perhaps that gust of wind was a message: *Take it off until you've earned it.*

He wore it in remembrance of his grandfather, but for the first time wondered if the old man approved. In response, warmth filled his heart. Eaglefeathers was pleased that he was doing his best to resume living the Cheyenne Way.

He made offerings and prayers every morning and night, but until he acted upon the last impression to examine the truck, he hadn't asked for anything other than for the weather to cooperate.

It often felt as if his brother and grandfather were standing beside him. Were they guiding him to something else he was supposed to do?

Another possibility struck. Perhaps evil ghosts known as *chinde* caused the accident, not mortals. If so, how would he seek revenge?

Curses could manifest numerous times. Men would continue to die as a result of their folly. But he never expected it to be so personal. Bryan hadn't exploited anyone. If it was his time, he could have gone in any number of ways or places. His gut told him it wasn't a coincidence. Surely there was some purpose.

But what?

For now, Bryan was gone and he remained. The cold stone of sadness that invaded his chest weeks before hadn't shrunk, much less gone away. Moisture coated his eyes like the cool of night distilled the morning dew.

But warriors don't cry.

When you feel the point of the arrow, embrace it. Die with courage. Return home with honor.

The point of the arrow.

He knew it well.

When his father, Littlebear, died. Then Eaglefeathers. Then his marriage.

Each impaled his heart and part of him had died.

Could a heart die with courage?

So far it simply died.

More of the warrior's creed sprang to mind: *Should you survive, seek your revenge.*

Bryan was a martyr, not unlike those who died over a century before. Murdered by those of the same mind who'd ravaged his people.

Anger swelled, consuming his grief as dawn conquers the night. He would make sure that at least one life sacrificed at Dead Horse Canyon would be avenged.

He set his jaw and pondered who the guilty party might be. His thoughts returned to the truck and the undeniable impression to investigate.

Tomahawk Creek flowed for most of the summer, usually until early August. Most years it dried up about the time snowfall resumed in higher elevations. As recently as the day before it was still too muddy. Hopefully good weather would continue and dry it out.

A falcon's sharp cry overhead snagged his attention. As eagle's smaller brother, it hunted closer to the ground, saw more details. It dove earthward until it disappeared among the pines in pursuit of some unfortunate prey.

He set his jaw. Signs were everywhere. He would pray even harder for the weather to cooperate.

They have vanished before the avarice and oppression of the white men, as snow before a summer sun.
—Tecumseh, September 1811

12. FLASHBACKS

BENTLEY RESIDENCE
RURAL FALCON RIDGE
June 7, Thursday
7:24 p.m.

Sara braked, staring open-mouthed out the windshield. An ostentatious gate accented with an enormous letter *B* blocked the way. On either side red brick pillars interspersed with wrought iron spikes stretched in both directions.

Her nose wrinkled. How many unfortunate elk and mountain lions misjudged their jumping abilities and had been impaled on one?

She spotted the voice box, where Angela greeted her by name. The pretentious barrier swung inward, dirt road yielding to paved asphalt.

Out there in the Styx that seemed a bit much.

Or was it business as usual in Texas?

The driveway wound through towering pines and an aspen clone for a few hundred yards before the Bentley's sprawling estate came into view.

Its location was ideal, elevated enough to see Lake Wilson to the west while Eagles Peak rose skyward to the east. She parked in the circular drive, grabbed her purse and sweater, then stood beside her car to admire the majestic panorama. Every direction offered a spectacular view.

Eagles Peak's crown of snow brought a flash of déjà-vu—
they'd been cross-country skiing!

The hum of an approaching vehicle distracted her to Liz's white Escalade pulling in behind her. The woman got out, waving and displaying her usual cheery smile, red hair gleaming like copper in the westering sun. The two exchanged a casual hug.

"Are you okay, dear? You look a little rattled."

"Hi, Liz. I'm good, actually. I just remembered something about the day of the accident."

"How exciting! What came back?"

"We were cross-country skiing. That isn't a big deal since we did that quite a bit. But it fills in one small piece of the puzzle."

"It's a start. Maybe more will come back soon."

"I hope so. I guess I should drive out where we usually went to see if it triggers anything else." She stopped as they reached the porch's flagstone steps.

Liz offered her hand. "Do you need some help?"

"Oh! No, I'm fine. I was just thinking. I haven't driven out there since the accident."

"I'd be happy to go with you, dear. We can take my car. You know, speaking of cars, you probably ought to get a better one, if you plan to stay here year-round. That little sedan isn't going to do too well in the snow."

"True. Our truck was four-wheel drive, so I never thought about it before."

French doors adorned with leaded glass etched with another stylized *B* greeted them at the top. Angela opened it with a flourish and beckoned them inside. Her Texas Big Hair was in full bloom, a gaudy turquoise necklace adorning her freckled chest.

Vaulted ceilings and travertine floors accented with oriental rugs awaited inside. Windows were everywhere, admitting the breathtaking view, interrupted only by an ornate marble fireplace. Leather couches and intricately carved tables further graced the room, like the lobby of a five-star hotel.

Angela's husband, Bob, looked up from a thick, leather-bound book, then got up to greet them. His imposing height and abundant girth fit both Texas and judicial stereotypes. Hooded, deep-set brown eyes commanded attention, distracting from the dark but greying comb-over straining to cover his head

"Welcome, ladies," he said, his voice reminding her of a bulldozer pushing a load of gravel. Certainly well-suited for issuing verdicts and prison sentences.

Angela showed them where to leave their purses and wraps, then escorted them to an array of *hors d'oeuvres* and finger foods in the dining area.

"Y'all help yourselves. Be sure to get some peach-Champagne punch. It's absolutely divine!"

After filling their plates and goblets, they sat around a walnut poker table inlaid with pink granite.

"Did y'all hear?" Angela said. "Miss Rhonda Wheeler got herself arrested."

Liz's hand covered her mouth while she finished chewing. "Arrested? Whatever for?"

"*Way-ehl*, bless her heart, this time she was pouring sugah into someone's mailbox."

"Why?" Liz asked.

"Ah suppose she was fixin' to attract ants or bees or something. But the mailman caught her. Meddlin' with mail is a federal offense. So, they arrested her."

Sara never heard of an adult doing anything so foolish. "Wow. I wonder what the punishment will be?"

Bob volunteered a response without leaving his chair. "Probably just a fine, provided there wasn't any property damage." His laugh, like his voice, was in the subwoofer range. "Country mailboxes all but invite such things. I remember putting roadkills in a few myself, back when I was a youth. Dead possums and armadillos fit in there just right."

Angela rolled her eyes. "Oh, Bob. How could you? From what I heard at the salon, she went berserk. Kicking and screaming and resisting arrest. By the time they got her to the police station, she was so worked up she had a seizure. So they took her to the hospital."

About then, Ida arrived, frizzy hair in its usual disarray. Bob let her in and showed her to the buffet table. She loaded up two plates and hefted herself up on one of the stools, diving right in while she caught up on the conversation.

"I'm glad they finally caught that crazy bitch," she commented. "One time she got mad at me for some unknown reason and took all the washers out of our hoses. Sam went out to water and got soaked. She was over on her porch puffing away on a cigarette and laughing her crazy head off."

Liz looked skeptical. "Are you sure it was her?"

Ida wiped her mouth with the back of her hand. "Who else? There's something not right with that woman."

"Years ago she was in an accident and had a serious head injury. That could explain it." Liz barely got the words out when her attention shifted to Sara. "Oh, no, my dear, I'm sure you're just fine. If you were crazy, surely you'd know by now."

Sara froze. Were her conversations with her dead husband tripping the edge of crazy? "Well, I don't remember everything I'd like to, but I sure don't plan on playing silly tricks on anyone."

"Did you ever get your water tested?" Ida asked, making little grunting sounds as she devoured another ham and cheese roll.

"I sent it in after the last time we played," Sara replied. "As of yesterday the results weren't back. I'll check again on the way home."

When everyone finished eating they cleared the table and set up the game. They broke the wall, chose their tiles, then passed their discards in the Charleston.

Sara sorted hers into the different suits—dots, bamboos, craks, and dragons. Something about the bamboos teased her eye. An image flashed—a tower. Not for cell phones, something entirely different.

The single dot blinked, too, its concentric rings pulsing with eerie familiarity.

Liz cleared her throat. "Sara? Your turn, dear."

The impressions evaporated.

"Oh! I'm sorry. I just had another flashback." She drew from the wall and discarded.

By the time the evening ended, Ida was all aflutter at having won. On her way home Sara went by to check her mail where she found a manila envelope with the lab's return address.

When she got home and compared it to the baseline the difference was startling. Previously benign levels of heavy metals had bolted significantly for lead, mercury, and copper with the pH far too acidic. Traces of chloride, sodium, barium and strontium were also noted.

She double-checked it again, then called Liz.

"Guess what? The water test results were in my mail. They're insane! I can't believe the horrible things that are in there. Nothing like this was there before."

"That's crazy! What are you going to do?"

"I think I'll go into the health department tomorrow and report it. Someone needs to test Edna's well to see if hers is like this, too. Heavy metals can cause kidney failure. They should check Rhonda's, too. Lead and mercury can make people act crazy."

"That's incredible. What else should we do?"

"I'll put up a notice at the store and on *myneighbors.com*. News travels fast, so that should do it. Maybe the Belton county health department will do more."

"What about the police?"

"Good point. If there's something going on around here that might cause it, they should know."

"I'll call Angela and Ida and a few other people. I'll tell Jim to test our water, too, just in case. They're supposed to notify us, but who knows? I'll call them, too."

"Great. I'll make copies of the report for everyone and let you know how it goes with the county and the police."

After she hung up she checked the figures yet again.

What caused such a potentially lethal spike?

Look abroad over their once beautiful country, and what see you now? Naught
but the ravages of the pale-face destroyers meet your eyes.
—Tecumseh, September 1811

13. TROUBLE

TOMAHAWK CREEK
June 8, Friday
6:57 a.m.

Charlie's expression was grim as he pushed his canoe into Tomahawk Creek. The weather-induced delay tried his patience to the limit. That, at least, was over. Yet, while he desperately wanted to know what happened and why, his gut roiled with anticipation.

Was this how warriors felt going into battle?

His jaw tensed as he got settled and paddled out to catch the current, mind focused on the task ahead. The sun was up, but not enough to breach the shadows or dismiss the misty morning chill. All he had was a small ax, so hopefully no fallen trees or debris blocked the path.

At least no beaver dams existed in contaminated water. There were few, anyway, loss of habitat killing off any that survived trappers from the previous century.

Eaglefeathers told him his great-grandfather fished that stream. Since then, fish had disappeared as stars before the rising sun. Toxic algae coated the rocks, vegetation once hugging the shore reduced to ghostly branches. The water wasn't even clear, but murky with an unpleasant odor.

A short time later he spotted the wreckage up ahead. Water churned and spit around its crumpled remains as if angered by the intrusion. Fortunately, that portion of the creek was wider, the stream only a foot or so deep.

He beached the canoe, placed his hat in the bow cavity, then clipped on the tool belt he bought when he worked construction a few years before. He peered up the cliff face to where the truck first landed, then up to the roadway.

A foreign object of some sort hung among the brush, a short distance below the spur. Too straight to be natural, probably a couple yards long. Then another. And another.

Skis.

Air left his lungs. Of course.

He sat there a moment as the gravity of what he was about to do settled upon him. Another deep breath, then he snapped his shirt pocket to secure his cell phone, took off his boots, rolled up his jeans, and stepped into the creek. Deeper than expected, icy water seared, then numbed his legs, joining his willfully frozen emotions as he waded toward what remained of Bryan's beloved Silverado.

The truck rested on its side, roof toward him, passenger door facing up. He made his way around to its exposed undercarriage where he used the driveshaft, then exhaust system to boost himself up. His jeans clung to his thighs, the denim's excess weight matching the truck's effect on his heart.

Decades worth of road trips and adventures pummeled his mind. Bryan loved that truck. A gift from his father when he got his master's degree. It was over ten years old, but he'd kept it in pristine condition. If he were still alive, he'd be devastated to see it like that. As Sara reminded him, his "trusty steed."

He exhaled hard.

His original intent was purely forensic, the emotional jolt unexpected. Sorrow punctured his heart like a snake's fangs pierce its prey. *Tseteshestahese* words for missing his brother, *Náoseema'xè-hoónòsé'ota*, blared through his head, capturing the emotion better than the English word *grief.*

He shoved it away and concentrated on reaching the handle. He pulled himself up and knelt on the door, feet hooked over the cylindrical after-market nerf bar.

The one he'd helped install to make it easier for Sara.

The window was shattered, but still in the frame. He pulled the hammer from his belt, covered his eyes with his left arm, and smashed it, then plucked out the shards with pliers. Both tools back in place, he peered inside.

The dash, headrests, seats and deflated airbags were all blotched with dark stains. Grief assaulted him again, as chilling and relentless as the surrounding water.

Blood.

He admonished himself, purposely in English. *Okay, I miss him, a lot, but that's enough. Stop. Get to work.*

He took a few photos of the interior with his phone, then got out his knife. Shattered plastic and glass were everywhere. The rearview mirror dangled toward the driver side, swinging slightly as he shifted his weight. He tucked the wilted passenger-side airbag behind what looked like the remains of a phone holder.

More photos, then he dropped his feet back on the driveshaft to try the door. No luck. The tortured frame jammed it in place, plus gravity would have challenged him as well. Dealing with a flipped over vehicle wasn't simple. Like mounting a horse lying on its side.

He pulled himself back up on the door. Lying flat on his belly and hanging onto the nerf bar with his feet, he reached inside far enough to push aside the other airbag. He tucked it behind the steering wheel, its column contorted grotesquely. With that out of the way he could see most of the door was missing, jagged edges already rusting beneath the water.

The water was relatively still, but too filled with silt to see. Probably nothing, anyway, with that gaping hole. Making sure his feet were secure, he reached inside far enough to release the console latch. A stray piece of glass cut his finger, a few drops of fresh blood joining the dried ones.

Blood brothers to the last, he thought grimly, wiped it away, then pried the compartment open with his knife.

Bryan stored CDs in there along with maps, basic tools, and usually an energy bar or two. When they went fishing, that was where he kept his cell phone, too. He leaned in as far as he dared, but still couldn't see if anything was inside. He got out his phone, hoping the camera might work as a periscope of sorts. He reached in as far as he could. The angle was too awkward to see anything. Maybe in selfie mode. He tilted the phone toward himself, then down until he could see inside.

E-éhpehá? Empty?

How could it be? Did everything spill out and fall through the hole in the door? Perhaps the glovebox. He tried the latch. Stuck. He pried it open.

Nothing.

He thought back to the truck's descent. It landed on the ledge, probably nose first, then righted itself, held in place by that tree. At that point, anything in the cab, including the console, should have been on the dash or maybe the floor. It was doubtful the glovebox would have opened at all. If it had, gravity would have kept its contents in place.

During rescue operations if anything was right there it seemed they would have grabbed it.

Or not.

It was a precarious rescue, their focus on the victims. When the vehicle fell the rest of the way, no telling how it descended. All the weight was in the engine, suggesting it would have descended nose first, even if it rebounded off the canyon wall on the way down. Any loose objects had a wild ride, but would have settled to either the dash or the far side.

And out the hole in the door.

Maybe so, but he was going to check, just in case. Much of the side remained, including the area next to the pedals. Something could be caught there, or toward the back, since it had an extended cab. There was no way he could get in back, but if anything was within reach, maybe he could retrieve it with his fishing net.

He dropped back in the water to retrieve it, the stream's embrace frigid again as he sloshed his way back to his canoe. Sara told him the cop claimed nothing was recovered. Why would he lie? Did someone loot it?

Possibly. Other than the weather, he didn't have any trouble getting there.

Maheo told him over a month before that evil men murdered his brother. This left no doubt. Someone purposely caused the wreck and destroyed any evidence.

The impression from the aspen that answers could be found in the truck echoed through his mind. So far what he found wasn't an answer, only confirmation.

Was that all he'd get? What good was it for identifying the culprit?

He sat down inside the canoe and prayed for help, which he'd failed to do earlier. He listened a moment for words of inspiration. The only response was the ripple of troubled water and leaves rustling in the morning breeze.

Maybe there was nothing to find. The truck's condition validated Bryan was murdered, nothing more.

Several weeks' anticipation all in vain. He may as well go home. He picked up his socks, then started to pull them on.

No!

He stiffened. Within the wind arose the distinctive chiming of aspen leaves. He tilted back his head, eyeing the cliff face from the water's edge to the roadway above. There she stood, leaves in a wild dance. Answers were there.

He set his jaw, grabbed the net and waded back. Resuming his place on the door, he poked around with the handle. Not a single thing, other than the usual debris. It was impossible to tell if anything was caught between the clutch and brake pedals. Not likely, anyway.

Nothing. Absolutely nothing.

Impossible.

No pickup cab was that clean. Even Bryan's. Neat freak or not, there were always items under or behind the seats, especially with an extended cab, intentionally stowed or otherwise. Same with pockets in the door panels. What truck didn't have something stashed in there? Gas receipts, candy wrappers, anything. It was simply impossible that everything either fell out or washed away. Even the keys were missing, ignition in the locked position.

Among the chunks of debris, back-lit by fractured glass, a metallic reflection caught his eye from the dashboard. An electronic component of some sort stuck between the defrost vents and what was left of the windshield.

Using his knife he picked it free, then grabbed it with needle nose pliers. What was it? Some sort of data storage device? Considering the condition of the dash, it could be anything, but at least it appeared intact. He dropped it in his pocket.

More photos, inside and out, then he made his way through the frigid water to his canoe one last time. He sat inside, shivering, and put on his hat, convinced the excursion was a total failure. Other than that one tiny component. He took it out of his pocket, scrutinized it again.

He shrugged, then slipped it under the reinforcement band inside his hat for safekeeping.

Maybe the photos. He brought them up, checked each one. Nothing jumped out. Perhaps full-size on a computer would reveal something.

He got out, shoved the canoe back into the water, and paddled back upstream. Gradually, his mind shifted to what, if anything, he should do. Maybe go back later to check the canyon side for anything stuck in the brush or shallow water.

The effort of going against the current dissipated some of his frustration. About a third of the way back his peripheral vision caught movement. He jammed the paddle into the streambed to hold his position and turned his head. A raven watched from a nearby tree. The bird's head cocked to one side, as if mocking his chagrin.

Tseteshestahese thoughts flowed once more. Ravens were not good omens. They were clever, usually maliciously so, and at times indicated conflict with a person's shadow where painful experiences festered. Answers often lurked in darkness, whether hidden deliberately by others or occulted by his own refusal to see.

He pondered Raven's message for the remainder of his journey, more convinced than ever that his suspicions as well as the responses he received from *Maheo* were correct.

Something was very wrong.

As he stepped into the creek to push the canoe to shore it felt as if some unknown force were holding him back. Hackles rose on the back of his neck. He peered up to where he parked, view obstructed by brush. As far as he could tell, his truck was still there, tailgate down as he'd left it.

Every nerve on full alert, he dragged the boat out of the water, then sat inside to pull on his boots. He dragged it up the steep embankment by the portage yoke. When he got to his truck, he tipped it up, pushed it into the bed as far as it would go, and secured it with rope.

Then he saw it.

A police car in front of his pickup, blocking the road. A heavyset cop got out, stepping carefully and deliberately down the rock-littered incline. The same one he spoke with at the hospital. He froze as the man approached.

"Show me your driver's license and truck registration," he demanded.

The words sounded foreign and he had to consciously switch to English before responding. He took out his wallet and handed over his license.

"My registration's in the glovebox."

"Fine. Get it."

The cop drew his gun as Charlie opened the door and retrieved the paperwork. When he held it out, the man holstered his weapon and examined the documents.

"These are for New Mexico. And expired."

"I know. I plan to go back and take care of it there."

"Is that so? *Hmmph.* You're Charles Littlewolf?"

"Yes. What's the trouble, officer?"

"The trouble is yours, Littlewolf. You're under arrest."

BENTLEY RESIDENCE
RURAL FALCON RIDGE
June 8, Friday
9:46 a.m.

As soon as Angela's Jaguar disappeared down the road on the way to her weekly hair appointment, Bob emitted a snort of relief. He couldn't even take a decent crap in peace with that woman around.

He marched into his office, unlocked the top drawer of his sprawling mahogany desk, and removed a sealed manila envelope. One thing for sure, he didn't need her hovering over his shoulder, ready to broadcast its contents to the entire civilized world. With her around, much less that nosy redhead down the road, who needed CNN?

He slit it open with the gold-plated letter opener his father gave him when he graduated law school, and extracted its contents. He adjusted his half-moon reading glasses to ride the end of his nose.

Sure enough. Goddamn it.

The same contaminants found in that Reynolds woman's well were in both the Brown-Sinclair system and his own.

What the hell?

At least his elegantly primitive albeit sophisticated sand filtration system took all that crap out. Anything good enough for the Brits proven to work over hundreds of years was good enough for him.

He read the results again and exhaled, hard. What did they screw up? If Gerald knew, which he should, why hadn't he been told?

iPhone in hand, he scrolled past his brother's office number to his cell, not wanting to deal with his over-protective secretary. About the time he thought it was going to voice mail, he picked up.

"What the hell, Gerald? I'm looking at a water quality report that makes the Houston ship channel look potable. I'm not talking the usual acid mine runoff, either. There's all sorts of crap that implicates our drilling operation. What's going on?"

"*Wahll, yee-haw.* Howdy, Bob."

He closed his eyes and shook his head at his exaggerated Texas drawl.

Bob had quickly learned to turn his accent on or off at will while attending Yale. For some reason, his brother found that irritating. As if being able to speak like an educated man, albeit a Yankee, betrayed his heritage.

Perhaps Gerald wasn't smart enough to recognize the advantages of choosing his diction style. It all depended on to whom he was speaking and what he wanted—sometimes an Ivy League-educated attorney, others another good ol' boy.

It wasn't like he couldn't sound as red-necky as the next guy when it served his purpose. For now, his point was strictly business. This was serious stuff.

"Good ta hear from y'all," Gerald rambled on. "How's the family? All y'all doin' just dandy up there yonder in yer Coll-er-adda mountain RE-treat?"

Bob worked his jaw, determined to keep his temper, even though his older sibling's little game had gone on long enough.

Such antics weren't anything new.

Problems went way back. Ever since Gerald ran over his dog, then refused to admit it. For decades. To this day he refused to believe it was an accident. More recently, it was no secret Gerald was pissed because the family business paid them equally. But unlike his brother, Bob didn't have to get his hands dirty.

At least not physically.

Figuratively? Well, that was another story.

Bob exhaled hard through his nose. "I assume you know about this?"

"Of course." The heavy drawl disappeared.

"Why wasn't I notified?"

"Well, it appears I didn't need to, bro, 'cause y'all found out all by yourself. Fu'thermore, I've been busy doin' damage control, plus keepin' on top of the investigation."

"Does that 'damage control' have anything to do with the local water company? Who hasn't informed its customers that their septic tank's field-line runoff is safer than what's coming out of their tap?"

"Don't exaggerate, Bob. I can *abso-fuckin'-LOOT-ley* guarantee no coliform bacteria what-SO-ever could survive in y'all's water."

"Cute, Gerald. Very funny."

"What do you care? Your water's fine, with that fancy-ass system y'all's got."

"You're right, my water's fine. And I don't give a rat's ass about the other people on that system. I'm pissed because you didn't tell me. Not because of the water, but because it's a dead giveaway to what we're doing up here. There could be financial implications if EMPI or, heaven forbid, the government is dissatisfied. You understand how forgiving they are, right?"

"Okay, listen. The water company got instructions and a nice chunk of hush money. By next quarter when they test, most of it should be gone, since we capped it off. If not, their usual mailing will include scaled down versions of the violations. Most customers don't read that crap, anyway. If they're worried about contamination they filter it themselves. It's not like it was pristine before. It was messed up long before we got here. Most people in those parts don't have a clue."

"Well, one woman up here had her well tested when some locals got sick. One actually died, another one's hospitalized and on chelation therapy. If their families get wind of this data, it could mean serious trouble."

"They'd be hard-pressed to prove anything that would hold up in court. You, of all people, Bob, should know that."

"Of course they'd lose in court. People with private wells are responsible for their own water quality. Our project's flowback hasn't been subject to the Clean Water Act since 2005, thanks to our buddies at Halliburton. Yada, yada, yada. That's not the problem.

"The noise they'd make, however, *is*. Getting the environmentalists all stirred up, the press attacking the entire oil and gas industry, more investigations, and ultimately, everyone's worst nightmare, the public finding out what's really going on up here."

"Yeah, yeah, I know. We're banking on it not being a big deal, based on the sparse population and general ignorance of such things."

"You'd damned well better hope so, Gerald. If our mistake blows EMPI's promise of secrecy and PURF becomes public knowledge, there'll be a shit storm neither of us can survive. Perhaps literally."

"Tell me something I don't know, Bob. You're preaching to the choir here, cowboy. I've been a tree full o' owls every goddamn night for weeks."

"Okay, fine. So what happened? What caused it?"

"Drilling up there ain't simple. Geology's a nightmare. We're dealing with layers and layers of different strata, different densities. Constant kickoffs. Dodging fault lines while using them for injection wells, lots of sidetrackin', all sorts of maneuvers like that."

Bob put the phone on speaker and strolled over to his den's wet bar, a bit earlier than usual with it still before noon. He selected a bottle of eighteen-year-old Glenmorangie and poured a generous shot.

"This isn't your first Colorado rodeo, Gerald. There's plenty of drilling sites up in these parts."

"Most of them's in flat areas fu'ther south. Plateaus. High elevation, deep bedrock, less tectonic action. Think of mountains as a crumpled-up piece o' metal as opposed to a flat sheet. How easy is it to go straight through all them changes without gettin' bumped around on the way down?"

"Thanks for the geology lesson. Now tell me what happened." He inhaled the liquor's enticing vapors, then took a sustained sip.

"The bore hole was too close to the deep injection site for the flowback. It triggered a minor tremor that fractured the casing, plus opened up a channel to the aquifer."

Bob licked his lips, regarded what remained briefly, then finished the shot. He closed his eyes, relishing the effects as the amber liquor transported him somewhere between scotch nirvana and fracking hell.

"Brilliant. Absolutely brilliant. Seems a first-year geology student could've seen that one coming."

"Yeah, yeah, I know. Shit happens. So sue me."

"Oh, shut your face, Gerald. I'm glad you're so amused. I'm sitting up here in the line of fire. They're already stirred up from that security breach a while back. They thought they took care of it. From what I hear, the job wasn't clean. Supposedly there's still a mess out there to deal with. Everyone's in a pissy mood already. Lonestar Ops don't need to be the one rockin' the boat right now, get it?"

"Yeah, yeah. I know. We fired the geologist and got a different PhD onboard who knows the area better. Former USGS as well as some time with the state geological agency."

"Why'd he leave a secure government job to work for us?"

"Seriously? That surprises you?"

"Yes."

"Even when we tripled his salary?"

Bob chuckled. "Right."

"Okay, now listen. Other than that little screw-up, Maguire says the prospects up there look promising. Damn promising. This could be just what we've been looking for. Expand it into a play before they figure out what happened in Oklahoma and raise the severance tax."

"Good point."

"Put on your landman hat, Bob. See what we can get a hold of for expanding operations. Before one of our competitors gets wind of it and snatches it up. I hear tell they've been sniffing around like a buck during rut."

"We already own quite a bit and Dad can see to it we lease as much federal land as we want. How much are you talking about?"

"Anything privately held. Whatever y'all can find. If you encounter any resistant landowners, remember our horizontal drilling radius is around a mile. Even if they have a land patent, they're not going to catch on to us drilling right under their asses some distance away and a mile or so down. If possible, get a geo-engineer to check it out, too. Try the Colorado School of Mines. Billy John's overseas or I'd send him up."

"Okay. I'll see what I can find."

"As soon as possible. Have a nice afternoon, Bob."

"Thanks. Same to you." He poured himself another shot, knocked it back in a single gulp, and huffed out an alcohol-saturated breath. "Give my love to Doris and the kids."

Before the pale-faces came among us, we enjoyed the happiness of unbounded freedom, and were acquainted with neither riches, wants, nor oppression. How is it now? Wants and oppressions are our lot, for are we not controlled in everything, and dare we move without asking, by your leave?
—Tecumseh, September 1811

14. ERRANDS

EN ROUTE BELTON COUNTY
June 8, Friday
10:04 a.m.

The thirty mile drive to Belton was familiar. Just under fifteen miles south of Falcon Ridge, it was the county seat and populated enough for all the major stores to be represented. Bryan made countless trips there for materials and supplies while remodeling the cabin.

Sara parked behind the two-story stone structure that housed all the county offices as well as the courthouse, then went inside. The water reports she'd found in the file box as well as the most recent one were tucked under her arm in a manila folder.

Along the way to the main lobby she passed the county clerk's office, reminding her she needed to transfer ownership of the cabin to herself. The building directory indicated the health department was on the second floor. Before the accident she would have taken the stairs. This time she opted for the elevator.

Belton County Health Department stared back from the door's frosted glass. Three people stood at the counter, another two seated against the wall. When her turn arrived she greeted the clerk and spread the reports on the counter. "I recently had my water tested. It has numerous heavy metals and chemicals that weren't there before. Where should I report this?"

The heavy-set, dark-haired woman scrutinized the two reports. "Yes, these look worth reporting. However, we don't get involved with private systems or wells. If the problem is pervasive in your area, we'll check with any local water masters and make sure their tests are current and within limits. This is quite common in the Colorado Mineral Belt. Meanwhile, I recommend you get a good filtration system."

"Fortunately, I have one. These tests were run on the input line. I'm just alarmed that things changed so drastically."

"Is your well in mineralized bedrock? They usually have a bigger problem than those in an alluvium stream."

Sara's brow wrinkled with thought. "I don't know. I need to look more closely at the original drill report."

"That should help you figure out where the problem is. You might want to check with the EPA. Find out if there's any Superfund activity nearby that may have opened up an old storage area. That could be what's tainting aquifers in your area. If that's the case, they may not be aware of the problem."

"Thanks. I will."

The woman eyed the papers with a thoughtful expression. "Do you mind if we keep copies of your reports for our files?"

"No, not at all." Sara shifted her weight as the clerk stepped across the small office to the copier. Standing still for any length of time still aggravated her back and hip enough to protest, sometimes rather loudly.

The woman returned and handed back the reports. "All that mining back in the 1800s sure caused plenty of trouble for us while people back then got filthy rich," she stated. "However, a few things mentioned in your report aren't related to mining. Things like selenium, benzene, and strontium. That implies the increase is related to industrial activity, usually fracking. Good luck figuring it out."

"Thanks."

After returning to her car she sat there a while, trying to determine if there was anything else she should do while she was in town. Going by the big grocery store certainly wouldn't hurt, so she put together a quick list and headed in that direction.

Along the way, she pondered what the woman said about mining. She'd heard that before, but this time it made an impression. Since Bryan installed such a robust filtration system, he was undoubtedly well-aware.

She picked up her groceries, stopped at a Wendy's for a quick bite, then headed back home, remembering her intent to stop by the police station.

Would they even care?

Did it have any relevance to their accident?

Probably not.

On the other hand, they asked to be notified if she remembered anything. Could that strange tower-like structure be some sort of Superfund activity? If that was all they saw, then it shouldn't have been a big deal.

Again her memory rang with Bryan's parting words.

Get away with what?

The empty feeling in the pit of her stomach asserted they'd seen something significant.

Something bad.

But what?

As always, the harder she tried to remember, the less came to mind. The previous two revelations came when she'd been thinking about something else. Maybe getting back into her meditation and yoga routine would help.

When she got back to Falcon Ridge she parked in front of the police station, then waited a moment to collect her thoughts. Was what little she remembered even worth reporting? Maybe that tower. Perhaps they knew what it was. Could the tower relate to the water? It wouldn't hurt to ask.

She got out, walked up the few steps, and pulled open one of the heavy double doors.

"Hi. Is Officer Fernandez in?" she asked the desk sergeant. "He's working on my accident investigation and I have something that might be relevant."

"Which case?"

"I'm Sara Reynolds. Auto accident. My husband was killed, our pickup lost down a ravine."

"Right." His look turned pensive. "Actually, someone we detained relative to that case has been trying to get in touch with you."

She straightened, mind racing. "With me? Who?"

"Someone we arrested earlier today. Hold on." He picked up the phone and punched a speed dial key. "Mrs. Reynolds is here. Says she has some information for you."

Her heart pounded. Who on earth could have gotten arrested and been trying to reach her? She giggled to herself when Liz came to mind. Was she up to something and her husband refused to bail her out?

She checked her cell, discovering it was still on mute since Mah Jongg the night before. Three missed calls and as many messages. Before she had a chance to check either, Fernandez appeared, wearing a look that made her skin crawl. She dropped her phone back in her purse.

"Are you sure you want to bail this guy out? He's a suspect in your case."

Her jaw dropped, dumbfounded. "What on earth are you talking about? I came here to tell you I remembered a few things about the accident. Who's a suspect in my case?"

"Charles Littlewolf. He was arrested this morning for trespassing on a crime scene and suspicion of tampering with evidence."

"Charlie? Oh, my God! What did he do?"

"Surveillance video caught him at the site where your truck landed. He broke into your vehicle, then tried to tell us there was nothing inside. We suspect if he found anything that he hid it before returning to where he was parked."

Sara stared at him, turbulence in her mind stealing any lucid response.

"You have additional information?" She nodded. "C'mon back to my office and I'll take your statement."

She did as directed and dropped heavily into a folding chair across from his desk.

"So what did you remember?"

"Nothing much. Just fragments. We were cross-country skiing. I think we saw some strange looking tower structure, or something like that. Whatever it was, it didn't belong there."

"Do you remember where that was?"

"Not really. But I know the general area where we usually skied." She proceeded to describe it, which resulted in an area of about eight square miles. "Do you have any idea what it might have been?"

"No."

"Is there any Superfund activity in that area? I'm not familiar enough with the process to know what that would look like."

"That's possible. We'll check it out." His professional demeanor switched abruptly to a look drenched with suspicion. "Do you still want to bail Littlewolf out? You're the one he insisted on calling."

Irritated by his attitude shift, she matched his look with one of her own. "He was a close friend of my late husband's. I'm sure he was only trying to help. At least someone around here is trying to solve his murder. Yes. Of course I'll bail him out."

He held her gaze a moment before looking away. "The JP set bail at $450 plus a $50 fine for expired out-of-state vehicle registration. I'll get the paperwork."

Sara stared into space, stunned. A distinct impression that Charlie was innocent washed through her like a strong cup of coffee. Her tension dissolved with the comforting, albeit irrational feeling that somehow she wasn't alone.

FALCON RIDGE PD
June 8, Friday
1:18 p.m.

Mike Fernandez watched the unlikely pair leave, then get into the woman's car, body language indicating they were comfortable with one another.

"Do you think they're in it together?"

He frowned at his superior, Captain Steve Urbanowsky, whose once-blond hair was rapidly succumbing to grey. "How? She could've easily been killed as well."

"Maybe he has plans to take care of that little detail."

He exhaled sharply. "She's already collected the insurance money. It would be a lot more complicated now."

"Not if he married her."

"Good point." Mike fingered his mustache. "You do realize how bogus this is, right? I think she saw right through it, too."

"Why do you say that?"

"She made a rather sarcastic remark that at least someone was trying to figure out who killed her husband. And she's right."

Steve's expression hardened, grey eyes cold. "We were told, in no uncertain terms, to proceed as if this were a normal accident investigation. A little creativity never hurts to keep those people off our butt. That Indian guy *is* unemployed and behind in his child support, which gives him motive. They're going to check on us, make sure we did as we were told. Before we close this case, we need to make some effort at an investigation, bogus or not. Otherwise, we could be next."

Mike tailed his boss into his office and sat down on the corner of his desk. "I'd sure like to know what's going on, what made them a target. She seems so young and innocent while neither she nor her husband has any criminal record whatsoever. Spotless military service, steady job, not even a parking ticket his entire life. Nada. He was an Eagle Scout, for heaven sake."

Steve rocked back in his chair and set his feet on his cluttered desk. "That's what makes you a good cop, Mike. Wanting answers. Curiosity. Never satisfied with anything less than the truth."

"Yeah. And that's exactly what pisses me off about this bullshit."

The Cheyennes are those who have been fighting with you. They did it in broad daylight, so that all could see them. If I had been fighting I would have done it by day and not in the dark.
— Satanta, October 1867

15. PHOTOS

FALCON RIDGE
June 8, Friday
1:20 p.m.

Sara's thoughts spun with disbelief. "What do you mean, the truck's cab was empty? How could it be?" She unlocked the car with her key fob and got inside.

Charlie climbed into the passenger seat, set his hat in his lap, then pulled on his seatbelt. "I don't know. But it was. Nothing. The console was empty and so was the glovebox. Nothing but broken glass and plastic debris. Windshield and passenger side window were shattered, but in place. Driver's side was face down, most of the door missing, so I suppose stuff could've fallen out. But not everything. Especially the closed compartments."

"Who could've done that?"

"Someone who thought there might be evidence of some sort, I suppose."

"Oh! That's right! When we were skiing we probably took pictures. My camera and our phones could have contained evidence of whatever we saw." She gasped with another thought. "Maybe that's why someone caused the wreck!" She pulled out and headed for the main road. "Do you want to go home or somewhere else?"

He flinched. "I'd appreciate it if you'd take me to the impound lot to pick up my truck."

"What? They didn't just leave it where you were parked?"

"Nope. They had it towed. I got handcuffed and thrown in the back of the patrol car. They even fined me for having expired New Mexico plates."

"It's not like you'd committed some violent crime! That's ridiculous. Where's the impound?"

"Hold on." He pulled a piece of paper out of his pocket. "Turn left on the highway. It's just down the road a few miles. So, you remembered you were skiing. Bryan actually mentioned that was why you were coming out. It's where I figured you were. Until you never made it back. Have you remembered anything else?"

"I had a flashback yesterday of some sort of tall structure. Different than a cell tower. No antennae and vertical sides. Also something big and round. I'm talking huge. Any idea what they could be?"

"Not offhand, but I'll bet it's still there. It doesn't sound like something that would be temporary."

"Dad works for a company that collects satellite data. I wonder if he could find out?"

"Sounds like a good place to start."

"By the way, I had my water tested. It has elevated levels of all sorts of contaminants that weren't there before. Mercury, lead, cadmium, and arsenic, plus selenium and strontium. I reported it to the health department, but they don't do anything when it's a private well. They suggested checking to see if any Superfund activities are active around here."

"I've heard about those projects. Sometimes they make things worse."

"Figures. Do they use towers of any sort?"

"Anything is possible. They might drill a hole that's deep enough to dispose of it underground. The impound lot is up ahead, about a quarter mile."

"Okay. Hey, you're on a well, right? You probably ought to have it checked, too."

"I've used bottled for years."

"Oh. Good." Gradually, her agitation coupled with the day's events started to settle. "Charlie?"

"Hmmmm?"

"Thank you so much for checking out the truck. I don't know why the police made such a big deal of it. I wonder if they're the ones who cleaned it out?"

"I doubt it. They set up video surveillance on the site, though, and put more police tape up by the road. Since I came in by canoe, I didn't see it. I didn't realize it was still an open case, much less a restricted area." He snorted. "Not that it would have stopped me. There's the impound, right up there."

Sara pulled into the lot and stopped beside a small cinderblock building. The adjacent area was surrounded by a ten-foot chain-link fence topped with razor wire. A variety of cars and trucks were inside, some severely damaged. Their truck probably would have been there, too, if it had been recoverable.

He opened the door and got out, then leaned back inside, dark eyes sincere. "*Néá'ešemeno.* Thanks for getting me out of there. I promise to pay you back. I hated to ask, but didn't know anyone else who'd help."

"No problem. How much do you think these people are going to charge to get your truck back?"

His dark eyes reflected surprise. "Oh. Right. I hadn't thought of that. I have no idea."

"Go find out. If you need help, I'm here." When he started to protest, she objected right back. "Bryan would want me to. Surely you know that. You need your truck. Now go find out how much."

He hung his head a moment, then went inside the squat building. He returned a few minutes later with a troubled look. She rolled down her window.

"They want $257.36, cash only. Includes towing and storage fees. Ridiculous. It's been here about six hours. That heap isn't even worth that much."

"Ridiculous, alright. Okay, get in. I need to find an ATM."

"I'm so sorry, Sara," he said as he got settled again in the passenger seat. "*Ná-amèhahtomēvo.* I owe you."

"Don't worry about it. This isn't your fault. You were trying to help. I have the feeling that nothing being there is important."

The ATM in the small shopping center had a two-hundred dollar limit, so she went inside the grocery store to cash a check for the rest. Moments later they were back at the impound. As he got out, he thanked her once again, his stoic expression failing to hide his humiliation.

She held up her hand in dismissal. "Not another word. Bryan would expect me to help."

"Thank you, Sara. Stay safe." He donned his hat and headed for the building, posture dejected.

On the way home her mind raced with what to do next. First, call her father and bring him up to date. Hopefully, he could find satellite pictures that would solve the mystery of the strange structure.

Information about Superfund sites should be online. If one related to the water issue, that would solve that, at least. Would the EPA be liable for Edna's death? Rhonda's crazy behavior?

When she got home, she collapsed into a kitchen chair. The usual aches and pains, further exacerbated by the stressful day, raged. Her body begged for a nap, but her brain refused to cooperate.

Maybe she could kill two birds with one stone.

Get out her yoga mat and assume the lotus position—which she could finally achieve again—and search the web. Bryan's laptop would be easier to use and more efficient than her tablet.

Satisfied with her plan, she laid out the mat, then went to retrieve the computer.

The sprawling oak desk and shelving unit built into the far corner of the living area struck her with a fresh wave of nostalgia. Bryan had designed it to his own specifications, then put it together, piece by piece.

What a renaissance man he was. There was absolutely nothing he couldn't do.

A small moan escaped as she lowered slowly to her knees and opened the cabinet portion on the right. Her shoulder and back muscles complained as she leaned far enough inside to reach the very back. A few twinges later she managed to release the latch to the false bottom. Since they were often absent from the cabin for months, he created a secure place for anything of value. He always left a spare laptop there, being a computer geek with a clear addiction.

The spring released and false floor elevated.

Bryan's computer, as expected, was nestled inside.

They always agreed not to mess with the other's machine. It was beyond annoying when someone else changed the settings, often inadvertently. Oddly enough, she felt as if she were intruding or breaking that pact. With a heavy heart, she lifted it out, apologized aloud for the violation, then got in position on the mat.

It booted right up. She connected to her phone's hot spot and opened Firefox. A handful of different tabs came up. Some work-related, eBay, and his Facebook page. She clicked on the last one, thinking she should shut it down along with all his other social media sites.

It finished loading.

The cover and profile shots were new.

A panoramic view of snowcapped peaks, his profile picture replaced with a shot of the two of them.

Both taken the day of the accident.

An onslaught of goosebumps tickled her arms and the back of her neck.

How did he do that?

She tried to think. Maybe with his phone. But the picture quality was far beyond that, not the typical distorted wide-angle. She scrolled down to where he added it, finding a post made with his phone.

I love my wife's new camera. Is this an awesome shot or what?

Her mind tripped through a log-jam of thoughts, data, and implications. Her camera could do that? Did he ever mention that? Not that her brain was exactly helpful these days.

Was it possible it didn't matter the camera was lost? Could the pictures they took be in cyberspace somewhere?

She clicked on the folder icon, hoping it would be easy to find. "My Pictures" contained a multitude of subfolders. One was called "Olympus."

She opened it.

Everything was familiar, taken before the accident.

Back to File Explorer. What was the one called OneDrive? Its icon looked like a cloud.

She clicked.

Several folders came up. Within was another one, also named "Olympus."

Another single folder lay within.

Its title the date of the accident.

MONTGOMERY RESIDENCE
BOULDER
June 8, Friday
3:10 p.m.

Will Montgomery couldn't understand a word his daughter was saying. Was she in danger? Or just excited?

"Calm down, Sara. Calm down." He repeated it, over and over, until the chatter gradually wound down and eventually stopped.

"Are you okay?" he asked.

"Yes, Dad. I'm fine. But you'll never believe what I found!"

His shoulders relaxed, relieved, then his jaw tensed. She should have stayed with them instead of out there in the boonies. If she were in some sort of trouble, it would take at least an hour and a half to get there—longer on Friday, when hoards of city dwellers headed for the mountains.

"Okay, Sara. Try me. What did you find?"

"The photos we took! The day of the accident! I had no idea my camera could do that. But I'm not that sure what I'm looking at. Or what to do. I need your help."

"Wait a minute, back up. Your camera did what?"

"It uploaded the photos! Everything's on Bryan's computer."

"So you think you have something important?"

"I think so. We must have seen something significant. Bryan understood what it meant, but I didn't. Or maybe he told me and I don't remember. But you might. For all I know, it's what got him killed."

Will stiffened, instincts screaming trouble.

"Okay. Listen. Download the folder with those pictures right now to a flash drive. If they're that implicating, there's no telling whether someone else might be able to find them or delete them. If they're important, I'm surprised they're still there. Do it now. I'll wait."

"Okay, hold on."

He sat chewing his thumb nail, mind doing backflips as he speculated on what they might reveal. Moments later she was back.

"Alright. They're on a flash drive. Should I delete them in this OneDrive?"

"Is anything else there?"

"Yes."

"Copy everything. Confirm you've got it, then go ahead. No sense leaving them out there for someone else to find. Empty the *Trash* folder, too."

"Okay. Done. Now what? Should I email them to you?"

"No! Especially not from Bryan's computer. If there's something shady going on, it may have been hacked."

"Wouldn't they have taken these pictures down if it had?"

"Good point. Maybe. Or it might be a unique account set up for that computer. Either way, shut it down. And no, don't email them. I'll come out tomorrow to take a look. If they're that sensitive, the less internet exposure they have the better."

"Should I tell the police?"

"No. At least not yet. I don't trust them, either. Wait until I take a look and we figure out what they are. Then we'll decide."

"Okay, Dad. I sure hope they solve at least part of this mystery. By the way, some other things have happened that I was going to call you about."

"Such as?"

"I remembered a few things. We were cross-country skiing. That's where we took these pictures. I had a flashback about it, and now I have photographic evidence."

"Okay. What else?"

"Charlie went to the wreck site in his canoe to see if he could find anything. Our truck was already cleaned out. Every single thing! The glovebox and console, both empty. My camera should have been there, Bryan's cell phone, my purse. And the cops told me back in the hospital they didn't recover anything. So who did?"

"Could the door have opened? Were the windows broken out?"

"The driver's side door was mostly gone. The glovebox and console were still closed, but empty. Oh! And he got arrested for being there, too. Accused of tampering with evidence at a crime scene, or something crazy like that."

Will's heart slammed against his chest.

The cab cleaned out?

That was beyond bad news. They'd definitely stumbled on something they weren't supposed to see. If so, it was a solid bet she was still in danger.

"Alright, Sara, listen very carefully. What you're telling me has me convinced that, whatever you saw, it was not only wrong, but dangerous. You need to stay with us until we figure this out. Pack up what you need and come home, *now*. It's early enough you can get here before dark."

He could tell by the long silence on the other end that she was going to argue. He set his jaw and deepened his tone to *I'm-your-father-don't-argue-with-me* range.

"Sara? I mean it. *Now*."

"But Dad. . ."

"No buts. *Now*. Bring Bryan's computer and anything else you think is too valuable to lose. This is serious. I'm not kidding."

It took a while for her to answer. He closed his eyes, projecting his intentions in her direction.

"Okay, Dad. See you in a few hours."

"Good girl. Text me when you hit the road."

"I will."

16. JOBS

SARA'S CABIN
RURAL FALCON RIDGE
June 8, Friday
3:21 p.m.

Sara scowled at her phone. Will hadn't been so commanding since her teens. What set him off? Obviously something or he wouldn't have insisted she head to Boulder at this time of day.

She closed her eyes and sighed. As if she weren't worn out enough already from everything else. Making that drive was the last thing she felt like doing.

Dare she not go?

No.

If anything happened she'd never hear the end of it. She sighed again, this time with resignation, then made a mental list of what to take. Mainly the computer and clothes for a few days. If she needed more, she could pick some up from her condo. Or just go shopping.

The flash drive in the USB port caught her eye. She ejected and removed it, marveling at its tiny size versus capacity. Where would something no bigger than a fingernail be safe and not get lost?

Something relatively small, yet secure.

A contact lens case in the guest bathroom, one of the spares they kept for friends who forgot their own, fit the task perfectly. She snapped it closed, then went back to the kitchen and slipped it into the makeup bag in her purse.

The manila folder on the kitchen table caught her eye. Yes, that should go, too. She hadn't even told him about the water.

Should she tell Charlie where she was going? He put his butt on the line for her, so she owed him. She grabbed her phone and sent a text. And what about Liz? She probably should.

Or not.

She liked Liz, but so far she was just a new, casual friend who seemed sweet, but was a bit of a busybody. The woman had her cell number. She usually texted before she came over, making it an easy decision not to bother. Nosey as she was, she'd want to know why she was going and Sara didn't want to explain, much less lie.

That decided, she trudged upstairs to gather some clothes. Even though she felt better she continued to sleep downstairs, between the stairs and that huge, empty bed. She grabbed the usual casual clothes and underwear from inside the dresser, then went to the closet where she slid her favorite hoody off its hanger.

Knowing Will and Connie, they'd want to go out for a nice dinner. Shorts and t-shirts wouldn't do for that.

Her eyes shifted to the garment bag that held the only dress she had up there. The one Bryan bought. A royal blue, slinky silk sheath with a huge, sexy slit up the side. Left at the cabin for their special times together. He loved it when she dressed up for him, especially out there in the wilderness. If left up to her, she'd have brought nothing but sportswear and her favorite hiking boots, not four-inch heels.

Candlelight dinners. Watching the sunset. Its silky folds in a heap while they made love on that sheepskin rug in front of a raging fire.

Her vision blurred.

She bit her lip, hard. Indulging in another meltdown was a really bad idea. Not with a long drive ahead.

No. Absolutely not. Not now. Suck it up, buttercup!

Steeling herself with a deep, determined breath, she grabbed the garment bag off the closet rail, then placed everything else in a canvas weekender bag. Back downstairs she collected Bryan's computer and the rest of her things.

Good to go.

She loaded everything except her purse and the water records in the trunk. Texted her father, who responded they'd go out to eat when she arrived, so she could drive straight through.

She smiled. So predictable.

Besides, a decent meal instead of frozen lasagna or burritos from canned refried beans had tremendous appeal. Bryan had done a lot of the cooking and fixing a meal for just herself was such a bore.

Yes, getting away for a few days was a good thing. Maybe staying at the cabin was a bad idea after all. Like Liz said, if she stayed for the winter she definitely needed another car. She could give that some thought while she was there, too.

A change of scene might be just what she needed to clear her head.

Heart, too.

Her dad and Connie understood better than anyone what she was going through.

Except maybe Charlie.

CHARLIE'S CABIN
RURAL FALCON RIDGE
June 8, Friday
3:26 p.m.

When Charlie got home from the impound he hung his hat on the dust-ridden elk antlers over the mantle, then collapsed in his recliner. He gritted his teeth and snarled like a cornered wolf. In reality he felt more like that dead raccoon on the side of the road.

Trash-bandits were smart, clever, and aggressive. Yet their fate as road waffles was a common sight.

Did he likewise set up his own demise?

Exhaustion, anger, and suspicion pressured his senses like an approaching storm front. He fumed further when the classic phrase *White man speak with forked tongue* came to mind.

Since when did Bryan's wreck become a crime scene?

That alone spoke volumes.

Obviously, he wasn't the only one who knew he'd been murdered.

Furthermore, how could what he'd done be considered damaging when the pickup was beyond totaled? All he'd found was that little electronic component.

He got up and took it out of his hat, then returned to his chair to examine it more closely. Between the humiliation of getting bailed out and picking up his truck, he'd completely forgotten to tell Sara what he'd found.

What was it?

His last cell phone had something like that. That's what it looked like, alright, a memory card. But to what? The truck was a 2008, so had limited electronics. Bryan used the GPS on his phone, so it wasn't from a navigation unit. His camera, maybe? Or more accurately, Sara's? Maybe it contained the pictures she wondered about.

His phone chirped—a text from Sara. It was good for her to get away. He liked her father and knew Bryan had, too. Should he tell her what he found?

No. It could wait. They'd both had enough for one day.

The guilt at having to ask her for help raged. He had to pay her back as soon as possible. She was right, Bryan wouldn't have thought a thing about it. Neither would he, if it were reversed.

But this was different.

Taking money from a woman—any woman—grated against him like sand in his boots. He should be protecting her, not the other way around.

His savings were just about gone and paying her back would wipe it out. He had to find a job, and fast. Since it was well into tourist season, he needed to leave his number as a guide with the store, local motels, bait shops, and any other businesses in the immediate area.

It was time to get out of this self-imposed cave of grief-stricken exile and find work. This was totally unacceptable warrior behavior. He could almost feel Eaglefeathers's glare.

The leaky tap in the sink reminded him what Sara said about the water. Actually, he ought to get serious and apply for a job at one of those water labs, even though it would mean a substantial commute. If there was one in Belton, that wouldn't be so bad.

Maybe if he had a real job again he'd get more respect.

In spite of his bachelor's degree in Environmental Management and minor in chemistry from the University of Colorado, he had the feeling he was still viewed as another stupid Indian. Other than those years with the Forest Service, he never had dependable employment.

As fate would have it, when he got furloughed, it turned and stung him like a scorpion. His child support was calculated on his previous salary. Thus, that obligation, of which he was only paying half, consumed his savings at an alarming rate.

His thoughts gravitated to his two daughters. He missed them. A lot. They talked at least once a week. It tore him up the last time. Both were crying because they couldn't come see him. And it was his own fault.

Between his survival skills and being comfortable with his primitive living conditions, his lack of income hadn't concerned him. There were too many back on the reservation who got by with far less. His humble home was more than enough.

But an ancient one-room cabin with no bathroom door was not suitable for two young girls. Carla was ten, Charlene, thirteen. Summer visitation this year wasn't going to happen. Other years since the divorce he'd gone down to see them in New Mexico and stayed in a motel. In addition to his ailing finances, his ex nixed that idea, saying it was inappropriate. They needed their own room.

He hated to admit it, but she was right.

Which gave him even more incentive to find work.

Real work.

He looked back at the electronic component. Where was a safe place to keep it? He eyed the stone fireplace. Above it hung a bow and quiver of arrows that belonged to his great-grandfather and the rack from his first elk hunt.

Below them on the rough-hewn mantle stood a small whitewashed clay jar decorated with the Diné orange and turquoise zig-zag design. A handmade gift from his maternal grandmother—his *amasani*—when he was a child. Where he kept small treasures he found, like turquoise chips left over from those who fashioned jewelry.

Perfect.

He got up and gently lifted its lid, smiling to see its former contents still in place. He placed the memory card among them, then cradled it in his hands and offered a prayer of protection upon it. Then set it back in place, still wondering at the memory card's contents.

When Sara got back, they'd figure it out.

BKSS LLC
ALBUQUERQUE, NM
June 8, Friday
3:31 p.m.

"Hey, boss. You busy?"

Keller closed his eyes and braced himself. "Never too busy for you, Johannsen. What's up?"

"First, some good news."

"That's refreshing. "

"Yeah. I talked to our handler at the NSA. I told her what was going on. She agreed things were potentially urgent, so she upgraded us. They fixed the mic on the Reynolds chick's phone so we can track her, hear her conversations, plus anything going on in the immediate area, even if she's not on the phone. We now have a channel to monitor all that, so we'll know what's going on real-time."

"Great."

"So, thanks to that, we got some more intel on the case. Going on right now. She just had an interesting conversation with her old man."

"I'm listening."

"Turns out that camera we found in the truck uploaded the pictures to the web. She just found them on the dead guy's laptop."

"Laptop? What laptop? How in hell did you miss that?"

"Don't know, boss. Maybe it was in her car or something. Anyway, she has no idea what they are, but even as we speak, she's getting ready to head for Boulder and show them to her old man."

"That can't happen. You know that, right?"

"Roger that. We're on it, watching her place right now and making sure anything in that car doesn't get there intact. We'll track her enroute."

"Don't kill her, okay? I'm talking surgical here. Do you hear me, Johannsen? Destroy the evidence and scare her, that's it. Her old man's going to be pissed, but if she's okay, he'll get over it. Do it right and he may not even suspect anything."

"Sure, boss. That's the plan. But I'm pretty sure from their conversation that he already does."

"Figures."

Keller pressed his fingers to his temples. Whatever pictures they got were only part of it. The main security issue was below ground. If the Corps of Engineers had gotten than damn thing out of there on time, the drilling tower wouldn't have been that hard to explain. She may not know what that monstrosity was, but her father would. Once they got all that heavy equipment and logistics crap out of there, above-ground security wouldn't even be necessary.

"Okay, listen," he went on. "Make sure you find all of Reynolds's accounts and check everything he downloaded or stored online. Everything, you hear me? Use whatever means necessary to get all you can from his ISP and phone records. Have you checked with EMPI cyber security yet about how he managed to get unauthorized access?"

"We pinged them. Haven't heard back."

"Keep after them. Granted, Reynolds was an IT whiz kid. With his background he could've gotten in anywhere. But we need to make sure they're secure. No telling where he got all that information, but EMPI offered one-stop shopping.

"We also need to find out how he discovered it in the first place. There's gotta be a leak somewhere. I need to give Steinbrenner an update. While I'm at it, I'll tell him to get off his lazy ass and make sure his system admin's doing his job."

"Roger that."

He ended the call, hoping to bloody hell they didn't screw this one up. Meanwhile, he needed to report the latest to that asshole project manager. He'd encountered plenty like him over the years, but that guy took the cake. He didn't care how obnoxious someone was if they were competent. In this case, his personality was a neon sign advertising an IQ in the turnip range.

Bernie worked his jaw as he found the number and punched it in, wondering how much that worthless bastard was making off this job.

As expected, it went to his squeaky-voiced secretary. "Mr. Steinbrenner's office. How can I help you?"

"This is Bernard Keller, PURF special ops. I need to talk to him. *Now!*" He snarled the words, using his harshest drill sergeant voice.

"One moment, please, Mr. Keller."

He cringed at her sticky sweet reply. At least he was past the first hurdle. While he waited, he finished off the last bite of his bologna sandwich and washed it down with a swig of scorched afternoon coffee. His nose wrinkled with disgust when the man picked up.

"Hi, Bernie. What's up?"

He gritted his teeth. The only person allowed to call him that was his mother, with the possible exception of his wife during moments of passion, which were few and far between.

He gritted his teeth, mimicking the man's condescending tone. "Hi, *Virg*. You need to know the latest. That is, if you're interested."

"Sure. But make it quick. I've got a meeting to get to."

"Fine. You remember that security incident back in April, right?"

"Refresh my memory. I have a lot on my mind, you know."

"Right. You're the only one with that problem, right Virgil? Okay, listen up. A sensor went off on the property. Skiers. They'd supposedly wandered into our territory. We found his parked truck, tracked it, and neutralized the target. The woman, however, survived. We found evidence that indicated they knew about PURF beforehand. Remember now?"

"Yeah, right. What about it?"

"Seemed simple, right? Well, it wasn't. They took photos. When we cleaned out the truck, we got the camera, but turns out it uploaded the pictures to his computer. The woman just found them and is planning to show them to her old man. Who's former FBI."

He rolled his eyes at Steinbrenner's startled sputter.

"Since Reynolds had documentation on the project, which he downloaded from *your* server, it's obvious he was looking for tangible evidence. Get it now, Virg? We have a major security breach that started on *your* turf. You need to confirm your cyber security guys fixed the vulnerability and see if they've seen any further suspicious activity. You'd better hope that's not the case."

"Okay. Fine. Anything else?"

"You realize, Virg, that you've already been hacked once. Cyber security is a biggie that's your responsibility. The guy involved had high-order computer skills, so it's possible it wasn't entirely your fault. But bear in mind the NSA won't be happy if someone got in because the system wasn't properly secured."

"I assure you my system administrator has it under control."

"You'd damned well better hope so. Let me know, alright?"

"Yeah, yeah. Got it."

Bernie's instincts blared like a Klaxon alarm as he hung up. For some reason he believed Steinbrenner was telling the truth. At least as far as he was aware.

But in the classified world being naive or stupid was a far more serious violation than being a good liar.

> *The Nez Perces never make war on women and children; we could have killed a great many women and children while the war lasted, but we would feel ashamed to do so cowardly an act.*
> —*Young Joseph "Chief Joseph", 1879*

17. I-70 EAST

INTERSTATE 70 EAST
June 8, Friday
3:42 p.m.

As soon as Sara turned onto the interstate eastbound, she tried to relax. There were less traveled roads that were shorter, but taking I-70 as far as the 470 Loop outside Denver, then taking Highway 36 the remainder of the way was appealing in its direct simplicity.

It was a beautiful, scenic drive she usually enjoyed. This time of year the mountains were still green, courtesy of melting snow. Jagged peaks loomed around her, drop-offs earning occasional adrenaline spikes, in spite of hefty guardrails.

Would it have done them any good, if there had been one at Dead Horse Canyon?

Something told her no.

As her nerves settled into the route's familiarity, she wondered what her father knew, or thought he did, that alarmed him so much. Then again, if she and Bryan had seen something that got him killed, it made sense. Being a target herself was not something her suppressed instincts allowed her to believe.

Miles streamed by as the two lanes wound gracefully through pediments and passes presided over by endless crags. Before she knew it, she was inside the Eisenhower Tunnel crossing the Continental Divide. Her heartrate doubled, the enclosure always aggravating her claustrophobia.

Her shoulder muscles relaxed when the gaping hole in the mountain's side appeared in the rearview mirror; which she checked frequently, half-expecting to see a black SUV on her tail. The nearest vehicle was an eighteen-wheeler, a quarter-mile or so back. Hopefully it would stay there. She hated those behemoths, especially when driving her Honda.

Those heading west into the Rockies to enjoy its many wonders made traffic onerous on Fridays. At least eastbound was relatively light.

Except that wouldn't last. About the time she got into town it would be the height of commuter hour. One thing she definitely didn't miss.

Her thoughts shifted to Charlie and his arrest. It was too weird that he'd found nothing in the truck.

Nothing!

How could it be?

Did she imagine the cop telling her they didn't recover anything? She had to ask again. If the local police didn't have it, then who did? Charlie said no one else would have any business down there, unless they were specifically checking the truck.

It was all far too troubling, nerves kicking in. To take her mind off it, she turned on her favorite Sirius station. Soon she was enjoying the drive again, zoning to soft rock for the better part of an hour. By that time, she'd left the Front Range behind and was on flatter ground approaching Lakewood.

Whew. No more yawning ravines with an appetite for cars.

Then, to her horror, Sarah McLachlan's heart-wrenching song, *Angel,* started to play. While her meltdown at the cabin had been averted, this time her eyes defied her will. Tears gushed from their confines, her throat constricting within seconds of the opening riff.

No, no, no, no, no! For heaven sakes, man-up, Reynolds. No crying at seventy miles per hour! Suck it up! Suck it up!

That song made her cry every time, long before she'd lost Bryan. Whether she could ever endure it again was the question now. She switched stations and reached over to get a tissue from her purse. An ear-splitting roar swelled beside her. She glanced over to see the eighteen-wheeler's tractor amble by in the inside lane.

She grabbed the steering wheel with both hands as the car shuddered from the semi's multi-ton vibrations. The beastly tractor rumbled past, hauling a trailer loaded with logs. When it started to move back into her lane too soon, she cried out, horrified, its axels at eye-level as the second trailer edged toward her.

She cranked the steering wheel hard right and slammed on the brakes. Metal screeched as the looming trailer bashed into the Honda's front fender, then continued on, seemingly unaware.

The car tipped sideways, balanced precariously on two wheels. It righted itself with a jolt, then bolted off the highway onto the unpaved shoulder where it skidded toward a drainage ditch. More screaming metal announced the front passenger side fender striking the guardrail. The back end swung around, smashed the barrier broadside, then came to rest, leaning to the right at a forty-five degree angle.

The airbag deployed with a pop.

Everything went black.

When she came to moments later, stars swam before her eyes. Flashing blue lights filled the rearview mirror. A police car. Good. But why were its lights tilted? She groped for comprehension. The smell of gasoline finished the task as a voice screamed inside her head.

Get out! Get out, Sara! Now!

Which was easier said than done, considering the car's awkward position.

The cop was at her door, tapping on the window.

"Are you okay, miss?"

Sara stared at him wide-eyed, panic compounded by disorientation. She could barely hear him, between the window and traffic noise. "I-I don't know. I, uh, think so."

"Hold on. I'll open your door and help you out. Don't undo your seatbelt. Wait until I have a hold on you."

"Okay." She waited, heart thudding against her chest.

"You need to unlock your door, ma'am."

She fumbled for the button on the dash, couldn't remember which one it was, so simply yanked the handle. The lock released and the cop pulled it open.

"You sure you're okay, ma'am?"

She stared at him, mouth agape. "I, uh, don't know. Just g-get me out of here!"

"Can you swing your legs toward me, outside the car?"

It was awkward and far more difficult than expected. The airbag restrained her chest, plus the seatbelt was locked. She braced herself against the center console with her elbow and moved one leg, then the other.

His voice was calm and soothing as he reached toward her. "Okay. Hold on to me with your left hand." She grabbed his arm and he likewise gripped hers. "Now release the seatbelt."

Click.

She fell into his arms, then held on as he lifted her to her feet. Flares dotting the roadway belched acrid smoke, traffic stacking up as lane closures brought normal flow grinding to a halt. Traffic whizzed past in oncoming lanes, screeching tires implicating rubberneckers not keeping pace.

He helped her to his patrol car where he opened the back door. She lowered herself slowly to a sitting position, feet outside on the ground. Pain jabbed her right side. Her left hand gripped it instinctively. Most likely a broken or dislocated rib. Great. Her eyes closed, the stench of gasoline, diesel fumes, and road flares triggering a dull headache that turned her stomach.

The cop was up front calling in, then came back around, holding a tablet. "Can you tell me what happened?"

"I sure can." Her heart pounded as she struggled to restrain the gorge rising in her throat. "A semi. With a double trailer. Loaded with logs. Ran me off the road. He passed me, then pulled into my lane. Right into me! I tried to get over. Out of the way. Ha. Didn't work."

The patrolman got back on the radio and put out a bulletin to watch for and detain the offending tractor-trailer. "We'll find him, miss. He's gonna be in huge trouble. Not only for being reckless, but for leaving the scene."

"I sure hope so." The headache worsened, her hands shaking. "I hate those things!"

A minute or so later, a cacophony of sirens screamed from down the highway, backed up traffic edging out of their way. A firetruck and an ambulance arrived, blinking a chorus of blue, red and white emergency lights, joined moments later by a tow truck likewise decorated. The fire engine pulled in front of her car in the ditch, ambulance behind the cop car, tow truck behind that. Three more cops showed up, lights and sirens in full emergency regalia.

The ambulance attendants headed her way, bearing a stretcher and backboard. The patrolman stepped back. "I'll catch up with you at the hospital to get the rest of your statement. I'm Officer Leonard. I need to finish locking down the area and start the investigation."

One of the EMTs stepped in front of her. "We'd better move you onto this, ma'am, until we get you to the hospital and they check you out."

"Okay," she agreed weakly, then started to get up. She held up her hand. "No, wait. I'm sorry. I'm g-going to throw up." She sat back down and leaned to the side where she vomited on the ground, barely missing her shoe. One of the attendants handed her a wet wipe. It felt cool against her face, its citrus scent strong and decidedly unpleasant.

She swallowed hard, then got up the best she could. They lowered the gurney enough with the back board in place for her to sit, then helped swing her legs around and lie down. Strapped in, they raised it again.

Before they reached the ambulance, panic surged—the very reason for the trip itself remained in her car!

"Wait! Wait! I need my purse. It's on the front passenger seat. And that envelope, too. I need my phone, to call my father. He's expecting me, up in Boulder. He's going to freak out!"

"Okay, ma'am. Hold on," one of the attendants said. He returned moments later and handed her the purse and manila envelope, then helped his partner load her onboard. One reached over to close the doors.

"Oh, no! Wait! I need my other stuff, too. In the trunk. A garment bag, an overnighter, and a computer. Especially the computer!"

The attendant gave her an exasperated look, but dutifully stepped back outside. He returned moments later, expression somewhere between apologetic and frustrated.

"I'm sorry, ma'am. The fire department won't let me near your car. A significant amount of gasoline has spilled, possibly into the trunk. They're afraid opening it could create a spark and ignite an explosion. If they can prevent that and secure the scene, I'm sure you'll be able to collect your belongings later at the police station."

"Oh, no! I have to have that laptop! I absolutely can't lose it! Isn't there something you can do? Anything?"

Before he could respond a muffled explosion shook the ambulance, a tell-tale orange glare flickering within its interior.

"Sorry, ma'am. I'm afraid that's a definite no-go."

"Oh, no," she moaned. "They sure better find that idiot trucker!"

"I hope so, too. You have no idea how many wrecks they cause."

"This is my second one this year. I swear, someone's trying to kill me."

His look shifted to suspicious scrutiny, probably caught between whether she knew how to drive versus the possibility it was true. He made sure everything was secure, then the driver turned on the siren, pulled out onto the highway and headed for Lakewood.

She didn't know whether to cry or scream. Yet, as the anger cooled, bone-chilling fear took its place.

What if someone *was* trying to kill her?

She attempted to lift her head to dig out her phone, but the backboard had her trapped. Plunging her hand inside her purse, she groped around until she found it. Unlocking it with her thumbprint, she voice commanded it to call her father. He answered on the second ring.

"Hi, Sara. Where are you?"

At the sound of his voice she reverted to being a little girl again. Her chest ached and eyes burned.

"You won't believe it, Dad."

Any subsequent words succumbed to a sob, tears streaming down the side of her cheek into her ear. She coughed, mouth still tasting horrible from barfing, heart collapsing in defeat.

"Sara? What's wrong, Kitten?"

"I-I was in a-another wreck, D-dad."

"Oh, no. What happened?"

She sniffled, his voice assuming is usual comforting effect. "Some idiot logging t-truck with a double trailer r-ran me off the road. I'm in an ambulance. On my way t-to Lakewood R-Regional." Silence on the other end. "D-Dad? Are you there?"

"Yes, I'm here. Are you okay? How badly are you injured?"

"Airbag knocked me out, so my head hurts, maybe another whiplash." She shifted, trying to get comfortable, wincing at the pain in her side. "Maybe a broken rib. The Honda's totaled. Plus it caught fire."

"My God, Sara! What am I going to do with you?"

"Oh, and it gets worse, Dad." She wiped her eyes and rubbed her forehead, discovering a rising bump.

"Uh, oh. I'm afraid to ask."

"Bryan's laptop burned up with the car."

He muttered something she couldn't understand.

"Could you repeat that, Dad?"

"Never mind. As long as you're okay, we'll work around it somehow. Don't worry about that for now. I'll get there as soon as I can. It's well into commuter hour, so it's going to take a while."

She flinched as she rubbed the back of her neck. "I'm sure those poor people tied up from my wreck won't be very sympathetic."

His laugh sounded good. "You're probably right. See you soon."

Once they reached the ER, Officer Leonard showed up a short time later. He got her contact information, both at home and at Will's, then told her he'd let her know the results. He admitted her side of the story sounded implicating and straight-forward.

So far, they hadn't been able to track down the offending semi, but he assured her they would. After the ambulance left, one witness traveling behind the semi looped around and reported what he'd seen.

"We'll be in touch," he promised. "I hope your recovery goes well." He patted her arm for reassurance, stopping to chat briefly with ER personnel before he left.

Sara closed her eyes and tried to relax, fury a distraction from the pain while she awaited being seen by a doctor and her father's arrival.

Such a government has something wrong about it. I cannot understand why so many chiefs are allowed to talk so many different ways and promise so many different things.
—*Young Joseph "Chief Joseph", 1879*

18. EVIDENCE

FALCON RIDGE
June 8, Friday
7:18 p.m.

Mike Fernandez's boss, Steve Urbanowsky, listened patiently as he indulged in his daily rant. "Our pledge is to protect and to serve. How can we do that with crap like this going on?"

Urbanowsky's chair squeaked as he leaned back as far as it would go. "I hear you, buddy. Every word. Unfortunately, that's just the way it is. There are lots of things people just don't need to know."

"I'd sure like to know a few things, like what they did to be targeted like that."

"They must've stumbled onto something hot. No telling what. There's a lot of federal land up there. Rumor has it there could be some black project. There's no other explanation for the heavy equipment we've seen, especially the guys on graveyard. They've escorted all sorts of things in the wee hours. Stuff that took up the entire road. Real fun, getting through these narrow, winding roads. Some of it had to be brought in with heavy-lift choppers."

Mike exhaled through his nose. "That's total bullshit. What could it be?"

Urbanowsky shrugged. "Who knows? Anything's possible. Look at all the rumors about the Denver airport. All those unexplained tunnels and other weird stuff, like that apocalyptic mural. It caused such a stir they eventually got rid of it."

"Right. Crazy stuff. You know, I thought working up here would be relatively peaceful. Rescuing skiers, an occasional drug bust or meth lab. Burglaries of unoccupied cabins. Missing kayaks. Worse case, an occasional drowning. Stuff like that. Not hit men and government agent gag orders."

"I violently agree, Mike. But that's just—"

"—the way it is. Yeah, yeah. I know. It really pissed me off lying to that Reynolds woman about not recovering anything."

"Actually, it wasn't a lie. Not technically." He righted his chair, hands flat on his desk. "*We* didn't recover a thing. *They* did."

Mike let fly with a derisive snort. "I couldn't believe it when that SOB laughed about how convenient it was the truck landed on a ledge. And I expect more dignity from those people than high-fives."

"Mercenary types. Amateurs. Not government. Hired guns. Contractors. Unprofessional as hell."

"I wonder what evidence they got? And what happened to it? Do you think they destroyed it? Or have it locked up somewhere?"

"I'm sure they gathered as much personal information as possible on the victims, then destroyed any evidence. Why would they hang onto it? If everything's secret, they're not about to press charges. If anything, that woman's life could be in danger, too. They probably didn't expect, much less want her to survive."

Their dispatcher, a trim but aging blond in her mid-fifties, knocked on the door frame, interrupting the conversation.

"This just in," she reported. "A car was totaled in a wreck with a tractor-trailer on I-70, just outside Lakewood. The driver's been hospitalized for observation. There's an APB out for the semi, which left the scene. It's in the news feed."

Urbanowsky nodded thanks and brought it up on his computer. His eyes narrowed. "The registered owner of the wrecked car is Sara Reynolds. Looks like they *do* want her dead."

LAKEWOOD REGIONAL MEDICAL CENTER
LAKEWOOD, COLORADO
June 8, Friday
8:20 p.m.

It was an unwelcome rerun as Sara fiddled with the seat controls in her father's Benz. Just what she wanted was another cervical collar when she'd barely gotten rid of the last one. The pain meds did a pretty good job but, as usual, weren't doing her brain or gut any favors. Between another mild concussion and the pain pill, she felt as if she were trapped in a recurring bad dream.

It took forever to get released from the ER. Her injuries weren't life-threatening, placing her near the bottom of the triage list. As it turned out, they did little more than the EMTs besides issue the cervical collar, offer to tape her broken rib, which she refused, and give her a prescription for pain meds she'd probably throw away.

At least now she was on her way to Boulder, leaving the noise and gut-wrenching hospital odors behind.

She closed her eyes, attempting to stop the dizziness. Nothing, however, helped what codeine did to her stomach.

Her father reached over and patted her hand. "You doing okay, Sara?"

"I suppose. I'm still so frustrated about the laptop. No telling what was on it. My clothes and other stuff I can replace, though I really hated to lose that dress."

"By the way, what did you do with that thumb drive with the photos? Please tell me you didn't leave it in the computer."

Her brows lowered with concentration. "No. I took it out. I know I did. Give me a minute."

It had only been hours, yet felt like weeks. Strained muscles protested as she retrieved her purse from the floor. Finding her makeup bag, she triumphantly displayed what was in the contact lens case.

"Ta-dah!"

"Good girl!" Her father reached over again to squeeze her hand. "There may have been something else on his computer, but this could be the most important."

"If there's one thing Bryan taught me it was never to keep backups in the same place as the computer. The farther away, the better. You know, I'll bet there's a backup of his computer somewhere else, too. I just need to find it. I must say, having my own built-in help desk was handy. I'll miss that. He loved that stuff, not only for what it did, but how it worked."

"He was head of IT and cyber security at that credit union, wasn't he?"

"Yes. He loved it. He redesigned and programmed their website, plus took great pride in making sure it was secure and unhackable. He was one of the first to set up a second level of log-in security via text messaging. Several of his coworkers have emailed or posted on Facebook expressing their condolences and telling me how much he's missed."

"I'll bet. He's pretty irreplaceable."

"*In the arms of an angel,*" she quoted quietly. "Oh, Dad, I miss him so much."

"I know, Sara. And it might not be much consolation, but we're two of the lucky ones. We may have lost someone we loved deeply, but at least we had that experience. Not only of being loved, but caring for someone with all your mind, body, and soul. Believe it or not, few ever find that. And those of us who do are often separated too soon."

"I suppose." She sniffled as she dug through her purse for a tissue, hoping to find one this time.

They met Connie for dinner at their favorite Italian place on Boulder's north side. Sara's stomach was still performing forward rolls, but felt better after a few bites of salad, still-hot-from-the-oven sour dough bread, and a forkful or two of chicken alfredo. She scooped the rest into a take-out box as they got ready to leave. As usual, no one had room for dessert, but got some to-go.

Since Connie had her own transportation, she offered to stop by Target and pick up a few essentials for Sara to wear.

Meanwhile, she and her father headed back to the house, where he helped her up the stairs and into the room that had been hers growing up. She felt like a teenager again as she laid down, everything familiar, safe, and comfortable.

Eyes closed, her mind was nonetheless abuzz. Achy but restless, she sat up, realizing how thirsty she was. When she returned downstairs to get a drink, her father got up from the living room couch to join her.

"Do you feel up to looking at that flash drive, Sara?"

His voice was nonchalant, but his eyes were saturated with salivating curiosity.

"Sure, Dad. Why not? It might be a good distraction. I'm tired and hurting, but too wound up to sleep."

He set his jaw and rubbed his hands together. "Okay, great. Let's see what we've got."

She followed him back upstairs, retrieved it from her purse, then went into his den. Heavy crown molding rimmed the upper reaches, walls lined with burgeoning built-in bookshelves. A walnut computer hutch occupied one side, his desk the other. He pulled the desk chair over to the computer and patted it. Her offended rib shot a dagger through her side as she lowered onto it.

"Is that seat okay?" he asked.

"It's fine. Sitting up straight actually feels a little better."

"Okay. If you get tired, just say so."

"I'm good, Dad. I'm anxious to hear what you think."

He inserted the tiny drive into a USB port, then opened the Olympus folder. The screen filled with dozens of picture icons. The first one opened on a panoramic vista of snow-covered mountains deep within the Gore Range, snow-dusted pines and spruces visible on distant mountains.

Some included her, Bryan, or in a few cases, both of them. Her throat ached. Little did she realize at the time they'd be the last ones, ever, of them together. After viewing a dozen or so, Will enlarged the thumbnail-sized icons to expedite finding what they were looking for.

She pointed at one where the terrain was disturbed by various geometric figures.

He clicked.

Her hands flew to her mouth, memory instantaneously restored. A relatively flat area, peaks forming a bowl around it, a host of heavy equipment marring the snow. A tall, straight-sided tower was off to one side, a huge monolith of a machine toward the left.

"What do you think, Dad? What is that?"

He folded his arms. "Probably a fracking operation. That tower looks like a drilling rig surrounded by a tank farm. But that big thing there, that's a boring machine. If all they're doing is fracking, they certainly don't need that."

He zoomed in until it pixelated, then pointed to a dark blur toward the back. "See that? That's a moving vehicle." She swallowed hard at the implications.

He right-clicked, bringing up its properties. "Great. We have the time, 15:51:18 on 17 April, plus GPS coordinates."

He cut and pasted them into Google. "I'm pretty sure that's a restricted zone. One where we redact any pictures taken with our satellites, or at least limit their release to low resolution."

Will grunted when moments later the search confirmed exactly that. "It looks like you and Bryan stumbled upon some Top Secret project."

"That's why they want us dead? So we won't talk? That's outrageous! Why couldn't they just tell us not to say anything?"

"People always talk. Always. Whatever that project is, they're not taking any chances. This isn't good, Sara. Let's see what's in those other folders."

Nothing else seemed important, mostly work-related contact information and project notes.

"No wonder they arrested Charlie," she said. "I wonder if he's targeted now, too?"

"Since he only saw the wrecked truck, possibly not. If he found anything, that would be another situation entirely. He needs to avoid going anywhere near that area. You should give him a heads-up. Black ops goons might already have him in their sights."

LAKEWOOD P.D. LAB
LAKEWOOD
June 9, Saturday
8:26 a.m.

Anita Nguyen loved her job as Lakewood PD's lead technician in the forensics lab. Especially cases like this, that challenged everything she knew about chemistry. She rubbed her eyes, then studied the pyrolysis data from the gas chromatograph and mass spec again. Gasoline residue and other compounds common to vehicle fires were expected. But if this was the routine wreck suggested by the initial report, what she was seeing was entirely anomalous.

The tipoff came from the fire crew, who'd witnessed the explosion and knew from experience there was more involved than the gas tank. Their initial report stated the computer's lithium-ion battery exploded, igniting spilled fuel, but that sounded like putting the chicken before the egg.

Besides, plastic explosives had no place whatsoever in such a scenario. However, it did explain why the dogs went crazy in the impound lot when they towed in the burnt-out chassis. Investigators were still sifting through the ashes with the pyro crew revisiting the accident scene.

The car was struck by a semi towing a double trailer. A witness saw the whole thing. Was it coincidence that it triggered an explosive device?

Something in her gut said no. Such things were a dead giveaway.

This was too exotic for anyone outside the military. So much so, she'd never seen anything like it before, except in text books. She bit her lip as she gathered her notes to show her boss and get his opinion. He was in the far corner of the lab on the phone, expression unreadable. She stopped a polite distance away and waited.

As soon as he hung up, she stepped forward. His expression indicated more than recognition. He gestured toward his office.

"Come with me," he said. "Update on that Honda explosion."

She hustled to keep up with his long, determined stride. "I found a few things I wanted to talk to you about, too."

When they arrived at his office, he gestured for her to go inside, then closed the door.

He never did that, except during employee evaluations. Did she mess something up?

He settled behind his desk and pursed his lips.

"We've been called off the case," he stated, brown eyes locked on hers. "We're to turn all evidence, including all analysis data, over to someone representing the NSA, then close the case."

Her jaw dropped. "Why?"

"Simple. They said so."

It is with shame, I acknowledge, that I have to notice so much corruption of a people calling themselves Christians. If they were like my people, professing no purity at all, then their crimes would not appear to have such magnitude. But while they appear to be by profession more virtuous, their crimes still blacken. It makes them truly to appear to be like mountains filled with smoke; and thick darkness covering them all around.
—William Apes, January 1836

19. FETISHES

CHARLIE'S CABIN
RURAL FALCON RIDGE
June 9, Saturday
6:10 a.m.

Charlie's eyes opened just after dawn, a nauseating wave claiming his awareness. The bed's metal frame creaked as he sat up. Still half asleep, memory of a similar dizzying sensation broke free.

When he'd been furloughed from his ranger job.

He and Bryan were supposed to go trout fishing the next morning, really early. The hour was his idea; Bryan hated getting up in the dark.

Then Charlie was a no-show. Plans made several days before, he'd forgotten. Bryan came over. Found him passed out amid a half-dozen randomly discarded beer cans and a nearly empty pint of cheap vodka. His brother cleaned up the mess, made a pot of coffee, then poured a glass of ice-cold water all over his face and chest.

He bolted awake, ashamed and embarrassed. Hung his head as he sipped black coffee, braced for an ass-chewing he thoroughly deserved.

Instead, Bryan told him he was better than that. He'd never accomplish anything if he turned to booze every time life got a little tough.

Eaglefeathers told him much the same thing. Years before, when he left for college. Words which blared through his head yet again, like the two times he indulged, as if he were under some sort of curse.

"Grandson, sit down and listen to what I am going to tell you. Listen real good to what I am saying. I'm telling you what I do not want you to do: Grandson, alcohol is nothing good for you. You don't take it. Leave it alone. Alcohol is not made for *Tseteshestahese* people. White people made it for themselves.

"Alcohol is a poison for you. It will take everything from you. First your spirit. Then your job and money, your children, family and home. You will have nothing to make *Maheo* proud of you.

"My grandfather, Silver Sky, spoke these words to me and told the truth. I have seen this happen to good *Tseteshestahese* men and women.

"Grandson, do not forget where you came from. My teachings are the ways from *Maheo*. Follow his ways.

"Grandson, I will repeat so you hear and remember. Alcohol is a poison. It's not made for *Tseteshestahese* people, it's made for the white man."

The two times that Charlie went on "open bar pity parties," as Bryan called them, he was depressed and humiliated, so he'd isolated himself. Keeping secrets from his white brother, however, was impossible. They were too close, able to read each other's minds and hearts.

The only other episode, when Bryan also intervened, was when Rosina left. That time his brother arrived in time to help finish the six-pack, then proceeded to tell him all the reasons he was better off without a woman.

Charlie reminded him of that list a year later when he told him about meeting Sara. His only response was that crooked grin.

He rubbed his face with both hands, distancing himself from when he'd disappointed two of the most important people in his life.

Now fully awake and stone-cold sober, the eerie vertigo sensation persisted. Multiple items struck the floor amid a medley of sounds, some as wind through summer leaves, others clattering like arrows missing their target. Dishes rattled. Another thud.

It stopped.

His confusion yielded to recognition—an earthquake.

They didn't have many, but they weren't unheard of, either. It wasn't bad, probably three-something, maybe less, on the Richter scale, depending on the epicenter. They'd come more frequently the past few years, reflecting the Earth Mother's disgust with her resident humans. The area's worst tremor in history occurred in 1882, a few years after the curse.

Had it been related? Was this another sign?

He lit a lantern, its glow revealing a variety of items scattered across the floor. The clay jar on the mantle, his first concern, remained in place.

Again, questions besieged him regarding its contents.

What was it from? A phone? A camera? What else could it be? His old Apple computer had no means for reading it. It had to wait until Sara returned.

All secrets are revealed in time.

He froze as the words settled like gently falling snow.

The mess cluttering the floor included the quiver of arrows. It had belonged to his great-grandfather, Rides the Wind. He picked it up, holding it reverently as he withdrew one from its buckskin pouch. Its straight, smooth shaft would not be deterred by the wind, but maintain its course, unwavering and true.

Its hand-crafted arrowhead was sharp. One that would easily pierce its target. It was oriented horizontally, perpendicular to the nock—one intended for war. Hunting arrows were oriented the other way. Would its victim have fallen with dignity and honor? Greet death fearlessly as the deer or bison at their moment of sacrifice?

Charlie closed his eyes and envisioned how his ancestors hunted buffalo, riding swift hunting ponies beside an animal two times their size. The target area to the heart behind their quarry's shoulder was a mere twelve inches in diameter.

Then white men came with rifles and slaughtered them by the millions, often from onboard a moving train. They stripped them of their hides and tongues, then left them to rot on the plains.

His jaw tensed as he returned the arrow to the quiver, then rehung it above the fireplace. Waste like that was unconscionable. Bison were essential to his people. Life itself. Food, shelter, clothing, even tools from their strong bones. They weren't worshipped, but they were revered.

Several fetishes had likewise fallen: mole, wolf, and badger. Carved by the neighboring Zuni tribe, that he'd collected while living in New Mexico. Their craftsmanship was remarkable. He often thought to fashion some himself. Such a task would teach him patience, something he lacked. He was already inclined to be a perfectionist, so the intricate work would be challenging as well as satisfying.

Did these particular ones fall for a reason? While the sacred red pipe sent his prayers to *Maheo*, the fetishes were helpful, too. Coupled with meditation, they prompted insights that led to inspired answers. Eaglefeathers taught him that most answers resided within.

Accessible without bothering *Maheo*.

He lifted his medicine wheel from the hook next to the chimney, then gathered all six spirit animals. As he settled cross-legged on the floor, he chastised himself for failing to feed them and promised to be more diligent. By doing so daily, he'd be more attuned to their call and not require an earthquake to snag his attention.

He set the medicine wheel on the floor, the cross separating its red, yellow, white, and black sections oriented to the cardinal directions. Next he set the fetishes facing center from their guardian positions: Mountain Lion, North; White Wolf, East;

Badger, South; Black Bear, West; Eagle, Upper Regions; and Mole, Lower Regions.

His mind wandered back to when his grandfather taught him about spirit animals. They could manifest as spirits, in real life, dreams, or even symbolic form. Not only these six, but all living things: Turtles, frogs, ravens, rats, lizards, snakes. He taught him where the creatures lived, what they ate, whether they were dangerous, and how they cared for their young. The lessons weren't rote, but experiential.

He met Eaglefeathers for the first time when his grandfather came to New Mexico for an extended visit, several years before his father went back to Colorado, never to return.

Charlie was a boy, going into his seventh winter, and awestruck by the man's stature and demeanor. How ancient he seemed, with his long, grey braids and colorful clothing adorned with quill work, beads, and feathers.

Lots of feathers.

He remembered sitting with him by the fire, warmth caressing his face while the chill of desert evenings assaulted his back.

"Tell me about lizard," Eaglefeathers said.

"He has four legs and crawls on the ground. He eats bugs," young Charlie replied.

"Yes. But what does lizard know?"

He squinted at his grandfather as if he were crazy.

Eaglefeathers patted the ground. "Lie on your belly. Flat on the earth."

He obeyed, sneezing when dust tickled his nose.

"Now, make your arms and legs like lizard."

He cocked his elbows and spread his knees a bit, getting into the role play.

The old man's voice grew softer. "Now walk. What do you see?"

"I see rocks. Grass. A sage bush." He sneezed again.

"How does earth feel beneath your belly? Do you hear anything? Feel anything? Something that might be good to eat? Or might eat you?"

He giggled. His grandfather cleared his throat, not amused in the slightest. He focused back on his task as he realized this wasn't a game. By the time the exercise was over, he felt as if he *did* understand what lizard might know, how it might feel.

The lessons continued over several nights before the fire, eventually covering not only animals known to inhabit the area, but more exotic ones as well. The tutorial taught him to be observant. Not only to their presence, but to recognize their strengths, vulnerabilities, talents, and unique wisdom. To know which to consult for answers. More importantly, to ponder its meaning upon seeing one in the wild.

More words touched his mind like a breeze through tall grass.

There are no coincidences.

Like raven, on his return from Tomahawk Creek.

He began the ceremony by lighting a sweet grass braid. He smudged himself and offered its smoke to the four directions. He set the smoldering braid in a shallow pan, then focused all his attention on his cadre of advisors.

Which were calling him? All did not always have anything to say. Mole had demanded his attention with the earthquake. He inhaled deeply, closed his eyes, and became a mole.

He meditated on the Earth, the smell of rich soil, the texture, far below, where moisture resided.

Her vibrations were disturbing.

Anger. Rage. Exploited.

She'd been violated. Neither honored nor appreciated. Her power rippled through him. The earthquake a warning. A reminder. All life depended on her. Humans were mere guests. Nothing compared to her. She could cast off offenders as a dog shook off dirt and fleas.

He absorbed Earth's unrest, then regarded the others. Did they, too, have a message?

Eagle and Mountain Lion were silent, but White Wolf beckoned. He imagined four paws, a thick coat of fur, an acute sense of smell for seeking prey. Unfailing loyalty to family and the pack, the many inflections and meanings of its soulful howl.

As Guardian of the East, he pictured himself as Wolf sitting tall and confident on an outcropping awaiting the dawn. Wolf didn't know what would happen that day or any other, but he faced it with courage and accepted its lessons.

He must do the same.

He didn't have the truth, but must sniff it out. Watch with a sharp eye for it to make itself known. With gratitude he released wolf's persona and regarded the remaining fetishes, Badger and Bear.

He sensed Badger's call. He contemplated the energy he sensed in its hide, the animal's link to *Novavose*. He assimilated its sleek, muscular body that hugs the earth, long claws and razor-sharp teeth. One of the few animals ferocious enough to take down a bear. A diet mostly comprised of prairie dogs, carrion, berries and other vegetation—whatever was available.

Badger's unconquerable spirit coursed through him, strengthening and comforting his wounded heart. Since his arrest he'd felt helpless and ashamed, then humiliated by Sara's assistance.

Badger reminded him not to feel like a victim. It was within him to be deadly and aggressive when the time was right. A time he would recognize as more truth was revealed.

His attention turned to Bear. He, too, remained silent. Thus, he meditated on what he'd received from Mole, Wolf, and Badger.

His conviction expanded. The curse was culminating in a way that wouldn't be mistaken for anything else.

Neither myth nor coincidence.

Bryan's death started it, he would finish it.

Startled by the impression, he'd barely absorbed it when another followed.

He had much to do. Much to learn.

Could he do it on his own?

His grandfather taught him a lot about herbal medicine and spiritual healing. He had the old man's medicine bundle and sacred red pipe. He'd already received guidance from the grandfather spirits about the accident and the truck.

Heritage or not, however, he didn't feel worthy. Or capable, of becoming a medicine man.

Perhaps by now he would have been—if he hadn't been so foolish as a youth. He cringed as he remembered college, when doubts first crept in. He'd studied chemistry and treaded too far in the white man's path.

His first experience with the world of spirits was horrifying. His Christian girlfriend back then told him it was of the devil. Thus, he backed off.

Later, he reflected on how his people were treated by those who professed to be Christians.

Whose beliefs and actions reflected those of devils?

His grandfather not only encouraged him to obtain a white man's education.

He demanded it.

Being immersed in that world, however, lured him too far into their way of thinking. He'd attempted the impossible. To stand upright with each foot on a different pony, one red, one white, running with the wind.

While heading in the same direction, balance was easy.

When the ponies diverged, however, he tumbled to the ground, an outcast from both worlds. His own people accused him of being an *apple*, those red on the outside, white on the inside. To the white man he was just another uncivilized Indian.

His grip on his own beliefs back then was tenuous. While both his parents were indigenous, Diné were matriarchal, *Tseteshestahese* patriarchal. The differences tore his parent's marriage apart and contributed to the failure of his own.

As a child he was continually caught in the crossfire, trying to please them both. His stomach clenched as he recalled how his mother criticized and demeaned his father. Especially his tribe-specific rituals and ceremonies. Before, but even more so after he left.

Whenever Charlie failed to meet her expectations, she accused him of being just like him.

As if being like Littlebear were a bad thing.

He worshipped his father.

Never thought he'd ever be half the man he was.

And if he listen to his mother, why would he want to?

Now, more than ever, he appreciated what a remarkable man his father was. Intelligent, trustworthy, and courageous. A brave Cheyenne warrior who, as soon as he graduated college in 1968, enlisted in the U.S. Marine Corps where he was commissioned a lieutenant. Such young officers were trained, but lacked experience, which tended to result in mistakes followed by heavy casualties.

Not Littlebear.

As a platoon leader on the front lines in Vietnam, his warrior blood allowed him consistently to outsmart the enemy. His superiors were astounded by his bravery and skill. He was awarded the Medal of Honor, two Purple Hearts, and an Expert Marksmanship badge.

Following an honorable discharge in 1972, he returned home to a hero's welcome. Eaglefeathers's pride in his son was evident when he gave a richly detailed account of the powwow they held in his honor. Charlie heard the story so many times it felt as if he'd been there. The Busby Community Hall was packed with families and dancers who came to show their support.

Kingfisher, the most senior elder, prayed for the Cheyenne people, their family, and a blessing on the food. White Buffalos were host drum. Coco, the lead singer and drummer sang a special honor song for him. Then the victory dance began. Littlebear in his dress uniform led everyone in a circle, including several veteran elders, also in uniform. Those present removed their head gear and stood to show respect. Then the feast and giveaway started. White Buffalo Singers received a table gift with star quilts for their inspiring songs and expert drumming.

Nevertheless, the war took its toll.

Littlebear had been exposed to Agent Orange.

Eaglefeathers treated him with Cheyenne medicine. They prayed together in many ceremonies and sweats over the course of two years, asking *Maheo* that he might be healed in body and spirit. Eaglefeathers went so far as to ask for his medals and even told him to leave his uniform in the hills, attempting to eliminate the bad spirits.

Littlebear, being the man he was, overcame a lot. By the mid-1970s he was teaching school and attending pow-wows during the summer.

Which was how he met Charlie's mother.

Big mistake.

Her hostility toward Cheyenne ways combined with Littlebear's lingering health issues made it clear that his father's birthright to follow in Eaglefeathers's footsteps wouldn't happen.

Thus, his grandfather concentrated on training his younger son, Charlie's Uncle Joe Whitewolf, as his successor.

Charlie often wondered why he was frequently included in his uncle's training. He helped with sweats and other rituals, such as fasting on *Novavose* and the sun dance. He was present at all healing ceremonies, often assisting with the buffalo rattle.

Years later, like so many veterans of that era, Littlebear developed cancer. He fought valiantly for almost three years before he crossed over, when Charlie was fifteen. Many soldiers who served under him and even a few of his superior officers had kept in touch and sent their condolences.

A year after that, Charlie and Eaglefeathers left the reservation for Colorado and Whitewolf became the tribe's medicine man. He never understood why they left, only that there was a lot of tension between his uncle and grandfather.

His father's death devastated the old man. Tears filled his eyes whenever he spoke of him. Then Charlie added to his heartbreak and compounded his disappointments.

Bad decisions flew in his face like a cloud of locusts destroying a cornfield. One planted to nourish his people. Since turning his back on his heritage, his world had crumbled. Broken to pieces as a shattered vessel.

Now his grandfather was dead. His chance to learn from him gone.

Forever.

He'd held the old man in his arms and watched his eyes lose their fire as he crossed over to the world of spirits. With his dying breath he pleaded with him not to abandon *Maheo* or his people. As the chosen son in Black Cloud's line, they were depending on him.

At the time it hadn't made sense.

As the warmth of a spring breeze caresses one's face while snow still covers the ground, a glimmer of hope dawned.

Eaglefeathers still lived in the land of spirits.

He could still access his wisdom, as he had at the accident site. By obeying his teachings he'd already received answers. His guilt for taking so long lingered, but a sleeping ember ignited as more words drifted into his mind:

Embrace your destiny. We will not allow you to fail.

He completed his meditation with a prayer for strength, protection, patience, and guidance. Peace settled over him.

His messengers resumed their sentry positions on the mantle. Remembering his promise, he found the tiny drawstring bag behind their stations and placed a few grains of ground blue corn before each one.

He thanked them again, Sara's ring tone hauling him back to the present.

"Charlie. It's Sara. Are you okay?"

"As far as I know. Why?"

"Just checking."

"We had a minor earthquake. Just a tremor. No big deal."

"Listen, I'm at my father's in Boulder and not sure when I'll be back. I got in a wreck and totaled my car on the way in."

His heartrate doubled, intuition screaming. "Are you okay?"

"I'm back in that dreadful neck brace, but other than sore muscles, more or less fine."

"What can I do? Do you need anything?"

"Nothing for now. I'd love some of that herbal muscle balm, though. I just wanted to let you know I'll be here for awhile so you wouldn't worry. If you could pick up my mail while I'm gone, it would be great."

"No problem."

"Great. I'll be in touch."

The call ended.

There was more. Something she didn't want to say on the phone.

But what?

20. REPORTS

MONTGOMERY RESIDENCE
BOULDER
June 9, Saturday
8:31 a.m.

A volatile brew roiled inside Will's gut as he watched Sara pace his den. Protective instincts tore through him, even stronger than when she'd gone off to college. What loomed before her now was far more dangerous than any frat party.

Doe-like eyes, so like her mother's, met his own. "What am I going to do, Dad?"

"Don't panic, Sara. I have a few ideas."

His jaw tightened. The last thing she needed to know was how worried he was. It was nothing short of a miracle she was still alive.

"I can't possibly hide from these people for the rest of my life."

"I know, Sara."

Depending on the situation, calling in a favor might not be an option. The last thing clandestine programs wanted was publicity. Her status ultimately depended not only on how much she knew but what it was about.

If the black ops people were professionals they knew his background. That was probably good, and could be why she was still alive. Maybe the best course of action was to convince them she wasn't a threat.

"I have Top Secret clearance. I see things with my job that require it. I have a few connections with people who buy our data. If I hire you as a consultant, there's a chance of getting you similar status. That might be enough for them to leave you alone. The main caveat is *need to know*."

She cocked her head to the side. "Dad. I already know. Not the details, but that something is going on."

He winced. She'd definitely inherited her mother's dry sense of humor.

"Not exactly how it works. However, plenty of people have seen things they weren't supposed to. The usual protocol, short of killing them outright, is put them under oath to keep quiet. Sometimes for a specific time period, sometimes forever. Violations tend to end badly."

"Jeepers, Daddy, I don't even know what I saw! What would I tell anyone? Who would even care?"

"You'd be surprised. Some people can't get through the day without reporting every move on Facebook. You didn't, I hope."

Her eyes met his, tinged with concern. "Bryan updated his with photos from that trip."

"Did he say or show anything, uh, sensitive?"

"No. Just snow-covered mountains. Generic Rocky Mountain snowscape."

He blew out a breath. "Okay. You need to shut that down. What about that water issue? It could be related and open up a real can of worms. Reporters snooping around can stir up serious problems. Environmental violations are big news."

"Well, there's nothing secret about that. At least one person died as a result, and I suspect another one's a step closer to the Funny Farm, thanks to lead and mercury poisoning. Everyone in my neighborhood knows about that."

"Like who?"

"I've been playing Mah Jongg with some local women. They know. Two of them have what I consider influential husbands. One's a semi-retired Federal judge, the other a retired Air Force colonel."

"Bird colonel or light colonel?"

Her squinty-eyed look was one he remembered from her teens. "I don't know, Dad. I've only seen him in a golf shirt and jeans, not dress blues. What difference does it make?"

"C'mon, Sara. Your husband was in the Air Force." He massaged his chin, pondering how either man could work to their advantage. "What's your opinion of them? Are they trustworthy?"

"I don't know them at all, just their wives. I'm friends with the colonel's wife, Liz. She's given me great moral support. In fact, I should call and tell her where I am so she doesn't worry. When I left I forgot we were supposed to go shopping today. I don't know about the judge's wife. She's snooty and standoffish. They're from Texas and seriously loaded. *Seriously!* You should see their house. I can't imagine what their place in Dallas is like. Probably one of those mansions with the columns out front."

He smirked, picturing the old television show by that name. Right—*who killed JR?* In this case, who killed BR? "Do you think any of them will say anything?"

"I don't know. There's something about that judge that creeps me out. When Liz has Mah Jongg at her place all I ever say to the colonel is hello or goodbye. He seems okay. Usually he just sits there, glued to Fox News or some sports channel. Bryan knew him when they were stationed at Colorado Springs. He never said anything bad about him. I like Liz. I don't think she'd say anything, at least to the news media. She's a bit of a busybody, but I don't think he'd let her go to the press."

"Alright. Good. I think for now, just lay low. Make it clear you're not a threat. It's apparent that someone is watching you, probably listening to everything you say and do. Act innocent. Don't say anything sensitive to anyone, especially online, on the phone, or within earshot of it. Inside your house, either. Give me your phone. We need to turn off the microphone."

"They're spying on me?" she replied, open-mouthed, then headed for her room to retrieve it.

She handed it over and he showed her how to cut off the mic in the settings.

"There. That will help some. Assuming they caused the wreck, how do you think they knew where you'd be? We need to figure out what Bryan discovered. He must have known what he was looking for when you went skiing. You were with him so they're going to assume you're an accomplice. That'll determine how much of a threat you represent."

He exhaled. What might lurk inside *that* potentially deadly can of worms?

"You mentioned before that he was diligent about back-ups," he went on. "Where did he keep them?"

Her face scrunched up in a pensive frown. "His laptop, which is gone. If it's on a flash drive, no telling where it might be. Maybe somewhere in our condo, or even the cabin. Maybe at his work. Or knowing him, all of them, plus some. Who knows?"

"I suppose it's good you don't know. Yet, on the other hand, we need to find out what he knew. How sensitive it really is, and what he intended to do with it, if anything."

She bit her lip, expression clouding. An alarm went off in his head. She was hiding something.

"What?" he prompted.

Her shoulders drooped. "There's something I haven't told you. About when he died. Whatever he knew was bad. Incriminating in some way. To, uh, powerful and important people."

She wrung her hands and stepped over to gaze out the window.

"When he, uh, well, died, he asked me to do something."

He stiffened. Wary, but not surprised. "What did he ask you to do, Sara?"

"He said, 'Don't let them get away with it.'"

When she turned around he lowered his chin and peered over the top of his glasses. "When exactly did he say that, Sara? The coroner's report said he died instantly from multiple blunt force trauma injuries."

Her eyes filled with tears and she started to weep. He got up and took her in his arms. She buried her face in his chest, shoulders trembling. He guided her over to the chair and crouched down in front of her.

"What, Kitten? Did you remember something? When did he say that?"

The sobs diminished, but the tears didn't. "We were both dead, Dad. We were in the air, looking down on our bodies in the truck. He told me not to let them get away with it. Then he left. Forever." She buried her face in her hands, sobbing.

His mind raced. *What the hell?*

The EMTs stated they'd resuscitated her in the ambulance. Technically, she was dead. The doctor even said they "brought her back."

From where?

Both statements collided with everything he believed. Was she crazy or was he missing something?

He patted her knee and got up, taking his turn at the window while she got a handle on her emotions.

Was it an illusion?

Hallucination?

Wishful thinking?

On the other hand, she had no reason to lie or make up such a thing.

Skepticism dismissed long enough to take her statement at face value, he had to admit it fit. Bryan knew something. She probably did, too, prior to the accident.

Anger flared. His renegade son-in-law stuck his nose where it didn't belong, got himself killed, and left her to clean up the mess.

A mess she couldn't even remember.

If they knew she had amnesia why was she still a target? On the other hand, her latest wreck suggested they were only trying to scare her. Unless they were a bunch of clumsy idiots who couldn't do the job right. Or was it actually a random accident? The police report should shed some light on that.

Her sniffling tapered off, then finally ended with a weighted sigh. The pleading look that remained conveyed this wasn't the time to question something she believed.

They had more important things to deal with for now. Things that were real, not imagined.

"Well, Sara, there's nothing you can do about anything until we find out what 'it' actually is. Those backups should do that. While you figure out where they might be, let's find out how your accident report is coming along."

If his suspicions were correct there wouldn't be one. If so, he'd have a better idea what to do next.

While her father checked with the police, Sara went to her room to clean up. She spread a touch of moisturizer under each eye, then used a tissue to dab away the smeared mascara. Did he believe her or not? At least he hadn't rolled his eyes or made her feel like a delusional child. It felt good to have it out, one way or the other.

When she felt sufficiently back in control she called Liz, who answered before it even rang on her end.

"Hey, Liz. It's Sara." An accident reminder dinged her side as she sat on the bed.

"Sara! Hello, dear! Are we still on for today? There's a great sale at that cute little boutique. Up to fifty-percent off."

"No, I can't. I apologize for not letting you know. I'm in Boulder. Something came up with my Dad."

"Oh. I'm sorry to hear that. Is everything okay?"

"Yes, everything's fine." She grimaced at the lie. "But I'll probably be here awhile."

"Did you hear about that wreck on I-70? Traffic was tied up for hours."

Huh? Where did that come from? How could she possibly know?

Or maybe she didn't. Either way, it was a strange comment. Admitting she was the star would evoke too many questions.

Questions she shouldn't answer, even if they were face to face. Fortunately, Liz was the one who told her to get a better car, so coming home with a different one wouldn't be questioned.

"Sara? Hello? Are you still there, dear?"

"Yes, Liz. I, uh, saw it on the news." Her nose wrinkled at the even more blatant lie. "Must have happened sometime after I passed Lakewood."

"Oh. Good. Well, enjoy your family. Hope to see you again soon."

"Same here, Liz. Bye."

"Bye, dear. Take care."

She set down her phone. Why did she have the feeling Liz didn't believe a word? Then again, she always was a terrible liar.

Oh, well, no matter.

The important thing was that she hadn't said anything that wouldn't be considered *normal*, no matter who was listening. Except for lying. She grimaced. Things were just too complicated lately for her addled brain. She was just putting the phone back in her purse when her father called from down the hall.

"Come here, Sara. I have some rather interesting news."

HUDSON RESIDENCE
RURAL FALCON RIDGE
June 9, Saturday
9:12 a.m.

Jim Hudson glanced at Liz as she set the phone on the table between their matching loungers. She was a good woman and he loved her dearly, but her knack for inflating the simplest thing into a crisis was downright nerve-wracking. How'd she ever survive when he was TDY fighting sundry wars on the other side of the globe?

"That was Sara Reynolds," she declared. "Someone's trying to kill her. First the accident that killed her husband, and now an eighteen-wheeler ran her off the road outside Lakewood."

His eyes shifted back to the weekly Dow averages parading below CNN's talking heads. "Oh? That was her?"

"She wouldn't admit it, but I'm sure it was. That car we saw on the news looked exactly like hers."

"You're good, Liz. All I saw was a ball of flames. You should work for the police department, maybe even the FBI."

She folded her arms. "I don't care what you say, she was involved somehow. I could tell."

"If so, I'd say she's pretty unlucky."

"I don't think that's it, Jim. I was with her when she remembered where she and her husband were, right before the other wreck. They were cross-country skiing, somewhere northwest of here. They came across some strange looking industrial site and took pictures. She couldn't remember what it was, assuming at one time she knew. I'll bet it's some sort of secret government thing."

His attention remained fixed on the TV, checking how Tesla, SAIC, and Halliburton had done. Hopefully better than the week before.

"Jim, listen to me. Something funny's going on. I just know it."

If what she said was true, it was a volatile situation. A new site in that area? Such things didn't spring up overnight. Surely he would have heard. He was retired, not dead. One of his old friends would have tipped him off to something so close to home.

That was how he knew about some of the goings-on in Nevada. They were under an uncomfortable amount of scrutiny the past few years from UFO buffs and were downsizing. They turned some operations over to the Army at Dugway and Fort Hood, others were already at Wright-Patt. In reality, there were secret facilities all over the country. Most had plenty of expansion room.

Why would they build a new one? They already had Cheyenne Mountain and various other outposts in the Rockies. Why not simply add additional space to existing ones?

"So what do you think? Why would they want to kill Sara and her husband? Jim? *Hey!*" She got up and stood between him and the television. "Colonel Hudson! Did you hear me?"

He shifted up his eyes without moving his head. "Yes, dear. Every word."

Which was true, though he was still processing what she'd said. "It does sound rather odd. But eighteen-wheelers cause wrecks all the time. These roads are treacherous. Maybe she's just someone who attracts catastrophes. I knew people like that in the service, of all ranks. You stayed away from them, as far as possible. Catch my meaning, Liz?"

Mouth agape, she dropped back into her chair. At least no sound was coming out. When they lived in Colorado Springs she had more friends to jabber to besides him. Since he'd retired, which was undoubtedly a mistake, she'd latched onto him like a tick. It was nothing short of a miracle that those sticky-sweet chick flicks on the Hallmark Channel hadn't given him diabetes. There were days when he wished another big conflict would come along so he'd get called back up.

So far, this was one of them.

Her reaction, though delayed, was more forceful than expected. "How can you say such a thing? That poor woman! My God, Jim, she just lost her husband. Now it looks like someone's trying to kill her. And you think I should abandon her? How could you?"

He exhaled. "Listen. If what you suspect is true, what do you think you can you do about it, Liz? Nothing. Absolutely nothing. And in my experience, there's a good chance some of that ill-fortune will splash on you. We came up here to get away from that sort of drama. It's not your problem. Leave it alone. Don't get involved."

Her eyes flashed with defiance, exceeding any he'd witnessed in over three decades of marriage. When his red-headed mate got this stirred up his best tactic was to retreat. He froze in place when she got back up and stood before him again, wagging an accusatory finger in his face.

"No. You listen to me, James Hudson. When you were overseas, especially in a warzone, who do you think took care of me? Who do you think took care of the women whose husbands came home in pieces, in a box, or not at all?

"We took care of each other! I'm not going to abandon that sweet thing to whoever or whatever is trying to hurt her. I have no idea what I can do, but she's going to know I'm her friend and she can count on me. And if you don't like it, you can kiss my big, white ass."

With that, she turned on her heel and sashayed into the kitchen.

The Keurig snapped, wheezed, and hissed.

He groaned. The last thing that woman needed was more caffeine.

21. UNDERCOVER

MONTGOMERY RESIDENCE
BOULDER
June 9, Saturday
9:30 a.m.

Sara hadn't seen her father so agitated since her mother was diagnosed with ALS years before. He stared out his den window, gnawing his lip, projecting a medley of unexpressed emotions. Several tense moments passed before he turned to face her.

"You remembered taking those pictures once you saw them. Anything else? Anything Bryan said at the time, before the wreck? What he knew about what you found?"

Her mind hadn't stopped racing since hearing about the accident report. How could there not be one? It was even on the news! Yet, the police claimed there was no record, not even of where her car was taken.

How could they lose her vehicle? *How?*

Who was that Officer Leonard, who helped her out of the car? He even came by the hospital. If he wasn't Highway Patrol, then who or what was he?

He seemed so nice. Was he one of *them?*

"Concentrate, Sara," her father prompted. "Relax and think. Maybe we should look at the photos again."

She inhaled deeply enough it hurt her side. "I'm trying, Dad. I really am. But I'm overwhelmed. I can't think straight. I haven't felt like myself since the first wreck. I don't know." Her eyes burned with a fresh wall of tears. "I just want this to be over. I don't know how much more I can take."

He crouched down and squeezed her fingers. "You're not alone, Sara. Stay here as long as you want. Until you feel like yourself again. However, it's critical for us to figure out what's going on. Do you think it's the concussion? Or don't you want to remember?"

She straightened. "That's possible. Maybe I *am* suppressing it. I feel frustrated, not remembering, yet part of me is scared. Terrified, actually. If it's serious enough to get Bryan killed and now come after me, it must be horrible."

Connie joined them, carrying a tray of steaming blueberry muffins and a pot of coffee. "Hey, you two," she said as she set the tray on the desk. "Any progress?"

Will exhaled through his nose. "Not so far. No easy answers, I'm afraid."

Connie walked around behind Sara and massaged her shoulders. "You need to get away. Get your mind off it for a while. You can use more clothes since your overnight bag burned up. Why don't we go shopping?"

Sara laughed in spite of herself. "Retail therapy. It might actually help. Nothing else has."

Her father's expression grew solemn.

"What's wrong, Dad? Do you disapprove of us shopping together? Or something else?"

His features relaxed.

"I think that's a fabulous idea. Acting normal. Just be careful. If you take your phones, watch what you say. Turn off the microphones and location functions. That won't stop them if they're good, but it'll make it more difficult. Better yet, leave them here. While you two do your girly thing, I'll go into the office to see what I can unearth. If it's secured beyond my clearance level, that alone will tell us plenty."

They ate at a leisurely pace, chatting about neutral topics, including Charlie's earthquake report.

"That reminds me. I'm going to write him about what happened. I asked him to pick up my mail and I think he understood it was more than a random request. He needs to be aware what's going on. They're probably watching him, too, after getting arrested."

"True," Will said. "Slightly safer than the phone or email."

Connie grinned. "You could even disguise it as junk mail."

"Perfect!" she agreed. "We can work on that tonight."

When they finished eating, they went downstairs where Will grabbed his keys and started to leave. Both women insisted on a hug and a kiss before they let him out the door. Phones on the counter, they followed him out to the garage and got into Connie's Cherokee.

"We have to get you another car," Connie noted as she pressed the ignition. "I love this one. You need one with four-wheel drive if you plan to stay out there. Do you have any idea what you want?"

Sara guided her seatbelt beneath the cervical collar. "*Hmmph.* I'm thinking a Humvee. Fully armored with a machine gun on the roof."

"I like it. But seriously, I don't think staying out there by yourself is a good idea, even if you had a tank."

"I know. I'm not sure, either. Yet I feel like I should, as if that's where I belong. Or I might not ever remember or find out what's going on."

Connie backed out, closed the door with the remote, then headed for Rock City Mall while Sara checked out the SUV's interior, contemplating the features she wanted.

Her scrutiny landed on the dash cam. Bryan had one in his truck. Charlie said there was nothing left inside. Was it possible anything it recorded was likewise in The Cloud? Her neck tensed, a spasm stabbing her shoulder as she considered what it would contain.

In spite of her own best efforts and Connie's enthusiasm, she had no interest in clothes shopping. Her back hurt and the neck brace was a nuisance when trying anything on. Furthermore, the last thing she felt like doing was wandering around a mall.

"Why don't we just go by Target? A mall has as much appeal as a marathon."

"Sure. No problem. This is supposed to make you feel better, not worse."

When they got to the alternative destination she picked up a few basics. Back in the car, Connie gave her a look she couldn't quite read.

"I have one more stop in mind, if you're okay with it. I promise it doesn't involve walking. But I'd like it to be our little secret."

Sara took off the contraption supporting her neck and tossed it in the backseat. "What? A male strip club or something?"

Connie's hearty laugh warmed her heart. "Heavens, no! Unless you think that would cheer you up."

"Probably not. A well-built man would just remind me how much I miss Bryan. In more ways than one. Heaven help any man who has to compete with that."

"No, this is something entirely different. But speaking of good-looking men, your Native American friend is quite a hunk. He reminds me of Daniel Day-Lewis in *Last of the Mohicans*. Hubba hubba!"

Sara's laugh morphed into a gasp.

"Are you okay, honey?"

She inhaled slowly, eyes closed. "Yes. Stupid rib. I suppose Charlie's a nice enough specimen. I love his long hair. But I've never thought of him that way. He's just a friend. The main thing we have in common is losing Bryan and trying to figure out what happened. Why else would he have gone down there to check out the truck? Which reminds me. Don't let me forget to write him that note when we get back."

They drove in silence for a while before Connie spoke again. "I can't help but see some parallels in my life to your situation. Don't forget how I came to hook up with your dad. That would have never happened if, well, you know."

"I suppose. But you two weren't from different worlds. And it didn't happen overnight."

"It would have been disrespectful to your mom and downright tacky if it had. And that's not where our heads or hearts were. But when people share a strong emotional bond, especially in grief or some other traumatic experience, it can shift to something more. I wouldn't discount the possibility."

"I try to keep an open mind about most things, so why not? I'm actually not even sure if he's still married. Seems like he has a wife and kids, but they might be divorced. Anyway, what's this big secret you have in mind?"

"You may not be comfortable with it. If not, just say so. I'm good, either way. But it might help. You never know."

"Okay. You've definitely tweaked my curiosity. So, tell me. What is it?"

Connie pulled into a shopping center and parked outside one of the shops. She turned off the engine and pointed to the storefront beyond the windshield.

"This!"

HEWITT IMAGING SERVICES
BOULDER
June 9, Saturday
10:08 a.m.

The cipher lock at the Hewitt Imaging Services employee entrance scanned the magnetic strip on Will's badge, then flashed green when he tapped in his access code. He pushed his way into the eight-story building, paused to clip his badge to his collar, then headed for the elevator.

Upon exiting on the fifth floor he glanced around. With luck, except for the 24/7 crew on the next floor manning the satellite room, the place should be all but empty with it Saturday as well as a beautiful day.

His office was off a secure area guarded by a retinal scanner. The device approved his entry into an expansive, windowless room. He dodged mainframe computers and analysis stations to reach his office, where he sat down and logged in.

If Sara and Bryan happened upon some black project like Google implied, there would be additional information in any number of satellite views. The equipment in their photos indicated something substantial. If it was just another fracking operation, that was no big deal. Whether people liked it or not, it was increasingly commonplace. Certainly insufficient to paint a target on their backs.

Sure, a lot of environmentalist groups were up in arms about it. But it wouldn't be protected by black ops people authorized to use lethal force.

That boring machine was another matter. What on God's green earth did they intend to do with that? He, along with any fans of The History Channel, were aware a network of tunnels existed nationwide, even though the general public dismissed it as rumor or another lame conspiracy theory. Little did they know there was a whole lot down there, far beneath the surface, giving a whole new meaning to the term *undercover.*

Expansion of such facilities took place underground and in such a manner there was little, if any, evidence at the surface, other than an occasional seismic disturbance. A new facility was big news.

What was it? And for whom?

His thoughts shifted to that earthquake, small though it was. Induced or natural? It didn't take a geologist to know both fracking and boring presented that potential. Natural occurrences were possible as well, but it was worth checking out.

First, he needed to confirm that those coordinates on Sara's photos matched the blackout area. He pulled up the visual scans, selected the ones he'd noted, and zeroed in. He folded his arms— restricted. Only low-resolution pictures from high altitudes would be released to services such as Google Earth. They'd see mountains, valleys, roads, and that was about it. Nothing smaller than a train car would be visible, about the same as from an airplane at thirty-thousand feet.

That didn't mean high resolution scans weren't available. Some would be released with restrictions, others to those who instituted the security level in the first place. He could access raw data, though he rarely bothered. It was a tedious process. Even more so when you didn't know what you were looking for.

But if that's what he had to do, so be it.

His primary job was sales, working with customers to determine what type of data they needed, such as resolution and any specialized scanning besides the visual spectrum. The National Weather Service wanted real-time visual, radar, temperature, and so forth. Oceanic temperature data were most popular with NOAA, along with jet stream patterns. Ironically, the satellites themselves were often government owned, but they collected, processed and cataloged the data, even when it was sensitive or classified.

What they collected was vast and expanding rapidly as developing technologies brought new methods to examine the planet. The U.S. Geological Survey was one of their customers who maintained a wealth of data. Unmanned aerial systems, a.k.a. drones, added a plethora of high resolution data previously inaccessible from space, even with the best possible optics.

He needed geophysical tomographic data. It provided layered images using different frequencies of a penetrating wave useful for atmospheric science, geophysics, oceanography, and numerous others. Most were on a small scale using x-rays, *e.g.*, computed tomography, or CT scans, like used in healthcare.

Seismic tomography, however, covered vast geographical regions. It required *in situ* sensors to take the measurements. The big question was whether that type of data had been collected in the target area. Such information would be gathered prior to construction, then perhaps afterwards to map progress. If so, that could reveal whether it was simple interest in the area or something more.

He pulled up the USGS website and checked for any such data. If there was any, it was probably provided by his employer, but easier to find on their site as opposed to Hewitt's data repository.

All he could find were location references related to earthquake fault lines and volcanos. He checked for any in the area. A few, but no major ones, such as the San Andreas or Hayward faults in California, much less the New Madrid to the east. He exhaled through his nose. That earthquake was most likely induced.

He rested his chin on his fist. His only remaining choice was to dig into Hewitt's imposing store of data. Their indexing was vague, purposely making it difficult to find specific data, thus protecting it from hackers, should they penetrate their extensive cybersecurity.

His lips compressed with the realization he was edging into that realm himself.

Need to know be damned. Sara's life depends on it.

First, he searched on the latitude and longitude to see if anything came up.

A huge listing filled his screen.

His victory collapsed to frustration when the data turned out to be raw. Column after column of numbers from over three year's worth of seismic measurements.

Did Hewitt do the data reduction or simply sell the data?

He scrolled to the bottom of the page, hoping for a link to further refinement.

Nothing.

He checked on who'd placed the sensors and ordered satellite data collection.

Classified and inaccessible.

Arms crossed, he glared at the screen. That wasn't what he was hoping for, but it was useful data. What lay underground remained a mystery and defied identification.

Which pointed toward some black project after all.

The question now was whose?

BKSS LLC
ALBUQUERQUE
June 9, Saturday
10:15 a.m.

Bernie took the last drag of his cigarette and ground it out in a tuna can repurposed as an ashtray. He stared at Johannsen's email on his laptop, read it again, and smiled.

It was about freakin' time they got a break. The second wreck had gone perfectly, access to the house in Boulder a piece of cake. Turned out they had that key, too. As a bonus, two cell phones were sitting on the counter. The NSA's fix would have even higher resolution and sensitivity than before thanks to a few hardware modifications.

Maybe this job would turn out okay after all.

He slipped on his prosthetic leg, put some weight on it, then shifted until the stump settled in place. As soon as he grabbed Terminator's leash from the hook by the door the dog was up on all fours, tail whipping side to side.

"C'mon, boy," he said. "Let's go for a walk."

> *The universe is full of magical things patiently waiting for our wits to grow sharper.*
> *—Eden Phillpotts*

22. PATRICE

BOULDER
June 9, Saturday
10:20 a.m.

The storefront window displayed colorful artwork with a New Age flair. *Cosmic Portals* beckoned from its midst, surrounded by stylized images of stars, planets, and a plethora of unfamiliar symbols. Sara got out of the car to check out the menu posted beside the door, Connie right behind her. Not much other than coffee, herbal teas, smoothies, pastries, salads, and a few sandwiches, all with space-themed names.

Connie slipped her arm around her waist "What do you think?"

"What is it? Some sort of Starbuck's wannabe?"

"Somewhat." A conspiratorial tone crept into her voice. "But that's nothing compared to what's not on the menu."

Sara raised an eyebrow. "Like what? Specialty bagels? Or joints?"

The woman's green eyes sparkled. "No. They don't sell them. But they've been known to happen. There's a dispensary just off the Diagonal, if you're interested. You certainly have justification, medically and mentally. That thing around your neck alone broadcasts you deserve a break."

"C'mon, Connie. You know I'm partially brain-dead. What is this place?"

"Well, they do have the best coffee in town. As good as any I had in Vienna, actually. But the bonus is the back room. The proprietor, Patrice Renard, is an astrologer. She doesn't make enough from that alone to maintain the place, so she sells a variety of light refreshments, provides free Wi-Fi, and bits of interesting reading material. So, what do you think?"

"An astrologer? I had no idea you were into this sort of woowoo stuff. Does Dad know?"

Connie's guffaw said it all. "Of course not! Do you know anything about astrology, Sara? Besides those dreadful daily horoscopes?"

"Not really. I know I'm a Gemini, but that's it. I've certainly never been impressed by those horoscopes. How could they possibly fit everyone?"

"You're right. They don't. But it's different when its based on you, personally. Calculated for when you were born. Then it works amazingly well. It sure surprised me." The woman's demeanor grew uncharacteristically serious as she continued.

"Not everything about life is logical, honey. When there are no sensible answers, sometimes you can find them in alternative ways. Other dimensions, if you will. I started coming here right before your mom passed. I needed to know why my best friend was being taken away by such a horrible disease."

Sara's intrigue deepened. "And you got what you were looking for?"

Connie's expression grew wistful. "Yes. Maybe not as specifically as I'd like, but answers that satisfied me enough that it was easier to accept and move on. It gave me the comfort of knowing that life isn't random or unplanned. That our lives have meaning and unfold when and how they're supposed to."

"Do you believe in reincarnation?"

"I do now. It makes things much easier to accept. Think about it. No matter how horrible a person's life may be, isn't it nice to think they might get another chance? I believe in God, Sara, but for me to put my trust in him, I need to know he's fair. Having more than one lifetime does that for me."

Sara bit her lip, pensive. "Do you remember any of your previous lives? Have you done regressions?"

The crease between Connie's brows accented the faraway look in her eyes. "I've thought about it. There's a woman in Denver who does them. Former nun turned mystic, but a trained psychologist. In a way, I wasn't sure whether I wanted to know. What if they were horrible? There's a reason we forget. A clean slate, if you will. A fresh start."

Sara nodded agreement. "I know now, without a doubt, that we don't really die. Our body does, but part of us remains. I know it wasn't an hallucination when I saw Bryan and watched him leave. For all I may have forgotten, that's one part I never will. It feels as if it's stored in my heart rather than my head. At least it served as a goodbye." She stopped to swallow when her throat constricted. "I know I'd feel even worse if I didn't have that. But I still wonder why I had to stay here?"

Her voice broke and she dug inside her purse for a tissue.

Connie rested her hand on her arm. "Listen, honey. We don't have to do this if you don't feel comfortable. I just thought maybe it could provide an answer or two. Maybe even why you had to stay. It's entirely up to you. You can trust her completely. Everything's confidential."

Sara stepped back to the car's side-view mirror to check her mascara. Satisfied, she stared back at the window where Connie stood, expression etched with caring concern.

"Okay. I'm game," she decided. "I sincerely doubt I could feel any worse. It might even help me remember something important."

"Alright. Great! Let's do it."

As the establishment's name implied, the interior resembled another world. Soft, meditative music played in the background. The tables and chairs were wood, not metal or plastic, the counter and coffee bar topped with granite. A hint of sandalwood mingled with the euphoric fragrance of freshly brewed coffee. Elevating it to an olfactory orgasm was the irresistible aroma of freshly baked cinnamon rolls.

Sara closed her eyes and inhaled. "Wow. This must be what heaven smells like. I think I gained five pounds already."

Connie gave her a one-armed hug. "Why don't we start with a cup of chamomile tea and one of those sinful pastries? Then we can see if Patrice is available."

They sat at the counter, Connie eyeing the bakery goods while Sara studied the menu. A college-age girl with short blond hair greeted them.

"What can I get you ladies?" she asked, her voice unexpectedly deep.

"I'd like a medium Cosmic Caress with extra cream and a Lunar Eclipse," Connie replied. She laughed at Sara's puzzled expression. "Chamomile tea and a dark chocolate cupcake with strawberry-mango frosting."

Sara pointed to the menu. "Bring me one of those cinnamon rolls. And a mocha latté."

"One Spiral Galaxy and a Lyra coming up," the girl said.

"Is Patrice booked this afternoon?" Connie asked.

"I don't think so. Let me check."

The beaded strands that separated the cafe from the reading room tinkled like tiny bells as the girl slipped through to the back. When she reappeared she gave them a thumbs-up. "Go on back whenever you're ready."

Moments later they received their orders. Sara savored the latté's energizing effects and sugar-laden treat, but nervous anticipation remained.

What on earth had she agreed to? What if this Patrice person told her something that made her feel even worse?

She picked up the last few crumbs with her fingers, then looked up to see Connie's confident smile. Surely her step-mom wouldn't set her up for anything traumatic. At least not intentionally.

"Ready?"

Sara inhaled slowly, still deciding. Connie's smile vanished.

"I promise it will be good," she said. "Trust me, honey."

She blew out the breath, feeling as if she were skydiving for the first time.

"Okay."

Connie's smile returned. She stepped over to hold the beads aside and beckoned her through.

A tall, elegant-looking woman stood to greet them, sixtyish, based on her long, flowing platinum hair. Wisps of violet highlights throughout were stylish, not garish, and brought out similar colored flecks in her dark blue eyes. She not only looked the part, but emanated an aura of timeless wisdom.

"Well, look what the cat drug in," she said, as she gave Connie a hug, then held out her hand. "And who have we here? Welcome. I'm Patrice Renard."

"Sara Reynolds." The woman's grip was firm, yet warm and friendly.

She returned to the other side of a round table, its tablecloth boasting silky shades of turquoise, magenta, and purple. An arrangement of eucalyptus, dried flowers, and teasels in a crystal vase stood to one side. Connie motioned for Sara to sit in the armchair opposite Patrice and dragged over another for herself.

Patrice rested her hands flat on the table. "So, tell me. What brings you here today?"

"Sara's my step-daughter," Connie explained. "Back in April she lost her husband in a horrible accident."

The astrologer's smile disappeared as her eyes shifted to Sara. "Oh, I'm so very sorry!"

"She was in the vehicle, too, and suffered numerous injuries, including a serious concussion," Connie went on.

"You don't remember it?" Patrice asked.

Sara shook her head. "Only fragments."

"But that's only the tip of the iceberg. It wasn't an accident. It was deliberate," Connie continued. "Then, yesterday, on her way here, an eighteen-wheeler ran her off I-70, and that wasn't an accident, either."

"Oh, no! So your life's in danger?"

"It seems to be," Sara answered. She filled her in about skiing, the photos, Charlie's visit to the wreck site and arrest, along with everything else she could remember.

The woman leaned back in her chair, concern lining her features. "That's quite a story. How can I help?"

"I'm hoping maybe you could provide some insights or answers. My memory comes back in tiny flashes, but it's still a puzzle with missing pieces."

"I'm sure I can find something. Do you know your own as well as your husband's time, date, and place of birth?"

"I was born June 17, 1986 at 6:28 p.m. in Boulder, and Bryan was born September 9, 1981 at 6:03 p.m. in Denver."

The astrologer grinned. "Perfect. I'm impressed you know his exact time. Most people don't even know their own."

"He was meticulous about everything. He refused to celebrate his birthday until that exact time every year and made me do the same. Otherwise it made him feel guilty. He complained he hadn't been born in the middle of the night so he wouldn't have to wait."

Patrice laughed. "Sounds like he was a dyed-in-the-wool Virgo." She entered the information in her computer, then read it back to confirm it. "What about the accident? Do you recall the date, time and place?"

"I couldn't forget if I wanted to. April 17, around 4:17 p.m. just outside Falcon Ridge. At least that's the time the police said the OnStar notification came in. It's easy to remember with the date and time numerically identical."

"That's certainly unusual. I don't think I've ever seen anything like that before. Hold on a second while I check something. *Hmmm.* Using numerology, the date and time boil down to an eight. That suggests the event conveyed some sort of power to those affected. Interesting. Okay, let's see what was going on astrologically."

The computer screen changed to a circle divided into twelve sections, some populated with symbols and numbers. Patrice stared at it a moment, printed it out, then set it on the table between them.

"Do you know anything about astrology?"

"Only that I'm a Gemini and Bryan was a Virgo. And that we weren't supposed to get along." She smiled. "We did, *most* the time."

Smile lines crinkled the corners of Patrice's eyes. "I can tell by how you speak of him that you were very close."

She pointed at the chart, her tapered nails similar in color to the streaks in her hair.

"This is a horoscope. It shows the location of the Sun, Moon, planets, and a few asteroids at the time of the accident. It's an interesting chart. Without going into a bunch of detail that would put you to sleep, I must say it has the imprint of a fatal accident. You don't remember anything about it?"

"Not the crash itself. All of a sudden Bryan and I were floating above the wreck." She bit her lip, grappling with an onslaught of emotions. "He told me he loved me and that I shouldn't 'let them get away with it.' Then he disappeared into the light. The next thing I knew, I was in an ambulance hurting all over."

"Oh! So on top of everything else you had a near-death experience. I can see that here, actually. Did that help you deal with losing him, at least to some degree?"

"Yes, a lot. I feel as if he's still here. I get these weird impressions. Things popping into my head that I couldn't have known." She went on to explain about the contaminated water.

"Okay. Hold on while I print out how the transits for the accident fit Bryan's chart."

"Transits?"

"I'm sorry. I forgot this is all new to you. Transits represent where in the zodiac the Sun, Moon, and planets were located at a specific time. In this case, the accident. When I compare it with Bryan's chart—which shows where everything was when he was born—it shows the energy exchange between him and the Universe at that moment."

The printout showed Bryan's chart in the middle with a second set of glyphs surrounding it. She pointed to a blue line connecting the two sections. "This tells me it was fated, not random. Wow. Pluto in the 12th, getting ready to station retrograde in less than a week. Plus a partile quincunx to Bryan's Phaethon."

"Huh?" Sara and Connie giggled at their shared confusion.

"Sorry! There I go again, babbling in astrologese. Mythologically, Phaethon was the son of Apollo who crashed his father's chariot into the sun. I call it the 'crash and burn' asteroid. It frequently represents someone taking on more than they can handle. It shows up a lot in accidents or crashes, figurative or otherwise.

"Pluto rules death and the Underworld. He was in the twelfth house, which includes things that are unseen. The spiritual realm, hidden enemies, your subconscious mind, and self-defeating behaviors. Angels and demons, if you will. Besides all the fated stuff, I can see this took place in a moving vehicle."

Sara's eyes widened. "That's incredible. What does it say about what happened to me?"

Patrice printed out another pair of nested charts. "This is your chart with the accident's transits. It shows that you would recover. You have Phaethon right next to your natal Sun. And Phaethon was next to the Sun for the accident, too, which is interesting. Similar energies, making them stronger. Are you a bit of a risk taker, Sara?"

She tilted her head, thinking. "I guess. Sometimes."

"It shows accidents would have a strong impact on you, that your life and goals would change. I don't mean to be nosy, and you don't have to answer, but did you get some insurance money as a result?"

"Actually, I did. More than I expected. You can see that there?"

"Yes. I see a financial new beginning that will give you the means to pursue something you care about a lot. Have you experienced numerous surprises and upsets in your life?"

"Oh, my. Let me count the ways." She rolled her eyes. "My life has never been boring."

"I'm not surprised. Here's another interesting feature of both Bryan's and the accident chart. There's a star in the constellation

Virgo called Vindemiatrix. Some astrologers consider it the widow's star. Saturn's location in his chart is in that same location and Saturn in the accident chart squares it. A square is an unfriendly aspect that can bring a crisis, plus Saturn tends to be harsh. Seems to fit."

"All too well. So you're saying that whomever Bryan married was going to wind up a widow?"

"Very likely. But the compatibility between your charts implies that was bound to be you."

Sara's jaw dropped. "Thank you for that. I always believed that, but thought it would be for a lot longer."

"Is there anything specific you'd like to know?" Patrice prompted.

"Can you tell if I'll find out who's responsible? Or why they killed Bryan and are trying to kill me?"

She hit a few keys and a new chart appeared. "Hmmmm. It looks as if you will, but not through conventional means. In other words, it's not likely the police or anyone else will be the ones to find out, or perhaps tell you, if they do. It's likely to be something quite contrary to what you expect. You do need to be careful. Is your father involved with trying to figure this out?"

Connie straightened beside her as Sara responded, "Yes. Is he in danger, too?"

"I don't think so. But I suspect he'll find out at least part of your puzzle. The person who cracks it wide open will be someone you know who's a bit unconventional or outside the mainstream in some way. He, or perhaps she, either has information or will obtain what's needed to figure it out. Any idea who that might be?"

"I'm thinking Charlie. He's the one who got arrested down by the wreck site. He's Native American."

"Check with him. I'll bet he knows something important. He may do something that could be, well, rebellious or illegal, possibly even related to his culture to find it. Maybe already has."

Her mind wandered back to when he got arrested. Maybe he saw something important, just didn't realize it at the time.

After chatting a while longer, Connie paid cash for the readings. Patrice gave Sara one of her cards and told her to call anytime. Then she and Connie left, stopping to pick up Chinese takeout for dinner later.

Connie cleared her throat as they pulled into the driveway and waited for the garage door to open. "Remember what I said earlier?"

She cocked her head. "Remind me."

"Not a word to your father. Unless you want a lecture about science and common sense we don't want to hear."

She nodded, wincing when it triggered another spasm. "I'm sure you're right. Mum's the word."

23. OFFERS

FALCON RIDGE
June 9, Saturday
12:35 p.m.

Charlie stood outside the bait and tackle shop in Falcon Ridge's lone shopping center, trying not to look like a wooden Indian selling cigars. Showing tourists where to catch trout didn't pay much, but it was easy work that brought cash-in-hand. Applying for anything better required updating his résumé, which meant borrowing Sara's computer. Meanwhile, he needed to do something.

A black Lincoln Navigator with tinted windows and Texas plates pulled in a short distance away. A large, serious looking man with deep-set eyes climbed out and lumbered toward him, comb-over standing up like a cock's comb in the breeze.

Rather than wearing the expected designer suit, he was in khaki shorts and a pricey Columbia sportsman's shirt. While he tried to decide if and how to approach him, the man saved him the trouble.

"Howdy, son. I'm fixin' on doin' some fishin'. Do you know your way around here well enough to show me where I can catch some trout?"

Charlie nodded. "I've been showing tourists where to fish for most my life."

"Super. Actually, I live around here, too, at least for the summer. Haven't gotten out for a while, though. Needed to get away from the little woman, if you know what I mean. Figured fishin' was as good an excuse as any."

"Nothing beats fishing for that."

"I'm Bob Bentley," the man said, extending his hand. "What's your name, son?"

Charlie smiled to himself. 'Son' was exactly what he was called the first six years of his life. Then his grandfather named him *Okohomoxhaahketa*, Cheyenne for little wolf. The official naming ceremony never took place, however, due to protests from his Diné mother. His *amasani* called him *Naalnish*, which meant "he works."

Which he had, all his life.

But no doubt this white man simply wanted to know his anglicized name, originally required for census purposes.

"Nice to meet you, Mr. Bentley. I'm Charlie. Charlie Littlewolf."

"Pleasure to meet you, Charlie. Call me Bob. Too many people call me Mr. Bentley. Or worse."

"Whatever you prefer."

"My equipment's in the car, but I need to get a license and pick up some bait or lures that'll work in these parts. What do you recommend?"

"I'll be happy to show you."

He led the man inside and pointed out those that most closely resembled his personal favorites, which he tied himself. While Bentley filled out the paperwork and paid for everything, he waited outside. Ironically, being behind in his child support, his own license was suspended.

The fact he even needed one was grating enough, considering the area once belonged to his people. On tribal lands, it wasn't required, but around there, it was. In some cases, "usual and customary" sites allowed Indigenous access, but whether this area qualified he didn't know.

His ancestors lived there, but it was a small band who'd broken away during one of their forced relocations. The Dead Horse Canyon massacre ended that. Years later, a tribal representative was sent periodically to watch over and renew the blessing on the site, starting with his grandfather.

His gaze wandered to the man's car, resentment knotting in his gut. Pushing past it by hoping for a good tip, he couldn't imagine that shiny beast on the pothole-infested roads that led to the spot he had in mind.

Bentley exited the shop, folded up his license and tucked it in one of his shirt's many pockets, a small bag in hand.

"If you wouldn't mind, we should take my truck, humble though it may be," Charlie suggested. "It's a pretty rough road getting to where I have in mind."

"I appreciate the offer, son. The four-wheel drive would do just dandy, but there's no decent place to get it washed and detailed, even in Belton. The little woman would pitch a fit if I brought it back all mucked up."

Bentley transferred his fishing poles and tackle box from the Lincoln to the back of Charlie's old Ford, then settled into the passenger seat and pulled on the seatbelt.

"You know, Charlie, I learned to drive in an old pickup a lot like this one. Brings back some mighty fine memories of simpler times."

Charlie couldn't imagine the man beside him in such a truck. Another white man with too much money and too little life. He backed up, got on the highway, and headed west.

"Is this what you do for a living?" Bentley asked.

"For now. I'm between jobs. I enjoy it a lot, just doesn't quite pay the bills."

"Surely you don't have a car payment, eh?"

He smiled at the attempted humor. "No. But I have an ex-wife."

Bentley scoffed. "I know how that goes. So what else do you do for work?"

"I was a forest ranger in New Mexico until a couple years ago. Fires took out my area. Cutbacks came along and next thing I knew, I got furloughed."

"Tough break. So you have a degree?"

He nodded. "University of Colorado. Bachelor's in Environmental Management, minor in chemistry."

"No kidding? You know any geology?"

"Some. Took a few classes. I know enough to understand what's beneath my feet, if that's what you mean."

"Think you'd be interested in doing something not as fun as fishing, but a lot better paying?"

He glanced over to meet Bentley's probing brown eyes. "What do you have in mind?"

"I'm a partner in an oil company out of Fort Worth. We're doing some work up here already, so since we have the crew and equipment, we're fixin' to do some exploration."

Anger bolted through him like a lightning strike. He should have known. Bentley personified the white corporate slime who got rich raping his Earth Mother.

"So far the geology's promising," he went on. "We've got one wildcat rig working out purty good, so we're shooting for a play. Ever work an oil patch?"

Charlie forced his jaw to relax and willed composure, though his eyes remained hard as he watched the road ahead. "No, actually I haven't." He braced himself, wondering if Bentley detected the edge in his voice.

"We've been doing seismic work and are fixin' to start drilling. Our geotech came down with appendicitis. He had surgery, but he'll be laid-up a while. He's back in Texas recuperating and wants to stay. So we're looking for a replacement. Can you run a gas chromatograph?"

"Actually, yes. I can."

"How much experience do you have?"

"Close to a thousand hours. In college I was on a work study program to help with expenses. I was assigned to a geology professor doing research. All I did for over a year was prep core samples, then run the results through analysis programs. Did a little field work with seismic and sonde data."

"That's perfect. You have family around here?"

"No."

"How'd you feel 'bout good food and lodging in a bunk house plus fifty dollars an hour when you're on-shift? What do you think?"

Fifty dollars an hour?

He was lucky to make that in an entire day.

But the oil and gas industry?

His heart collided with his stomach at the thought.

He scowled as he braked, then turned right on the dirt road to the fishing area.

"There'd be some long days—twelve hours, sometimes more. But our geologist's an ex-civil servant who insists on weekends off." Charlie assumed the ensuing snort was an editorial on the guy's work ethic. "We Texas folk don't do cold weather, so unless we find somewhere to set up permanent-like, we'll finish up by the time weather turns bad."

Charlie's mind growled with more silent derision, picturing the winter conditions his people endured on reservations. The truck bucked through ruts and over rocks, not unlike the thoughts assaulting his brain.

All that aside, at that beyond-tempting rate he could catch up his child support in a few weeks. Maybe even still see his girls, plus be back on his feet by the end of summer. Then he could worry about finding work that didn't conflict with his morals.

But the oil business?

He winced at the thought.

"Thanks for the offer, Bob. If you don't mind, I'd like to think about it for a day or so."

"What's to think about? Not enough money?"

The stifled laugh came out as a snort. "No, nothing like that." He debated on telling him, but didn't know how it would go over. Indians were screwed hard for centuries when they were honest.

Bentley chuckled softly. "I get it. You people are the original environmentalists. I don't like it, either, Charlie. But I inherited the business and the money's good. Beautiful country out here. I live here, too. We're doing our best to be responsible. Use the best equipment, latest technologies, follow the regs, and try to do as little damage as possible.

"It's essential to the economy, you know. Buying oil from camel jockeys in the Middle East cripples our policies and finances terrorists. I figure finding it here is my patriotic duty to help us be independent as far as energy's concerned. By the way, my great-grandmother was full-blooded Cherokee."

He glanced over, suspicious. *Did he make that up to win him over?*

"Indians in Oklahoma make a boatload of money off the oil industry, son. They don't seem to have a problem with it."

Charlie concentrated on the road ahead, slowing to a crawl for a massive washout that jolted the cab, hard. He exhaled through his teeth, resolve crumbling.

It wasn't exactly a bad feeling. More like the anticipation of jumping off a cliff into an icy spring-fed pond. Perhaps *Maheo* was looking out for him, dropping such a lucrative opportunity right in his lap. He pressed his lips together as he caved completely, feeling as if he were betraying his own mother.

"I guess I can't argue with that. Okay, sure. Why not? I'll give it a try, Bob. When do I start?"

"How about Monday at oh-six-hundred? I'll give you a map to the site. Talk to the GM, Trey Maguire. I'll make sure he's expecting you."

"GM?"

"General manager. Head honcho for the team."

"Okay. Thanks. I'll be there."

He stared at the rough road ahead, hoping he hadn't just made a huge mistake.

HUDSON RESIDENCE
RURAL FALCON RIDGE
June 9, Saturday
5:08 p.m.

Jim Hudson stared blankly at Fox31's six o'clock news, not hearing a word. Liz hadn't talked to him since her explosion that morning. While being freed from her incessant chatter was somewhat pleasant, the tension wasn't. That woman's anger projected like a plutonian isotope ready to go critical in a nuclear bomb. The question was whether she'd fizzle out or explode again.

Deep inside he knew she was right. She was a caring, compassionate woman who'd put up with him for decades. Being career military, he'd been gone—a lot—and if she weren't such a strong person the marriage never would have survived. Most of his peers went through at least one divorce long before retirement.

He owed her. Not only his love and respect, but some modicum of moral support. If she wanted to be there for that Reynolds woman, then he should be there for Liz.

Besides, he was hungry.

Based on over thirty years of marriage, she wouldn't fix a thing for dinner until he apologized.

Admitting defeat, he hauled himself out of his chair and trudged into the kitchen for a can of Mountain Dew. He popped it open and took a swig. Then, like going into a battle he was sure to lose, he set out to find wherever it was she went to pout. At least she hadn't gone shopping.

He strolled down the hall and peered into the extra bedroom they shared as an office and sewing room. She wasn't there, so he continued to the guest room. There she was, back to the door, tying a baby quilt for their daughter who was expecting her second child in November.

He cleared his throat. She turned around, wearing a look that registered somewhere between hurt and anger on the ginger scale.

"Look. I'm sorry. You're right. Okay? If you want to be buddies with that gal, that's fine with me. Her husband was a good man. When we were on TDY he was the comm guy. He patched in calls to the states for the troops. A bit outside regs, but good for morale, so we turned our heads. I'm sure his widow is a good person." Stifling the snort failed as he got to the point. "Besides, you'll do whatever you want, anyway."

Her frown dissolved into a victorious smile. "Yes, I will. But I prefer to have your blessings."

"Yeah. Me, too."

She got up and they exchanged a hug. She stepped back, arms interlocked with his. "Can I ask you something, Jim?"

"Do I have a choice?"

She responded with that wicked smile he knew too well. "Not if you're serious about a truce."

"Okay. What?"

"If there's something going on, isn't there some way you can find out what? You have a high level clearance, don't you?"

He took a swig of his soda, then exhaled through his nose. "Yes. On active duty I did. But you have to understand, Liz. That doesn't mean I get to know everything. Only those things that were relevant to my assignment or mission. No one knows everything, not even the president."

"Well, if there's some secret facility in our own backyard it seems that should qualify as relevant."

He chuckled, yet, had to agree.

"Okay. I see your point. I have some connections at the Pentagon who owe me a favor or two. I'll call Monday and see if I can find anything out. But assuming I do, in order to tell you, I may have to put you under oath not to say anything."

Her look switched back to that fire-eyed demon. "Then what good will it do if I can't tell Sara? Can we put her under oath, too?"

"Let's just see what, if anything, I find out, okay?"

"Okay. I suppose."

His chest heaved with relief. "Great. So. What's for dinner?"

MONTGOMERY RESIDENCE
BOULDER
June 9, Saturday
5:20 p.m.

Sara and Will sat across from one another at the kitchen table while Connie got out dishes, utensils and a bottle of low-sodium soy sauce. They passed around the reheated cartons of Chinese food, each taking a generous portion, then settled in to eat and share their day, though hers and Connie's would be heavily redacted.

"So, what did you find out, Dad? Anything?"

He shook his head. "Not much. I did confirm that the coordinates correspond with some classified project. Exactly what, I don't know. I found some raw seismic tomographic data for the area, but couldn't make any sense of it. However, that confirms someone's interested in what's below the surface."

"Could that just relate to the fracking operation?"

"It's possible. There are faults in the area, so I can see how they wouldn't want to trigger any earthquakes."

"A little late for that."

"True. But minor tremors are to be expected. Sometimes they're actually a good thing. Small ones release tension which can ultimately prevent a big one. Or so they say."

"Why would fracking be some big secret?" Connie asked, joining the conversation as she sat down next to her husband.

"Good question." He helped himself to more fried rice. "There must be more to it than that, considering that boring machine. They must be building some sort of underground facility. If they're digging and blasting, then they'd need to know. As soon as we're done eating, let's take another look at those pictures. Zoom in until it pixilates and see if there's anything we missed."

"I need to write Charlie, too. I hinted that I'd send him some information. And I wonder what he knows that he hasn't told me."

Her father gave her a quizzical look. "What makes you think that?"

Connie kicked her under the table. Sara blinked hard, trying to side-step the slip. "Oh, uh, I just have this feeling. Maybe he found something that he forgot to mention. With all the hassle of being arrested and all."

His expression lingered, suspicions apparent, but much to her relief, he didn't pursue it.

They finished eating, then went upstairs to reexamine the pictures. Zooming in confirmed the likelihood of a fracking operation, but little else. Her memory likewise refused to budge.

"How should I disguise this letter so anyone snooping around in my mail doesn't suspect anything?" Sara mused aloud. "You suggested junk mail. What do you think?"

"How about an ad for new cars? You're going to need one, and that might clue him in."

"I like it. And if I send it to Charles Reynolds at my address, he should figure it out."

"I'll get busy on Photoshop to create the ad while you figure out what to say," Connie volunteered. "I should have heavy photo paper to print on."

"Perfect. By the way, Dad. I thought of something else. Several months ago Bryan installed a dash cam in the truck. Do you think whatever was on it could be out there like these photos?"

Will's eyes narrowed. "Excellent point. If so, it probably would have been in the same place, just a different folder. You copied everything there, right?"

"Yes."

"Then probably not. Those things accumulate a huge amount of data. Probably too much to store. They're usually set up to overwrite old files after a certain amount of time to save space."

"Oh, well. It was just a thought."

I am like one on a high snow bank: the sun shines and continually melts it away, and it keeps going down and down until there is nothing left.
—Struck by the Ree, August 1865

24. MEMORIES

CHARLIE'S CABIN
RURAL FALCON RIDGE
June 9, Saturday
9:32 p.m.

Charlie sat cross-legged in front of the fireplace, wool blanket draped around his shoulders. In two days he'd start work with Lone Star Operations.

Was there any other way he could make that kind of money? No. Absolutely not.

The prospect, however, shadowed his mind like a storm front. In response a random thought tickled his psyche.

This is something you must do.

The justification, however, remained buried beneath any conscious awareness.

Besides the industry itself, what concerned him most was the thought of living with those people. Like when he left for college.

Harassment stories along with the racist views that characterized the industry constituted modern tales of cowboys and Indians. Working with them all day would be bad enough. But bunking with them as well? He didn't want to think about the pranks he'd be subjected to.

He pulled the wrap closer, fingers entwined in its soft texture. June or not, nights were brisk at seven thousand feet. Its earthy scent, including a hint of lanolin, unfurled memories of three decades past, when he was living on the Diné reservation in New Mexico.

His very first job.

An assignment he resented.

He could still see Littlebear leaning against the horse corral, arms folded across his chest.

"No, son," he'd said. "You have only six winters. You are too young for the javelina hunt. You must stay and help your mother and *amasani*."

Charlie hung his head, thinking he'd sneak away somewhere for the remainder of the day.

"Look at me," his father commanded. When he obeyed, his intent collided with the probing eyes of a knowing parent. "When I return you will tell me what you did and they will tell me if you did it well."

He pouted, looking back at the ground. Not hunting with his father was disappointing enough. That edict made it even worse. The teasing he'd suffer from his cousins and friends for doing the work of squaws would be merciless.

Moccasins shuffling in the dirt, he trudged back home to find his mother. As soon as he stepped inside their hogan she took one look at his sour face and shooed him away.

Outside again, he stifled a smile, vindicated to pursue his original plan. Then he remembered. His work was subject to review. His grandmother, one of the tribe's weavers, was his other option. He'd watched her work a few times, but progress was slow and tedious—far too boring to hold his interest for any length of time. With luck, she wouldn't be busy and would tell him one of her wonderful stories. He especially liked those about mischievous coyote.

But when he got to her little house, she wasn't there.

It sounded like a big commotion over by the training corral. Sheep bleating along with people talking and a variety of other unfamiliar sounds. Curiosity tickled, he headed that way.

The characteristic smell of sheep was strong with so many confined to a small area. That, along with all the dust, evoked a giant sneeze. He wiped his nose on his sleeve, then climbed up on the fence to watch the antics of one of the lambs. That held his attention until he spotted his grandmother a short distance away.

What was she doing, poking around what looked like dozens of flat, dead sheep?

Then it a registered: Shearing time.

He watched one of the men use clippers to peel away a year's worth of wool from one of the ewes. It came off in what looked like a solid piece. His grandmother spotted him and waved him over.

Maybe this wouldn't be so bad after all.

"I'm supposed to help you today, *amasani*," he said.

Her weathered face, round like the moon and likewise bearing the grooves and craters of life, broke into a broad smile. "I'm so glad, grandson. What think you of all this wool?"

"I think it smells funny."

"I like it," she replied. "Sheep are almost as important now as buffalo were long ago. They give us meat and they give us wool. This is one of my favorite days, when I pick the fleeces I want before the rest go to market."

"Aren't they all the same?"

"No. Each is very different. Certain parts are better than others, too." She took his little hand and led him over to those she'd set aside. "Let me show you."

She pointed out the different parts of the animal from which the fleece was removed. Some areas were much cleaner and the fiber longer.

"I have a very special project I must do. I need you to separate the shoulder section from the ones I've chosen. Do you know why?"

He looked closer. "Because it is cleaner?"

"Yes. It is also the longest, which makes it easier to spin."

That task finished, he thought he was done. Little did he realize his work had only begun. The raw wool needed to be prepared for spinning. She showed him how to tease each lock by pulling it apart.

His reverie paused as he rubbed his thumb and forefinger together, remembering how they squeaked when coated with lanolin. To his surprise back then, it also softened the callouses he'd earned practicing with his bow.

Next came combing the teased wool with a pair of carders that looked like giant-sized dog brushes. The resulting bats went into a reed basket, miniature clouds of fluff awaiting his grandmother's skilled hand.

As the day wore on, his arms ached and he couldn't card quickly enough to keep up with her spinning. She prodded him to work faster, her hand moving the spindle relentlessly as she twisted the prepared fiber into yarn.

As it turned out, the project lasted into summer. By then he earned her name for him, *Naalnish*. Once enough yarn was spun, the fun began. Now he could do some exploring while he gathered the dye materials needed to produce a variety of warm colors. Best of all, the collection process for some required a knife or ax, a worthy task for a young brave.

Cottonwood leaves, yarrow, and oak bark were some of the things she requested. Among the most challenging were cochineal beetles which, when dried and ground into powder, yielded shades of red. It took an entire day or more to collect enough from their cactus homes for a single batch. To both him and his *amasani*, however, it was time well-spent.

When she was ready to start the dyeing process, he hauled water from either the iron-rich spring north of their village for reds, or the alum-rich one to the east for yellows. The resident minerals affected the final hue and were necessary for the fiber to retain its color—the '"why" of which planted the seed for his interest in chemistry.

When she had sufficient dyed yarn, he helped warp the loom constructed from tree trunks, tie the warp rods that helped create the pattern, then wind the different colors on smooth sticks that served as shuttles.

Then, at last, weaving began.

He marveled day by day as she lifted the warp rods and alternated shuttles, colorful geometric patterns emerging with each row, until their collective labors produced a finished blanket that was not only functional, but a work of art.

His heart swelled as he remembered the day it came off the loom. She folded it carefully, hugged it a moment, then handed it to him with a sparkle in her eyes.

"Where should I put it for you, *amasani*?"

"In your hogan, *Naalnish*. By where you sleep."

"Why?"

"Because it is yours."

Only now, as a grown man, did he appreciate the love and wisdom of that experience. Especially when he discovered that most blankets, at least those offered for sale by members of the tribe, were not made the old way, but with commercial dye and machine-spun yarn.

This was one like none other, made expressly for him with his *amasani's* love and his reluctant assistance.

It was far more than the work itself. It was what it taught him. Not only about the old ways, but of cycles. Of going full circle from the vegetation the sheep ate to grow wool to dyeing the yarn with some of those same plants. The process was tedious and long, yet the result was priceless.

From that first bat of carded wool to its liberation from the loom, it instructed him in the ways of life. It taught him patience, perseverance, and appreciation—for hard work and simple things.

The Diné believed part of their soul went into such creations and always hid a loop somewhere in the tight weave for their soul to escape. So far, it was so cleverly hidden he'd never found it. His fingers caressed the soft fiber, wondering if he ever would. It felt softer each year, improving with use, unlike so many things that didn't last. Analogous to the earth itself and his connection to it.

All thanks to the wisdom of an old woman, who at the time was not much older than he was now. Whose kind heart would forever live in a cherished wrap that kept him warm for what would soon be thirty *haigos*, including many spent in the frigid Colorado Rockies.

How many white men had such a treasured possession?

Man was part of nature. Stewards, not conquerors. Unlike those who stole their land and forced indigenous populations to settle in inferior regions. Then drove them off again when a wealth of silver, gold, copper, lead, and other minerals were discovered beneath what his people considered sacred ground.

The *Tseteshestahese* word for "white man" was *vehoe*, their term for "spider"—a creature that made a web over all things for himself alone. Proven accurate as they continued to benefit from exploiting and abusing the entire area. When done, the aftermath remained from leaching and other methods employed to separate the metals.

Rather than extracting and processing minerals in a way that honored the earth and showed gratitude for its abundance, they raped the land, leaving gaping holes and tunnels behind. In time, the toxic drainage killed all aquatic creatures and drove away wildlife that depended upon such channels—like Tomahawk Creek.

No telling what happened to the one where he'd taken Bob Bentley earlier that day. A stream previously loaded with fish. Now it, too, was barren.

He felt like an idiot. What kind of a guide took a client to a dead stream? The last thing he expected was for Bentley to be understanding. He was flabbergasted when the man told him it was okay, that he really didn't care about the fish, his main objective to escape from his wife for a few hours.

Charlie didn't expect to be paid, much less a generous tip.

He took the hundred-dollar bill out of his shirt pocket and looked at it again. He'd never seen one before and felt inclined to save rather than spend it. Especially now that he had a job.

A job working for a company that did much the same as the miners years before.

In spite of what Bentley said about being responsible and such, he stiffened, wondering again at his decision.

Why did thoughts of his blanket come at this critical time? The first thing that came to mind was that he'd initially resisted helping *amasani*, yet he'd benefited greatly. Would LSO surprise him in a pleasing way, too?

His thoughts shifted to Eaglefeathers. In the days before he crossed over, he gave him much counsel. In particular, he remembered the old man's serious demeanor when he explained why he pressured him to continue his schooling.

"Grandson," he said. "I have pushed you to attend school for education. My heart is humble for you going to college. The white man teaches his knowledge in his books. You must learn that knowledge so you can live a good life and care for your own family one day.

"Grandson, now I must tell you the truth of why I made you go to school. My reason is I do not have education. I cannot read a white man's book. I want the best of two worlds for you, to provide and care for your own family and teach your children and grandchildren a way of life with knowledge and wisdom.

"My father and mother sent me to the government school, the Busby Boarding School, when I was ten years old. They wanted to cut my long braids off. They said I could not speak Cheyenne, my only language. They said I was to live in the dormitory with many young people, some older, some younger. My father and mother could visit me on Saturday only.

"So the night before they cut my long braids I ran away. I walked in the dark to get home. I was scared all the way. When I made it home, I cried in front of my father and mother and told them what they were doing to me.

"My father became very angry and went the next morning to speak with the school boss. I don't know what he said, but I did not have to go to school anymore."

Using his education to support himself was what he was expected to do.

But with a company with no reverence for the Earth?

His thoughts turned to the medicine wheel. Could it tell him to proceed? Or whether he was making a major mistake?

He set the blanket aside and got his sage bundle from the mantel. He lit it, waited for it to smolder, then smudged himself and the four directions. As the familiar scent cleansed the room, he felt his anxiety dissolve, confident he'd receive the guidance he needed.

He lifted the wheel from the nail on the wall and gathered the fetishes. Positioned again on the floor, he set each in place. The rock figures glistened in the fire's light, tiny eyes sparkling as if alive.

A cold draft from beneath the front door prompted him to return the blanket to his shoulders. His eyes closed as he offered a prayer to *Maheo*. Feeling peaceful and receptive, he regarded them, expecting mole to beckon.

Nothing. Was mole offended?

He sat up straighter, surprised a call came from Eagle. He closed his eyes and imagined soaring high above on powerful wings, earth spread out below. Eagle's sharp eyes spotted its prey from a great distance. Yet over all, it was the big picture. A distant perspective, background to its primary goal. The great bird feared nothing. It would dive into a herd of sheep to gather a lamb, flaunting its speed and strength to humans guarding the flock.

Eagle took what he wanted.

His jaw tensed.

No wonder the white man chose it to represent their plundered country.

Sometimes, however, Eagle's arrogance delivered his own demise. He remembered a juvenile eagle fishing in Lake Wilson. It hooked a huge fish, probably a large-mouth bass, that it could barely lift from the water. It struggled to fly, but couldn't, its catch too heavy for immature wings.

Eagle talons could only release their prey on solid ground. This assured they wouldn't drop their meal before arriving at their nest. But in this case it delivered destruction. Exhausted by its vain attempts to fly, the bird eventually fell into the water and drowned.

There was some figurative prey for him to capture. But he should be cautious, not take on more than he could control. Flying into the white man's domain was required, but he must maintain his ability to escape.

Was it a warning? A reminder not to sacrifice his values and be drawn into the white man's world? Or something else?

Badger's wink reminded him of his previous advice. Take what you need, then be ruthless defending yourself.

Black Bear, Guardian of the West, demanded his attention. He assumed the persona of a bear—strong, powerful. The bear was one of the few animals that ate its prey alive rather than killing it first. It lumbered about on all fours, except when threatened, when it arose on its hind legs, declaring its dominance.

Bears knew about preparation as fall and winter approached, when they found a secure place to hibernate. They yielded to nature, to seasons of change. Like badger, it was omnivorous, eating everything from berries to other animals, even man.

Other than its diet, there were things that could not be changed. In many ways, he felt as if he'd been hibernating emotionally. It didn't mean he was weak, only retreating from the harsh realities of life. Bear's acceptance of seasonal cycles acknowledged the power of earth to heal. Bear couldn't prevent winter from coming nor stop the advent of spring. Earth and nature prevailed.

Whatever man did to the earth, nature could resolve. He needed to understand what he could and could not control. For now he was to appear as a teddy bear, cute and harmless. Bentley's token Indian. Yet within, he had the spirit of a mother bear protecting her cubs. Just because he'd submitted for now, didn't mean he lacked an abundance of strength and power.

He thanked Black Bear, then sensed Mountain Lion's call. He assimilated her grace, strength, and power. Her territorialism, the ferocity with which she defended her boundaries.

Just because he was going into the white man's world didn't mean he had to accept or absorb their lifestyle, much less their way of thinking. He would defend his own, should the need arise. If he found they were being irresponsible in their exploitation, he would speak up, albeit respectfully. Maybe he could teach them something as well.

He continued his meditation, sensing that Eagle had something more to say. With a jolt he realized he'd perceived the raptor's lesson, but not its symbolic representation.

A strong admonition fell upon him to honor his Cheyenne heritage and birthright with more dedication. An image of a small domed structure came to mind, a sacred place that confirmed and blessed who he was. One with a function honored for over three hundred years.

His efforts so far to connect with *Maheo* were missing an integral part of all ceremonies—the sweat lodge. The message was clear:

Restore the one he and Eaglefeathers built decades before.

Here, like all new comers, I experienced that even with a university degree it was not an easy task to convince the people that you can do anything.
—Carlos Montezuma (Apache) 1912

25. PROMPTINGS

MONTGOMERY RESIDENCE
BOULDER
June 10, Sunday
7:09 a.m.

Rather than get dressed, as soon as Sara woke up she went directly to the den computer. The photos still looked vaguely familiar, further details hidden behind persistent fog. Like pictures in an old album. Some triggered vague recollection, but lacked context.

Her heart ached that she couldn't remember the last thing she and Bryan did together. The selfie they took showed how happy they were. She zoomed in, examining his face, then his eyes. Something was there beyond his usual boyish mien.

Fear, perhaps? Acceptance of his coming demise?

She panned over to her own. If only she could speak to the woman she was then. It seemed so long ago. What advice would she give? As she stared into her own eyes the usual carefree vacation look was likewise missing.

If Patrice saw the wreck in the moment's cosmic imprint did something inside them both sense it as well?

Its timestamp indicated it was taken prior to the ones that captured the fracking tower and boring machine. Those, in turn, were taken less than an hour before the wreck.

What happened in between?

She closed her eyes, trying to remember. A fragment or two teased her mind. Rushing back to the truck. Bryan explaining something. Her heart raced as a few things slammed back. He'd discovered a scandal he claimed was huge, mentioned something about a server.

Server? What server?

They each had computers, but no server. Was that where he found something? Or hid the data?

Patrice's words trailed through her mind, that Charlie knew something. Which reminded her to mail her covert warning. She retrieved it from the desk on the other side of the room, smiling at its disguise—a colorful ad for new cars and trucks on glossy photo paper. She started to take it downstairs, then stopped.

No.

Maybe she should send it from the post office, rather than the mailbox out front. If anyone was watching her, it might not get to him. And surely a supposed piece of advertising in the outgoing mail from a private residence would scream it was something else.

Her paranoia made her question her sanity, yet it was justified. Bryan's teasing voice jumped from memory:

Just because I'm paranoid doesn't mean no one's following me.

Her brow crinkled. At the time she thought it was a joke. But what a strange thing to say. As her mom always said, "Many a truth is spoken in jest."

She pondered what he may have been implying as she returned to her room and tucked the note in her old University of Colorado backpack. Maybe she should skip mailing it entirely and deliver it in person. Or just tell him. She felt guilty after Connie's clever work, but it was safer not to have it in writing, anyway. That decided, she returned to the den and fed it through the shredder.

It crunched away, her thoughts cycling: *What did he know?*

Back in her room she pulled on a new pair of olive-green shorts, then a pink and green camouflage top she bought the day before. She ached all over, but shunned the neck brace. Doing her best to be sensible, she got down on the floor to do some gentle stretches, then slipped on her flip-flops and went downstairs.

Her father had already left to play a round of golf with a colleague. Connie was at the counter, pouring a cup of coffee.

"Good morning, honey," she said, giving her a hug. "Can I fix you some breakfast?"

"No, thanks. Maybe a piece of toast. My stomach's still pretty queasy. The only thing that sounds good is one of Patrice's cinnamon rolls. What did she call them? Spiral galaxies? We should have brought some home."

Connie handed her the bread. "True. But knowing your father, he'd want to know where they came from. So how do you feel today? Well enough for some car shopping?"

Her nose wrinkled as she operated the toaster. "I think, given my propensity lately for wrecks, that I should rent one for now. That'll give me time to make up my mind. It also might be harder for those spooks, as Dad calls them, to find me."

"Tell you what. Why don't we put it on my credit card? Then it will be even harder."

"Good idea. Thanks. I'll write you a check."

"No big deal. It's the least we can do. So what do you want to do today?"

"I want to kick back and take it easy. Get plenty of rest, relax, see if I can remember anything. Then maybe rent a car this afternoon. Actually, I think I'll head home tomorrow."

"Oh, no! Please don't leave. Don't you want to stay until you feel better? Until we know you'll be safe there? Besides, maybe Will can find out more about that strange site."

She wrinkled her nose, debating. "I'm torn." The toast popped up and she took it to the table to butter it. "It's always comfortable here and I appreciate your help so much. But I feel compelled to go back. I need to remember as much as possible, which I'm more inclined to do there. Plus, I want to talk to Charlie. Figure out what Patrice alluded to."

"So you liked her? We didn't get much of a chance to talk about it yesterday. Did what she said resonate for you?" She took a coffee mug out of the cupboard for Sara and filled it. "Cream and honey?"

"Just cream. Yes, I liked her a lot. She felt like someone I've known forever. Have you been going to her very long?"

"Several years. I go quite often for what's called horary questions."

Sara tilted her head to the side. "What on earth are they?"

"They're amazing. Even Patrice is fascinated by them. You formulate a question. Based on the date, time, and location, she runs the chart. Then she reads it to provide the answer."

"You're kidding. And it works?"

"Absolutely. I've been astounded by how on-target she is. In fact, yesterday, when you asked if you'd ever find out who was doing this and she ran that chart? That was a horary."

"The one where she said Dad wasn't in danger and that Charlie has some answers?"

"Exactly."

"Wow. I'll remember that. I'm sure I'll have plenty more before this is over."

CHARLIE'S CABIN
RURAL FALCON RIDGE
June 10, Sunday
7:32 a.m.

Charlie stood on the south side of his cabin, coffee mug in hand, gazing upon what remained of the sweat lodge he helped Eaglefeathers build decades before. Its skeleton was in shambles. Weeds and small bushes, even a young Douglas fir, had overtaken it to the point of being unrecognizable.

Like his grandfather, it had returned to the Earth. Now a sacred place. Disturbing it didn't feel right.

He should build a new one.

He went inside his cabin to get what he needed for an offering. As the tobacco touched the ground he asked the Earth Mother for permission to use some of her resources and prayed that his efforts would be accepted by *Maheo*. He sat back on his haunches, sobered by the memory of his first ceremonial sweat.

Stumbling through a vast field of grass that towered above his head. Legs moving full speed with the predator's breath hot on his tail. He was a mouse who'd wandered too far from its den fleeing the fangs of a hungry fox. Other nightmarish visions assaulted him as well. Fiery eyes. Fangs dripping with venom.

He exhaled hard, trying to dismiss it and any potential for a rerun, when its symbolism abruptly made sense—running aimlessly away from the safety of his roots while the white man's world tried to consume him.

A clear message he wasn't ready to recognize, much less accept, back when he was a stubborn, rebellious youth lost between cultures.

What a blind fool he'd been.

Times changed. He changed. No longer renounced his heritage, which offended the grandfather spirits. This time would be different. Now *he* was different, not the same person he was back then.

Building a sweat lodge needed to be done according to specific traditional procedures. The first time was when he was fourteen. Uncle Joe Whitewolf's ritual fast on *Novavose*. Accomplished according to his grandfather's directions, then he served as its door keeper. It was a lot of hard work, something he was instructed to do. This time his efforts would confirm the commitment he'd previously lacked.

Peace swelled in his heart with the firmest of convictions there was nothing more important he could do that day.

Determination renewed, he fetched his tool belt and a band saw from inside, then perused the ground around his cabin for the right place. Intuition led him to a relatively level grassy area surrounded by a grove of trees.

He closed his eyes and thought back to helping his grandfather construct the old one, also when he was a youth. Its memory prompted him to sing the Badger Song, a tradition for when such a task was begun. A request and invitation for Badger's blessings and access to *Novavose*.

While he sang a warm glow settled upon him as if to welcome him home. Another prayer asked that the site be acceptable to and protected by *Maheo*, then forever after revered as a sacred place.

Sweat lodges were usually built at the onset of spring, when the rising sun guided the structure's eastern orientation. With it now closer to the summer solstice he hoped compensating for the calendar violation with a compass was acceptable.

He measured and roughed out the structure's eight-foot diameter, including a two-foot circle in the center for the stone pit. To his relief, the good feeling he had earlier resumed as he confirmed the cardinal directions with a compass, then dug in his heel to mark each point.

Eighteen choke cherry trees would form the structure. He glanced around, trying to remember where he'd seen any that were tall and sturdy enough. Another intuitive nudge led him to just such a stand where their branches stretched to at least three times his height. His hand grasped the trunk of the nearest one, satisfied with its girth when his fingers failed to meet.

He removed the saw from his tool belt, then thanked each one for its sacrifice before he severed its trunk several inches above ground, leaving a few lower branches to give it a chance to rejuvenate.

Upon closer examination, he realized some had done just that. He smiled. No wonder he felt as if he were led there. This was the same stand from which he and his grandfather built the last one.

After dragging them back to the site, he set two of the largest trees three feet apart on either side of the eastern heel mark for the door. Then, exactly opposite them on the west, he lined up two more.

He secured all four firmly into the ground, then bent them over and tied east and west together with hand-tanned buckskin. The two resulting arches formed the first section of the dome.

Next, he secured one on the north side mark and another opposite on the south, then bent them over and tied those two together.

After that he added two more trees on both sides of the north center tree, two on both sides of the south, then tied them together over the top. The dome was now complete with two ribs running east to west and five north to south.

The remaining four trees would serve as stringers, secured parallel to the ground to reinforce and stabilize the structure. He began at the left side of the doorway and tied one to each of the ribs on the south side fifteen inches above the ground.

With another tree, he did the same from the right side of the doorway along the north side, then tied both trees together in the rear. He repeated the same reinforcement process with the last two trees, this time thirty inches above ground level, then tied them together in back.

He checked all the ties, tightened them one final time, and added additional ones until he was satisfied all eighteen trees were lashed together into a sturdy structure.

Brave Wolf and wife beside their sweat lodge, June 20, 1901. (Photograph by L. A. Huffman)

It was essential that the fire pit, located five steps outside the door, line up toward the east with the stone pit inside. He marked the stone pit's center with a stick, then used another one to mark the fire pit's proposed center. When checked with the compass, their orientation was slightly off so he adjusted the markers accordingly.

The next step entailed stacking the wood. He hoped there was enough already cut and split. Building a sweat lodge was usually a tribal activity. A time of bonding, sharing, of mutual support and cooperation. Loneliness settled around him, missing the comradery, yet doing so alone served him right.

He'd shunned such things, back when he deemed sweat lodges torture chambers rather than sacred places for physical and spiritual renewal.

The sun and his stomach told him it was nearly noon, so he returned to his cabin to grab a bite to eat. There was just enough elk roast left for a couple sandwiches, which he ate with some tortilla chips. As he consumed the last one he realized he'd be starving by suppertime.

He took his last venison roast out of the fridge's small freezer, put it in a pot with the contents of a bottle of water, then set it on the propane stove's smallest burner to defrost and simmer while he worked.

The afternoon promised to be hot, so he turned to grab a few water bottles, then realized he'd poured the last one over the roast.

Great.

His well-water was fouled and unsuitable for a sweat. It would offend the gods and possibly kill him with toxic vapors, depending on which pollutants it contained.

He grabbed his keys and headed for the store. He returned with three cases of bottled drinking water, enough in gallon jugs for when he did a sweat, plus a bag of produce for the stew.

He turned the frozen roast over in the pot, added more water, then went outside to check the woodpile. Enough remained with a six to eight inch diameter for at least one sweat.

To heat the stones initially required the blaze to last for an hour and a half, then another hour and a half after that to keep them hot for all four rounds.

The first four logs became the base. He laid the four-foot lengths side by side, oriented east to west, made sure they were straight, then stood, rolled his shoulders, and stretched.

Now for the stones.

A small-scale, individual sweat could get away with using twenty-eight. He winced at the thought. Eaglefeathers frowned upon such deviations.

Do it right or not at all.

Gathering up the needed forty-four, one to honor each of the Cheyenne chiefs, would take considerable effort. It wasn't as simple as collecting big rocks the size of a grapefruit. The only ones acceptable were volcanic in origin and thus capable of withstanding extreme heat. The prospect loomed as a daunting task in both time and energy.

Maybe he could use the stones from the one he and Eaglefeathers built.

When he returned to the old site he stood there a moment, touched as never before. His vision blurred, heart aching. What he wouldn't give to be with the old man one more time. He wiped his eyes, then pushed aside the overgrowth to make his way inside.

The stone pyramid in the lodge's center, as expected, was undisturbed. Goosebumps chilled his neck and arms, breath stolen by an involuntary gasp. He knelt before it, mesmerized. How many times did Eaglefeathers bless those very stones?

Memories besieged him.

Sweet grass smoldering, fragrant smoke rising.

Soulful strains of the Grandfather Song.

No.

More than ever he recognized the site was sacred. Disturbing it was still wrong.

Ashamed of being too lazy to collect new ones, he got up to leave. Grandfather spirits fell upon him as autumn's first snow blesses parched ground.

Use the stones, grandson. They bind us together in ways you cannot know.

He fell back to his knees. Tears kissed the stones during his grateful prayer. He opened his eyes, yet remained a while longer to absorb the moment. Gentle hands caressed those on top, then lifted each one with the same reverence bestowed upon the ceramic jar given to him by his *amasani*. Then, one by one, hefted them to the fire pit.

The best ones served as grandfather stones which were placed in the four corners and center of the log base. The remaining ones filled the space within, then stacked to form a pyramid.

He checked it's stability, then cleaned up all the leaves, twigs, wood chips, and other debris from around the lodge, inside and out. Not to be wasted, it filled gaps between stones, then as kindling. After that he surrounded the pile with upright four-foot lengths of split logs.

Satisfied at last, he returned to the cabin to retrieve his grandfather's sweat lodge buffalo hides to cover the structure, which took a few trips due to their size and weight.

After tying the last one in place for the door he stepped back and exhaled hard. He wiped the sweat from his brow and smiled. He'd just built a sweat lodge entirely by himself. Not because he had to, but because he wanted to. Certainly a step toward becoming an honorable *Tseteshestahese* man.

Of critical importance was the fact it was constructed strictly according to *Tseteshestahese* tradition. A worthy abode for the grandfather spirits.

"Good work, *Naalnish,*" he declared aloud. "You earned *Amasani's* name for you today."

His warm rush of accomplishment mingled with the approval he felt coming from Eaglefeathers, whom he'd sensed nearby since retrieving the stones.

He ducked inside and sat cross-legged on the far side of the stone pit facing the door. It was darker than night. The smell of freshly hewn choke cherry branches and buffalo hides provoked memories that flickered like the shards of light teasing the door.

Tired but content, he sang the sweat lodge completion song, feeling as if he weren't alone. He finished with a prayer that *Maheo* and the spirits would be there, then remained a while longer, soaking up the sense of peace before going back outside to admire it again.

Its readiness beckoned, but it would be at least a week before he could use it. Loneliness flared again that he'd be its sole occupant.

If you follow the way of Maheo, *as I have taught you, Okohomoxhaahketa, then you will never be alone. He will always walk with you and be with you.*

Gradually the memory and satisfied glow transitioned to reality: His job with LSO started the next day.

By the time a week passed he would need its ritual cleansing.

MONTGOMERY RESIDENCE
BOULDER
June 10, Sunday
6:03 p.m.

The pot roast filled the room with mouth-watering aromas. Sara closed her eyes a moment to savor it, appreciating the home-cooked meal. While Connie loved to go out, she was nonetheless no stranger to the kitchen. She'd miss that, but couldn't stay, motivation fueled by impatience.

What did Charlie discover?

"It's not even six o'clock and light until ten," she said as she set the table. "If I leave right after dinner I'll still have plenty of time to get home before dark."

Her father's smirk puzzled her. Behind his back, Connie stopped stirring the gravy, her scowl indicating she was likewise confused.

"How exactly do you plan to do that, Sara?" Will asked. "Uber?"

Her eyes locked with his across the table for a long moment. Her determination crashed back to reality.

Thanks to that long nap she took chilling out that afternoon car shopping never happened.

"Right," she agreed, rolling her eyes. "I guess I'm just anxious to get back home."

"Why? What's the hurry?" he asked.

Over by the stove Connie glared, free hand zipping her lips. *No Patrice!*

Sara glanced from one to the other, brain frozen.

"Uh, I don't know, Dad. Just a feeling, I guess. And I think I'm more likely to remember something there. Here I get too comfortable lounging around living in the past."

"I suppose that makes sense," he admitted, but his eyes remained on hers, suspicious and probing her mind.

Connie tossed her another look as she brought the food to the table. Sara shifted her eyes to the roast and speared a chunk, then passed the platter along.

"I was looking at those photos again and managed to remember a little. But again, only fragments," she said, changing the subject.

"That's progress, nonetheless," her father said, loading up his plate with mashed potatoes. "Eventually all the pieces will fit together. What did you remember?"

"I vaguely recalled high-tailing it back to the truck. The timestamps on the pictures show less than an hour between the last one and the wreck. Bryan was saying he'd discovered some scandal that was 'huge' and something about a server. But I have no idea which one he was talking about. We didn't have one at home. Just our laptops, tablets, and so forth."

His expression indicated wheels turning in his brain.

"A server, eh? *Huh.* Bryan and I had some pretty interesting conversations. He understood all that IT stuff inside out. There wasn't much, if anything, he didn't know how to do. A few times I, well, wondered about some of the things he said. When I'd question him, he was always, uh, well, evasive."

Something about his voice's strange inflection triggered an alarm. She set down her fork and stared at him, hard.

"Oh? Like what?"

His eyes were troubled as they met hers. "The last time you both were here, he and I were upstairs watching the Superbowl and having a few beers. He mentioned how his job at the credit union was pretty boring. Sometimes he did some exploring. Some of what he mentioned is only found on the Dark Web or classified sites." His lips compressed in a line, as if holding something back.

"And?" she prompted.

He exhaled, hard. "I think he was doing some hacking."

Her heart rate spiked. That made perfect sense. It also had an oddly familiar ring.

"You think he found something that relates to all this? Something so classified it cost him his life?"

Will's attention fixed on his plate, then slowly met her questioning look. "It's a strong possibility, Sara."

"Oh, my God! Why didn't you say so before?"

His voice remained steady. "I don't like jumping to conclusions. Until now, I didn't have enough information to support that. Since those photos were taken relatively close to your cabin, it was possible you just stumbled upon something you weren't supposed to see. But combined with what you remembered and I've found so far, it sounds as if the discovery wasn't random."

"If that's true, what should I do now?"

"Keep trying to remember. Figure out more about that server. Did you ever replace his cell phone?"

"No. I had no reason to. Why?"

"Get it replaced. There might be a clue in Cloud Storage or on the Google account on his phone. He probably erased his tracks, but you never know. People think of their phones as an extension of their brain. On the other hand, if there was anything there, the spooks probably took it down."

"True. And you're right. Bryan always knew exactly where his phone was. At all times. I used to accuse him of being addicted to it. He blew it off. If it had incriminating information on it, then it makes more sense." She held her temples. "So what he did was against the law?"

"Accessing classified information or cyber snooping is definitely not legal. Often it's a federal offense. Some people have gone to prison. Others have left the country to avoid prosecution. At least he doesn't have to worry about that."

"Right. They killed him instead. And tried to get me, too!"

"They naturally assume you know this dirty little secret."

Her thoughts raced, absorbing the implications. Seconds later, she sat up straight, eyes flashing. "How could he do that to me? I loved and trusted him. And he nearly got me killed!"

"I sincerely doubt he expected such an outcome. He was a bit of an idealist, naive in his own way. He would never deliberately put you in danger, Sara. I'm sure of that."

"I don't know, Dad. He told me it was *huge*."

"There are lots of things that could be *huge* without carrying a death sentence. But all the evidence indicates this did."

Her appetite fled. Her own husband, the love of her life, nearly got her killed. Without hesitation, she'd literally trusted him with her life. Hot tears of fury with a side of betrayal filled her eyes.

She excused herself and plodded upstairs to her room where she sat on her bed, caught in the unhappy flux of a love/hate interface.

"Damn it, Bryan!" she growled aloud. "How dare you expect me to finish your dirty work! What's the matter with you? You owe me a *huge* explanation, buddy. If you weren't already dead, I'd kill you myself."

But dead he was.

And her father was right.

Bryan could be idealistic.

It was what made him such a hopeless romantic. A part of him she cherished. He'd never deliberately harm her. She knew that. Like her father, she shouldn't judge him or the situation without the facts.

Gradually, her heartrate returned to normal

At least a few things were starting to come back.

What server? Where? Was there one at their condo she didn't know about?

He'd always taken care of their computers and all things electronic. There could be one, where all their files were backed up, that she didn't know about. Or did he stash it on his work computer? Or the credit union's server?

Before she forgot, she decided to call about replacing his phone. She gave them the account information, then waited for what seemed a long time. A different person from the customer service rep came on the line.

"Mrs. Reynolds?" The voice was deep and authoritative.

"Yes."

"I'm sorry. We have no record of that number."

She stiffened. "What about my phone?" She provided the number, which was still listed, but any record of his was entirely gone.

"Okay. Thank you."

Her teeth ground with frustration as she went back downstairs and joined Will and Connie clearing the table.

"Big surprise," she said. "AT&T has no record of Bryan's number."

His lips compressed like before, as if holding back what he wanted to say. Several seconds elapsed.

"Getting the phone company to make such a claim isn't easy, Sara. That, combined with the lost police report, proves once again we're not dealing with amateurs. This is serious stuff. Damn serious."

"I know, Dad."

Will's expression remained solemn, eyes penetrating. "You still have that Glock I gave you a few years ago, right?" She nodded. "When's the last time you took it out?"

She grimaced, fully aware where this was going. "It's at the condo. I, uh, well, I guess I haven't taken it out for, well, a while."

"How long?"

"I'm not sure. Probably a couple years."

His glare reeked disapproval. "We need to refresh your skills. Furthermore, you need to stay with us, at least until we find out exactly what's going on. Enough is enough."

She bristled, about to argue, then realized he had a valid point. Two wrecks within a few months, both orchestrated to kill her, was certainly enough.

Did she owe it to Bryan to exact some sort of justice on the perpetrators or not? If this was as big as it seemed, what could she possibly do to keep them from "getting away with it?" By all appearances, they already had.

Maybe she should forget the whole thing. Did her dead husband actually expect her to risk her life doing so? She closed her eyes and swallowed hard.

"Maybe you're right. But more than ever we need to find that server. With luck we can solve this thing, once and for all. Then we'll have a better idea what to do. What would it look like? Maybe there's one at the condo I didn't know about."

His commanding look softened. "A regular desktop CPU can be configured as a server. It doesn't have to be some huge mainframe with its own lightshow. If there is one, he may have kept it out in the open. Or tucked away in a closet, if there was a power source nearby. If there's one there, it shouldn't be hard to find."

"Okay. Tomorrow after I'm no longer auto-impaired, I'll go by my place to see what I can find. I might just spend the night while I decide whether to stay with you or go back to the cabin."

Will opened his mouth as if to speak, but Connie jumped in. "Would you like us to go with you?" she offered. "I don't like the idea of you going there by yourself."

"I insist," Will stated, making it unnegotiable.

She held her chin, considering. She hadn't been back since the accident. And now, besides the emotional side, there were personal safety issues. If Bryan violated federal law, there was a good chance whoever was trying to kill her was watching the place.

She nodded. "You're right. Yes, I'd appreciate it if you'd go, too. Plus, you can help me look for this elusive server."

26. LSO

LONE STAR OPERATIONS (LSO)
LOGISTICS OUTPOST
RURAL FALCON RIDGE
June 11, Monday
5:47 a.m.

First light crowned Eagles Peak as Charlie reported to the Lone Star Operations work site at o'dark-thirty Monday morning. A week's worth of clothes were in his truck, but he hoped to live home. His bachelor's degree and transcripts were in a manila envelope to confirm his qualifications.

A small trailer alive with lights beckoned. He climbed the built-in metal steps to the door and knocked, not wanting to appear too presumptuous by walking in.

A deep voice yelled, "C'mon in."

He twisted the knob and stepped inside. It looked like a messy office. A few desks topped with computers. File cabinets adjacent to a copy machine. Water cooler, coffee maker, white boards scrawled with notes and schedules. Cork board cluttered with notices of sundry colors and sizes.

A big white guy stood behind a table strewn with maps and diagrams. A little taller than Charlie, around six-four and two-forty. His white moustache and matching hair staging a retreat bespoke experience more than age. He froze as if his visitor had dropped in from another dimension.

"Can I help y'all?"

Charlie swallowed hard, wondering if he was expected or whether Bentley had been messing with him. He introduced himself and mentioned Bob telling him about a job. The guy broke into a huge grin and held out his hand.

"Welcome aboard, Littlewolf. I'm Trey. Trey Maguire, general manager. Am I glad to see y'all! Here, set yourself down." He motioned to a chair beside the table, sweeping the maps and such aside. "I'll get the new employee paperwork. Would y'all like a cup o' joe?"

Charlie sat down as instructed. "Yes, coffee would be great."

"Okay, let's get this here show on the road." Maguire extracted a stack of pure bureaucratic joy from a file cabinet and dropped it in front of him, then brought over a mug filled with steaming brew.

"When y'all's done with that, the next step's to run into town for a drug test. They'll email the results back to me by the time you gets back. We'll get y'all badged up, then there's a boatload of online training you has to complete and—might I add—*pass*. After that, we'll get y'all outfitted proper like, then go out in the field. Ever work an oil patch before?"

"No, sir. Studied geology in college, did sample prep for one of the professors for a couple years. Did a little seismic and sonde field work. Analyzed a few core samples as part of the class lab, but that's about it."

"Well, that's a helluva lot more than some guys come in here aknowin'. Y'all's familiar with the area, though, right?"

"Yes, sir. Been roaming these mountains since I was a teen."

"Perfect. For now, y'all's job will be to work with our geologist. He'll tell y'all what to do."

Maguire explained the paperwork, took his driver's license and other documents to photocopy, then went back to scrutinizing the maps while Charlie filled everything out.

When he got to the emergency contact information, he started to fill in Sara's number, then stopped. After what she'd been through, the last thing she needed was to be the first to know if anything bad happened.

Then who? His ex?

His lips compressed. Right. She'd be too busy celebrating. Maybe Sara's father. Yes, that would work. He thought he'd saved his number from texting while Sara was in the hospital, but couldn't find it. He finally gave up and used hers. He could always change it later.

It took almost an hour to drive into Belton for the drug test and back. Passing it was the least of his worries. When he got back, he started the safety training, which was mostly common sense. His people had practiced situational awareness for millennia. They called it survival.

There were a few things he hadn't thought about before, however. Like hitting a pocket of hydrogen sulfide, which could kill in a matter of seconds. There was also a host of equipment issues. Explosive hose disconnects or failing machinery spewing projectiles. Blowouts sent shrapnel flying at hypersonic speeds along with oil and drilling mud loaded with toxic chemicals.

Before he'd be allowed near the rig itself he needed to complete several hours of OSHA training. Considering the risks, the generous pay made more sense than ever.

It was after ten by the time he finished the training and took the exam. After pointing out the location where he'd clock in and out, Maguire took him over to the barracks trailer a short distance away.

It housed about twenty, some bunks neatly made, others in disarray. Shoes and clothing spilled from wooden lockers beneath the beds, a few crumpled soda cans around as well. The unpleasant odor of sweat, dirt, and oil, was far worse than any gym or dorm.

Worst of all, it felt like a prison. His gut lurched, his own concerns knotted with ancient confinement horrors entrenched in his DNA. Sleeping outside on the ground would be better than that.

Maybe the answer would be *No*, but he felt compelled to ask.

"Uh, Mr. Maguire? I, uh, appreciate the offer, but it only takes me ten or fifteen minutes to get here from home. Would it be okay if I just came in every morning rather than stay here?"

The big guy grinned. "Sure ain't no Hilton here, now is it? Some of these roughnecks don't have a home anywheres, much less nearby, so we puts 'em up. But it ain't required. Punctuality, however, is. Comprenday?"

"I understand." His mouth twitched, trying to smile with relief, but he kept it at bay.

After seeing the chow hall and its scheduled hours, they crossed the compound to a metal shed to pick up his gear: A flame-resistant yellow Kevlar monkey suit he'd wear over his regular clothes, orange safety vest, hardhat, steel-toed boots, goggles, a gas mask, hydrogen sulfide monitor, ear protection, and gloves.

"Alright. Gear up," Maguire stated. "Then y'all can get to work."

He pulled on the monkey suit, then sat on a nearby bench to change into the boots. He set the hardhat in place, a far cry from his usual head covering, and strapped on the equipment, feeling like a warrior preparing for battle. Maybe if he did a good job, Maguire would add an eagle feather to his hardhat.

"Looks like y'all's good to go." Maguire slapped him on the back. "Oh. Yeah. One more thing. How's y'all feel 'bout a good fight?"

His response was a questioning look. "No, thanks. Had enough of that in college. Why?"

"Just checkin'. I have a strict no altercation policy. I expect my men to solve disputes peacefully, period. Get into a fight, at least here on the worksite, and y'all is gone. Get into one in town, it better not keep y'all from showing up for your shift."

"Works for me."

Another concern evaporated, chest lightening with relief. The others could hate Indians all they wanted as long as they liked keeping their job more.

"Okay, great. Does y'all have any questions?" Charlie shook his head. "Okay. The guy ya'll needs to talk to up there is the toolpusher, Dick Duncan. I'll get the roustie over here with a ride." He got on the radio. "Hey, Tommy. I need y'all to take the newbie out to the site. We's over by the equipment shed."

"Roger, that," came the scratchy reply.

"There's a road we dug to the site to get the equipment in, but it's a lot longer that way. It's quicker with an ATV."

Charlie nodded, then waded through a final wave of guilt and misgivings while the mantra *fifty dollars an hour* repeated inside his head.

A short while later the guy arrived driving an eight-wheeled amphibious all-terrain vehicle. Maguire introduced them and while Tommy shook his hand firmly enough, his grey eyes revealed thinly veiled contempt. He hopped in beside him and pulled on the seatbelt, grateful for the no fighting policy as he pondered what lay ahead.

The ride was far from smooth, but nothing short of mature trees could stop it. The vehicle bounced over rocks, blew through a small stream, then thrashed across more rough ground. When they reached the final ascent, a pounding, mechanical commotion rose above that of the engine. The volume increased as they came to a relatively flat area where a truck-mounted drilling rig dominated the scene, a half-dozen roughnecks in various positions on and around it.

"This is it," Tommy yelled.

He'd barely climbed out when the ATV took off. His attention shifted to a cluster of workers twenty yards or so away from the rig. A stocky guy with a shaved head, probably in his early fifties, waved him over. His chin was wider than the top of his head, neck non-existent. His piercing pig-like eyes were nonetheless intelligent and most likely didn't miss a thing.

"I assume y'all's Littlewolf." He held out his hand. "I'm Big Dick. Toolpusher and head swingin' dick 'round here. And yeah, that's my name *and* my title. Callin' me Dickhead is a compliment."

Charlie laughed politely, wondering how much this guy would live up to his name.

"C'mon, I'll introduce y'all to Doc Phil Stafford, the geologist y'all will be workin' with. I hope havin' y'all around will get him to shut the hell up. His whinin' 'bout havin' too much to do's drivin' me batshit crazy."

Charlie sensed from his tone that the geologist wasn't the most popular team member as they walked to a thirty-foot trailer some fifty yards away. Before stepping inside, he checked his feet for mud. Then he saw the floor, well-tracked with brown scuffs on what was once light-colored linoleum.

It was outfitted wall-to-wall with lab equipment, most of which he recognized. To the right a large table contained several printouts of seismic surveys. Another held a core sample, the plastic sleeve cut open with signs of being picked through.

"Yo, Dr. Phil."

Stafford's attention remained fixed on a gas chromatograph. He was slight of build, head covered with unruly brown hair tickled with grey. Thick heavy-rimmed eyeglasses dominated his sharp features. Other than the missing hardhat, he was dressed like everyone else.

"This here's Charlie Littlewolf," Big Dick said. "The grunt y'all's been bitchin' 'bout."

"It's about time," he replied without looking up. His voice rang with a high-pitched whiney quality similar to fingernails on a chalkboard.

The toolpusher smirked, slapped Charlie on the back, and left. He stared longingly at the door for a moment then, accepting his fate, stepped over to see what the guy was doing. The machine was newer and more sophisticated than what he'd used years before, but similar enough to recognize.

Disturbing someone engrossed in an analysis was against lab protocol anywhere, so while he waited he looked over the mass spec and other equipment, including a scanning electron microscope. Playing with such toys was why he'd gotten a minor in chemistry. A welcome surge of anticipation rippled through him. Maybe this would work out okay after all.

At length, Stafford swiveled around, wearing a look that reeked with unveiled skepticism. Charlie held his gaze, feeling as if he were wearing a breech cloth instead of Kevlar.

"You've worked a lab before?"

"Yes."

"What's your experience?"

He explained, to which the man replied with a series of unreadable expressions. He proceeded to the table with the core samples where he instructed him on what to do.

Before he had a chance to start, the racket of the eight-wheeler joined that of the rig in a raucous duet. Dr. Phil headed for the door, gesturing for him follow.

"C'mon, Chuck. Time to eat."

He cringed. That name released unpleasant college dorm experiences he'd worked hard to forget. He sucked back his annoyance as he stepped outside, the momentary glimpse of optimism already fading.

The nerve-wracking drone of the rig dropped to an idle as everyone hustled over to the ATV. Tommy was back with box lunches.

At that point, Big Dick took advantage of everyone being together by introducing him to the rest of the crew. A dozen roughnecks, the driller, and various other scruffy-looking characters. The type he previously met in sundry nightmares and other unpleasant encounters. He maintained steady eye-contact balanced somewhere between a lack of intimidation versus aggression.

Policy or not, no telling what went on behind Maguire's back, especially at night. He sent a silent prayer of thanks to *Maheo* he could live at home.

The crew grabbed their food, then sat around on the ATV and other equipment. All seats were taken, the entire area laden with mud, natural as well as the grey, chemically laden drilling variety. He admonished himself for acting like a white man and plopped down cross-legged on the driest piece of ground he could find.

Mountain Lion advised him to maintain his boundaries and authentic self, which he intended to do. He pictured his father and grandfather watching, determined to make them proud. Hopefully they'd forgive him for being in cahoots with people in the same category as the miners over a century before.

The food was superior quality, better than plenty of restaurants he'd been to, which managed to tip his opinion back another notch toward the positive. He didn't spend that much on food, anyway, normally eating relatively simple meals. Being well-fed on the job was a definite plus.

The roughnecks consumed their food in a few bites, then a handful wandered off to have a smoke. As soon as Dr. Phil, who'd parked his skinny butt on the trailer steps, went back inside, Charlie followed.

After that, neither said a word for hours. He prepped dozens of samples as he was told, though it differed slightly from the way he did it before. The man's response to the results was a series of unintelligible sounds, which he assumed to be approval.

They were going to pull core one more time before shutting down for the night, so Dr. Phil sent him out to watch. He stood a hundred feet back, eyeing the portable monstrosity. Its tires alone dwarfed the workers, the tower enclosing the drill higher than the surrounding trees.

The engine started, emitting a whiff of diesel exhaust followed by a deafening roar, nerve-wracking in spite of the ear protectors. He braced himself, then flinched when the drill penetrated the ground.

What are you doing to my mother? bellowed through his head in Cheyenne.

The teeth-rattling vibrations beneath his feet translated to screams he heard as audibly as the driller's instructions to the roughnecks.

How could they not hear it? Did prolonged exposure to this horrific mechanical din blow their eardrums?

No.

They were deaf.

But not from impaired hearing.

What he perceived came through his heart and connection to the Earth. The physical world was all the white man acknowledged, like their view of the stars and heavens above.

The affliction resided in their souls.

The bitter irony that such an attitude originated with the period in history known as "The Enlightenment" was a fact he always considered with the utmost disdain. Denying the spiritual connection between all living things, of which the Earth herself was part, contributed to the disconnected attitude that led the white man to such despicable deeds. Their entire purpose in life was to conquer—their fellow humans, animal life, their Earth Mother, the Universe itself.

He didn't know which was louder, the monolith beside him or the voices in his head protesting the blatant exploitation. Echoes of Black Cloud's curse, perhaps? Whatever their origin, how he'd endure this job for even another day was edging beyond comprehension.

True, it would relieve his financial straits. Did that make him no better than the white men ravaging the planet? Was his Earth Mother's pain something he needed to experience? Something that would expand his perspective and allow him to understand more deeply? He thought back to the Medicine Wheel and the insights he gained before starting the job.

No wonder Mole had been silent.

> *The best people possess a feeling for beauty, the courage to take risks, the discipline to tell the truth, the capacity for sacrifice. Ironically, their virtues make them vulnerable; they are often wounded, sometimes destroyed.*
> — Ernest Hemingway

27. THE CONDO

MONTGOMERY RESIDENCE
BOULDER
June 11, Monday
10:24 a.m.

Early the next morning Connie rented Sara a dark grey Lexus GX. So far she liked it, other than the fact it felt like driving a tank without the benefits. Fortunately, she had a month to decide whether she wanted to buy or lease it. She'd have a better idea by the time she drove out to the cabin, whenever that might be.

For now she was cruising along I-25 South toward Denver, a familiar drive. So much so, it presented a timeless quality. As if she were returning home after a casual visit while Bryan was TDY.

And while the flames of outrage that he'd placed her in so much jeopardy had reduced to embers, the heat remained, evaporating some of the grief. She knew anger was part of the recovery process, but this was different. Not only did he abandon her, but left her in a precarious position of his own making, whether he was aware of the consequences or not.

Deep inside she knew he'd never hurt her. At least not intentionally. He undoubtedly discovered something for which he became a martyr. She could almost hear him pleading with her not to allow his death to be in vain, softening her heart. If she quit now, she'd let him down.

How could she live with herself knowing that?

Her father's edict that she stay with them replayed through her head like an earworm. It made sense, just didn't feel right. Of course he wanted to keep her safe. Being doted upon in her childhood home the past few days was comforting, to say the least. But crawling back into the womb wouldn't make the situation go away. She was a grown woman and needed to act like one.

Furthermore, this was her mess, not theirs. Dragging them into it could put them in harm's way as well.

By the time she exited the Interstate on East Hampden her mind was made up. This was her problem and she would deal with it herself.

Left on South Maple, then into the gated entry to the condo complex. She instinctively reached up to the empty visor. Right—both remotes were lost.

Could she remember the code? She pulled forward, reached for the key pad, and let muscle memory take over.

The gate slid to the right.

She drove through, turning to pick up the mail as she always did when she got home from work. With little effort she remembered that combination as well. There was more there than expected, including what looked like several cards. She set the burgeoning stack in the passenger seat, then wound through the labyrinth of driveways to her unit.

The condos were nondescript, a simple five-sided geometry like the houses in a Monopoly game. The grey siding was likewise nothing special. Its best feature comprised the green space surrounding the buildings. Evergreens and shrubs of all varieties lined paved walkways well-suited for walking or jogging, which more than compensated for its bland appearance.

She pulled into her parking space, turned off the engine, and stared at the front door. As if she'd just been there the day before.

So normal, yet not.

Her chest tightened.

While she waited for Will and Connie she started going through the mail. Most were sympathy and get-well cards. One from Bryan's office mates contained several notes from different individuals, causing her eyes to tear-up.

Her heart shot into her throat when a vehicle flew into Bryan's parking spot to her right.

Will's silver E-350.

She wiped her eyes with her hand, stuffed the mail in her purse, and got out. Connie took her hand as they walked to the door. Will sorted through his keys, a reminder she couldn't have gotten inside, anyway. Another thing on her list to do before she left.

She braced herself as he fit the key in the lock.

His hand rested on the latch. Solemn eyes met her own. "You realize, Sara, that things may not be as you left them. If they're looking to destroy evidence—"

"I know, Dad. It could look like my room when I was a teenager. Let's just get this over with."

He pushed open the door, finger to his lips. They stepped inside. Everything appeared normal. Neither she, nor especially Bryan, liked coming home to a mess. As always, they left the place clean and uncluttered, though the air was stale.

One thing that attracted them to it initially was being an end unit. The downstairs boasted a high ceiling and windows on two sides, giving it less of the "tunnel" look some condos couldn't avoid. The open floorplan included an expansive living area, relatively small kitchen, formal dining room, and half-bath.

Built in the 70s, it had been upgraded with hardwood floors downstairs, plush carpeting in the bedrooms upstairs, and granite countertops. The navy-blue leather sofa hosted a multitude of colorful throw pillows with a crocheted afghan her mother made across the back. The IKEA end and coffee tables dated back to when they first got married, topped with a few books and stacked magazines.

It looked the same, yet felt different.

Empty.

Abandoned.

Sterile and unfamiliar.

They headed upstairs, Will in the lead. At the top, the doors to the two bedrooms and guest bath were open, as usual. The nearest one led to the guest room, which doubled as their office. They filed inside. Everything appeared normal. Their two desks, file cabinets, bookcases, and futon appeared undisturbed.

Will pointed to the baseboard. An electrical cord painted the same peach color as the room snaked along the top. He traced its origin to an outlet behind her desk, then back along the woodwork and through the wall, closet on the other side. Sara opened the door and flipped on the light.

The trio exchanged startled looks. No sign of the cord. She never thought about it before, but the cathedral ceiling downstairs offered numerous potential cubby holes easily disguised by sheetrock on the second floor.

The perfect place to hide a home server.

A box with old computer components—Bryan's "electronic graveyard"—and a rainbow of plastic storage containers were stacked on the floor against the suspect wall. She pushed them aside, revealing a metal access panel.

Will's fisted hand mimicked a twisting motion.

Already on task, she returned with both flat and Phillips head screwdrivers. He removed the screws, then the panel. The business end of a power strip stared back from the otherwise-empty space beyond. The dustless computer-shaped footprint beside it on the plywood subfloor spoke volumes.

Her mind exploded.

Their home had been violated.

What else did they take?

At first glance everything else in the closet seemed in order. Shelves of packaged printer paper, software CDs in their original packaging, boxes of photographs, three-ring binders with newsletters that covered everything from naturopathic medicine to strategic investing.

It took a few moments to notice, its usual space occupied by a box of manila folders. Hand over her mouth, Sara pointed to it.

At her father's blank look, she grabbed a pen and pad from the desk and scrawled, *My laptop! It's gone, too!*

Will scribbled: *Where's your gun?*

She pointed to the bookshelf. She scowled back, defensive. How was she to know her home would be broken into? The neighborhood was gated and never had a crime problem. If anyone in the complex was robbed, a notice would go out.

She removed a large book and opened it, revealing the inside was hollowed out.

Like the server cranny, it too was empty.

Connie grabbed the writing materials. *Did you have it at the cabin?*

She shook her head, then held up a finger, thinking, then wrote: *Maybe. But this was mine. He had a Ruger. Why take mine?*

Will pointed at what she said and gave her a questioning look. She wrote, *Nightstand* and waved them toward their bedroom.

"Well, that's certainly original," Will muttered, then scrawled, *Where's the ammo? In his sock drawer?*

This time she ignored the sarcasm and was in their bedroom before she had a chance to freak out. Focusing on the problem at hand, she proceeded to the small chest of drawers on the left side of the bed. She pulled open the top drawer to its full extent, reached underneath to release the catch, then removed it and placed it on the bed.

She stifled a moan as she squatted down to reach inside. Her fingers closed around the case and lifted it off the hook. It felt too light. Her heart pounded, not surprised when it, too, was empty. She gaped at her father.

He bit his lip and worked his jaw. "Let's go out to the car, Sara. I have something to show you."

She gave him a puzzled look, then exchanged a look with Connie. Will ripped off the pages with their notes, stepped back into the office to feed them to the shredder, then led the way out to the parking lot. He kept going past their respective vehicles to the other side, beneath a towering ponderosa pine.

"You're clearly dealing with professionals," he said. "You actually did a reasonably good job stashing everything. But that's assuming they absconded with it. We don't know for sure whether Bryan had anything with him versus being taken."

She rested her chin on her knuckles, trying to remember. All that came to mind was pure speculation. "He could have had his gun in the truck console, but I don't know why he'd take mine, too. And I doubt he moved the server. Unless he told me, but I can't remember. We should check our bedroom closet. It's even bigger."

Will looked thoughtful. "Good point. We'll check when we go back in, but they probably would have found it, anyway. With both handguns missing you need to file a police report. With no evidence of forced entry, it may be hard to convince them they were stolen, especially since Bryan may have taken them to the cabin. But if you find them up there, you can always let them know."

He worked his jaw. "Speaking of forced entry, you lost your purse in the wreck. There's a good chance whoever did this has your keys."

Her mouth fell open, the revelation evoking another unsavory surge of fear coupled with rage. "That's right! How convenient, right?"

"We need to change the locks. We'll do that before we leave."

A discomfiting tingle coursed through her veins. "This is creepy, Dad. My home has been violated in some evil way. But there's no evidence, other than the guns and my laptop missing. And maybe the server. But you're right, they probably have my keys. And the remote for the gate." She exhaled hard. "Should I ask the cops to come out or just drop by the station?"

"That's a tough one. We've got to assume your place is wired. So if the police come here, the bad guys will find out you discovered those things are missing. On the other hand, it could have been a robbery, since you've been gone for quite a while."

He paused, teeth clenched, a breeze ruffling his thinning hair.

"Okay," he went on. "It would be more convincing to have the police come out and complete a full report. Show them where the weapons were kept and explain the situation. Part of it, anyway. Leave out your suspicions of why or who the culprit might be. As far as the police report is concerned, you were away for a while recovering from an accident and came home to find them gone. That's it."

"Okay. But I must say, my experience with the police so far has been as suspicious as everything else."

"I know. They cave to the feds. But you still need to follow standard procedure. If you don't, it leaves you vulnerable. What if someone used one of those weapons to commit a crime? It wouldn't take much to frame you as the perpetrator. People have gone to prison with less evidence than that. Actually, if the people you're dealing with are as good as it appears, they could even set up something like that to get rid of you indirectly. Let you rot in prison for a crime you didn't commit."

Her stomach lurched.

"On the other hand, there's a chance this has nothing to do with the other," he continued. "With you gone so long, a robbery is credible. A rather targeted one, I must admit, but possible. We just don't know."

She rolled her shoulders, trying to ease the tension. "Great. Thanks, Dad. That makes my day. But my gut tells me it wasn't a robbery."

"Me, too. It just gets better and better, doesn't it?"

"Yeah." Her lips compressed as she fought to contain her indignation. "I may as well call them now and be done with it."

She made the call, less than happy when they said it could take a few hours before an officer arrived for a nonemergency.

Brow wrinkled, she assessed her options. "As long as I'm here, I may as well gather up some clothes and toiletries to take back to the cabin. I'll check our closet for any panels while I'm at it."

"Seriously, Sara?" Will stated. "You're going back? Even knowing government goons are on your tail? You must be kidding."

She set her jaw. "I have to. I appreciate you wanting to protect me, but I'll never solve this if I stay at your place. I have this gut feeling the answer lies back at the cabin. I have to get back there and see what I can find." She glanced at Connie who gave her a narrow-eyed reminder.

"Absolutely not," Will said. "There's no way you're going back out there alone. I can't allow you—"

"Dad! I'm a grown woman! This is my battle. Needless to say I'm scared, confused, and angry. I'm hurting, tired, and more frustrated than ever that I can't remember what happened. Yet. But I remembered the code to get in here and for my mailbox, so it's coming back. But with all this, more than anything I want to—need to—know why."

"Damn it, Sara, be reasonable. At least wait until next weekend. Then I can go with you."

"That could be too late. If there's anything there, these so-called goons may find it first."

"If they haven't already."

"I don't think they have. You stayed there while I was in the hospital."

"True," Connie agreed. "We were gone most the day, but there was still snow on the ground. We would have noticed any tracks besides our own."

"Maybe," Will muttered. "They could have traced our steps."

"As far as I can tell, nothing was missing. For example, Bryan's laptop, which was hidden in that desk he built. They found the secret compartments here, so they probably would have there, too. But they could be there now, with me down here."

"Sara, listen to me—"

"No, you listen, Dad. My husband's blood is on their hands. They killed him. My life will never be the same. To honor Bryan's memory I need to pursue this. Even if I don't succeed, even if they kill me, too. I can't betray him or let his death be in vain."

"What about your life? You have no idea how dangerous this is or who you're dealing with."

"You know what? I think if they wanted me dead, I would be. Either that or I have some guardian angel, maybe even Bryan, watching over me so this big secret, whatever it is, can get out."

He narrowed his eyes and started to speak, but Connie interrupted. "Hey, you two. Check it out. You've drawn quite an audience."

For the first time Sara noticed how many people in and around the parking lot were watching.

"Oh, what the bloody hell," she muttered, and started toward a green area, Will and Connie on either side.

"I have to find that information," she went on, lowering her voice. "He was meticulous. Detail-oriented. He didn't jump to conclusions without substantiated data. That was just how he was. He was also anal about backups, so I know that data is out there somewhere. I'll find it, I know I will. Once I know what's going on, then I'll have a better idea how to proceed. For now, I just have to get the facts and understand why it was important enough for him to lose his life."

"Be reasonable, Sara. You saw the pictures and what they imply. The scope of this is potentially massive. From what I can tell it's some government complex. It's being protected by skilled security people. You need to back off and leave it alone. Get on with your life. Let it go."

"No. I can't," she argued. "I don't care what they're doing out there. They didn't have the right to kill Bryan or come after me. I'm sick and tired of the government looking out for themselves, corporations, and the elite at the expense of ordinary people. This is not what this country is supposed to be about."

She huffed out a breath. "The ones who work hard and made this country great are continually exploited. That corruption is now very personal. I'm furious. I don't know what Bryan discovered, but he said it was 'huge.' He wouldn't have asked me to expose it if it weren't a big deal."

She stopped beneath a stand of towering spruce and turned to look him square in the eyes. "It's out there somewhere, Dad. I can feel it. Bryan was no dummy. I may not know what he was dealing with, but he did. He knew how to find secrets and he knew how to keep them. Why do you think he built furniture with hidden compartments? It's there somewhere and I'll find it, if it's the last thing I do."

"And it might be. You're playing with fire, Sara."

She folded her arms. "So what? I'll take that risk. If they kill me I'll be with Bryan. I wanted to go with him, anyway. The way I see it, either way it's win-win."

Will expelled an exasperated breath. "Alright. You've made up your mind. Twenty years ago I would have grounded you and sent you to your room. Obviously that option's gone. Just promise me you'll be careful. One thing I absolutely insist upon is replacing your handgun and going to the range before you go back. Deal?"

Her mouth hung open as if she had more to say, but it was now moot. "Deal," she agreed with a nod. Their eyes met again, this time without their well-matched determination. He spread his arms and she fell into them, arms tight around him.

"I'm just worried about you," he said. "This is serious business."

"I know. I'll be careful. And I'll always welcome your help and advice. But this is something I need to do."

"Eating is something *I* need to do," Connie stated. "If you two are finished, let's order pizza or something. I'm starving."

They walked back, called Domino's, then, while they waited, Will searched the place for microphones and any other devices. After a while, he motioned Sara back outside across the parking lot, Connie tagging along.

"They planted bugs in a few light fixtures, the upstairs smoke detector, and all the heater vents. There might be more that I missed. Today's electronics are so small they can be nearly impossible to find. There could also be a boom microphone outside somewhere, which would pick up anything you say with the windows open."

He pointed up at one of the security lights. "Those things provide a perfect place for one, especially the one outside your kitchen window. If you're going to stay at the cabin, I'm not sure its a good idea to remove them. Then they'd know you're on to them, which might make them ramp things up. Even if you're pursuing this, I think it's in your best interest to appear as innocent as possible."

She scoffed. "Great. Did you find anything in the bathroom?"

"No. I didn't check for a two-way mirror though. At least they're not perverts." He smiled at her derisive snort. "Just watch what you say and where. Try to act normal."

"Whatever *that* is these days."

"True enough. Innocence aside, you need another handgun. I'll get you one after you take care of the police report. Then we can go practice a bit."

"I think I can buy my own gun, Dad."

"Maybe not," he retorted. "You may well be on file as a 'person of interest.' You might not pass a background check."

Her hands flew to her hips. "You're kidding, right?"

"I'm afraid not. Rather than get on their radar, why don't I just do it? For all I know, I might be on their watch list, too, by association. If that's the case, I may as well find out."

"What about me?" Connie suggested. "I could buy it. I never changed my name on my driver's license when we got married. Maybe Connie Watkins isn't on their radar, at least not yet."

"That's actually a great idea," Will agreed. "If you're on there, we're screwed for sure."

The three of them laughed, though the attempt to relieve the tension was as effective as eliminating the stink of a feedlot lagoon with a can of Febreze. About then, the pizza driver showed up. By the time they finished eating outside on the patio, Detective Martin McDaniel arrived.

A personable, medium build black man, he photographed where the guns were kept, examined all the doors and windows for any evidence of forced entry, but, as expected, found none. He pointed out that patio door latches were a cinch to breach and advised placing a heavy dowel in its track to physically restrain the door. He dusted both entries, the hollowed out book, and gun case for prints, then took Sara's statement. He listened attentively and took copious notes as she recounted her abridged story of the accident and being out of town since mid-April.

When he asked if they noticed anything else missing, Sara mentioned her laptop. Her eyes met her father's. His expression blared a big fat "No" regarding the server, which made sense. She had no personal knowledge whether there'd ever been one or not, so couldn't give a detailed description.

McDaniel finished his report, shook hands, and left.

Before she forgot, she went to the hall closet to retrieve the looped duster Bryan bought for cleaning the ceiling fans. She unscrewed the brush and stuck the handle in the track for the sliding door.

The bad guys would still get in if they wanted, but no sense putting out the welcome mat.

28. SHIRAZ

SARA'S CONDO
DENVER
June 11, Monday
3:47 p.m.

fter that, they drove to a small gun shop with an indoor shooting range. Sara picked out a .40 caliber Glock with a laser sight. Connie gave her personal information to the proprietor for a background check while the others continued shopping.

"I guess I'll need a shoulder holster, if I'm going to pack this thing around," Sara commented.

Will laughed. "The last person who wore a shoulder holster was Don Johnson on *Miami Vice*. You need a paddle holster. And something to carry a spare magazine. Unless you plan on keeping everything in your purse."

"Very funny, Dad."

The hefty, bearded store owner, who could easily pass for a time-traveling mountain man, got one out from behind the counter and handed it to Will. He explained how it rode the side of her butt. When she went to draw the weapon, however, she winced, broken rib and other injuries staging a loud protest.

"Alright, try this," he said, reconfiguring it until he noticed what she was wearing. "Those elastic waistband shorts need to go. You'll need to wear a belt for this to work."

She made a face, having switched to them for comfort, but assured him she had plenty of khakis and jeans, which she could wear with one of Bryan's belts. She added a spare magazine, then made it two, and a holder for it as well.

"Maybe I should just get a bandoleer," she quipped, rolling her eyes when her father appeared to be giving it serious thought. He set two cases of ammo on the counter, one for each of them. As an afterthought, she added a pad of targets.

Will tapped them with his finger. "Where do you plan to use these?"

"At the cabin." He shook his head. "What? Is that a problem?"

"If you make a big show of being some modern Annie Oakley it could make any confrontation more aggressive."

"More like Lara Croft, Dad. What if I add a silencer?"

"Wouldn't matter. They're watching you, remember?"

"Well, crap." She wrinkled her nose at the thought and put them back. "So how do I practice? Add online gaming to my new life?"

"No, but close. What you need is a laser trainer cartridge. Then you can practice inside, plus they're silent. A laser dot shows where the shot would have landed. This also lets you know if you tend to move when you pull the trigger. They come with a snap cap so dry firing doesn't hurt the gun."

"Sounds perfect. Except if they're watching me they'll see me anyway. And probably know I'm here, getting a new gun."

"Did you leave your purse and phone in the car?"

"Yes."

"Then they don't know that for sure. Just wait until I come out to sweep the cabin before using it."

"Fair enough."

After adding it to her other purchases, background check clear, the owner rang everything up. Connie whipped out one of her credit cards to do the honors.

"Okay, let's test this baby out," Will said.

Using the foam ear plugs offered by the facility, they entered the indoor range behind the store. Sara interlocked her fingers around her new best friend and aimed at the silhouette on the paper target. Its firm kick took her by surprise, but sufficiently reminded, subsequent shots formed a tidy grouping.

"That's my girl!" Will said, grinning as she reloaded.

Connie's eyes, meanwhile, were wide. "Wow. You're good, honey."

"Just like riding a bike," Sara replied, smiling for the first time all day.

The last time she'd gone shooting with Bryan she'd commented what a great stress reliever it was. Back then it was more of a game. Now it wasn't. When she reloaded the clip and slapped it into place it felt good. Real good. Already she felt less vulnerable. In this instance, she had to admit, her father *did* know best.

On the way back they stopped to pick up new deadbolt locks plus three prepaid burner phones, one for each of them. Will explained if they were watching her it wouldn't take long to find its signal. However, it might give them a little privacy for a day or so, especially if she only used it a substantial distance away from home and not near her car, in case they were tracking that as well.

When they got back to the condo, Will changed out the lock while Sara watched, so she could do the same at the cabin. By the time he finished, it was too late for her to leave.

"Do you feel comfortable staying here alone?" Connie asked.

"I don't know what bothers me more, spooks or ghosts," she said as she walked them to their car. "But I'm good. I feel better with my new toy. Thanks for that. I'm a big girl and need to act like one. I'll text you on the burner when I get back to the cabin tomorrow."

Will shook his head as he waved both hands back and forth. "No, no, no! Not from home, remember? Use your regular cell for simple stuff like that. For the burner, either make sure you're away from home or save it for something sensitive that can't wait. Once you use it, they'll be on it."

"Right. Got it. It's hard to get used to being watched. Now I know how celebrities feel around the *paparazzi*."

After hugs all around the couple left. Sara watched them drive away, caught in the uncomfortable space between liberated and lonely. Then, setting her jaw, she went back inside where she grabbed the gun case, ammo, and bag of accessories and took it upstairs to her bedroom. She started to place everything on her dresser, then stopped.

Bugs.

What a pain.

She took everything into the adjoining master bath, then gathered the clothes she wanted to take back, directing her thoughts away from anything sentimental.

That done, she returned to the bathroom and examined the paddle holster, deciding she may as well get used to it, plus break it in. She changed into a pair of khaki shorts, then went to the closet to get one of Bryan's belts. She stood there a moment, gazing at his clothes. Her practical side knew she needed to get rid of them. For now, she couldn't bear the thought.

His tie rack included hooks for belts. She removed his favorite and caressed its embossed leather. Bought during one of their ski trips to New Mexico. She exhaled hard, then returned to the bathroom where she threaded it through the belt loops, holster, and magazine pouch.

The image of his clothes refused to leave her mind. Her vision blurred. His dying request beckoned from memory, shoving her from melancholy to determination. Her thoughts meandered back to her teens, when she wanted to work for the FBI. Like her dad, but as an operative, not some boring analyst.

For years, her heroine was fellow Gemini, Angelina Jolie, in the original *Tomb Raider*. For a while she even pretended to change her first name to the lead character, Lara Croft, by writing her name with a creatively stylized *L* that barely passed as an *S*.

She heart skipped a beat.

It felt far different being the target instead of the asset.

She set her jaw and buckled up, then adjusted the holster so it rode her left hip. She ejected the magazine, loaded it, and slapped it back inside the grip. Then she loaded one of the spares and slipped it inside the holder. Safety engaged, she slipped the gun in place, a *click* announcing it was properly situated. She reached over to practice a cross-draw. Her shirt was in the way, result far from what she intended.

Huh. Good to know.

She practiced several times in front of the mirror, lifting her shirt with her left hand, then drawing with her right. She repeated the motion until it became mechanical, muscle memory initiated.

Fueled by grief, anger, and outrage she had no doubts she would use it if necessary. Wearing a loaded weapon felt good.

Less vulnerable.

Almost powerful.

She still wondered if Bryan's gun had been in the truck. It seemed unlikely that the spooks would have found it in the nightstand's secret compartment. He was as comfortable with a weapon as she was, having been a sharpshooter in the military, even though his assignment didn't require it.

Would he have undertaken such a risky endeavor unarmed?

On the other hand, having a shootout with a security force was unlikely to end well, one way or the other. He looked more like a computer geek than a criminal and was a good talker. Maybe he figured being armed would be to his detriment if caught and make any charges more serious.

No telling. She thought she knew him. Now she wasn't so sure.

She donned a sweater to cover her piece, then went downstairs to the kitchen. After finishing the two leftover slices of pizza, she went outside to the patio where she sat on a wrought iron chair with a bottle of Shiraz.

The sun descended in dramatic shades of red and orange, sinking toward the barely visible edge of the Front Range.

It was quiet, but by different standards than the cabin. Rather than the chirp of birds and melodic duet of aspen leaves and pine needles, she was immersed in the faceless white noise of the Denver 'burbs. The distant swish of traffic on I-25 was constant and hypnotic.

Until the din of an eighteen-wheeler evoked an involuntary shudder.

Likewise, the occasional squeal of tires when someone braked hard for the light on East Hampden, usually followed by the irate blast of a horn.

Within the complex came the muffled sound of car doors as her neighbors got home from work or happy hour. Muted conversations drifted on the evening breeze, cut off by the thump of closing their front door.

She and Bryan spent nearly every evening out there. Their after-dinner ritual, even when it was so cold they bundled up. In winter, it was gluhwein, something they'd discovered in Germany on their single European vacation.

His last R&R before he was discharged.

By the time fiery clouds hugging the horizon conspired with the Rockies to consume the sun, she'd finished the bottle. She got up unsteadily and shuffled inside. After locking the patio door, she clumsily dropped the brush handle in place, then dragged herself up the stairs, head lost in an alcohol-induced fog.

Her hands clung to the rail until she arrived at the top, where she swung around the banister, almost playfully, toward their bedroom. She shed the gun, shorts, sweater, and top, then pawed her way into an oversized Grumpy Cat nightshirt.

Their king-size bed loomed before her. Heart-wrenching nostalgia erupted from the depths of her soul.

"Nope. No way. Can't do it."

She giggled at how badly she'd slurred the words, not caring in the slightest who heard it.

She grabbed her pillow, then wobbled down the hall to the office. It took some fumbling around before the futon dropped flat with a *clunk.* She opened the window for some fresh air, then flopped onto it, face down. Within moments she fell into that zone somewhere between drunken stupor and dead sleep.

She awoke a few hours later, dizzy and disoriented. Security lighting streamed through sheer curtains billowing in the breeze. She turned over, trying to get comfortable so she could go back to sleep. Chilly, she pulled a blanket out from one of the storage drawers underneath.

Snuggling into its fleecy folds, she no sooner got settled when she heard her name. Her eyes flew open.

What was that?

A dream? Hallucination? Or was someone there? She turned to her back, listening, heart racing.

Sara...

The light coming through the window brightened, then coalesced into an apparition. The silhouette and its familiarity encompassed her heart in warmth that defied the room's evening chill.

The room swirled as she propped herself up on her elbows. "Bryan? Is that you?"

He didn't answer. Didn't have to. As they had after the accident, his words came directly into her heart, embracing every cell.

I'm so sorry, sweetheart. I never should have put you in danger. I never dreamed it would get so ugly. Please understand. I would never hurt you. I'll always protect you, as much as I can.

The apparition started to fade.

Shock induced sobriety jolted her fully awake.

"Wait! Wait! Was there a server, Bryan? Where? Where is it?"

The vision froze, mercury vapor security light visible through his transparent personage.

Yes. Of course. I worked on it all the time. Everything you need is there.

"But they took it! It's gone!"

Not to worry, sweetheart. I always kept a backup. Of everything. Everywhere.

"In that OneDrive Cloud folder? I found the photos. But now our laptops are gone, too."

There's one place they'll never find. But you will. It's all written in the stars. Sleep well, Sara. I love you.

"No, Bryan. Wait!"

He was gone.

She clutched the covers to her chest.

What just happened?

Was it real? A dream? Or was she really that drunk?

She swung her feet to the floor and waited for the dizziness to halt before she staggered over to the light switch. Her eyelids slammed shut at the sudden blast of light. She squinted through her lashes to the fully lit room.

She felt awake.

Was she? Or was this a dream within a dream?

Grabbing the notepad they'd used earlier, she recorded what she remembered, not trusting herself to retain it by morning. By then, she'd be convinced it was no more than a dream. If when she got up the page was blank, then she'd know that's all it was.

Yet dreams could contain messages, too.

What did he mean, there was one they'd never find? Written in the stars? What kind of crazy, cryptic clue was that? Bryan always loved puzzles, something she didn't appreciate, especially under the circumstances.

Damn it, Bryan!

It was bad enough he'd left her. Teasing her from the grave was not amusing.

The adrenaline burst faded to extreme fatigue.

She turned off the light and laid back down, snuggling into the covers to resume a deep state of slumber.

Maybe it would make sense in the morning.

Try as much as possible to be wholly alive, with all your might, and when you laugh, laugh like hell and when you get angry, get good and angry. Try to be alive. You will be dead soon enough.
—William Saroyan

29. COLLEAGUES

HUDSON RESIDENCE
RURAL FALCON RIDGE
June 12, Tuesday
7:25 a.m.

Jim Hudson's fingers drummed his desk. Liz was right. If some new government installation was in their backyard he had a right to know. Maybe it was another one of those bunkers for surviving an apocalypse.

Cheyenne Mountain included such facilities for high ranking military personnel and similar ones closer to D.C. for government officials.

But why would they need another one? Whatever for? And why there?

Maybe what that Reynolds woman saw was nothing, everything else she experienced mere coincidence. The whole thing sounded like something out of a Michael Crichton novel. Doubts aside, however, he'd promised Liz. To be honest, at this point, he was damn curious himself.

He pulled the printout of the latest contact list out of the top drawer and found his friend and former commander, Fred O'Reilly. Now a three-star, he'd known him since graduating from the Academy back in the 70s. With it two hours later on the East Coast he'd be there, even though Fred was never an early riser. One of those who went through multiple divorces and wasn't in any hurry to retire. He loved the military and had nothing better to do.

Was his own life any better?

He grunted.

Not really.

He picked up the house phone and tapped in Fred's private number.

The man answered with his usual panache. "O'Reilly."

"Hey, Fred. Jim Hudson. How are you?"

"Well, well. Colonel Hudson. Doing just fine, Jim. What's up?"

The general abhorred small talk, so he got right to the point. "I'm a little embarrassed to ask, but I promised my wife."

"Maybe if I'd kept more promises I'd still have a wife. What's the problem?"

He recounted the Sara Reynolds saga, Readers Digest version. "So, what we're wondering is whether there's some new installation going in up here?"

Fred was silent for several seconds. "I've heard rumors about something going on up there, Jim. All I can say is it's not military."

"No? What then? Civilian? What are they going to do, move the nation's capital here when the sea levels rise?"

"No. Not government, either. At least not *that* part of the government. Some new big-ticket item showed up in the black budget. No one's willing to talk about it."

"What do you think is going on?"

"I have no idea. But I'd stay out of it. Anything buried that deep, literally and figuratively, means trouble. Sounds like your neighbor found it."

"Seriously?"

"Dead serious. Leave it alone, Jim. Gotta go."

"Bye, Fred. Thanks."

The line went dead.

His jaw tensed, mind racing.

What was he going to tell Liz?

SARA'S CONDO
DENVER
June 12, Tuesday
7:29 a.m.

Morning light bolted through sheer curtains and screeched off peach-colored walls. Sara massaged her forehead, bump from the accident still tender, but definitely not the reason for the pain assaulting her head.

What a freaking idiot! What in the world was she thinking, sucking down all that wine?

She got up in slow motion and shuffled to the master suite, temples throbbing. In its adjoining bathroom, lights off, she brushed her teeth and washed her face with cold water. Her shoulder length hair was an unruly mass of angry curls. It hurt just thinking about brushing it out. She twisted it into a scrunchi and called it good.

The clothes she'd worn the day before beckoned, though the paraphernalia on the belt confused her. Remembering, she trod downstairs, desperate for a cup of coffee, but without the gun.

The way she felt, she didn't need the temptation to shoot herself.

While it brewed, she dropped two frozen waffles in the toaster and checked the fridge. They'd planned to stay at the cabin for two weeks, so cleaned it out. As if anything would be edible two months later, anyway.

She sipped her coffee, less than enchanted that her birthday was less than a week away. While she should be happy to be having one at all, it was still a day she couldn't get excited about.

Being a widow at thirty-two certainly wasn't part of her life's plan. Residual aches and pains still haunted her, always lurking beneath the surface, waiting to bite. This must be what it felt like to be eighty years old.

She needed to look up what was good for inflammation besides ginger and bromelain. Hyaluronic acid was good for joints, so that was probably a good idea, too. Maybe she'd ask Charlie.

Hopefully he could make her some of that muscle balm. He seemed familiar with tribal medicine. Maybe he'd have some other ideas as well. She admonished herself for leaving the medicine bundle he gave her at the cabin.

Fortunately, butter lasted a long time in the fridge, likewise maple syrup, so she dressed her waffles and poured herself another coffee. The food settled her stomach, but failed to fill the emptiness in her heart. She'd never believed alcohol was a depressant until now. It wasn't like she'd never been alone in the condo before. Yet, every fiber of her being ached with loneliness.

Never was she more aware that Bryan was not TDY.

Her appetite departed after a few bites, but it wasn't until she finished her coffee that she remembered.

She dumped what was left of her breakfast down the disposal, then dragged herself back upstairs.

The notepad was on her desk right where she'd left it, her semi-coherent scrawls barely readable. Nonetheless, there it was. She'd had some interesting dreams in her life, but never one where she wrote down what happened. People didn't do that in their sleep. Furthermore, her heart told her it wasn't a dream. Like when Bryan bid her goodbye high above Dead Horse Canyon.

She sensed his presence on a regular basis, sometimes questioning whether it was her imagination. But drunk or not, she knew what happened the night before was real. And certainly the most cryptic.

Why didn't he just say it in plain English?

Seriously!

Written in the stars? What on Earth was *that* supposed to mean? It's not like the microphones could hear him.

Could they?

Did she say anything sensitive out loud? Another thought struck: *Stars?* Was that a clue? Did that include the planets? Was it possible this was something Patrice could decipher?

Par for the course, her purse was downstairs. She trudged back to the main floor, taking the notepad. She parked on the couch, dug the astrologer's business card out of her bag's side pocket, and entered the number in her cell phone. She saved it, then started to press the call icon, when she remembered—*bugs*.

She growled silently as she grabbed her keys, then went outside. Achy and stiff, an occasional wince interrupted her progress as she strolled along the sidewalk past the next building to a green area. A bench beneath a flowering crabapple tree presented a welcome sight. Settled at last, she closed her eyes and pressed *Connect*, wishing she'd worn her sunglasses.

Hungover or not, she swore the sun was brighter than usual.

Patrice answered after several rings, her voice scratchy and disoriented. With horror she realized she'd woken her up.

"Oh, I'm so sorry, Patrice. I didn't even think about what time it is. This is Sara Reynolds, Connie's step-daughter. Remember me?"

"Oh, hi, Sara. I definitely remember you. What can I do for you, sweetie?"

"I had a strange experience last night. I probably drank a little too much wine, but I woke up in the night and saw my husband."

"That doesn't surprise me, actually. I suspect there's a strong inter-dimensional bond between you two. What did he say?"

At least the woman didn't think she'd lost her mind. "Well, a bunch more has happened since we saw you three days ago. We believe there's more information on a server somewhere. It looks like he had one in our condo, here in Denver, but someone broke in and stole it, along with our handguns."

"Wow! That *is* a big deal!"

"We were afraid the information was lost forever. But Bryan assured me it was somewhere else as well. Another backup. But I have no idea where it might be. Do you think you could help?" She crossed her fingers.

"I can sure try. So you're still in Boulder?"

"No, Denver. At our condo."

"And my clock says it's 7:48. Hold on while I jot that down. My memory isn't what it used to be."

"Tell me about it," Sara muttered.

"Okay. So tell me exactly what he said and what you want to know."

"He told me he worked on it all the time, that everything was there. That he always kept a backup. Of 'everything, everywhere.'"

"What do you think that means?" Patrice asked.

"I have no idea. I told him his laptop got burned up, mine stolen, and the server was gone. Nothing was on the OneDrive cloud storage thingy except the photos and some other stuff that meant nothing, so I have no idea what he meant by 'everywhere'."

"Okay. Did he say anything else?"

"Yes. He said no one but me would find it. That it was written in the stars. I have no foggy clue what that's supposed to mean. So I thought of you." She giggled. "I'm really sorry for calling so early, Patrice."

"It's okay. I'm as fascinated as you are at this point. Usually there'll be something in the chart that clarifies it. I'll take a look and call you back, probably sometime after noon or so. I have a client coming at eleven. Is that okay? Will that be soon enough?"

"Whenever you can is fine. I apologize for waking you up."

"Don't worry about it, sweetie. I've gotten calls at far worse hours. At least the sun is up. Oh! One more thing. Did you happen to notice what time this happened?"

"No. I didn't even think about it and there isn't a clock in that room."

"It's okay. I don't really need it. Talk soon."

Sara felt better already, confident she could throw some light on the subject. After going back inside, she rinsed her breakfast dishes and placed them in the dishwasher, then headed back upstairs to take a shower. While she was in town, she may as well go by her old job.

By the time she got dressed in one of her new outfits the headache retreated, her brain more functional. She eyed the gun, debating. Why not? She checked the safety and put it in her purse.

The drive to where she worked for over five years presented the same ethereal quality as coming down from Boulder. No doubt her neurons recorded individual commutes as one and the same, like saving an update of the same file.

Rocky Mountain Physical Therapy Associates was in an upscale shopping center about three miles away. She parked. Everyone was going to make a fuss, tell her how sorry they were, *et cetera* and so forth. She didn't want to fall apart, but if someone started crying, she would, too.

Yet, she needed to do this. Turn in her official resignation, if nothing else.

She climbed out of the car slowly enough to humor the various aches and pains, locked it with the key fob, then steeled herself as she approached the door.

Someone apparently saw her coming, most likely the receptionist, and had mustered a greeting party of four or five colleagues. As soon as she stepped inside they were all over her, talking at once, and giving her hugs. At least their dominant mood was friendly excitement, not maudlin sympathy. She hugged back, realizing how much she missed them.

A few peeled away to tend to patients, but the others herded her toward the breakroom. Not wanting to be a total drama queen, she downplayed the second wreck and all their suspicions that the first one was anything more than a hit and run. After a half-hour or so of chit-chat, she begged off, saying she needed to check in with human resources.

She sat down across from the director, Katy Carson, a fortyish, heavy set, dark-haired woman with almond-shaped eyes and cheekbones that hinted at Native American heritage. She repeated her story, then got down to business. She actually had another month of disability payments left, so she made her resignation effective when that ran out. She signed the needed paperwork, gathered up her copies, and prepared to leave.

"I don't know if I should tell you this or not, but there were some people asking about you a while back," Katy said. "It wasn't about the disability payments, but the accident."

"The accident? Did they show any ID?"

"Yes. Some Federal agency. Very vague. Not the FBI or NSA, just a generic government badge. They were quite imposing. Gave me the willies."

"What did they want?"

"Nothing much. Whether we'd heard from you, if you'd returned to work, if you'd come by, checked in, that sort of thing."

Sara's face reflected the woman's mystified look. "I have no idea. Have they been back? Are you supposed to let them know if I come back to work?"

"No. They just thanked me and left. But there was something about them that didn't seem right."

"Thanks for letting me know. I must say there's been too many weird things going on lately."

"Are you back in town for good?"

"No. I was visiting my family in Boulder for a few days, but I'm going to head back to the cabin later today. I haven't decided what I'm going to do in the long term. Once the snow hits, I might be back."

Katy's response was warm and sincere. "Well, if you get bored and want to come back, even part time, just let us know. Your patients keep asking about you. Everyone misses you a bunch."

"Thanks. I miss everyone, too. I'm still trying to get my head together. It's like hitting the reset button on my life."

"I get that. Oh! I almost forgot!" She got up and went to a closet behind her desk where she got out a box. "Here's everything, at least your personal items, from your desk. We needed the space for the new guy and figured if you came back, then we'd figure out where your station would be."

"At least you don't have to worry about that. Thanks again, Katy."

The women exchanged hugs, Sara picked up the box and started for the door.

"Oh! One more thing," Katy called after her. "I need to get back your key."

Sara froze. *Did those horrible people get in there, too?* She grimaced as she turned around.

"I'm afraid it was lost in the wreck. My purse and everything in it went over that cliff with the truck."

"Yikes. I can't begin to imagine what that was like."

"Yeah. Probably a good thing I don't remember."

"Okay. I understand. Here, just check 'Lost', sign this, and we're good."

She set down the box long enough to do so. "If those men come back, would you let me know?"

"Definitely. I'll see if I can find out any more regarding who they are, too. See if they talked to anyone else besides me."

"Great. I appreciate it."

"Next time you're in town let us know. We'll throw you a farewell luncheon."

Sara smiled. "I will. That sounds great. I enjoyed working here a lot. Who knows? Maybe I'll be back someday."

"That would be wonderful. Be safe."

"I sure hope so. Bye, Katy."

She waved at the others as she headed toward the front door, begging off lunch invitations. It was getting close to noon and she wanted to be home when Patrice called back.

Box in the back of the SUV, she drove off, stopping to pick up a Mexican pizza at Taco Bell before heading home. She brought the food inside, set it on the kitchen table, then went back out to get her work stuff. Not feeling like dragging it upstairs, she stuck it in the coat closet next to the front door.

She no sooner got settled at the table with a tall glass of iced tea when her cell phone went off. She picked it up, hoping...

It was.

Prejudices are rarely overcome by argument; not being founded in reason they cannot be destroyed by logic.
— *Tryon Edwards*

30. SIGNS

HEWITT SATELLITE IMAGING
BOULDER
June 12, Tuesday
11:23 a.m.

Will obsessed unceasingly on the seismic data. It dominated his mind like a crippling, albeit painless, migraine, shoving everything else aside. His gut screamed its importance. Who owned it? What was it for? Fracking? Then why was it classified?

He'd done data reduction years ago, before moving into sales. New collection methods and more sophisticated algorithms had been developed, but the principles were the same. It wasn't rocket science to figure out the parameters. After that, it was a matter of translating it into some sort of graphic representation.

The first 3-D graphing programs showed up back in the 80s. Such apps were even more sophisticated now. Not that it mattered. Data were data, the means for displaying them fundamentally the same. Hewitt developed generic in-house number-crunching programs used when a client's contract included processing. Surely one of them would work.

He saved the latest data in the comma delimited format used for most input files and started feeding it into the different programs. The first four produced nothing but garbage. The fifth swam in an infinite loop that required a hard reset.

His fingers drummed the desk, frustration at a peak. Then it struck. He slapped his forehead at his own stupidity. True, it had been a while since he'd performed such a task. But the admonition to *RTFM* struck like a bolt from the blue.

Even stranger, something about it sounded like Bryan. Memory, perhaps. They'd had that conversation about users who failed to "Read The Freakin' Manual."

Okay, stupid.

PDF files described each one. It didn't take long to find those used for seismic tomography. He brought one up, found the input screen, and fed it the data.

The computer chugged away, an annoying and hypnotic row of dots denoting its progress at glacial-speed. Not a surprise, considering the size of the input file.

His stomach growled. Hungry and ready to get something to eat, he hesitated to leave. What if his boss wandered in? There was little doubt he was messing with something beyond his clearance level. He stared at the progress bar on the screen, debating. At the rate it was going, he could grab lunch and still be back before it finished.

He added a password to his screensaver, just in case, grabbed his keys, and headed for the local deli.

SARA'S CONDO
DENVER
June 12, Tuesday
11:47 a.m.

Sara's hand shook as she swiped the icon to answer the call.

"Hi, Patrice. I need to call you back. Is that okay?"

"Sure thing, sweetie. No problem."

As soon as she started for the place where she made the initial call, she realized she'd goofed—big time.

Damn!

While she may have gotten away from the condo microphones, she nonetheless conducted the initial conversation on her regular cell.

What an idiot! Even though the mic was turned off, her father had warned her it wasn't absolutely foolproof.

Guarding her every move was such a pain. Being seriously hungover didn't help.

Berating herself for the careless mistake, she grabbed the burner, wrote Patrice's number on her hand, and started for the door. She froze. Maybe she should take her gun. While she was gone, even a few minutes, those sleazy spooks might come back and steal it, too.

She snarled as she climbed the stairs, disgusted with how complicated life had become. Maybe she really should forget the whole thing. She grabbed her purse and left, locking the door behind her. This time she went to a different green space, in case they noted the location the previous time.

At last she settled on a concrete bench beneath a trio of towering arbor vitae. She glanced around, relieved no one was within earshot. She punched in the numbers and pressed *Connect*. Patrice picked up on the first ring.

"Hi, Patrice. It's Sara. Did you find anything interesting?"

"Different number, sweetie?"

"Yes. But don't save it. It's a burner phone. I should have never called you on the other one. It's probably being monitored. Being watched is such a gigantic pain."

"I can imagine! Anyway, yes I found quite a bit. So much, in fact, I'm going to write it up so I don't miss anything. But I'll tell you the highlights. Meanwhile, give me your email, before I forget."

She sucked in her lower lip, debating. Everyone on the planet had a Gmail address and if hers was being hacked, that was probably the one. Should she create another one? Or maybe, since she was still an employee of RMPTA for another month, she should use that one. HIPAA healthcare confidentiality rules required their computers be highly secured.

Then again, depending on who those spooks were, they could get anywhere they wanted. Especially if they got into her personal effects at work. With luck, maybe they wouldn't look with her not employed there anymore. Maybe that's why they wanted to know if she was back. At the least, she'd change the password as soon as possible, preferably from a public computer.

Another nuisance inconvenience. *Ugh.*

"Okay, use this one," she answered. "It's more secure: smreynolds1@RMPTA.com."

"Got it. Okay. Are you ready? You might want to take some notes."

"Hold on a sec." She dug the notebook and a pen out of her purse. "Okay, ready. Oh! Is it okay if I record this?"

"Certainly. I will, too."

She tried to figure out how to set the phone on *record* without success. "Oh, no! Stupid burner can't do that."

"Don't worry, sweetie. I'll email the recording along with the written version."

Her eyes shifted skyward with relief. "Perfect! Okay. What have you got?"

"A lot. The information is hidden somewhere, perhaps related to his job somehow. Another possibility is anything else he worked on, maybe even for free. Volunteer work or a hobby, perhaps."

"That makes sense. He was system administrator at the credit union where he worked."

"Okay, along those same lines, it looks as if it's safe from any enemies, that they won't find it."

"Perfect. That's exactly what he told me." A chill ran down her spine, singing a duet with the goosebumps on her arms.

"I believe he *did* have a server at your house that you didn't know about, too."

"That's incredible you can see that. What else?"

"It looks as if one key to unlocking the mystery will be through a friend of his. Was he close to anyone at work who might know something?"

Her brow wrinkled. "Not that I know of. He worked alone. He felt safer that way. He was friendly to everyone, but kept his distance. He didn't trust anyone, other than his manager. And his boss didn't know the details, since he wasn't a techy type. Bryan didn't want someone embezzling, then pinning the blame on him."

"Hmmm. Whom do you think it might be?"

"The only person he was close to was Charlie, our Native American friend. Do you think he knows something? Like where this information is hidden?"

"Not yet. But it looks like he'll help find it. Native American, you say?"

"Yes. He and Bryan were tight, ever since they were kids."

"Is he close to his culture?"

"I'm not sure what you mean."

"Is he spiritual? Believe in divination, that sort of thing? Do you know if he's in touch with his tribe, whether they have a medicine man?"

"I have no idea. But I think he's spiritual. He didn't act surprised when I told him I talked to Bryan. He said he did, too. Oh! And a neighbor saw him out by the accident site, smoking some sort of pipe, if that means anything."

"Perfect. Okay. You need to talk to him. He should have some ideas for where you'll find the information. He may have to do something, well, unusual, to find it. Maybe already has."

She inhaled sharply, mind spinning. She hadn't thought of asking him to help. Did Bryan confide in him? He came up in the last reading, too. But that one related to who was responsible. Was this referring to the same thing? Or were all the answers in one place?

"Sara? Are you still there?"

"Yes! Sorry! I'm stunned. That makes perfect sense. What would I do without you, Patrice?"

"There are no coincidences, Sara. You were meant to find me. The Universe is working with you on this one."

"So is there any indication where this data might be? I keep thinking of Bryan saying it was 'everywhere.' Any idea what that could mean?"

"I don't know for sure, but it's not in an obvious location. My guess is electronic form somewhere. Maybe more than one place, more than one source. Or perhaps out on the internet."

"That doesn't narrow it down much, but at least it's still out there. Anything else?"

"No, that's it. If I think of anything else I'll include it in the transcript."

"I don't know how to thank you. How much do I owe you?"

"Nothing. This one's so fascinating, I'm excited to be part of it. Besides, if you're being watched, it might be better not to have any financial transactions between us."

"Right. They were probably listening when I called you the first time. I should have used the burner."

"Doesn't matter. They won't find it. Only you or your friend. Good luck. Let me know how it turns out, okay?"

"I sure will! This is so incredible. How does this stuff work, anyway?"

"I suspect it's related to the promise 'ask and ye shall receive.' Whatever's on your mind is reflected in the cosmos at that moment. Being timeless, it also contains the answer. I've been wrong a few times, but it's always been my mistake, not the chart's."

"Amazing. Thanks so much. I'm going to call Connie and catch her up, then head back to the cabin as soon as I get packed up."

"I can't wait to hear how it goes. Say hi to Connie for me."

"Will do. Bye, Patrice."

"Bye, sweetie."

She dropped the phone in her purse and covered her mouth with one hand, heart racing. It confirmed what Bryan said, right up to 'answers in the stars,' plus provided information she wouldn't have dreamed of otherwise. As she prepared to call Connie, she realized she had another problem.

How could she tell her father what was going on when Patrice was supposed to be her and Connie's dirty little secret?

Whatever.

She'd cross that bridge when she came to it. He'd probably think the dream was no more than a wine-induced hallucination, anyway.

HEWITT SATELLITE IMAGING
BOULDER
June 12, Tuesday
1:21 p.m.

Will came back from lunch and placed his mega-sized cup of iced tea beside the keyboard. The screen, as expected, was asleep. He sat down and wiggled the mouse to wake things up, then entered the password.

It looked like some sort of game. A fractal-like swirl of multiple circles branched out from a central hub. It certainly wasn't what he expected from data delineating fault lines and differentiated rock layers.

WTF?

He chuckled that he'd picked up the popular expression. In this case it certainly said it all.

He leaned forward and lifted his chin to peer through the center section of his trifocals. What the hell was it? Data or some sort of mistake? Maybe that program wasn't the right one. The only way to know would be to examine it more closely and see what other features it revealed.

The data strip at the bottom denoted a topside view, looking straight down at the ground. It was dated only a few weeks before. The finished project, perhaps, not preparatory to construction. He right-clicked. The metadata lacked the usual military coding system.

Visually, it reminded him of a UFO crop circle.

Coincidence? Had to be.

On the other hand, he shouldn't discount the possibility. A chill shot through him, doubling his heart rate. His thought process favored Occam's Razor, *i.e.,* the simplest explanation. However, nothing about this was simple. Not with the entire area highly restricted.

He examined the screen again. Maybe a conspiracy *was* the simplest explanation.

It didn't take long to eliminate it as an alien outpost. Rather, it looked like a retirement community. Yeah, right. But it reminded him of one of those assisted living places with apartments, a few separate houses around the perimeter, clusters of units closer in, then a centralized cafeteria and shopping area.

Like where Connie's parents retired.

A residential Area 51.

Yeah, right.

He laughed, then blew out his cheeks and thought some more. Probably a research facility. None of the sections looked spacious enough for manufacturing, few big enough to conceal a UFO. There was plenty of room for that at other outposts, anyway.

Maybe since so many facilities had come to light they were building new ones. Bioweapons development, perhaps. Or some special access cloning project for government officials so they could live forever.

He chuckled again, convinced he was watching too many *Ancient Aliens* and UFO programs to humor Connie's love of all that off-the-wall unexplainable stuff.

This, however, was real.

And very, very secret.

So much so, he could get in serious trouble for hunting it down.

What was it?

If it was a big enough deal to get his son-in-law killed and invite attempts on his daughter's life, then he'd better figure it out.

His thoughts turned to that hidden compartment in Sara's condo. It was the perfect place for a server. And the spooks found it.

What was on it?

If all Bryan knew was on those photos, it was doubtful it would have gotten him killed. They would have been easy to debunk as a Superfund mine clean-up operation, even with the boring machine.

Bryan must have found something more tangible. He was hacking and stumbled upon a project that was, as Sara said, *huge*— literally and figuratively.

The implications were grave. If Sara found the data, then what? Maybe it was a secret best left alone. Except those spooks undoubtedly believed she already knew.

The strange facility glared back like multiple, glaring eyes. Examining it from different angles indicated it was at least a thousand feet below the surface. Yet the rooms weren't as high as expected. According to the software, around twelve or fifteen feet.

Probably a lab.

But for what?

His thoughts shifted back to those conspiracy nut TV shows and their insistence that secret underground bases existed galore. Could it be?

Nah.

His eyebrows pinched together.

No better explanation came to mind.

In a closed society where everybody's guilty, the only crime is getting caught. In a world of thieves, the only final sin is stupidity.
—Hunter S. Thompson

31. BROTHER?

BKSS LLC
ALBUQUERQUE
June 12, Tuesday
2:19 p.m.

Bernie gazed out his window at a pair of dust devils birthed by the takeoff wake of a Southwest Airlines Boeing 737. What was taking Steinbrenner so long to answer? For two cents he'd take the guy out himself. He inhaled sharply when at last he picked up.

"Hi, Bernie. What's going on?"

"Listen up and listen good. Fire your systems administrator. *Now!*"

"What are you talking about? Why?"

"Fire your IT guy, *now*. Not tomorrow, not the next day. *Now!* Why? Your system has a back door the size of a B-1 hangar, asshole. As if that's not enough, you've got VASI lights leading right up to it. Fire him. Immediately. Understand? Like in yesterday. Get someone in there who knows what the hell he's doing."

"What are you talking about? He has thirty-five years experience. He *does* know what he's doing."

"Ya think? Maybe that architecture worked in the 80s, but any adolescent gamer today could hack right in. You don't even have an SSL set up. I'm not kidding. Get rid of him."

Dead silence.

"Steinbrenner? You still there?"

The ensuing sound reminded him of when he'd worked a hog farm in West Virginia as a teen. "Yeah, I'm here. Listen. I, uh, can't."

Bernie's head and what was left of his bad leg started to throb. "What are you talking about? Why the hell not?"

"He's my, uh, my brother-in-law." Steinbrenner's whiney voice was nearing dog-whistle range.

"So freakin' what? His incompetence could get both of you killed. I'm not kidding, Virgil. What part of *dead* don't you understand?"

"Look, Bernie. You've got to understand. He's my sister's husband. She's executor of our father's will. If I piss her off, I'm out. Do you know what that means?"

"You can't be serious."

"Serious as a heart attack."

How'd this idiot ever get to be a project manager?

"You know what, Virgil? If you don't take care of this—right here, right now—you won't have to worry about either a heart attack *or* an inheritance. Get the picture? Put your brother-in-law in charge of your goddamn lunch room. Hire someone who knows how to secure a network."

"Hmmm. That just might work. But who?"

"Someone like Bryan Reynolds, dumbass!" He closed his eyes, muttering a litany of profanities. "Tell you what, Steinbrenner. I'll call the NSA and have them send someone out."

"No, no! Don't do that. I'll take care of it, Bernie. I will."

"You have exactly twenty-four hours, understand? Not one second more. Hear me, Virgil? Twenty-four hours. You need to shut your system down *now* and get it fixed no later than 2:22 p.m. Mountain Daylight Time. Tomorrow. You got that?

"Yeah, yeah. Got it. No problem."

"I mean it. The NSA doesn't play nice with stuff like this. Get it?"

"No problemo, Bernie. Consider it done."

Keller slammed down the phone. His gut clenched, a sure sign this wouldn't end well.

Terminator sat up and rested his muzzle on his thigh. He scratched the rottie's head while he stared out at the desert, grinding his teeth.

Assholes like that shouldn't be consuming oxygen intended for those with a functional brain.

Jaw set, he picked up his cell and set an alarm for 14:22:18 the following day.

Two hours later he called his IT contact to check whether EMPI's intranet was still online. It was. He told him to notify the NSA to pull the plug on their IP address and then administer the appropriate discipline to the recalcitrant soon-to-be-ex-project manager.

He leaned back, arms folded. Stupid SOBs like that deserved it more than Reynolds. He would have loved to have a genius like him on his team. If he'd known how talented he was, he would have recruited the poor bastard instead of killing him.

Another frustrated breath carried an explosive F-bomb. The dog cast him another concerned look. He took his big head between his hands and kissed him on the nose.

"Well, that's it, boy," he said. "That asshole's no longer my problem. Let's go for a walk."

SARA'S CONDO
DENVER
June 12, Tuesday
2:48 p.m.

Sara sat in the nearest branch of the Denver City Library using one of their public computers. After logging into her work email, she downloaded the written version of Patrice's reading and the recording to the thumb drive that contained the pictures, then listened to it twice using headphones before heading home.

As she drove she pondered the new insights Patrice added. She simply had to share it all with Connie. It was still early. There was plenty of time. Rather than take a chance on the burner, she'd tell her in person. After that, she'd head back.

The thought of driving on I-70, especially in an unfamiliar vehicle, was so terrifying she'd already decided to take the state highways and back roads. That would be just as easy from up there, anyway. The fact the first wreck occurred on a back road gave her pause, but she nonetheless decided to stick to her plan.

Back at the condo she changed into a pair of jeans, finished gathering what she needed, then zipped everything up in Bryan's carry-on. Back and shoulders still too sore to heft and carry it, she dragged it down the stairs, each step producing a teeth-rattling jolt. She parked the bag at the bottom and closed all the blinds. The handle from the duster was already in place, though she couldn't remember doing it.

A wry smile tugged at her lips. No big surprise, considering.

She took one last look around, besieged by an onslaught of random recollections. In some ways, being back actually felt pretty good. Almost normal.

Whatever *that* was.

Resisting another crying jag, she grabbed her purse from the counter and slung its strap over her shoulder. It weighed a ton with its extra cargo. Was keeping the gun in there a bad idea? The last time she'd tried to get something out of it while driving hadn't ended well.

Not thrilled at going back up the stairs, she did, nonetheless, and retrieved another one of Bryan's belts and a long sweater, then came back down and got the gun situated in the holster.

Maybe she should get a concealed carry license. If she intended to keep it on her, she probably should. Would that trigger some sort of alert as well? Would they confiscate it if she were on a watch list? Definitely a question for her father.

She extended the carry-on's handle and dragged it outside the door. Locked the deadbolt, put the bag in the backseat, then got in and guided the seatbelt around the gun. She started to head for Boulder, but before reaching Highway Thirty-six, it dawned on her she should go by Bryan's work, too.

No telling what might be there. If not the information itself, maybe some clue regarding where it might be. What if the information was on the credit union's server? How would she get to it, much less explain the situation to his boss? Finding out he'd been hacking into secure sites on company time much less using their equipment would not be well-received.

A few minutes later she parked in front of the Denver City and County Employees Federal Credit Union. She turned off the car, a sick, empty feeling in her chest. How many times had she come by like this to pick him up for lunch?

The meltdown she averted at the condo broke cover and made a soggy exit from her eyes. A few sniffles later, the rearview mirror revealed substantial mascara runoff complementing the Shiraz-sponsored bags under her eyes. She was not only a grieving widow, but definitely looked like one. She wiped it clean, braced herself, then went inside.

As soon as she entered the lobby the manager, David Tompkins, rushed over and escorted her to his office. She guessed him to be a few years younger than her father. His full head of curly red hair was ticked with grey, but he had a runner's build. Bryan had mentioned he ran marathons all over the world, including weird places like Antarctica.

True concern colored his voice and posture as he offered her a cup of coffee. She declined and sat down stiffly. He got settled behind his desk and folded his hands on its polished surface. "How are you, Sara?"

A sigh escaped unbidden. "It's been hard. But I'll get through it. My family's been wonderful. I have some friends out at the cabin, too."

"So where are you staying? Back here in town or out there? Some of us dropped by a while back to see how you were doing, but your place looked deserted."

"I've been out at the cabin since the accident. This is the first I've been back, mainly to my dad's in Boulder. I decided to go by the condo to pick up a few things, and now I'm heading back. But I thought I'd stop by to thank everyone for the kind words on

Facebook, the cards, and to see if Bryan had any personal items from his desk that I should pick up."

The man's expression shifted, eyes questioning. "Bryan's belongings? Uh, well. *Hmmmm*. As I recall, someone who said he was his brother came by and got them a few days after the accident."

Sara's jaw went slack. "Are you kidding? Bryan doesn't have a brother."

"Do you?"

"No."

His expression froze. "I'm sure we have some record of it. Hold on." He got on the phone and asked to see the receipt for Bryan's personal effects. A short while later, a middle-aged woman came in and handed him a sheet of paper. He looked at it, then handed it to Sara. "Does this signature look familiar?"

Even her doctor's writing was better than that. "No." She handed it back. "There's a timestamp on there. I don't suppose you still have security footage from that day?"

Tompkins shook his head. "No. Sorry. That was almost eight weeks ago. We keep it for a month and that's it. I'm so sorry, Sara."

She gritted her teeth, mind racing. "You didn't ask for ID?"

"No, I'm afraid not. We had no reason to consider that anyone other than a relative would want his personal items. We went through it to make sure there was nothing there of a confidential nature. You know, work-related. Like passwords and such."

Her thoughts raced.

Did any of that "confidential" stuff include the hacked information? But how could she bring up such a thing? Should she even tell him about the sinister circumstances associated with the wreck?

"I'm sorry, Sara. Want me to check with the person who handed it over? See if he remembers anything?"

"Yes, please."

Tompkins squinted at the receipt, then dialed an extension and asked the person to come to his office. A young man with long, stringy hair sauntered in moments later. Tompkins showed him the receipt.

"Do you recall anything about the guy who picked up Bryan's belongings?"

The guy looked thoughtful, scruffy chin in hand. "Thirtyish, dressed in jeans and a polo shirt, wearing a Bronco's cap. Looked a little like Bryan, but a little taller. Is there a problem?"

"I'm afraid so. Turns out Bryan doesn't have a brother. We're trying to figure out who it might have been."

"Oh! Gosh! I, well, never thought. . ." He bit his lip. "Am I in trouble?"

The manager looked at Sara, who exhaled as if to rid herself of the troubling thoughts. "No, it's okay." She reached over to pat the guy's arm. "You had no way of knowing. The only thing I really wanted was his coffee mug. Don't worry about it."

"Gosh, I'm really sorry," he repeated. "We liked Bryan a lot. We miss him. The new guy's a total butthead. Freakin' know-it-all Yankee from some crazy place in Maryland. Gatoradesberg, or something like that."

She tried not to smile. "I think you mean Gaithersburg. I miss him, too. It's okay."

With a final apology, he left. Meanwhile, the rpm of the wheels in Sara's head was increasing. "How'd you find someone from Maryland?"

Tompkins shrugged. "One of those lucky breaks. He found the job on Monster.com and applied. Said his wife just got on at NIST. He had the right qualifications, so we hired him. So far he's done an okay job, in spite of his personality. Or lack thereof."

"So she works at the National Institute of Standards and Technology?"

"That's what he said. Do you think you know him? I know sometimes these IT types do a lot of networking. No pun intended."

"What's his name?"

"Jason. Jason LaGrange."

She shook her head. "Bryan never mentioned him."

"Do you want to meet him?"

"Not especially. Well, thank you for your time, David. I'd better go. I have a lot of driving ahead."

He stood to shake her hand. "I'm so sorry for the mix-up. Have a safe trip home."

"I sure hope so." *If he only knew.*

She got settled in her car, mind racing. That whole thing sounded suspicious, including Bryan's replacement. Like Patrice said, there are no coincidences. As soon as she got home she'd google him and see what came up.

Which reminded her she didn't have a computer. Fortunately, there hadn't been that much on hers. Her email was online, most pictures on her phone. Anything else could be replaced. She mainly used her tablet for random surfing and shopping. Another laptop would be handy for research, though. That Walmart along the way to see Connie should have one that was good enough.

As she headed for the freeway she kept checking her mirrors. A few random turns, just to be sure, then she got on Highway Thirty-six North, then the Diagonal to Boulder, where she stopped at Walmart. She grinned wryly as she pulled into the parking lot, remembering the protests when it first came to town. Tacky and unwelcome as they considered it back then, enough people shopped there now.

She rejected the sales person's banter and pointed at a Dell laptop. "That one."

She gave in to his suggestions for accessories, however, which included another high capacity thumb drive, carrying case, wireless mouse, USB Wi-Fi receiver, full-size keyboard, headset, and a set of adapters to read all sorts of storage devices.

Before long she was winding through a subdivision of upscale homes, then into the driveway of the one on Skyline View Drive that would always feel like home. She no sooner turned off the engine when Connie flew out the front door.

"What's wrong? Is everything okay?"

Sara gave her a conspiratorial smirk as she got out. "Oh, yeah. It's okay, alright. Patrice did one of those question thingies for me."

"A horary?"

"Yes. You'll never believe what she said."

Connie's green eyes sparkled as she grabbed her hand to drag her inside. "Tell me! What did you ask and what did she say?"

They sat on the over-stuffed livingroom couch, Connie hanging onto every word.

"There's one problem," she added as she finished the story. "This is critical information. I know Charlie won't have a problem with it, because he's okay with this other-worldly woo-woo stuff. But what about Dad? What should we tell him? I really don't like keeping secrets from him."

"Good question. Me, either." Connie exhaled through pursed lips. "Offhand, I'd say nothing for now. Go ahead and talk to Charlie and see what happens. If everything works out, then we can tell Will. By then, we'll have some validation. Then he won't have any choice but to accept it, even if he thinks it's a coincidence. Depending on what Charlie does or finds, we might not even need to tell him astrology was involved."

"I like that. Oh, by the way. I stopped by Bryan's work to pick up his personal belongings."

"And?" Connie tilted her head.

"*Hmmmph.* Get this. They gave Bryan's stuff to someone who claimed to be his brother. And his replacement is from Maryland. If I'm not mistaken, Spook Central is around there somewhere. I smell a rat. How about you?"

"I'll say. That definitely sounds fishy. Do you want me to tell Will or do you want to?"

"Go ahead. I'd better go. I thought I'd be on my way before this. I can't wait to get back and talk to Charlie."

"I certainly understand that. Sure you won't stay for a cup of coffee?"

"No. Then I'll just have to stop to pee. I'm going to take state highways back. I want to stay off I-70. I get a panic attack just thinking about it, especially that tunnel."

Connie nodded. "I can imagine. Oh! I almost forgot. You left your neck brace here. Hold on while I get it."

"Don't bother. I feel better without it, especially driving. And I have the other one at home, if I ever need it."

They exchanged a long hug, then Connie gave her a look. "You're wearing your gun, aren't you?"

Sara grimaced, realizing she could have been arrested for having it in the credit union. "Yes. It feels weird, but good. I need to ask Dad if I should get a carry license, though."

"I'll pass that along, too."

"Okay, great. If so, have him text me that the cat is okay. If not, that the cat died."

"Like that physics experiment."

"Exactly. Schrödinger's Cat. Somehow it fits, doesn't it? Thanks again for telling me about Patrice."

"My pleasure!" She stepped back to look her in the eye. "You drive safely now, girl. How do you like the Lexus so far?"

"A bit of a tank, but it feels safer than the Honda. Or even the pickup, for that matter."

"The main thing is no more wrecks."

"Right. No more wrecks!" she agreed, then climbed into the driver's seat. She waved, then backed out, filled with anticipation of what Charlie might add to the recent revelations.

Other than checking the mirrors more frequently than usual, the drive back was uneventful. She stopped in Silverthorne to stock up on some food, arriving at the cabin around seven-thirty. After hauling everything inside she decided tomorrow would be soon enough to talk to him, since she either had to drive somewhere with the burner or go by personally. She'd driven enough for one day.

She was tired, but anxious to set up the computer. The first thing she did after doing so was insert the thumb drive with the written and audio versions of Patrice's reading. She read it through again, highlighted some key sections, then sent it to the printer on the kitchen counter.

Next, she connected it to her phone's hot spot so she could download a virus checker and firewall that included a Virtual Private Network or VPN. She put a Band-Aid over the camera, then googled "Jason LaGrange." Several came up, but none from anywhere near Maryland, much less Denver, Lakewood, Boulder or any other town in the area.

Her lips tightened into an angry line.

If Bryan secured anything at work it probably hadn't been found yet. She closed the search as another thought struck. Once it either was discovered or determined nonexistent, she'd bet dollars to donuts that LaGrange would quit.

Should she say anything to Mr. Tompkins?

Probably not.

That would require telling him everything. Bryan was best remembered for the good guy he was.

This land belongs to us, for the Great Spirit gave it to us when he put us here. We were free to come and go, and to live in our own way. But white men, who belong to another land, have come upon us, and are forcing us to live according to their ideas. That is an injustice; we have never dreamed of making white men live as we live.
— *Sitting Bull, 1882*

32. HELIACAL RISE

CHARLIE'S CABIN
RURAL FALCON RIDGE
June 13, Wednesday
4:49 a.m.

As if cooperating with the hour's intent, Grandmother Moon lurked beneath the horizon while blackened skies strewn with stars awaited their demise at dawn. Charlie made an offering with his prayers, then sat cross-legged on the bare ground outside his cabin, facing northeast.

Dawn would commence just after five o'clock, sun breach the horizon roughly forty-five minutes later. Just enough time to get to work by six.

Morning air sharpened his senses as he tapped softly on the hand drum in his lap. The hypnotic rhythm quieted his mind much as his blanket warmed his body, a lullaby to his indigenous soul. He would have preferred buckskin instead of jeans, but might not have time to change.

Showing up looking like he'd just come from a powwow would stretch Maguire's "no altercation" policy to the breaking point.

As it was, he'd show up smelling like burnt sage. Certainly better than what emanated from those roughnecks.

His mind shifted to work, discomfort resuming. Immersing himself in the white man's world before brought catastrophic results.

Back then he deserved being called an *apple*.

Would he succumb again?

His white brother was killed by the same type of men who cheated his people out of their land, slaughtered the buffalo, and ran them off like wolves to desolate lands no one wanted. Bryan's dying request to Sara that they "not get away with it" pierced his heart like a fiery arrow.

Badger's admonition to his inner warrior was as clear as spring water.

For now, his view of the future was as dark as the predawn sky. The only thing working for LSO would help was his bank account.

Was it another betrayal?

Something told him it wasn't, if his heart remained true. The threads of fate were invisible, tying people and events together in tenuous ways. A decision that seemed simple could lead or, conversely, divert from, whatever it was *Maheo* wanted him to do.

Was he assisting the enemy in violating the earth?

Or invading their camp?

There was something to be learned there.

It certainly wasn't enjoyable. Dr. Phil was unpleasant, to say the least. He bristled with suppressed annoyance.

Chuck, indeed.

His thoughts shifted to the two main things that demanded attention: First, find out the truth behind Bryan's execution, and second, earn a living. In the white man's world, currency was necessary. He had responsibilities, many of which required a source of income. Like being a better father and seeing his girls. No telling what his ex was telling them.

He was older, more experienced with life. Intuition told him the job related somehow to what he was supposed to do, even if for now it presented a dichotomy. He was ready to bear the pressure of standing astride two ponies. This time if one diverged, he'd stay with the red one and honor his roots.

His gut told him to avenge his white brother's death, but not do anything foolish or impulsive. Maybe it wasn't yet time. When it was, their power would help him serve up the needed justice and restore balance.

The thought startled him.

Serve up justice? How?

That was no simple matter. Yet it held a kernel of truth. And for thus he sought the *Maheo's* counsel.

While the fetishes provided valuable insights, inspiration came through multiple channels. If he could discover more regarding how to fulfill his obligation to Bryan, all the better.

The scent of pine needles and soft chime of aspen leaves embraced him from the forest below while his eyes remained fixed on the eastern horizon,.

As he practiced what Eaglefeathers taught him of the *Tseteshestahese* way of life, he likewise remembered how the Diné sought answers. Both tribes honored the same Great Spirit, but through different rituals.

Dawn was a sacred time when Diné tradition declared one could seek wisdom in a special way. Why not take advantage of both? Surely *Maheo* wouldn't mind.

A pale glow caressed distant peaks, reaching toward heaven. Light fanned out and brightened, the time he was waiting for. The last rising star or constellation preceding the sun's appearance would deliver specific inspiration in those sacred moments before it was extinguished by the break of day.

His heartbeat merged with that of his drum, mind clear and receptive as he watched, waiting.

What appeared wasn't surprising. Stars known to the white man as Orion's belt. To the Diné they were the quiver of *Átsé Ets' ózí*, a strong, young warrior charged with protecting his family and people. His appearance in an heliacal rise was a call for action.

What that might be, however, was what he needed to know.

Opening his mind to *Maheo*, he braced for the moment's culmination, when a small splash of pinkish-red appeared between the peak-strewn horizon and the spreading light. Its energy stirred his soul, bathed in brilliance like the snow crowning high elevations.

A sharp cry shattered the still air like a lance—a golden eagle on its morning hunt.

Another call from Eagle.

He assumed the great bird's persona, acquiring its flawless vision that sought its prey, then swooped in for the kill before it could escape. Eagle didn't know where his prey would appear until it did. He rode the wind, searching, until it broke cover.

He kept drumming, maintaining focus, enjoining patience. The eagle plunged groundward, then ascended again, an unfortunate rabbit dangling from its talons.

An animal that depended on its senses to perceive danger, then use its wit to survive.

He thought back to hunting rabbits with his father. They were not always successful. While their arrows were swift and silent, their feet were not. Rocks, twigs, fallen leaves, perhaps the vibration itself, served as warning. Snares were far more effective.

This quest required that he hunt as the eagle. Maintain his instincts and be on constant guard with unwavering vigilance. Sharp of eye, his approach silent, swift, and deadly.

No warning.

Otherwise, he would fail.

He drummed a while longer as he watched and listened. The sun continued its journey, dissipating night and its shadows, stealing dawn's intrigue.

To discover what happened to Bryan required further action.

How his job with LSO fit in would come with time.

SARA'S CABIN
RURAL FALCON RIDGE
June 13, Wednesday
1:23 p.m.

The afternoon sun bathed the cabin's spacious interior with incoming light. The Southwest patterns on the Danish style couch were bright and true, defying its age. Combined with the room's timbered walls and sheepskin rug, the scene was worthy of a Colorado travel brochure.

Unaffected by the cheerful ambiance, Sara sat on the couch, fidgeting as impatience collided with concern.

Why hadn't Charlie responded? What was taking so long? She'd kept it benign, assuming it would be intercepted, wondering if that could be part of the hangup. She picked up her phone, ready to text again when it rang.

Finally!

"Hi, Charlie. I was getting worried."

"Sorry. I just saw your text. Is everything okay? How was Boulder? By the way, you didn't get any mail."

She leaned back, finally able to relax. "Everything's good. I found out some interesting things I need to talk to you about. In person. Are you busy?"

"Actually, yes. I, uh, got a job."

She straightened again, taken aback. "A job? That's terrific! Congratulations! Where?" Creases teased her brow when it took him a while to answer.

"You probably won't believe this," he said at last. "Lone Star Operations. An oil exploration company."

"You're kidding, right? Good grief, Charlie, what have you done? Gone over to the dark side?"

"Yeah, I know. But I need money. I took this guy out fishing. We got talking and the next thing I knew he offered me a job."

"That's fantastic, I suppose. Who was it?"

"A Texan named Bob Bentley."

Her jaw dropped. "Seriously? I thought he was a federal judge. I had no idea he was some sort of oil baron. I guess I should have known when I saw his house. I play Mah Jongg with his wife, Angela."

"Interesting."

"Yeah, small world and all that."

"So, what's up with you, Sara?"

"Well, I was hoping you could meet me on the trail, where we ran into each other last time. A bunch has happened, plus I found out a few things I wanted to share."

"Okay. It's pretty quiet. I should get off at five. I'll come by after that, say around 5:30?"

"Perfect. See you then."

The feeling they were on the cusp of something big fired through her again. She glanced at the time—barely 1:30. Plenty of time to go over what she wanted to tell him, maybe even get a few things done.

There was so much to catch up on. It felt as if she'd been gone for weeks instead of days. Most important was what Patrice said.

What did he know?

Impatience raged, fueled by burgeoning curiosity.

Wanting to listen to Patrice's reading again, she set up the computer on the kitchen table, put on the headset, then went through it slowly, pausing and rewinding a few times. Then she checked it against the written version, not wanting to miss anything. The exact wording was crucial if Charlie had any questions. Maybe he'd pick up on some subtle cue she missed.

There was so much to tell him. She started a list so she wouldn't forget anything.

> *photos in Cloud*
> *second wreck*
> *Patrice x2*
> *Dad's discovery at work*
> *vision*
> *server & guns*
> *Bryan's work stuff and replacement*

She sent it to the printer, then deleted the file without saving it. As she reviewed it to be sure she hadn't left anything out, she realized there were a few things her father wasn't aware of, either. Such as Bryan's dubious successor and government goons visiting both of their places of employment.

She'd give blood and pay money to know who'd picked up Bryan's belongings. Who that new guy really was, too.

How could she find out if he quit? Job postings perhaps?

Perfect. Maybe even get a notice when it opened up.

Which would require a qualified applicant.

A mischievous grin teased the corners of her lips.

She took out her phone and activated the hot spot. Crossing her fingers that the VPN would perform as advertised, she logged into Monster on the computer and searched for IT system administrators.

As expected, Bryan's résumé appeared. With it in the system, it would come up for any matching positions. Unfortunately, the notice would go to his email, for which she didn't have access.

No problem—open a new account.

She included his middle name so it was different enough for the system to accept. She copied his résumé from the original site and used her work email for notification. When the credit union came across it, they'd just figure he never closed his account. She, on the other hand, would get a notification whenever a matching job turned up.

Just to be sure, she posted it to Indeed, too.

Satisfied, she shut down the computer, then took out something for dinner. Charlie rarely refused something to eat. The only time was the day they scattered Bryan's ashes. She whipped up some coleslaw, then took some pork chops out of the freezer.

By then it was only four o'clock, so she decided to take a quick nap. Still avoiding the loft, she sprawled out on the bed in the guest room. The gun needed to go. She set it on the storage bench, then crashed quicker than expected.

When she awoke it was after five.

Near panic, she pulled on socks and hiking boots, then grabbed a baseball cap from a nail in the log wall. Mind racing, she sat on the storage bench to calm down. She stood up and tucked the Glock back in place.

At least it was starting to feel natural.

She grabbed her list, sunglasses, and the printout of Patrice's reading, then set her phone in airplane mode. She stopped. If Charlie couldn't make it or would be late, she couldn't receive a call or text. With it on, the spooks could track and, if her father was right, hear her. She gritted her teeth and snarled, turning it back on before dropping it in her pocket.

When he got there, she'd turn it back off.

Who cared if they knew where she was? They probably already knew from their conversation.

As she headed out the back door she realized she should lock it, something she'd only done previously when leaving for Denver. She went back inside to grab the key, secured the deadbolts she installed the night before, then was on her way.

What news did he have?

Goosebumps crept along her arms and met in the back of her neck.

With beauty before me I walk
With beauty behind me I walk.
With beauty around me I walk.
With beauty above me I walk.
With beauty below me I walk.
—Traditional Navajo prayer

33. THE MEMORY CARD

SARA'S CABIN
RURAL FALCON RIDGE
June 13, Wednesday
5:04 p.m.

When Sara got to the bend in the trail Charlie wasn't there. She sat on the boulder where she'd rested before. How could scattering Bryan's ashes seem like both yesterday and eons ago?

She drew in a breath, savoring the mountain air, sun warm on her bare arms. The vista was one few saw except for paintings and postcards. She scrunched up her nose. Was that some chemical smell, like natural gas? She sniffed again—it was gone.

Either the wind shifted or it was her imagination. Unless it related to Charlie's job. The thought of an oil well nearby made her stomach turn.

Wildflowers had yielded to early summer, a new crop coming in fall. Shortly after that, they'd be covered with snow, which fell as early as mid-August.

She studied what Patrice said again. What struck her most was that the information was hidden. She'd find it with his assistance.

But where?

"Hi, Sara."

Her heart bolted into overdrive. "Oh! Good grief, Charlie! You scared me half to death."

"Sneaking up on wildlife and white men has been in my people's DNA for millennia."

"Well, it might not be a very good idea to startle me these days." She lifted her shirt enough to show what she added to her wardrobe.

"Whoa!" he exclaimed, raising his hands and moving back so fast he nearly lost his hat. "I guess you *do* have a lot to tell me."

"I'll say. So much, I wrote it down. My memory isn't what it used to be."

"It's been a busy few weeks. You look much better than last time. Was the trip to Boulder good?"

"Other than the wreck, yes."

"Wreck? What wreck? Are you kidding?"

"No. Plus I came across new information I didn't want to go into over the phone. I'm apparently under surveillance."

"Surveillance? Sounds serious. So, shoot." He held up his hand. "Not literally, of course. What's going on?"

She rolled her eyes. "You have no idea."

She went through her list, one by one, except meeting Patrice. By the time she finished, his dark eyes were wide.

She waved the papers. "And it gets better."

He cocked his head, looking somewhere between curious and suspicious. "What's that?"

"While I was in Boulder, Connie took me to see Patrice, her astrologer. She did a reading for me regarding where I could find the missing information."

Questions danced in his dark eyes. "You went to see an astrologer?"

Her eyes narrowed, taken aback. Maybe he wasn't as in-tune with such things as she thought. "Don't you believe in astrology?"

"I believe in messages from the heavens. But it's a matter of whether they're authentic. So many don't know what they're talking about."

"Well, Patrice is legit. The night before, when Bryan came to me in that vision, he told me a few things, which I included in my question to her. She confirmed what he said and then some. You're key to finding out where the information we need is hidden. You came up in a previous reading, too, about whether I'd ever find out who was responsible for Bryan's death."

Curiosity colored his expression. "Is it okay if I see that?"

She handed it over and waited, monitoring his reaction.

"Huh. Okay, I see what you mean. And what's even more interesting, is that, well, she's right. I actually *do* have a few things for you, too."

The goosebumps staged an encore. "I knew it! What is it?"

"For one thing, this." He retrieved something from inside his hat and held it out. She picked it off his palm. An SD card.

"Where'd you get that?" she asked, handing it back.

"I forgot to tell you earlier, with all that jail hassle. I found it in your truck. Stuck between the dash and windshield, with a bunch of other debris. What do you think it came from? Your camera?"

"Maybe. Let's go back to the house and see. If it's from the camera, it's not a big deal because those pictures were uploaded to the Cloud and I got them. If we're lucky, it's something else. I'm pretty sure I got the cable adapter we need with my new computer."

"I took pictures of the wreck, too, while I was down there. Would you like copies?"

She hesitated. "I guess it wouldn't hurt."

They strolled back to the cabin and went inside. He parked his hat in its usual spot while Sara sat down and booted up the computer, then checked her phone to make sure it was either off or in airplane mode.

It was on.

She buried her face in her hands. Since he'd surprised her, she forgot. They'd probably heard everything. She rolled her eyes and turned it off.

He handed over his phone. She connected it to the computer and found the picture file, then transferred them to the laptop.

The first one opened. Her hand flew to her mouth. There it was, Bryan's beloved truck. On its side in a crumpled heap, surrounded by water.

Its decimated chassis and shattered windshield made her eyes burn. Then, as if that weren't bad enough, the next ones showed its blood-stained interior.

By the time she closed the last picture, her chest ached.

His faraway look and compressed lips revealed a similar reaction. He cleared his throat. "Pretty gruesome, huh?"

"Very. I need to show these to my father. Okay. Let's see what's on that other thing."

She dug through the accessory kit until she found the right cable, inserted it in a USB port, then plugged in the card. She bit her lip, a dark, portentous feeling churning inside as the computer connected to the new device.

"Alright. Here we go. Let's see what we've got."

He pulled up a chair and sat beside her. A new directory appeared on the screen. She clicked. Several folders came up. Their names looked like dates, including the day of the accident.

Maybe it *was* from her camera.

She clicked the first one. The files inside were MP4s.

They exchanged mystified looks.

"Movies? This definitely isn't from my camera. Those would be jpgs. It could take videos, but we never did. We used our phones. I have no idea what this is from."

She clicked the first one. Windows Media Player opened. Moments later the screen filled with the taupe-colored hood of Bryan's Silverado. It was facing their condo, accompanied by the soft purr of the engine. The building retreated as the view panned across the parking lot.

She clicked *pause*, mouth agape. "Charlie! This is from the dashcam! I had no idea it had sound, too."

Her hands flew to her mouth at the discovery's implications. First the pictures, now this. Tears stung the back of her eyes.

"I don't know if I can watch this. Oh, my God."

Another thought struck.

If the cabin was wired like the condo, she'd just announced what they found.

Where could they go to watch it?

She got up and waved him outside. Confusion defined his features as he obeyed and walked beside her a few dozen yards up the trail.

"We have to be careful what we say inside," she explained. "Dad warned me they probably installed listening devices here, too. Possibly even outside. I already blew it, but we should go somewhere else to watch it. Any ideas?"

His shocked expression shifted.

"Your computer runs on a battery, right?" She nodded. "Then I know a place. But we'll need to drive." He nodded toward his truck.

"Okay. I'll gather up everything."

Back inside, she shut down the laptop, then slipped it in its case along with the cable and SD card. What else?

She already had her gun. She slid the phones and her wallet in the zipper compartment, then decided to leave her cell behind. One final glance around, then she locked the place up. Careful steps carried her down the rocky drive and into the cab.

Her mind was too numb for conversation. He took a narrow but paved road toward Lake Wilson, passed a small burger place, then a few elegant lakefront homes. Moments later he arrived at a public park with a boat launch and small picnic area. A few pickups and SUVs with empty boat trailers were in the parking area. No one was around.

She grabbed the computer bag and the two of them headed for the picnic tables beneath a stand of pines. She scrutinized its branches suspiciously. Surely this place wouldn't be bugged.

Would it?

She'd never been there before, so the odds were in her favor.

While the Dell booted up, dread evolved to suffocating fear. By the time the screen settled, her heartrate and respiration staged a full-blown panic attack. Quivering hands crossed over her chest.

"I can't. . . watch these," she whispered between ragged breaths.

He sat beside her, hand on her shoulder. "We have to, Sara. Answers are here. If we want them, we have no choice."

She slid off the bench and took a few steps toward the lake. She wanted answers, but hadn't considered how painful they might be. Her hands flexed at her sides as she turned around, eyes fixed on the laptop as if it were a rabid wolf ready to strike.

Did she want to know or not?

If so, this would tell her. It also meant reliving the most horrifying experience of her life. Did her subconscious suppress it for good reason? She buried her face in her hands, then dragged them apart, flat against each side of her face.

"I don't know, Charlie. I just don't know."

He exhaled through his teeth. "Look. I understand. You don't have to. Probably shouldn't. I'll watch it. See what's there. If you don't want to, that's okay. I'll do it."

She walked around the table and sat on the opposite side. A breeze swept off the water, the surrounding trees whispering overhead as if poised to listen.

"Thank you. You watch it." She closed her eyes and braced herself. "Go ahead."

34. SNOOPING

BELTON COUNTY PARK
LAKE WILSON RECREATIONAL AREA
June 13, Wednesday
5:49 p.m.

C harlie shifted over in front of the computer. The first folder's date was a few days before the accident. Probably Bryan going to and from work. He opened the second one from the bottom, dated the day before. Inside were two files. He clicked the first one. The data strip along the bottom displayed the time and date.

It started at their condo, signs along the roadway indicating they were heading toward I-70 West. Bryan and Sara were talking. Normal chit-chat, happy and excited.

He glanced up at Sara across the table. Tears were coursing down her cheeks. He turned down the volume.

"No, it's okay," she said, wiping her eyes. "I have to listen. It should help me remember."

He set his jaw, not sure it was a good idea, but complied. Dealing with crying, much less hysterical, women was several miles outside his comfort zone.

Normal conversation continued for several minutes—talk about work, projects they'd left behind, looking forward to a break at their favorite place.

Charlie bit his lip while his thoughts cycled. Listening to this real-time would take forever. If he fast-forwarded, however, he might miss something important. The chatter diminished slightly

306

as they got farther from Denver. Miles of mountain-walled Interstate eventually streamed by, the familiar terrain and steady hum of the engine hypnotic.

Someone turned on the radio, a pop station, which made it harder to hear what they were saying. He skipped forward when there was no dialog.

More small talk.

That video ended when they stopped for lunch in Dillon. No telling what was said inside the restaurant. Nothing he could do about that. He clicked the next file.

On the road again, someone turned off the radio.

"I have a few things I need to do while we're up here," Bryan said.

"Work around the cabin type stuff?" Sara asked.

"Uh, no. Not exactly."

"C'mon, Bryan. We're supposed to be getting away from work".

"Yeah, I know. This is my own project. You, uh, probably wouldn't approve."

"Really?! And just what have you been up to now, Bryan Reynolds?"

"Well, you know how bored I get at work. Maintaining an IT system isn't that hard. You have to keep an eye on it, make sure everything's working the way it's supposed to. I work on improvements and revisions, hardware maintenance, software updates, that sort of thing. But I still have a lot of time to kill."

"Okay. I get that. So what's your point? What did you do? Play computer games? Nothing naughty, I hope."

Both laughed.

"No, nothing like that. I just snoop around a little. Surf the web. See what's out there. New products and stuff. Explore the dark web sometimes. That's where things get interesting."

"Should you be out there?" Concern tinged her voice. *"Could you get in trouble?"*

Bryan chuckled. "That depends on where I go and what I have to do to get in. Or if I get caught."

Charlie paused the video. Sara wore a pensive frown. He pointed to the computer and mouthed, "Do you remember this?" She shook her head.

He continued to alternate between watching her, then the video where the road whizzed by as their conversation continued.

"Alright, Bryan. You're up to something, aren't you? What have you done? Are you hacking into places you don't belong?"

"I, uh, suppose you could say that. Personally, I believe this is information the American people have a right to know."

"Oh? Like what?"

"I got into some interesting records. Stuff that could get some pretty high-up people in a lot of trouble."

"Such as?"

"Congressmen using taxpayer money to reward lobbyists and major supporters who finance their campaigns."

"Don't they just reward them with favorable legislation?"

"Yes, that's the usual channel, which is bad enough. But this goes way beyond that. More material compensation." He snorted. *"As if their sponsoring corporations aren't already paying them obscene salaries."*

As the video continued, he looked up again to check on Sara. Her entire face was etched with surprise.

"I don't get it. What are you saying?"

"Some powerful people have demanded the same level of protection as government officials."

"Like bodyguards? Secret Service stuff?"

"No. Bigger. Much bigger. You're aware that they have underground bunkers in various places where the president, his cabinet, and members of Congress will go in case of an apocalypse, right? The military, for example, has Cheyenne Mountain."

"I've heard of such places. I suppose it makes sense."

"Well, these powerful campaign supporters want the same benefit."

"Hmmmph. That sounds like some major misuse of public funds if they're using taxpayer money."

"*Exactly! Big time! They've tried to hide it in the black budget, where a lot of secret DoD projects are funded.*"

"*Does the president know about this?*"

"*Absolutely. He signed it. But he may not know the specifics. Did you know there's something like thirteen security clearance levels above the president?*"

"*Are you kidding? How can that be?*"

"*Just the way it is, Sara.*"

"*So what are you saying? You've uncovered concrete evidence of this?*"

"*Yup. A project they call PURF. Pearson Underground Residential Facility. Costing over sixty billion dollars.*"

"*Holy crap on a cracker, Bryan! What exactly do you plan to do about it?*"

"*I haven't decided. I figured WikiLeaks would be a good place to start. I can't trust the press or CNN with this type of thing. Some of them are into it themselves. I don't doubt they're the types who'll benefit.*"

Charlie hit *Pause*, meeting Sara's wide-eyed expression with one of his own.

"This explains a lot, doesn't it? I wonder if they knew what he was up to before they found you on the property?"

"Who knows? Oh, Charlie. No wonder they wanted him dead! And me, too, since they assumed I knew about it, too. What are we going to do?"

"I don't know. I know what Bryan would want."

She rolled her eyes. "Unfortunately, I do, too. First hand. He told me not to let them get away with it, remember?"

His gut wrenched at the ominous implications. "This is serious business, Sara. If we don't do it correctly, we're dead, too."

"I know. I don't know about you, but I'm terrified."

He nodded grim agreement. "We still don't know where he stashed the data. The only way we can do what he asked and blow this thing wide open is to find it."

"True. The data files have already been confiscated from the expected places. It may have been on his laptop, but it burned up in my last wreck. You wouldn't think there'd be even more backups, but supposedly there are. And we'll find them according to both him and Patrice. Hopefully this will tell us where else to look."

"Do you remember any of this?"

"Sort of. It sounds vaguely familiar."

"Okay. So you're good with continuing?"

"I suppose. We're in too deep not to at this point. They, whoever *they* are, already think we know, so we may as well find out all we can. If they're going to kill us, we may as well know why and have something to spill first."

"I agree." His eyes held hers a moment before he clicked *Play*.

"This is scary stuff, Bryan."

"I know. In a way I'm sorry I found it. But now that I know, it's my duty to put it out there."

"Do you have any idea how dangerous this is?" she asked, voice rising. *"Good grief, Bryan! This isn't some stupid video game!"*

"I know, sweetheart. I debated whether to tell you or not. But if something happens to me, you need to know why. That I was targeted for a reason."

Her gasp was so loud the soundtrack picked it up. *"Right. And by association, I'm on that list, too. Oh, my God, Bryan! What were you thinking?"*

"I wasn't, I guess. At first, I was just curious when someone at work mentioned her fiancé got a job with the Army Corps of Engineers somewhere around here. I couldn't imagine what it might be. So I started digging around. I was pretty surprised myself at what I found."

"So, what exactly did you find? Do you have actual, hard evidence, or is this all conjecture?"

"Oh, I have plenty of hard, very incriminating evidence."

"Such as?"

"Briefings. Emails. Legislation, both drafts and approved versions. Budget breakdowns. Construction plans. Contractor lists. Schedules. Maps. Numerous sources that all fit together."

"It's gotten that far, to the construction stage?"

"Oh, yeah. Big time. It'll probably be finished, at least the first phase, by the end of this year. And you'll never guess where it is."

"Why do I have this feeling I don't want to know?"

"Because it's virtually in the cabin's backyard. That's what I need to do while we're up here. Find physical evidence to back up what I've seen online and document it."

"With photos, right?"

"Yes. Complete with GPS coordinates to confirm it synchs up with the plans."

Their truck exited the Interstate and turned onto the local highway. Ironically, the one where the accident occurred.

"Well, you sure know how to ruin a vacation, Mr. Reynolds."

All was quiet until the dirt road that led to their cabin branched off a few moments later. As the road surface shifted, sundry thuds and bumps accompanied the conversation.

"After I get the photos I need, I won't mention it again. We can pretend it doesn't exist and just do our usual thing up here. Ski, drink some good wine, have our fill of great, hot sex. I can't wait to see you naked in front of a blazing fire and have my way with you on that sheepskin rug. Makes me horny just thinking about it."

"Hmmph. It better be great. It might be our last."

"We don't have to wait, you know."

"I suppose. But after what you just told me, I'm not exactly in the mood."

"Don't you want to play like we're Mr. and Mrs. Smith? *Didn't you want to work for the FBI when you were a kid?"*

"Shut-up, Bryan. I'm not amused. This is scary stuff."

The video ended when the truck pulled up to their cabin, surrounded by random patches of snow.

Charlie stifled a smile when he saw Sara blushing. Neither spoke for several moments.

"Wow. That was certainly more than I expected," he said finally.

She exhaled hard. "You and me both. I should've left well enough alone. Way too much information."

"Yes and no. It's not like ignoring this will make it go away."

"True. And while we now know what's going on and why they wanted us dead, we still don't know where he hid the evidence. Without that, we can't expose it, even if we wanted to. He may have told me in the cabin, but I can't remember. Listening to this was weird. I don't recall any of it, though it sounded vaguely familiar. Like when you sing along to a song and can remember the words, but couldn't without it playing."

He nodded, forehead wrinkled with thought. "You know, it's possible, if everything was on that server at your condo, that they'll assume they got it and are safe from exposure."

"If you were them would you take that chance and leave me alive?"

"Probably not."

"Besides, if they're spying on me they know I'm looking for it. Probably what I promised Bryan, too. I feel as if I'm skiing on a slope far beyond my skill level. And headed for a massive stand of trees."

"And I'm right there behind you, on a snow board."

They froze when a white Tahoe towing an over-sized pontoon boat pulled into the park. The driver attempted to back it up to the ramp, but was clearly an amateur. After jack-knifing the trailer numerous times, he finally figured things out and the boat eased into the water. A woman got out, laughing and shaking her head as she climbed up to release the craft while three young kids piled out the back.

"He should take driving lessons from the guy who hit me with that eighteen-wheeler," Sara commented, then covered her face with her hands and dropped them to her lap. "I need a break. Would you like something to eat? There's that little burger place back down the road."

"Sure. Sounds great."

After loading everything back into the computer case, they returned to the truck and headed back down the road.

The food stand, appropriately named "The Snack Shack," sold burgers, hot dogs, tacos, drinks, and a variety of chips. They picked up their order, grabbed a handful of napkins, then got back in the truck to eat.

Charlie held up his can of Dr. Pepper. "To Bryan," he said. "May we live long enough to curse his name another day."

She tapped his drink with her diet orange. "To Bryan," she muttered, eyes troubled.

When they finished eating he gathered up the mess and deposited it in the trash beside the order pickup window. He bought a couple bottles of water, then got back in the cab, turned the key in the ignition, and dropped the gear shift in reverse.

"Those people should be out on the lake by now. Same place?"

"I suppose. Unless you know somewhere else. We need to find out if it tells us where to find this incriminating evidence."

As expected, when they arrived back to the park the boat was out on the water with no one around. Once the computer was set back up, she resumed her place on the table's far side. She tucked her arms against her stomach, lips compressed.

The final folder with its two MP4s stared back from the screen. He exhaled through pursed lips.

"Okay. Let's do this."

No bright star hovers about the horizon. Sad-voiced winds moan in the distance. Some grim Nemesis of our race is on the red man's trail, and wherever he goes he will still hear the sure approaching footsteps of the fell destroyer and prepare to meet his doom, as does the wounded doe that hears the approaching footsteps of the hunter.
—Seath'tl "Seattle", 1854

35. TOTAL RECALL

BELTON COUNTY PARK
LAKE WILSON RECREATIONAL AREA
June 13, Wednesday
7:01 p.m.

The eerie cry of a loon out on the lake gave Charlie the chills as he poised the mouse over the file dated April 17. He clicked. It opened on stark white. Snow covered the hood, ground around the cabin, and peaks behind it. Two sets of footsteps marred the space between the steps and the truck. Deep trenches remained as it backed up and turned around, then bumped down the incline toward the road.

"Okay, Bryan. Let's get this over with." Her voice trembled.

"It's going to be okay, Sara. If I don't find any physical evidence, it's over. Kaput. Done. I'll destroy what I have and let it go. No one will ever know."

Fresh snow crunched beneath the tires as they jolted along their private road. As the elevation lowered, it became muddy and rutted, typical for the onset of spring. Upon reaching the main road they turned north, pavement quieting the ride.

"Promise?"

"Promise. C'mon! This'll be fun. We haven't been cross-country skiing since Thanksgiving. Fresh snow makes it perfect. We're combining business with pleasure."

"More like risky business, if you ask me."

"You always said I reminded you of Tom Cruise."

"Yeah. Except his movie exploits weren't real. Why can't you use your drone?"

"Too obvious that I'm snooping. This way we'll just look like a couple skiers. Furthermore, they could hack into it and steal it or shoot it down."

"Better it than us. So how are we going to find this place?"

"The plans I found have GPS coordinates. That's how I knew where the site is. Google maps will take us as far as possible on the highway. We'll go off-road after that, until the four-wheel drive craps out, then ski the rest. It should be a big site that's hard to miss."

"But if it's underground, will there be anything on the surface? Won't last night's snow cover everything up? We must have gotten eight or ten inches, maybe more."

"The plans call for a geothermal system, so there should be evidence of a drilling operation. Unless they're finished with that phase."

"What if they see us? Then what?"

"Good question."

"If it's such a sensitive project, won't they have security? Cameras, at least?"

"That's why I love you, Sara. You're one smart cookie."

"You didn't answer me. What if they see us?"

"I don't know. Hopefully, they'll just figure we're random cross-country skiers and ignore us. Maybe give us a warning."

"Seriously? You actually believe that? If this outpost is Top Secret or above? C'mon, Bryan. You can't possibly be that naive."

"Okay, you're right. But I think that it's in such a remote area that the risk of people like us happening by is so low that they won't bother. Cameras, maybe."

"Wouldn't they be monitored?"

"Good God, Sara! Do you want to go back? Forget about it? You've been watching too many goddamn conspiracy movies."

"Me? I've been watching too many? Ya think? What about you? Who do you think you are, Jack Reacher? This is no game, Bryan. Your little 'I'm bored at work' pastime could get us killed!"

The truck veered off the road and jerked to a stop, the sparse shoulder narrowed by a heap of aging, dirty snow.

"Okay. One last time. Do you want to turn back? Speak up now, Sara, or forever hold your peace. Sure, this is dangerous, but it's probably the only chance I'll ever have to make a difference in something. You know how much I hate all the crap that goes on. They're all so damned greedy and corrupt! This proves how bad it is and needs to be exposed. If done right, no one need ever know it was me, personally."

"Yeah, right."

"No, listen. Like I told you earlier, I'll go through WikiLeaks. Worst case, we might have to leave the country. Do you want me to give up the chance of a lifetime to do something important? More important than keeping hackers in some shithole country out of some dinkball credit union's accounts?"

"That's pretty important to the credit union members, Bryan."

"Right. Who don't even know I exist."

"You just said no one will know that you did this, either. You don't need to be a hero for your life to have meaning, Bryan. Especially to me."

Silence stretched for several seconds. Finally, "What do you want to do, Sara?"

All was quiet for several seconds.

"I honestly don't know. Only that I'm scared to death. Tell you what. Flip a coin. They say that reveals what you want to do. If you're excited at the result, then it's what you wanted. If you're disappointed, then you unconsciously wanted the other."

"Okay. Heads, we proceed. Tails, we go home." Shuffling noises, then a slapping sound. Another long silence. "Heads."

No one spoke. The truck pulled back onto the road, video silent again for a few miles. Eventually, it slowed down, left the road, bumped over the icy wall left by the snowplow. It thrashed *forward in fits and starts, continuing until its tires wheezed in protest, the slushy grade too steep, even for four-wheel drive.*

It ended.

Charlie's gaze met hers, equally solemn.

"Based on the flip of a coin," she muttered. "Amazing."

"Do you remember any of that?"

"Not really. It's like it happened to someone else."

His heart thudded dully in his chest as he directed the mouse over the final MP4. Would it reveal what they needed? Or another dead-end?

Literally.

He dismissed the sordid thought and clicked.

"All right, these photos prove what I found isn't a fluke." Bryan was talking fast, clearly excited. *"There's some sort of operation in progress up there. Now I just need to pull it all together and figure out what to do next."*

The truck bumped and thrashed back to the main road where it turned left, a winding, morbidly familiar two-lane road looming ahead.

The dashcam explored sheer drops, then panned to safety around hairpin turns. The video's digital timer read 16:15:08.

"What kind of information do you have? Are you sure it's irrefutable? That's a huge accusation, Bryan! If you don't have hard evidence, no one's going to believe you."

"I told you. I have documents galore. Transcripts from meetings that were off the record, construction plans, and financial data. When the American people find out what's going on out here, they're going to crap their pants."

"So where exactly is this evidence? Somewhere safe, I hope."

"Several places. You know how obsessive I am about backups. It's on my laptop and my backup flash drive, that I keep in the console, here in the truck. It's on the server in our office and I also have other backups on—"

—KABOOM!

The ear-splitting sound of a violent crash exploded from the speaker. Charlie jumped, cringing when metal screeched in protest at each additional impact.

He didn't know if Sara's screams were live or from the recording, maybe both. On the other side of the table, her face was buried in her arms, shoulders shaking. His eyes returned to the screen, mesmerized.

He'd asked *Maheo* what happened to his brother.

The answer was right before his eyes.

The truck stopped abruptly, dashcam directed at trees and the sheer drop ahead.

"B-Bryan?" Her voice was raspy.

No answer. Another loud thump, more screeches from traumatized metal. Sara screaming. The truck rocked. Another impact, then another and another. Slowly, the vehicle tipped sideways. Another blow and it tumbled slowly over the side, jerked to a stop moments later, camera staring into the depths of the ravine. Steam crept from beneath the hood.

On the other side of the table Sara's hands covered her mouth, tears flooding her cheeks. "Turn it off! *Please!"*

He didn't respond, mind fixated on the scene before him, camera still live.

Branches moving, water rippling below, otherwise eerie silence.

An unfamiliar male voice shattered the quiet.

"This is Jeff from your OnStar system. We've detected an airbag deployment in your vehicle. Are you okay?" The notification repeated. Then, *"Police and emergency vehicles have been dispatched to your location."*

Motion in the branches, water sparkling below, creaking and moaning from the truck and the lone tree holding it in place. What seemed an eternity later, sirens, then the racket of rescue equipment. Yelling, thumping sounds, the door opening, then the screech of a saw grinding metal.

"This guy's dead," a different male voice said. *"Just need to get him out of here."*

"She might be alive, but barely," a different voice stated. *"We'll need a backboard. She's lost a lot of blood, too. Get ready to type and match as soon as we get her onboard."*

A scratchy *"Roger that"* came through someone's radio.

Thumping and banging continued, then once more all was still. The siren resumed, then faded to silence.

The truck was still on the ledge.

When did it fall?

Did that tree give out?

He tweaked the recording forward, minute by minute, then stopped when more racket ensued. Dim voices, growing closer, different than the ones before.

Why was someone else there? A wrecking crew?

"You hit the bullseye on this one. Right in the driver side door. Good job."

"Thanks, Eddie."

"Alright. Get this thing cleaned out. Everything. Damn airbags! Shit!"

"Here's a camera. And a cell phone, there on the floor. I got the gal's purse, too. I'll clean out the glove box, you get the console."

"Got it. Shit, there's blood everywhere. Sticky, goddamn mess."

"Yeah, I know. Worst part of the job. Geez, this guy was pretty neat, though. Look at this. No beer cans, no candy wrappers, no fast food crap." He laughed. *"I'd hate to do this with my truck."*

"Yeah. Mine, too. Just make sure you get everything. Everything, understand?"

"Even these CDs?"

"Yeah, dumbass. Think about it. No telling what's on them. Might be data, not just music."

"Right."

"I've got everything on my side. How 'bout you?"

"Yeah, nothing left but busted glass and plastic."

"Alright, this thing's definitely gotta go."

"Home movies, anyone? Or YouTube?"

"*Good point. Be interesting to hear what they were talking about. I wonder if his last words were 'Oh, shit!'*"

The other guy guffawed. "*We'll find out when we get back. Supposedly pilots say that right before they auger in. Maybe the boss could use it to advertise our services.*"

More laughter.

"*No telling what good stuff is on there, you know. Could save a bunch of trouble sanitizing this mess.*"

"*Right.*"

The camera shook, jolted back and forth, forward and back.

"*Damn, this thing's on there good! What'd he use, Gorilla Glue?*"

"*Probably. And it's not plugged into the cigarette lighter, so it must be hard-wired to the battery. It's probably motion-activated. So it catches anyone messing with the truck.*"

Both laughed, hard. "*Ya think?*"

"*Uh, yeah. Hey, look. Ignition's still on. The camera's probably still running.*"

"*Perfect, Johannsen. We can show the boss our good work.*"

"*I like it. Excellent idea. One way or another, I need to get the goddamn thing outta there. Gimme the hammer. Not like we're gonna sell it on eBay.*"

Jerking movements linked to concussive sounds jarred what had been a static view. The camera whipped around in a dizzying arc, catching a glimpse of a blond, Nordic-looking guy with ice-cold eyes, probably in his late thirties.

Staccato strikes, shaking, and sudden jolts in multiple directions continued. Charlie flinched with every blow. The screen trembled, pixelated, then turned black.

Silence. As still as death. Gradually, time and place reestablished their presence, trailing echoes of the violent finale. Other sounds arose.

Sara's muffled sobs.

Whispering pine needles.

Wake-generated waves lapping the shore.

Heart pounding in his ears.

Grief-tainted rage seethed, filling the void Bryan's death had torn in his heart. It roiled and swelled, like storm clouds rolling in from the west, snarling with thunder. Moisture demanded release from his eyes.

Warriors don't cry.

He sensed movement as Sara's hands slipped away from her face. Red, swollen eyes met his, her expression horrible to behold. He swallowed hard, speechless.

With one final, heart-wrenching wail, her eyes rolled back and fluttered closed. She slumped forward, arms and torso strewn across the picnic table, breeze ruffling her hair.

At the sight of her limp form his own turmoil changed channels. The Cheyenne had a word for being overcome by emotional trauma—*É-áhanaxanéotse*. Like when his grandfather died in his arms, taking part of his soul with him.

The elusive nature of time swirled around him. Where did it go? What had he done that mattered since then? He'd pushed it away, ignored it. Wandered aimlessly, stumbling as a blind man along unfamiliar paths.

His thoughts drifted to his girls, then his Diné grandmother, still alive in New Mexico.

At least as far as he knew.

Many years had slipped past since he'd seen her. He'd been negligent about writing, partly because someone had to read it to her. While Eaglefeathers made him a man, *amasani'* made him a human.

Life was fleeting with no guarantees, future below the horizon, awaiting the rising sun.

> *Do the difficult things while they are easy and do the great things while they are small. A journey of a thousand miles must begin with a single step.*
> *– Lao Tzu*

36. TIME

BELTON COUNTY PARK
LAKE WILSON RECREATIONAL AREA
June 13, Wednesday
8:20 p.m.

Sara opened her eyes, surrounded by the soothing fragrance of rosemary. A hand rested on her shoulder, shaking her gently. "Sara? Sara. Wake up. Are you okay?"

She lifted her head, momentarily confused to see the lake a few yards away. She turned toward the voice. Dark, troubled eyes met her own.

It all rushed back.

Tears resumed, sobs erupting from the depths of her heart.

Charlie handed her a wad of napkins to wipe her face.

"It's okay," he said, placing his hand back on her shoulder. "You're here. You're alive. It's over."

"Oh, my God." Her voice trembled, words somewhere between a wail and a whimper. She buried her face in the napkins. *"Oh. My. God."*

The breeze picked up and troubled the pines, their whisper no longer hushed. A pinecone dropped and bounced along the ground. The distant growl of a boat, more waves lapping the shore.

The firm touch of his hand increased, reflecting the magnitude of what they'd shared, then he shifted his attention to his hat where he placed the sprig of rosemary in its decorative band.

She sniffled a few more times and blew her nose.

"I'm sorry," he said. "I should have listened to that alone. It's not like I didn't know how it ended."

He offered her a bottle of water. She accepted it, removed the lid and took a sip.

"It's n-not like I didn't, either. N-not your fault. I've been s-struggling to remember for months. That g-gap's been hard, too. So now I know. At least as much as I did before."

Her voice reflected forced control, though a tremor remained.

"Which isn't much," he said. "We still don't know exactly what he found. It sounds as if he had several backups, but most are gone."

"Even his laptop. It was hidden at the cabin. I was taking it to Boulder to go through with my dad and see what else might be on it. It burned up in the wreck. I don't doubt he had a flash drive at work, but they got that, too."

The wind caught her hair again. She pushed it out of her face and tucked it behind her ears. Took another swallow of water. Her eyes closed as an involuntary shiver ripped through her.

"Okay," she said, still breathless. "In that vision he told me the information was still out there. He said it was 'Everywhere.' That could be the internet. But where? A new site, an old one, a blog? Who knows? He built the website where he worked, so it could be on their server, but they planted someone there, too."

"They did? I thought they just picked up his stuff."

"No. The guy who replaced him wasn't random, I'm sure of it." She explained her suspicions about Jason LaGrange.

"How would you get to it on their server, anyway? Unless he left that information somewhere, too. I have no idea how to find something like that on the internet."

"Me, either," she said. "He sometimes worked from home so he must have had a back door. I doubt googling 'Bryan Reynolds conspiracy stash' would help."

"If all his backups were deleted or confiscated or even at his work, he wouldn't have stated you'd find it. It must be somewhere only you would think of or be able to look."

"Or according to Patrice, maybe you."

He took a long swig of water, then sat beside her. "Well, I suppose it's a good thing they didn't get this, at least," he said, nodding toward the computer. "I'll bet they were freakin' out when they realized they had the dashcam but not the recordings."

"Right. And at least now I know a lot more, even though I can't say I remember. Only what I just heard and the photos. Like watching through someone else's eyes. Or seeing a movie, one you saw before, but a long time ago."

"So you still can't remember what you talked about the night before?"

She gnawed her lip, thinking. "No. Not so far. It's still a blank."

"What should we do?"

"For starters, you keep the SD-card." She turned the computer around to face her, relieved the screen was blank. Her hand shook as she ejected the device, then removed it from the adapter and dropped it in his hand. "I need to tell Dad. He was pursuing some things, too. But calling him, even with the burner, seems too risky."

Waves walloping the shore in the early evening breeze joined the two-fold assault from crying and the onslaught of information. The sun leaned toward the horizon, reminding her how long they'd been there. An hour or so of daylight remained.

"We should leave," she decided, turning back to the table to pack up the computer. "I need to get my head on straight. Figure out what to do next. I'm sure Dad will have some ideas. What do you think we should do?"

He didn't respond, a faraway look in his eyes. Her throat burned, realizing how much those videos affected him, too. She only heard what they contained. He'd watched it.

Bryan once told her about witnessing one of his buddies get blown to bits by an IED in Afghanistan. He was devastated. Probably how Charlie felt now.

He mumbled something in a language she didn't understand.

"I'm sorry. What did you say, Charlie?"

"Oh. Right. Just thinking out loud. I'll call the grandfather spirits. Ask them for guidance." He didn't elaborate any further.

She shouldered the bag and they headed back to the truck immersed in thoughtful silence. Once inside the cab his dark eyes focused back on hers, an unexpected smile behind them. He started the engine, then laughed out loud as he pulled onto the narrow road back to the cabin.

She scowled, mystified. "What's so funny?"

"In the summers when we were young, sometimes I was so used to talking with my grandfather that I'd say something to Bryan in Cheyenne. He'd just look at me, blinking like an owl, until I finally heard myself. We'd both laugh, then I'd say it in English. I eventually taught him enough that he understood much of what I said."

Her eyes widened as his shifted back to the road. "Do you think he may have used Cheyenne in some way to hide the data?"

"I was thinking the same thing. It could be the name of a website." He laughed. "It would take them a while to find *Okohomoxhaahketa.com*."

"No kidding! What's that mean?"

"My name, Littlewolf, in Cheyenne. Or it could be used for a file somewhere we haven't found."

"I don't know about you, Charlie, but I have a feeling you're on to something here." *Just like Patrice said.*

"I feel it, too. But it could be just about anything. Who knows?"

"I know. But at least that narrows it down another notch. If that's the case, you're more likely to figure it out or recognize it. It could relate to something you two did together, some memory you shared."

"That makes sense. I'll think about it and see if anything stands out." The faraway look returned. "I will enjoy remembering."

By then they were back at the cabin where he pulled in behind her GX.

"Okay. Thanks so much for everything, Charlie. Next time you'll have to tell me about this job of yours."

He pursed his lips. "Yeah. Not exactly my dream job, but the pay's mighty close." His eyes met hers in a wordless exchange of emotion. "Are you okay, Sara, being here alone?"

"I won't say I'm not upset, because I am. But I'm okay. I need to figure out how to get this information to my father. My birthday's in a few days. That will work to get them out here. You should be there, too, so we can strategize together. I'll let you know." She opened the door and started to get out.

"Hey, wait." He shut down the engine. "Let me go in, too, and make sure everything's okay." He grinned. "Even if you're the one with the gun. You can protect me."

She laughed, but didn't argue. They walked up the steps, where she dug her keys out of the computer bag. He went in first, then they checked each room together. Everything appeared to be exactly as she left it. She walked him back to the front door.

"You're sure you're okay?" he asked.

She nodded. "Yes. I'm okay."

"If you have any ideas or need anything, text or just call me."

She watched from the deck until his truck disappeared among the trees. Back inside, she secured the deadbolt, then leaned against the door.

An unexpected calm fell upon her, dissipating the last remnants of shock. As painful as it was, it was better than that gaping hole in her memory.

And at last she knew—*it was time.*

She entered the guest room where determined hands stuffed everything in the carry-on bag she'd kept down there since returning from Denver. It bumped up the stairs behind her and into their bedroom where she stared at the king-size bed. Tears blurred her vision, but peace remained.

It was time.

REAGAN NATIONAL AIRPORT
WASHINGTON, D.C.
June 13, Wednesday
10:18 p.m.

EMPI Chief Operations Officer and PURF Project Manager, Virgil Steinbrenner, took his phone out of airplane mode, got up from his first-class seat on Frontier Airlines Flight 548 out of Denver, and removed his garment bag from the overhead compartment.

His eyes scoped out the shapely flight attendant while he waited to proceed to the jet way. The Airbus's heavy door swung outward, and he trudged out of the aircraft toward the terminal.

It would be close to midnight by the time he got to the Crowne Plaza in Arlington. Reagan National contained a wide variety of restaurants where he could grab something to eat. He stopped at the first place that was still open, sat down at the counter and ordered something quick to prepare—a bottle of Heineken and a hamburger.

He glanced at his watch. The Metro only ran until eleven on weeknights, which didn't give him much time. Oh, well, so what? If he missed it he'd catch a cab.

He wasn't sure what to expect from this trip. No one told him much about the upcoming meeting, which wasn't surprising given agendas weren't published. He wouldn't see that until eight o'clock the next morning when he entered the secure meeting room in the Capitol basement where the House Ways and Means Committee discussed black projects.

He wasn't due to report for another six weeks. He couldn't help but wonder what this was about. Maybe that IT security thing. As far as he knew, it was fixed, so it shouldn't be that.

His brother-in-law didn't seem to mind his sudden demotion or being reassigned to monitor the lunchroom's vending machines. Thus, it appeared everything was okay there as well.

He hadn't mentioned the deal he and LSO cut with the EPA Superfund. That could be construed as double-dipping.

Screw 'em.

That was a separate transaction.

No different than contracting with a municipal water company.

Splitting the proceeds with the oil company was just the way it was done. So far, both were satisfied, making it unlikely it had anything to do with that. None of their damn business, anyway.

His beer arrived and he took a swig, ignoring the glass. The liquid felt good on the way down, hydrating his mouth, dry from the flight.

His mind meandered through the progress they'd made the past few months. Creating a huge network of underground compartments nearly a quarter mile beneath the surface finished months before. They were able to use some of the old mine shafts by expanding them to a more symmetrical architecture. The tailings were reduced by the usual means using cyanide and mercury, any metal that remained extracted and auctioned off.

Infrastructure was almost complete. Waterlines were being installed, the source that same aquifer they'd accidentally sullied a few months back, thanks to that fracking debacle. They were tapping into it upstream from the injection well, so if it ever happened again, perhaps due to more tremors, the facility's water quality wouldn't be affected.

The guy behind the counter set his hamburger in front of him with its side of curly fries and a pickle. He squirted some ketchup on the plate, took a bite of the pickle, and finished garnishing the burger with mustard, a slice of tomato, and a sorry-looking piece of lettuce.

He munched away while his mind reviewed the work so far versus what remained, looking for any potential issues. According to the latest PERT there weren't any showstoppers. All critical paths were clear and progressing on schedule.

There was that one onsite security breach involving those two skiers. Except that was months ago. Keeping the project underwraps was critical, for any number of reasons.

Keller claimed that incident was closed. He didn't have the details, which suited him just fine. That was Bernie's problem, since BKSS was contracted to deal with such things.

All he needed to know was that it was cleaned. He had a pretty good idea what that meant, didn't particularly like it, but again, not his problem.

He popped the last soggy fry in his mouth, then tucked his American Express card in the folder. The server picked it up and was back moments later. He added a fifteen percent tip and signed it off, placing the card back in his billfold before picking up his bag and leaving the restaurant.

Back in the concourse, he headed for the entrance to the Metrorail system. He reloaded his fare card at a SmarTrip machine. From there, he sauntered into the station, estimating he'd make the last train by a fifteen-minute window. Arrows directed him to the blue/yellow line where he found a few others waiting as well.

Perfect timing.

He grinned to himself.

As a project manager such was expected.

The Metro tunnel's honeycombed structural design always made him feel as if he were inside a beehive. As an engineer, he appreciated the principle behind it, the strength it provided while reducing mass. A similar design covered much of the connecting tunnels back in Colorado.

The subtle vibrations of an approaching train brought him back to the present. He got off in Crystal City, rode the escalator to ground level, then walked across the sprawling brick plaza on South Bell, looking forward to relaxing in his room.

The air was warm but not uncomfortable, humid with the hint of exhaust fumes. Which was why he loved Denver's mountain air.

Trees in raised planters cast elongated shadows from the security lights, the open area deserted at the late hour. Office buildings walled the concourse, windows dark. He never came in this late and hadn't noticed before how far it was to the hotel.

Movement in the shadows raised the hairs on the back of his neck with the sudden feeling he was being watched. Sweat broke out on his hairless head, dribbling down his temples past his ears. He hastened his step, willing away his fears while he admonished himself for not calling a cab.

Next time he'd know better.

There wouldn't be a next time.

All men are made by the same Great Spirit Chief. They are all brothers. The earth is the mother of all people and all people should have equal rights upon it.
— Young Joseph "Chief Joseph", 1879

37. COINCIDENCE

CHARLIE'S CABIN
RURAL FALCON RIDGE
June 14, Thursday
6:19 a.m.

When Charlie arrived at work the next morning Big Dick sent him home. Something on the rig had gone "teats up" and it would take at least a week to fabricate the needed parts, then deliver them from Fort Worth.

While his boss and Maguire gnashed their teeth, it took serious effort to contain his elation. He kept it underwraps until he got into his truck, then his grateful grin burst free like a rabbit escaping a faulty snare.

Sleep the previous night had been shredded as cornstalks in a prairie hail storm. Dashcam videos blared unwelcome encores while he fretted over what to do next. Such distractions at work could result in a mistake, which would give Dr. Phil an excuse to fire him on the spot.

The guy obviously hated him. Why else would he taunt him by calling him Chuck? Maybe one of his ancestors got killed at the Battle of the Little Big Horn.

He steered toward home, still grinning, when an impression jolted through him with the heart-swelling witness of truth.

Maheo had *commanded* the rig to break down.

His satisfied simper collapsed to open-mouthed wonder. His insomniac pleas for help and guidance had been heard. Tears of gratitude coated his eyes. He knew exactly how to use this precious gift of time.

It wouldn't be simple. But having served as a door keeper, he knew the process well. There would be no one to tend the fire, heat the rocks, or carry water other than himself. If he didn't plan it out perfectly, such disruptions would diminish its effects. Even worse, mock its sacred purpose.

The first thing he did when he got home was make a tobacco offering to express his thanks. Then he checked the sweat lodge's fire pit. While it was stacked and ready, several logs needed to be added after each round to maintain the temperature of the remaining rocks. There was plenty of wood next to the house. But there was one problem—it was all a foot or more in diameter.

A heavy ax beckoned from its angled perch in one of the logs. He yanked it out, straddled the first trunk, and slammed it into its target, dual braids flying. The wood ripped apart with a loud crack, a few firm jerks and twists splintering it in two. Several whacks later it was suitably sized.

He kept chopping until he felt confident there was enough. He wiped his brow. The exertion alone provoked a good sweat. He hauled the wood over and set several more upright with the others, making sure the stone pyramid inside was entirely surrounded. Satisfied, he struck a match and ignited the tinder. Leaves and twigs crackled, smoke profuse. Fortunately, the west wind blew it away from the sweat lodge door.

He hunkered down to fan the struggling flames until they caught and clawed upward amid an angry cloud of acrid smoke. He walked the pit's perimeter for a safety check, then returned to his cabin to fetch a bucket of water, which he set to the side until it was time to move it closer to warm it up.

It would take an hour and a half before the stones would be red hot, giving him time to get everything else ready, including himself. He was hungry, but eating before a sweat was a bad idea. Fortunately all he'd had so far was coffee, having left LSO before stopping by the chow hall.

For the first time he realized he might not have everything he needed. The old man gave him many sacred items, most of which related to medicine man duties and responsibilities. Some were gifts, others inherited when his grandfather crossed over, such as his medicine bundle.

His uncle, however, who was living on the Northern Cheyenne reservation, had some as well. Such as Eaglefeathers's buffalo skull. Normally, it would be placed on a mound in front of the sweat lodge when it was in use. He pondered the dilemma a moment, then realized he could place the sacred red pipe on the sweat lodge roof above the door instead.

Other things were crucial, which he hoped to find in the chest at the foot of his bed. If not, he had to figure out some way to improvise. And quickly, since he'd already lit the fire.

When he got back, he knelt in front of the chest and lifted the lid. He took out his badger hide, on which the sacred red pipe would rest, then the medicine bundle. The next day he'd need the Cheyenne paints, so he unfolded the bundle, took them out, and set them aside. Hopefully he could remember exactly how to apply them.

The next layer in the chest was concealed by a colorful blanket. Not a cherished one like the one from his *amasani*, but one he'd purchased in *Diné Bikéyah* to keep at his ranger station.

His chest ached, its geometric design as imposing as a stone wall. After the old man died, he'd put it all away, every item another dagger of regret that advertised his failures.

He uttered a silent prayer for forgiveness, ashamed again.

Be at peace, Okohomoxhaahketa. For eternal matters it is never too late.

The prompting's source was unknown, but quieted his guilt. All he could do was hope it was true. He gulped back his unworthiness, heart still heavy.

Eaglefeathers often said, "Denying the past doesn't change the past." The usual context related to how they were treated by *Vehoe*. But like so many wise sayings, it applied to anyone and everything. Duly reprimanded, yet somehow comforted, his mind shifted to the task at hand.

He bit his lip.

Braced himself.

Lifted the blanket.

Familiar scents saturated with memories wafted from within. The vanilla-like scent of a partially burned sweet grass braid. A fringed and beaded leather bag with the old man's eagle bone whistle. A neatly folded hand-tanned deer skin.

He took them out, one by one. Held each to his chest a moment, as if to apologize for his absence. Then set it next to his badger hide. All were essential.

But so far no rawhide buffalo rattle or buffalo horn cap.

His mind hummed with possible alternatives as he eyed the fringed and beaded white deerskin shirt and pants below.

Eaglefeathers looked so handsome when he wore them for special ceremonies and celebrations. He stroked its texture, fingers leaving soft trails in its velvety nap. He lifted them to his face, inhaling the scent of fine leather mingled with wood smoke and a hint of cedar. His grandfather's fully beaded moccasins were there, too, another thing he needed for his fast tomorrow.

He set the clothes aside and turned back to the chest. Relief washed through him. The buffalo rattle and buffalo horn cap were right there. He got up and draped the pullover shirt and pants across the back of his living room chair, then took everything else over to the table.

Did he need anything else? He closed his eyes and mentally rehearsed the ceremony.

Yes. Several branches of man sage. Thanks to Eaglefeathers, many such bushes grew outside his cabin. He grabbed his hunting knife and went out to cut what he needed. He tied strips of red cloth around a few to use as a switch, the others left loose to serve as a cushion.

Man sage under his arm, he picked up the rattle, cap, and braid to take to the lodge while he checked on the fire. It was also time to start heating the water.

Right, *water*. He needed several bottles to drink between rounds, too.

Halfway along what was becoming a well-worn trail, the sharp snap of established flames welcomed him. He moved the bucket next to the fire, set his drinking water just outside the door, then placed everything else inside on the left side of the stone pit.

Which reminded him of something else he needed—a sturdy, forked choke cherry branch for moving the red-hot stones.

A thorough search of his cabin failed to produce the one Eaglefeathers gave him the first time he served as fire keeper. Sadness struck again as he wondered what happened to it, then grabbed the band saw and returned to where he cut the trees for the structure. He found one that would serve the purpose, then took it back to his cabin where he cleared the small branches with his knife and trimmed the larger ones with a hatchet.

The alarm on his phone sounded. The hour and a half required for heating the stones was over.

So far his timing was perfect.

He stripped down, then wound the deerskin around him twice, covering him from waist to knees. He tied it in place, hung the eagle bone whistle around his neck by its sinew cord, then gathered up the badger hide and pipe bag from the kitchen table.

When he got to the sweat lodge he hesitated. A sweat represented returning to the womb, further emphasized by the shape of the lodge itself. In most cases sweats were community events when the tribe banded together to support one of its members in achieving a specific purpose.

As when he built it, once again he longed for home, surrounded by his Cheyenne brothers and sisters. He promised himself that as soon as whatever he was there to accomplish was complete, that he would return to the reservation.

He spread the badger hide on the roof over the door with the tobacco and pipe on top, bowl facing east. After securing the door open, he picked up the bucket by its wooden handle and set it inside, then went out again to start fetching the rocks.

Heat blasted his face as he carefully pushed aside the smoldering logs with the choke cherry branch. Rocks glowed among the embers like miniature suns. Sparks flew as he edged the branch's fork under the initial stone, careful not to disturb the stack.

He lifted it slowly, flashbacks crackling as the fire. He turned and lowered it carefully to the ground where he rolled it in the dirt.

The first time he was fire keeper he'd forgotten, resulting in a cloud of ashes and debris riding the steam and irritating everyone's eyes, himself included.

He never forgot again.

Or the soul-scorching look his mistake earned from Eaglefeathers.

When all the residue was removed, he took it inside and set it down on the east side of the pit. He repeated the process, moving clockwise until a red-hot stone resided in each of the cardinal directions, plus one in the center. By the time he knelt down, eyes closed, sweat already dribbled from his temples.

The rigors and memory-fraught emotional toll of setting everything up alone produced a dissonant hum that disturbed both mind and body. He breathed deeply, waiting, until stress yielded to the peace radiating from his grandfather's stones.

He broke off a piece of sweet grass braid. Raised it high above his head in each of the cardinal directions. Lowered it in four steps, then placed it on the center stone. Blessed the others in similar fashion.

He smudged his body with the gathering smoke, directed it over the bucket, then throughout the lodge. Next, the eagle bone whistle and buffalo rattle each made four passes through the vapors. After a prayer of thanks to *Maheo* for the ways of his grandfather, he retrieved six more stones from the fire.

At last he closed the door and took his place to the left, sitting cross-legged on the man sage.

Where Eaglefeathers always sat.

A sultry red glow lit the lodge interior.

He closed his eyes to declare the sweat's original purpose: To understand how he should avenge Bryan's death.

The words refused to come.

Other thoughts flowed, their source outside himself.

All things, even tragedies, have a purpose. Maheo *is the Creator, you are the created. His ways are not your ways.* Maheo *is truth. Walk with a prayer for patience, guidance, protection and wisdom. Your grandfather is a very strong medicine man with powerful prayers.* Netsevoto, *who you know as Eaglefeathers, was chosen by his grandfather as he has chosen you to have his medicine.*

The words struck Charlie's heart with the harsh sting of truth. No matter how much he tried to deny it, deep inside he always knew.

For the first time he not only understood, but *felt* how much his arrogance devastated the old man.

Did he die of a broken heart?

How much longer would he have lived if he'd been willing to listen?

To learn? Been more humble? Accepted the honor of being chosen?

Instead, he'd seen it as no more than a lot of trouble and bother, an intrusion on his life for something he wasn't sure he believed in. Forced and trapped, his response was that of a cornered badger.

His heart ached as it split open and words flowed in Cheyenne.

"Maheo, I have forgotten who I am. I pray for your guidance to honor my grandfather's spirit medicine. My heart is ready. Teach me. I stand before you, pleading for strength and courage to make it right with you.

"I present to you the purpose of this sweat: It is to purge my past and help me live as an honorable *Tseteshestahese* man, as my grandfather did."

He dipped the buffalo horn cap in the bucket, then closed his eyes and prayed as he dribbled its contents over the rocks. Vapors issued forth, felt rather than seen, the pre-heated water producing softer steam that didn't burn like the explosive effects of cold.

He lifted the eagle bone whistle to his lips and blew, inviting the grandfather spirits to join him, then picked up the rattle and sang the Grandfather Song in welcome. Four songs accompanied each round, chosen by the lodge keeper. The words sent moisture from the corners of his eyes, down his cheeks, and onto his chest.

After a time he exchanged the rattle for the man sage switch to coax the toxins from his mind and body, alternating between the two. He sang the Badger Song. Wolf Song. And Buffalo Song.

The rocks grew dark.

He got up to retrieve the next eleven, one by one. He banked the fire, got a drink, then went back inside and blessed the stones with sweet grass.

It took a few moments to get settled again. As the heavy cloak of seething humidity folded around him, he remembered savoring those breaks of fresh air and a drink when he was door keeper. This time he would have preferred his prayers to be uninterrupted.

Again he blew the whistle, repeated his purpose, then shook the rattle and began to sing.

EL CHARRO MEXICAN RESTAURANT
DENVER
June 14, Thursday
11:54 p.m.

Bryan's former boss, David Tompkins, sat amid the midday racket in El Charro Mexican restaurant, watching for his wife, Susan. The relief he felt that the federal auditors were gone unleashed a strong temptation to celebrate with a frozen Margarita.

They'd showed up right after Reynolds died in that accident, even though they'd just been there a few months before. What that was all about, he didn't know. They didn't find anything, just like the time before, though their tactics were different, as if they were looking for something specific.

Oh, well, not to worry. Now they were gone.

Whew.

Any illegal antics on the part of his employees could jeopardize his job. He did his best to hire honest people, but human nature couldn't be trusted when millions of dollars were only a few keystrokes away.

Susan came through the door and stood there, looking around. He waved. When their eyes met she wove around the tables to the chair across from his.

"Well, you look more chipper than usual," he commented, voice mingling with the din of other patrons, rattle of dishes, and wait staff taking orders. "Good day at work?"

She shook her head, bobbed hair shaking. "Not exactly. Kind of exciting, though. Found out this morning our chief operating officer got murdered—shot in the head—on a trip to DC. They're saying it was robbery, but whoever did it didn't even take his Rolex. What kind of thief leaves something like that behind?"

"A smart one."

Her flawless brows arched. "How so?"

"Expensive items like that are often serialized as well as chipped." He punctuated the statement with a tortilla chip diving toward the salsa. "If they're tracked, stealing one isn't the best idea. To remove it would probably stop the watch."

"Oh! No kidding? I never would have thought of that."

"Yeah. Technology these days can trace just about anything. If it wasn't about robbery, why do you think anyone would want him dead?"

"I have no idea. He was overseeing some big project out in the front range somewhere, supposedly one that no one was supposed to know about. Maybe it had something to do with that."

He threw back his head and laughed. "No offense, Susie, but it couldn't be very secret if you know about it."

She snickered, then likewise dug into the chips. "There aren't many secrets in our office, David. Furthermore, he had quite the reputation for being lazy, so I'm sure his secretary was aware of everything that went on. It's an easy guess she was doing most, if not all, the work. Who knows who she said something to?"

"Hmmm. Interesting. You know, my bookkeeper's husband is with the Army Corps of Engineers working some big project around here. I wonder if it's the same one? Plus, one of my tellers mentioned someone coming in to make a deposit who said something that implied major construction in the area. It was a rather large sum and the guy said it was nothing compared to the bonus he'd get when it was complete. As I recall, he worked for EMPI."

"No kidding? Could have been Virgil or one of his lackeys. He promised the whole team bonuses. Big ones. Everyone in my department was jealous." She shook her head. "Except he was such a jerk, no one wanted to work for him, anyway."

"Any manager working a classified project, or anyone else for that matter, who'd say that to a teller would have to be a total idiot." Their server arrived. "The usual?" She nodded. "Stuffed jalapenos, chicken fajitas for two, and two ice teas."

He *really* wanted that Margarita, but it wouldn't be fair to Susan. Considering her day, she could undoubtedly use one, too.

The server left and the conversation picked up where it left off. "My IT guy was killed a few months ago in a bad accident somewhere out in the Styx. Also in the mountains west of here. His wife came by the other day to pick up his personal effects. But get this—someone who claimed to be his brother already had." His mouth shifted into a snide smile.

"And?" she prompted.

"He didn't have a brother."

Once again her eyebrows reached for the ceiling. "Wow. That sounds pretty suspicious, doesn't it? I wonder if the two events are related?"

"No telling. Small world. Anything's possible. Makes me wonder about the IT guy I hired to replace him, too." He took another chip and loaded it with salsa. "You know, thousands of people worked the Manhattan project for years without a single leak. What happened to good old-fashioned integrity?"

"That's for sure. I suppose everyone has their price. Speaking of IT people, I heard we're looking for one."

He grinned. "Perfect. Maybe this is my chance to get rid of this guy. His work is okay, but no one can stand him. Another one with a personality disorder."

"Go ahead and tell him. If he's a jerk he'll fit right in with that PURF bunch."

Their meals arrived and the couple dug in. When they finished the last bite, they wished each other a pleasant afternoon, then returned to their respective jobs.

When David got to his office, he settled in his chair, thoughts of a siesta teasing his mind. A letter-sized envelope was on his desk. He opened it up, curious, and unfolded the paper inside.

Spontaneous laughter exploded from his chest.

Jason LaGrange had resigned.

CHARLIE'S CABIN
RURAL FALCON RIDGE
June 14, Thursday
1:19 p.m.

The stones's subtle glow faded, the lodge's interior darker than night. Steam mingled with the scent of sweet grass rose silently from all forty-four stones, the only sound random crackles from the dying fire.

Drenched in condensation, tears, and his own sweat, Charlie no longer felt alone. It took a little over two hours, leaving him soaked and exhausted, yet cleansed and renewed, body and soul. Eaglefeathers was near and better yet, proud. Littlebear's and Bryan's presence were strong as well.

Water flowed from his eyes again, mind and heart still overcome by what he'd experienced during the third round. He was praying for Bryan. Promised to do anything he could to help Sara and avenge his death. Every emotion previously suppressed burst free from his heart, mingling with the sweat pouring down his cheeks.

As his supplication continued he heard the distinct sound of singing. The grandfather spirits leading the Journey Song for his brother. He opened his eyes, finding the veil lifted. Backlit by glowing stones, their ethereal presence was unmistakable within the sacred mists. He followed their lead as together they provided Bryan a safe journey home to his family.

While he retrieved the stones for the fourth round the veil closed, but their essence remained.

The fourth round and ceremony now complete, he declared his purpose again, sang the Thank You song with heartfelt sincerity, then offered another prayer. He sat a moment longer, heart overflowing, then got up and tucked the sweet grass braid between the structure and buffalo hide roof for the next time. He stretched, and stepped outside where he squinted up at the sun's glare high overhead, its rays and light somehow foreign.

He picked up the pipe stem and bowl from the roof and returned them to their bag, then rolled up the badger hide and tucked them both under his arm while he grabbed the empty water bottles from the ground with his free hand.

Back in his cabin he set the sacred items on the kitchen table, tossed the plastic bottles in the recycle bin, then untied the buckskin and slung it over the back of a kitchen chair to dry. The eagle whistle came off from around his neck, he pondered its power for a moment, then kissed it and carefully placed it in its bag.

After unbraiding his hair, he shook it free, then stepped over to the tiled area in the back of his cabin. With the help of the block and tackle hung from the rafters, the shower also worked for dressing out deer or elk. Most of the time he was thankful for the core of the old twenty-gallon water heater attached to the cabin's south side where the sun softened the otherwise frigid flow.

Bryan, the system's inventor, came to mind, also responsible for installing the in-line filter that reduced the well's impurities enough to bathe, at least.

After a sweat, however, was another story.

The cold water felt fabulous as it gushed over his face, through his hair, and down his back. He poured shampoo into his hand and worked it through his hair, savoring its tantalizing fragrance. He scrubbed his scalp, then leaned over and finger-combed the lather through his long hair. A distant memory flared of his wife doing just that after the first sweat they did together.

He scoffed at the reaction it evoked, the very one that caused history to repeat itself. If Littlebear had been alive, would he have been able to stop him?

Probably not.

Frigid water dispatched that issue in short order as he stripped both suds and memories to the tiled floor, then rinsed his hair until it squeaked. After washing all over, he toweled dry, but remained naked, feeling somehow liberated, shoulders and back savoring the cool caress of damp hair.

Hunger raged. He finished off the last of some venison stew, downed two bottles of water, then collapsed in his chair. The soft chorus of the buffalo rattle still whispered in his head. Eyelids too heavy to resist, he closed his eyes for but a moment.

When they opened two hours later, his mind was silent and still.

Fatigue conspired to lure him to bed, which looked far too tempting. The next day would be as important as this one, if not more so. Cleansed physically and spiritually, he was now properly prepared to begin a fast and petition *Maheo* for answers.

SARA'S CABIN
RURAL FALCON RIDGE
June 14, Thursday
2:32 p.m.

Sara sat on her favorite boulder beneath a sky that wore its signature shade of blue, undisturbed by clouds. Technically, it was her backyard, the property including as far as she could see of the surrounding land. The view was spectacular. With a touch of imagination, she could envision being airborne like an eagle, high above the jagged peaks.

The sun was high, its rays warm on her shoulders. Her pony tail peeked through the back of the dark green *Bitte ein Bit* baseball cap Bryan got overseas, the saying a popular slogan for a German beer. Sunglasses and her Glock finished her ensemble, which otherwise comprised the usual khaki shorts and polo shirt, also Bryan's. She often wore his clothes when he was alive, so didn't think much of it.

This place along the path, where she met Charlie last time, was where she went to meditate or talk to Bryan. Whether or not he answered she wasn't sure, but she often sensed his love or sometimes words that sounded like him came into her head.

The vocabulary and syntax fit, so she liked to think that it was, though logic claimed it was probably her imagination. So far he hadn't provided any clarification regarding what he meant by finding the answer in the stars, however.

She suspected part of it referred to Patrice, yet the woman hadn't provided definitive information, only clues. Then again, it wasn't like Bryan knew she'd go to an astrologer. Maybe it hadn't referred to her at all. She sure nailed it with Charlie, though.

At least so far.

So the information was "in the stars."

Bryan always loved astronomy. They spent numerous evenings stargazing, when he taught her most of the constellations. She was so excited that first time she saw Saturn through the telescope in all its ringed glory. The Moon, likewise, was glorious, especially the mountain shadows along the terminator, where its light and dark sides met.

A spark of inspiration flashed, like static escaping a doorknob on a cold winter day. City lights at their condo precluded a decent view of the night sky, or *seeing* as Bryan called it. Thus, they kept the telescope up there, in the closet on the landing outside their bedroom.

Maybe. . .

She got up, sorry to leave her perch, but too curious to wait. The descent went slower than preferred, but recent injuries reminded her to slow down. Once inside, she tossed her sunglasses on the kitchen counter and made her way up the stairs.

She opened the closet door, confronted by all their ski gear. She bit her lip. That wouldn't be happening again any time soon. Furthermore, her favorite skis were somewhere in Dead Horse Canyon. Going alone wouldn't be the same, anyway. She pushed their bunny suits aside, the fact two were missing another gut-wrenching reminder.

The huge telescope box stood upright in the far corner. She felt down its side for the leather strap that secured it and doubled as a handle. It wasn't so much heavy as bulky, but she groaned as sore muscles joined the rib's strident protest as she wrestled it out.

Once she dragged it into the bedroom, she tipped it onto the bed and opened it, not sure what, if anything, she was looking for. The telescope, mounting bracket, and tripod were all secured by sculpted foam, eye pieces in a separate box.

She opened it and peered inside—nothing but optics. A soft bag held their observation log. A planetsphere that showed the positions of the stars for different dates and times. A laser pointer. A small flashlight with red tape over the lens.

She took everything out and lined it up on the bed, looking for anything out of place.

So far, nothing.

Removing the foam from the box to check underneath revealed nothing there, either. She sat on the bed and folded her arms.

All his books on astronomy were downstairs. In the storage bench, where she found the old property and well records.

Maybe he hid something down there.

> *They that can give up essential liberty to obtain a little temporary safety deserve neither liberty nor safety.*
> — *Benjamin Franklin*

38. IN THE STARS

MONTGOMERY RESIDENCE
BOULDER
June 14, Thursday
3:08 p.m.

Will was supposedly working from home, but couldn't concentrate. That conglomeration of circles wouldn't leave his mind's eye. It had to be what Sara and Bryan stumbled upon. It was some big deal, or wouldn't have jeopardized their lives.

What the Sam Hell was it?

A raucous clamor sounded overhead. A chopper. A big one. Not the usual air traffic that frequented Boulder's local airports. The Diagonal Highway was often patrolled by news helicopters. With it only about three o'clock, a tad early for commuter hour, it could be covering a wreck.

He got up from his chair and adjusted the blinds. The racket increased. Definitely a military chopper, not Life Flight or news media. Windows rattled. Small items fell over on his desk, some clattered to the floor.

The craft loomed into view, no more than a hundred feet above ground. Far below the legal flight limit. Even more disturbing, it was black. Not a single registration mark. A Black Hawk that was clearly armed.

His heartrate spiked.

Was it going to land? Open fire?

Time froze as adrenaline-saturated blood slammed through his veins. The house shook beneath the rotors' thundering blades.

Window panes buzzed in their frames, vibrations so severe he expected them to shatter. He stepped back, just in case.

His vision blurred. *Why?* Blood pressure? Or trembling glass?

Still, the chopper hung there, dark and ominous, seconds like hours.

An eternity later, it banked and retreated toward the south, racket fading.

He exhaled hard.

What was *that* all about? Some sort of veiled threat?

His mind raced, as if trying to keep up with his heartrate. As much as he wanted to believe it was random, his gut told him otherwise. He was snooping where he didn't belong. Knowing those people, they always found out. *Always.* Such had already killed his son-in-law and targeted his daughter.

Was he on their list, too?

He thought of what he told Sara about laying low. On the other hand, if enough people knew, then the bad guys had fewer options. Then they just debunked the story, disparaged the witnesses, and waited for the problem to go away. At this point, however, not enough people were aware of the facts to implement that approach. So few were easily silenced with intimidation.

In some cases permanently.

Another factor struck—he'd taken security oaths. So had Bryan. That obligation didn't go away, often lasting decades or even a lifetime. Those who took solemn vows of secrecy acknowledged lethal consequences were possible. Waived their constitutional right to a fair trial. Even though their oaths were for different matters, the same principles applied. They were accountable for snooping, to say nothing of releasing classified information.

Phil Schneider came to mind. A Department of Defense contractor who'd gone public about an event he witnessed. A year or so later he turned up dead. Ruled a suicide—until his ex-wife insisted on an autopsy. Then it was clear he'd been strangled—not the usual suicide choice. They didn't take out everyone who knew, but eliminated the primary witness, sending a strong message.

Sara, on the other hand, did not take any such oaths, but was considered complicit to Bryan's actions, judging by recent events. Without the data, however, she couldn't do much. When she found it, however, her threat was equal to Bryan's.

He hadn't felt this helpless since Sara's mother, Ellen, wasted away before his eyes from Lou Gehrig's disease.

His reverie halted when Connie pounded up the stairs. She stopped dead on the threshold, wide eyes locked on his.

"What was that all about?" she asked.

He gestured for her to sit down. She dropped into his recliner, her usual cheerful demeanor nowhere to be found.

"I'm not sure," he said. "I suspect a warning."

Her mouth fell open. "What are we going to do, Will? Are we a target now, too?"

"I don't know. It's possible. Bryan obviously uncovered a real can of worms. Now we're in on it, too."

"What about Sara? Is she safer at her cabin or with us?"

"Good question. If they have us in their sights, it doesn't make much difference. My gut tells me separate is better for now. Why give them a single target?"

Her shoulders slumped. "That's not very reassuring."

"I know. I need to get in touch with her somehow. Find out what's going on. I wonder if she found something."

Her eyes snagged his again.

He knew that look.

"What is it, Connie? Do you know something you haven't told me?" Her nervous titter said it all. "Okay. Out with it."

"I think Sara's on to something, finding whatever Bryan discovered."

It was a toss-up whether to laugh or strangle her. He shifted to his most patient persona. "Go on."

"Promise you won't get mad? Or think I'm crazy?"

"*Hmmmph.* You drive a hard bargain, woman."

"Well?"

"I suppose."

"Okay."

She cleared her throat and squared her shoulders. He couldn't imagine what was coming, but it was going to be good. Her eyes locked with his.

"When Sara stayed at the condo she had this dream or something, where Bryan told her the information was 'out there.'"

He scrutinized her over the top of his glasses. "Out *there*?"

"Yes. He was very vague and mysterious. Even said the answer was, well, 'in the stars.'"

A sarcastic remark almost escaped, but he caught himself. He folded his arms. "What do you think that means?"

"Sara has no idea, either. Except. . ." Her expression turned pained, nose crinkled.

"Go on," he prompted.

"When she and I were out shopping, we, uh, made another, well, stop." She bit her lip.

He lowered his chin, but held her gaze. "Just say it, Connie. The suspense is killing me."

She flinched, then blurted out, "I took her to see Patrice. My astrologer. So Sara called her to ask about the dream."

His eyes flicked upward, but he bit his tongue. As weird as things were lately, answers from the great beyond might be exactly what they needed.

"An astrologer. *Ohhh-kaaay.* So. What did this woman have to say?"

"She basically confirmed what Bryan told her."

I'll just bet she did, he thought.

"She, meaning Patrice, thought that their friend, Charlie, may have some information. Or an idea where to find it. Sara was going to check with him when she got back. That's why she was in such a hurry to go back to the cabin."

Will pressed his lips together and collapsed into his office chair. "That's not a bad idea. He and Bryan were close. They may have talked about things he didn't tell Sara. Guy talk." She gave *him* a look. "Alright, we don't tell you gals everything, either. I admit it. So, have you heard anything back?"

"No. She may not know anything yet. And I hesitate to call. Just in case—"

"—they're listening," he finished for her. "And she may well feel the same way about contacting us, even with the burner. Not being able to use it at home is a major drawback. They probably have a tracking device on her new car by now, too."

"Yes. She may be saving the burner for a real emergency. Plus they don't have all the features of a regular phone. I've been playing with mine. I don't even think they can text."

Connie jumped when his fist slammed the desk.

"Damn! What's the matter with me? Besides the burners, we should have set up some sort of code and gotten new email addresses. We need secure communications, but must assume any electronic means will be compromised sooner or later. Technology has advanced exponentially since I was involved with any of that stuff. Their capabilities now are incomprehensible."

He growled with disgust. "And with those spooks all over us, there aren't many options. They could have bugged this place, too." He slapped his forehead. "Like when we all had dinner after her last wreck. *Damn!*"

Connie's expression switched to pensive. "That reminds me of something else. She wondered if she should get a carry license. If so, she said to text her that 'the cat is alive.' If not, that it's dead."

"Hmmmm. Have to think about that. I can think of pros and cons either way." He froze when his phone chirped. A text from Sara's regular phone.

"What?" Connie prompted. "Is it Sara?"

"Yes. *Huh.* She invited us out this Sunday. For her birthday."

"That's right! With all the excitement I plum forgot. That's perfect. She may have some news."

"I'm sure she does."

"What should we get her for her birthday?"

"I don't know, Connie. How about a case of forty caliber hollow points or an AR-15?"

SARA'S CABIN
RURAL FALCON RIDGE
June 14, Thursday
3:50 p.m.

After texting her father, Sara knelt in front of the storage bench and lifted the lid. She set the blankets and tools on the bed behind her, then spent a moment examining them. They were undoubtedly antiques and actually pretty cool. Great wall decorations.

Something to do later.

At least she could eliminate the old wooden box that held the property records. Others were likewise wood, darkened with age. Some were cardboard, newer ones colorful plastic. The wooden ones were probably more old stuff, perhaps clear back to his grandfather. Unlikely to contain anything she needed. She stacked them beside her.

She opened the nested flaps of one made of cardboard.

Family albums.

Old ones.

She took one out and flipped through it. Black and white photos. Bryan's parents, maybe even grandparents. Bryan as a baby, a toddler, an adorable little boy.

That same crooked smile.

Tears filled her eyes.

If only they'd had a child together. When he got out of the service they were thoroughly engrossed with being together at last, working, and saving for the future. Why on earth did they wait? She forced herself to close the box along with numerous vain regrets.

She added it to the growing stack of wooden ones and checked another similar one. Nothing but unlabeled photographs, mostly soldiers and memorabilia from some tropical area. Probably Vietnam. An envelope held his father's army discharge papers. She set it aside as unlikely to contain anything.

A blue plastic file case appeared more recent. She opened it. A rolled-up shoulder sash covered with embroidered patches—Boy Scout Merit Badges. A banner—*Order of the Arrow.*

Interesting, considering his closeness to Charlie.

An album contained Merit Badge documentation and numerous certificates he'd earned. The heading on one caught her eye.

The Boy Scout Motto.

"Be Prepared."

Indeed.

She turned each page, not surprised that his favorite, even then, involved astronomy. As a project he'd tracked a retrograde cycle of Mars, using photos to illustrate its loop in the sky and explaining the phenomena in a report printed out by a dot matrix printer.

In the stars. . .

Interest aroused, she thumbed through it. Nothing that resembled an electronic device.

Another album lay beneath. The front sheet protector contained his Eagle Scout certificate. The next page held his project approval application. His proposal comprised creating a website of comparative astronomy, that of the Navajos along with those popular in modern America.

Her heart tripped a faster beat.

Could it be?

Her hand trembled as she read through his suggested content. Most of the constellations were those he taught her. Ursa Major and Minor, Cassiopeia, Orion, Canus Major and Minor, and those that marked the ecliptic or path of the Sun, commonly known as the zodiac.

She smiled. Patrice would love it.

The last one was unfamiliar. A constellation called Argo. It contained a star second in brightness only to Sirius named Canopus. Navajos knew it as the Coyote Star.

Since he'd received his Eagle Award, he must have completed the website.

So where was it?

Such things lurked on the internet forever unless removed. Even then, they often continued to live in caches and mirror sites *ad infinitum.*

Dot matrix printed pages covered with HTML coding occupied the last several sheets. She pawed through them, eventually finding hosting information, the URL, and, most important of all, log-in data for editing purposes.

She closed the album with trembling hands.

Now what?

CHARLIE'S CABIN
RURAL FALCON RIDGE
June 15, Friday
4:01 a.m.

It was still dark when Charlie awoke the next morning. He braided his hair, then wrapped each one with strips of red cloth. His feet occupied his grandfather's beaded moccasins, deerskin wound and tied in place around his hips. Still damp from the previous day's sweat, the leather's cool touch magnified the predawn chill.

The earth paints needed for the fast were lined up on his kitchen table.

Blue. Yellow. Black. White.

A dream the night before refreshed his memory of when Eaglefeathers painted his uncle's body for his ceremonial fast on *Novavose*. He prayed to express gratitude for the timely reminder, an important component he'd forgotten.

The correct application of Cheyenne fasting paint demanded precision and the inclusion of many important details. Thus, he also prayed for guidance applying the symbols and colors in the proper manner.

He shook some of each color into separate bowls, added a little water, then mixed them with a tree branch until the powder dissolved.

He coated the tip of his index finger with blue, placed it on the top of his forehead, dragged it in a line to his ear, then straight down to the bottom of his chin. Repeating the same strokes on the other side created a diamond shape. The symbol that identified him as one of the Morning Star people.

With yellow he traced a circle over his heart. Wetting his finger with paint again, he placed it in the circle's center and moved outward in a spiral until the symbol on his chest was solid yellow, representing the sun. Inviting *Maheo* into his heart.

Returning to blue, he drew a quarter moon on his left chest/shoulder then a blue full moon on right.

Next came black, made from burnt cottonwood. Dodging the other markings he covered his face, neck, body, and both arms, then from below his knee to his ankle. Lastly, white dots representing stars decorated his neck, body, and arms.

When finished, his body was a work of sacred art. Tied to *Maheo's* creations as a child of the universe. Such a declaration drew the spirits more quickly.

He rolled up the sacred red pipe and eagle bone whistle in the badger hide, draped his blanket over his bare shoulders, then set out for the sweat lodge, flashlight lighting the way.

Warmth gathered around him, followed by a voice that whispered to his mind.

Grandson, I am pleased you remember my teachings. Your labors show your heart is sincere and you are ready to walk the Red Road as a Tseteshestahese *man. Continue as you were taught and you will find what you seek.*

Indigenous people recognized dawn was a sacred time when the dark of night yielded to the light of day. If everyone greeted the sun in the proper spirit the earth would know peace, which was how *Maheo* intended for people to live.

Amasani taught him Diné traditions, such as those in the Winter Stories about the stars and how they related to finding answers in a heliacal rise. The Cheyenne greeted the dawn and beseeched *Maheo* for answers in a slightly different way. Having both in his heart and blood was a great blessing.

When he reached the sweat lodge he retrieved the man sage cushion from within, then sat outside between the door and fire pit facing east, though sunrise would occur toward the northeast that time of year. The ashes retained a subtle glow and hint of warmth from the day before. He spread the badger hide on the ground, then placed the pipe stem and bowl in the center, tobacco to one side.

As more and more teachings came back, he realized how fortunate he'd been to receive answers from his previous fast. His early steps returning to his roots stumbled as a toddler learning to walk. But *Maheo* knew his heart and still responded after he'd fasted four days. This time he would do it correctly.

Would it still require four days?

He didn't know, only that he would remain in place as long as necessary.

A breeze rustled through the leaves and whispered through the pines. He shivered as he watched the sky, awaiting first light. When a hint of pink appeared he got up, removed the blanket from his shoulders, folded it, and placed it on top of the man sage forming a comfortable seat.

He picked up the pipe stem, held it in the crook of his arm. His grandfather's words flowed as water as he attached, then loaded the bowl:

Vehoe *stole our freedom, our land, and our lives. They cannot take* Maheo *from us. He gave us our sacred red pipe.*

The Sun burst free.

He held the eagle whistle to his lips and blew.

Its piercing cry broke the stillness, announcing his presence and humble request for an audience with the grandfather spirits.

He struck the match, touched it to the tobacco.

Blessed the stem and bowl with the first sweet breath of pungent smoke.

Maheo *is our creator. He created us to live in peace. He has opened your eyes to who you are. Your brother died that another truth be told. He was killed by evil men. You will soon know who murdered your brother. He wants the truth to be told to the people.*

The impression drifted through his consciousness as feathers in the wind. Soft, yet tangible. Forceful, yet filled with love.

Sacred smoke swirled skyward, carrying the thoughts, prayers, and desires of his heart.

Forgiveness for his arrogance, from both *Maheo* and Eaglefeathers. Strength to conquer his weaknesses. Wisdom to see beneath the surface. Understand his life's purpose.

For his daughters, Carla and Charlene. To be a better father. Improve his home so they could spend more time with him.

Have the means to pay back Sara for the bail and impound money.

Learn patience, particularly with Dr. Phil. Refrain from reciprocating the hatred he felt being sent his way.

Know why he stumbled onto a job that violated the Earth. What was he there to do? To learn?

Expose Bryan's killers. Help Sara find the truth of what he'd discovered, for which he died. Avenge his murder according to *Maheo's* will.

The high-pitched cry of a bird of prey pierced his awareness. His eyes opened. A pair of bald eagles circled the space directly above the sweat lodge complex, beckoning.

The grandfather spirits had arrived.

He reached out to join them with mind and heart. Moments later, he soared beside them. The domed structure shrank as his spirit ascended skyward. The forest stretched out below, treetops bathed in morning light. Vegetation yielded to a towering cliff.

Halfway down, a treacherous strip of road hugged its side— the blind turn overlooking Dead Horse Canyon.

A black Suburban approached the bend. It slowed, then stopped before completing the turn. A man got out. He stepped to the edge. Peered into the ravine. Then gave the driver a thumbs-up and got back inside.

The SUV crept around the turn to a look-out point hidden from oncoming traffic. It stopped, then backed up, facing the drop-off. A heavy brush guard, like those on law enforcement vehicles, protected the radiator. It sat there, engine running.

Waiting. . .

Bryan's moving pickup appeared, the size of a cricket. The Silverado approached the turn. The SUV burst from the shoulder in a cloud of dust, engine roaring.

"No! Lookout! No!" Charlie screamed, words an eerie wail that ripped through the forest below. He braced for the impact, eyes closed, but the vision persisted.

An involuntary gasp escaped when the SUV slammed the truck's driverside door. It backed up, then shot forward again to shove its prey over the side. Twenty feet down, it struck a ledge, nose first. It hovered a moment, bed in the air, then slammed down, upright again on its precarious perch. A small tree kept it from plunging to the bottom of the canyon.

Wounds that had barely begun to heal ripped open upon witnessing Bryan's brutal murder a second time. His heart ached and throat closed as the disturbing scene continued.

Instead of leaving, several men exited the SUV and looked over the side. They exchanged high-fives, then got back in their vehicle. It continued up the road and parked where Charlie left his truck during his original fast.

The men got out, opened the cargo compartment, and unloaded an ice chest. They opened it up, each retrieving a can of beer, then sat around, joking and drinking.

The shrill scream of sirens interrupted their revelry.

A police car arrived. Then an ambulance and the Belton Fire Department rescue team. One man left the SUV to converse with the cops, who soon left, then joined the others watching the rescue operation.

Fire Department personnel donned safety harnesses and rappelled down to the truck. The passenger-side door opened with a few sharp tugs. They removed Sara's unconscious body and secured her to a litter. Pulleys lifted it to ground level where they transferred her to the ambulance. It left, siren blaring and lights flashing.

The screech of an abrasive saw announced efforts to remove the driver's side door and recover Bryan's body, more difficult with it overlooking the yawning precipice. His limp, blood-covered body rode another litter topside. A second ambulance arrived. Their gruesome task complete, it departed at normal speed, followed by the rescue team.

The men strolled over to the accident site and belayed rappelling lines from the aspen beside the road. Two donned harnesses and descended to the truck. One went to each side and started extracting everything from the cab. A short time later each exited with a bag. One man took both, then yanked his rope, those at ground level hauling him back up.

Meanwhile, the other man removed a chainsaw from his backpack and cut partway through the small tree holding the truck on the ledge. Then he came around to the passenger side and yanked the tether. The topside team raised him several feet off the ledge to a small spur.

He kicked off, swinging on his harness. Oscillating back and forth, he repeatedly kicked the pickup's frame above the passenger door.

After several strikes, the truck listed to the side. The tree gave way. As if in slow motion, Bryan's pickup slid sideways, then tumbled over the edge. After a spectacular fall, it landed with an earsplitting crash, water spraying in every direction.

The men cheered as if their team had just scored the winning touchdown at the Superbowl. They hauled the second man to street level. Exchanged more high-fives. Then climbed in their Suburban and sped off in the direction from which they came.

The dashcam video had already provided similar, though less detailed information. Why see it again? As his mind sought the reason, once again he found himself seated between the sweat lodge and fire pit. He stared into the ashes, stunned, while his breathing and heartrate returned to normal.

His hands still trembled when, at last, he puffed again, prayers for clarity ascending skyward as his meditation continued.

Time collapsed amid the sensory bouquet of tobacco fumes, connecting him with earth and sky. At length, the vapors failed to dissipate. Rather, they spiraled, forming a blinding orb surrounded by starkest blue. It expanded, then burst, revealing a portal of dazzling white. A personage appeared, increasing in size as it floated toward him. While featureless, its identity was unmistakable.

His white brother beckoned. Charlie's spirit soared forth to join him in the light. It wrapped around them like a dancing shawl, folding back the years to when they were carefree youth.

The hour was late, the pair sitting before a dying campfire. Sparks flew skyward, blending with a sky so alive with stars it was difficult to distinguish individual constellations.

"What meaning do your people place on the stars?" Bryan asked.

Charlie stared into what was left of the fire, unsure how to respond. The summer sky was less known to the Diné. Astronomy and star myths were part of their oral tradition of Winter Stories, told from October to late February. Only then were such things discussed. The Upper Darkness was sacred. Its secrets known only to medicine men and a few chosen elders.

Amasani taught him the entire Universe was an interrelated, sacred organism. Rather than viewed as a scientific curiosity to be violated with instruments and space probes, it represented all of creation and how everything was spiritually connected. Integral to their existence. Traditional hogans and most sweat lodges were octagonal or circular, representing the sky, then oriented according to cosmic directions and principles.

"Do you see the star patterns as people?" Bryan prodded. "Or animals, with stories about them?"

He assessed the celestial dome ablaze with stars, awed by their mysterious beauty. His *amasani's* words haunted him, leaving him uncomfortable. It was summer, not winter. However, it was within days of the solstice. A time when it was okay to talk about some aspects of the heavens.

Thus, he reluctantly agreed.

"I'll start," Bryan volunteered, pointing north. "The Big and Little Dipper are two of ours that everyone recognizes. Their official names are Ursa Major, the Big Bear, and Ursa Minor, the Little Bear." He explained how to find Polaris, also known as the North Star, then asked, "Do your people have names for them, too?"

He smiled. "My father's name is Littlebear. Maybe that is where he is. Yes. We, too have a name for the stars that revolve around the one you know as Polaris. To the Diné it is *Náhookos Biko*, the central fire. It has two parts, one male, one female." He pointed to the male component. "That is *Náhookos Bi'ką',* the male revolving one, which is about the same as your Big Bear. The other side, *Náhookos Bi'ááá,* is the female revolving one. We see them as one."

"Interesting," Bryan replied. "We call the female revolving one Cassiopeia, the Great Earth Mother. Do you have a favorite constellation?"

Charlie stood and pointed south. "Yes. *Ma'ii Bizo',* the Coyote Star." He directed his brother's attention to the bright reddish star riding the horizon below Sirius. It was barely visible in Colorado, more easily seen in *Diné Bikéyah*, their traditional land in the American Southwest.

"Why?"

"As a child, coyote was part of my favorite stories. Many were lessons intended to scare us so we'd behave. As a trickster, he's not always good. Some believe he's a bad omen. I liked his clever nature."

"Like our cartoon character, Wile. E. Coyote. Except he gets his butt kicked by a roadrunner. I like that, a bird beating his enemy. I've been told I'm mischievous. But I hate being bored. I like adventure."

He marveled at how much he had in common with his white brother. "Does our Coyote Star have meaning for you as well?"

"Yes. We call it Canopus. It's a guiding star. In the south, opposite Polaris. Sailors used it for navigation. It's the keel of a great ship. Part of the constellation Argo."

Charlie blinked, startled.

He was back in the present, bathed in the full light of midday.

The pipe had burnt itself out. He closed his eyes, trying to absorb all he'd seen before lighting it again.

Great spirits have often encountered violent opposition from mediocre minds.
— Albert Einstein

39. CONNECTIONS

COSMIC PORTALS
BOULDER
June 15, Friday
1:42 p.m.

Patrice sat at the counter in *Cosmic Portals,* sipping her mid-afternoon chai latté, listed on her menu as a *Nebula.* Violet-streaked platinum hair graced her shoulders and back like drifted snow. An ankle length, multi-tiered skirt, vibrant in shades of turquoise, blue, green, magenta, and of course, purple, cascaded to the floor. It hid her bare feet, manicured toes curled around the stool's bottom rung.

Her reverie halted when she sensed a call coming in. Not her cell phone—someone tapping on her psyche. She wasn't clairvoyant or as psychically gifted as some of her peers. Spending as much time as she did in transcendental time, however, she was sensitized to such promptings.

Who was it? A friend? A client?

Usually it was one or the other, someone she'd hear from within a day or so. She closed her eyes and tuned in, trying to identify the psi-gifted visitor. The result presented an enigma. Someone she didn't know, yet familiar. The vibes were pure, clear, and uncluttered, different from the troubled people who sought her counsel. Instinct suggested someone in touch with the unseen realm. Perhaps with indigenous blood.

Of course! That friend of Sara's.

What was his name?

Ah, yes—Charlie.

She tuned in more carefully, trying to figure out why he was in her space. Something about Sara's reading. *Aha!* He was stuck somewhere between skepticism toward western astrologers and whether she were a witch, or perhaps a visionary.

She understood the holistic nature of Native American beliefs and their disdain for the white man's lack of spirituality. To many tribes, certain portions of the heavens were sacred. Revealing its secrets to the uninitiated was deemed highly offensive. Many indigenous spiritual leaders disapproved of astronomy for similar reasons.

Which explained a distrust of astrologers.

In reality, she couldn't agree more with regard to how man should live in harmony with nature. At least they had that much in common. Indigenous beliefs were based on animism. Everything had a spirit and all were connected. People, plants, animals, minerals, even the Earth herself. Not unlike The Force in the movie *Star Wars,* all of which fit her own beliefs.

Not wanting to be distracted by coffee shop patrons or walk-in clients, she picked up her latté and with a multi-colored flourish, glided toward the reading room entrance kitty-corner from the counter. She hung a *Do Not Disturb* sign decorated with a sleepy crescent moon on the doorframe, then rustled through the beaded strands.

This was going to be fun.

She sat down at her table, hands flat on its silk covering, and concentrated on the incoming vibes. When she sensed a clear signal, she responded with thoughts of greeting.

Namaste, Charlie. What can I do for you today?

She giggled at his startled response. *Do you have questions about what I told Sara?* When he didn't answer, she pinged him again. *Yes, I'm really here. I felt you thinking about me. What would you like to know?*

The beauty of such communications was that so much could be conveyed wordlessly, mind to mind, at the speed of thought. Furthermore, heart-felt questions carried an emotional link to the timeless domain of spirit. To help him feel more comfortable, she sent a blast of love, respect, support, and acceptance.

After a short delay, what came back was confusion about the astrological chart. He didn't understand what it represented. To refresh her memory she brought up Sara's reading on her computer. With such information confidential, she made no attempt to remember the specifics of what she told clients.

She projected the image and started to explain. The outer circle represented the ecliptic, or path of the Sun as viewed from the Earth. The horizontal line through the middle represented the horizon with east on the left, west on the right. The Midheaven near the top was where the Sun was at noon, directly below that where it was at midnight.

It took only seconds to imprint his mind with the glyphs for the signs of the zodiac, sun, moon, and planets, coupled with their respective energies. Then she projected another data dump explaining the astrological houses and how each represented specific parts of life.

He soaked it up like the proverbial sponge.

That is similar to our Medicine Wheel, he responded. *It is also oriented to the cardinal directions. What I don't understand is how you determined that I would be the one to provide Sara with answers?*

She explained, after which he shared the dashcam experience, leaving Patrice the one who was stunned.

He sought further insights, but they were elusive. He explained his visions at sunrise two days before, likewise those so far, during his spiritual journey. One revelation clarified what occurred during and after the wreck. The other was a flashback of him and Bryan exchanging their understanding of the constellations, years before.

Where is this Coyote Star? she asked. *Do you know our name for it?*

To you it is Canopus.

Ah, yes. The pathfinder star. Not always an easy journey.

Indeed it is not. You told Sara I could help her find the evidence. The dashcam confirmed the accident was deliberate. But we need the information Bryan gathered. Is it still out there somewhere?

Patrice turned back to the computer for another look. *I believe so. It's hidden, possibly in intangible form. Perhaps electronic. Or on the internet. Bryan told Sara in a dream it was in the stars. Does that mean anything to you?*

Not so far. But it must be important because my vision of Bryan also mentioned the stars. How it relates to finding the information, I don't know. Thus, I thought of you.

She sensed he was smiling. She did likewise, hoping someday they'd meet.

By the way, what is your name? he asked.

Patrice. So you had an impression at sunrise?

Yes.

It's a magical time, isn't it? Dawn teaches us that there is much light prior to the actual rising of the sun. In other words, if you're attentive, you can see the signs of what's to come and how to prepare. Were you watching to see which star would rise before the sun? His reaction indicated surprise.

Yes.

She grinned. Many cultures recognized the significance of a heliacal rise. *Which one was it?*

The stars of the constellation you call Orion.

What did this tell you, if you're willing to share? She crossed her fingers.

That I should take action. What that is, I do not know. Perhaps something that involves protection. To be a warrior.

Let me take a look at the chart for that time and see if anything else stands out. That was Wednesday, correct?

Yes.

She entered the approximate time for sunrise on June 13, around 5:30 a.m., then adjusted it until the sun was a bit below the chart's ascendant, so named for where the sun rises.

Okay, she responded. *Canopus, your Coyote Star, relates in some way. It is trine Neptune, which lasts for a long time. Canopus doesn't move and Neptune moves very slowly. This combination suggests it will bring inspiration that will help you know what to do. It will have a strong emotional effect. Sara may know something related to this star as well.*

Interesting. I'll check with her. Thank you. That confirms it has meaning.

Before you go, may I ask you something?

Of course. I have asked you many things.

Are you a shaman, Charlie?

All she sensed was a burst of static, suggesting confusion or surprise. Did she offend him? Certainly not her intent. She was about to apologize when she felt the gentle psychic ripple she recognized as sigh.

Actually, my people prefer to be called healers or medicine men. The answer is no. But I was supposed to be.

She frowned, surprised. *What happened?*

My grandfather told me I was to follow his path. I was young. Stupid. Torn between my people and the world of the white man. I studied the environment as the white man knows it, as science. Not a living being animated by spirits. I also studied chemistry. Everything I was told conflicted with the beliefs of my people. I felt foolish for believing the old ways. My heart failed in its ability to embrace my heritage. I rejected my grandfather's teachings. I accept them now and am trying to learn. But he crossed over years ago. He's gone. And I must make a living. I am again caught in the white man's world.

Patrice's heart sensed his ennui. *Charlie, listen to me. Your world is as real as the modern one. There are other dimensions. If there weren't, we wouldn't be having this conversation. Much of what they teach in college is lacking at best and wrong at worst. You have no idea how many clients I have who are educated. Medical doctors, engineers, mayors, people in all professions. They would be mocked and ridiculed for consulting me, yet they do. Why? Because astrology works.*

You are one of the fortunate ones, she went on. *You know both sides. You have the missing pieces that your people have known for millennia. If you don't mind giving me your date, time, and place of birth, I'd love to look at what the heavens were saying. Your cosmic birth announcement, if you will.*

She willed more caring his way, hoping.

I was born the same day as Sara's husband. September 9, 1981 at 9:31 in the morning. In Albuquerque.

She typed in the data, saved it, and seconds later the chart appeared on her screen. She laughed—hard—as she always did when her expectations proved correct. In this case, it was a configuration known as a yod that denoted a life driven by fate.

The three components included Neptune (spirituality) and Pluto (the underworld) at the base, with Chiron (the wounded healer asteroid) at the eye, which fit the calling of a medicine man perfectly, all of which was further emphasized by their house placements. Its influence was activated by the same heavy transits in effect for Bryan's accident.

With he and Bryan born the same day, the transits were transformational to both, but in different ways determined by the house placements.

Following your grandfather's footsteps is your destiny. What I see here tells me you are already a healer, you just need to learn the particulars. It's a configuration sometimes called "the finger of God." It's shaped like an arrow with an asteroid we call the "wounded healer" at the point of the arrow.

Her heart swelled, witnessing the statement's truth, a similar reaction reflected back from him, particularly at her reference to an arrow.

Tell me about this wounded healer, he said.

It's an asteroid named Chiron, after a mythological centaur. His meaning suggests some wounds never heal. What we suffer prepares us to help others who are experiencing similar pain. Does that fit the role of a medicine man?

Yes, very much, he replied. *I have heard that great suffering is to be expected along the path. Perhaps it is not too late.*

Her feelings toward him warmed even more.

It was written in the heavens when you were born. Thus, it's never too late. This part of your life was activated the day of the accident, so now is exactly the right time for you to pursue it. Whatever happened to keep you away before doesn't matter. It was experience you were meant to have. Now is your time. If you deny it again, however, you will pay. Probably in a very unpleasant way.

His energy felt troubled, like funnel clouds before a violent storm. *I have been paying,* he responded. *Life has been hard since I turned away. Very hard. Now it makes sense. You are right, Patrice.*

I work with the same energy, Charlie. In the same dimension, just in a different way. In that respect, we speak the same language. Listen to your heart. Like they say, when the student is ready, the teacher appears. Now is your time. If I can ever help, call me anytime.

Thank you. I will save your contact information.

Patrice tucked a strand of silver hair behind her ear and grinned. Intrigued by the similarities, she promised herself to learn more about the Medicine Wheel.

She sensed they would meet relatively soon, but the circumstances felt ominous. She noted the yod's degrees and bit her lip. The New Moon, known to trigger events, connected with it a few days before.

Would it bring a pleasing fireworks display? Or a nuclear bomb?

BKSS LLC
ALBUQUERQUE
June 15, Friday
4:09 p.m.

Bernie leaned against the outside wall of his office and took a few baby hits from a joint while Terminator took a dump, then ran off some pent-up canine energy in the weed-infested lot behind the building. His thoughts wandered back to fighting overseas, of firing up a doob and watching bullets fly in slow motion on the way to their target, before the advent of tracers. Days of zig-zag paper and wheat straws, weed rolled the size of cigars. Another world from today's pussy boys with their pinch pipes.

Nothing was the same any more, even the dope.

He took another hit, then studied its smoldering tip. Actually, this batch was pretty clean. Stronger now, no buds or seeds. Really smooth. Good shit.

His eyes remained on his dog, but his mind and gut screeched in a discordant duet that so far marijuana hadn't squelched. Now he faced a different foe. Not paying attention to details had turned what was supposed to be a cake-walk into a cluster-fuck.

Key words in his contract blared through his head like a klaxon alarm: *Assure the security of the PURF site.*

Period.

Perimeter security.

Make sure no one intruded on the property.

A no-brainer.

Set out a bunch of electronic intrusion alarm devices and watch for violations. As isolated as it was, it should have been easy money. It's not like it had the allure of Area 51 or some other secret site that sucked in UFO buffs or other nut-jobs like a diesel powered sump pump.

Now in addition to simply securing the property, they were tasked with protecting the data.

No longer simple.

Not even close.

Furthermore, when the additional responsibilities landed on his head like bird crap during a casual walk on the beach, it blew their budget to smithereens.

So much for any bonus.

All as dictated by that asshole, Steinbrenner, whose organization was responsible for the data leak in the first place. The idiot couldn't even provide industry-standard cyber security, much less what was required for classified government work.

Without that major screw-up—one that bordered on criminal negligence—the problem wouldn't even exist.

At least now that idiot was out of the picture. The Corps of Engineers would manage it to completion. The lead guy seemed like a straight shooter unlikely to run off with the money.

He took another thoughtful hit, still awaiting the onset of its calming effects. Some fifty yards away, Terminator took off after some unseen quarry. He whistled. The dog froze. His massive head turned toward him, then back toward his target. He whistled again, louder. Gave the hand gesture to return.

The rottie took another longing look afield, then loped toward him at a leisurely pace. When the canine returned, albeit reluctantly, he got a treat and a pat on the head. He gobbled it down, then sat beside Bernie's prosthetic leg and emitted a jowl-flapping canine sigh.

His ponderings resumed, turning to Reynolds, who had the hacking skills to find the incriminating data in their original repositories, much of which he'd done. Going through the man's confiscated files, however, suggested that knowing what to look for and where was handed to him like a treasure map by EMPI.

How'd he even know to look there in the first place? No telling. It had to be leaked from someone at EMPI. They were geographically in the same area. All it would take would be one person blabbing information they considered inconsequential being overheard during happy hour.

So that was screw-up number one. Not even his responsibility. That was bad enough. However, it could have—*should have*—ended right there. And would have, if he didn't have a second-rate team who were gaining real-life experience at his expense.

It was a damn shame that woman didn't die in the first wreck. EMPI's goof aside, the data issue wouldn't have escalated any further if his team had done the job right and disconnected the telematics in Reynolds's truck.

At least they'd dodged a bullet for using lethal force on what appeared to be cross-country skiers. It was a gift from above when they discovered they had illegal foreknowledge of the site.

Things continued to go south, however, when they discovered the chick's father was former FBI.

What next?

As an independent special ops team it was a really, really, *really* bad idea to piss off anyone with connections to an alphabet agency. Being black-balled meant automatic rejection for any lucrative contractor jobs—like this one was supposed to be. Definitely bad for business.

Their abysmal luck didn't stop there when the Reynolds chick not only survived, but got the bright idea to carry out her husband's intent to expose the project.

If that happened, everyone was screwed.

Not just him and his team, but all the way into the upper echelons, to those with a vested interest in PURF.

Preventing exposure of any variety was what EMPI and BKSS were responsible for in the first place.

Yeah, right.

With the security work escalated, he desperately needed a research assistant. To provide timely data of critical facts. Like Reynolds having that mountain cabin. His guys sucked at anything beyond boots-on-ground operations. And truth be told, only marginal at that. Except car wrecks. That they could handle. But crashes didn't solve everything.

At least now they had real-time monitoring on numerous channels.

Great.

Except he didn't have the resources to keep up, or even go through all the transcripts. No doubt they'd miss stuff. His greatest fear that it would be something big.

Like the chick finding the data.

When her father figured out what was going on, he'd given her some tips for staying under the radar, which made Bernie's job more complicated. Furthermore, now she was packing, putting his team at risk. Hurting her was a really bad idea, but now his team was in a sorry position if they couldn't shoot back.

He hoped buzzing her old man's place with that Blackhawk would scare them off.

If it didn't, there went another huge, budget-busting mistake.

The only way they could save their collective asses was to find any remaining data stashes before she did. However, according to that crazy star-gazing witch, the Reynolds chick would find it first.

They absolutely had to track her every move. Confiscate it as soon as she found it. Before she has a chance to go public. He could call in NSA assistance, but their services were billed against his contract's charge number. If they weren't careful, he could wind up paying the government instead of *vice versa*.

Speaking of dumbass goofs, another top contender was the dashcam SD card. No telling where that thing wound up. Hopefully lost in that stream where the truck landed. If their quarry got a hold of that, they were screwed in more ways than one.

Johannsen's dumbfounded look when he'd asked where it was would have been hilarious if it weren't so potentially devastating. Seeing his team in action on the evening news during a supposed covert operation topped his list of worst nightmares.

The local police swore that Indian arrested at the site had nothing on him. But how hard was it to stash such a thing? Would cops in such a dink-ball town even recognize it as evidence? What did that sneaky devil expect to find, snooping around down there, anyway? No telling what he was up to.

They needed to check the surveillance video again to see if he'd found anything. So far, they'd only used it to tip off the cops, assuming the cab had been swept clean. Ignoring his soldier instincts early on, when that Indian spent so much time smoking some weird looking pipe at the wreck site, had clearly been a mistake. Hackles teased his arm hair as the eerie feeling staged an encore, defying his efforts to dismiss it as superstitious nonsense.

An approaching plane snagged his attention and he watched it execute a flawless touch down. Would his team pull off a similar landing? Or go down in flames?

He extinguished the joint, took a matchbook out of his pocket, and tucked the butt inside next to the fold line. It went into his wallet for later, while his mind wandered back to which asshole had stolen his roach clip, way-back-when.

Back inside, Terminator resumed his usual post under the desk while Bernie settled in his chair. He felt calmer now, the break worth it. He slipped off his prosthetic leg and leaned it against the wall, then resumed reading the phone transcript between that crazy witch wannabe and the Reynolds chick.

While skeptical of such flakey methodology, he'd been around long enough to see crazier things work than astrology. He'd be as irresponsible as everyone else if he ignored it. Furthermore, since the Reynolds chick summoned the other key players to her place for a birthday celebration, it stood to reason she'd found something.

Then again, maybe not.

It actually *was* her birthday.

Was it really a party?

Or a ploy?

Were they deliberately taunting them into checking it out? What would they do, invite them in for some cake and ice cream? Check your automatic weapons at the door, please?

Another possibility struck. Could it be a trap? Would their own cadre of mercenaries challenge them to a shootout? No specific time was mentioned for this alleged party.

Was that an indication of some sort as well?

He exhaled hard through his nose, peaceful feeling yielding to reality. These people were smart. That made it difficult to stay one step ahead. If it was premature, they could blow the whole thing. His only option was to plan the operation, monitor the feed, and warn Johannsen it could be called off at the last minute.

Maybe that's all it was, a party.

More than ever, everyone's browsing records were critical. If the incriminating data were stored online somewhere, which seemed more and more likely, and the chick managed to find it, they'd be checking it out.

Once his team found out where it was, they could retrieve the files, shut down the relevant IP address, then make sure it disappeared online, once and for all. Tracking down backup and mirror sites wasn't easy, however. For all they knew, Reynolds could have stashed it somewhere on a government server. If he could get in and snoop around, he could just as easily leave something behind. Including a scheduled email to WikiLeaks with instructions on how and where to retrieve it.

It was so considerate of his widow to leave for a few days so they could wire her cabin. So far, the recordings didn't contain anything they didn't already know. The astrologer's prediction that she would be the one to find any further evidence suggested it was in their personal effects somewhere.

Too bad they didn't know about that place earlier. It would have saved a lot of trouble destroying his laptop. Hell, they could have torched the place and been done with it, all evidence destroyed. Maybe they still should.

Unless it actually *was* online somewhere.

That left two options: Raid the place or wait for her to find it. The latter seemed most practical. Let her do the work. Which meant monitoring her activity 24/7.

On the other hand, what if she already had it? If so, how much of a time window did they have before they went public?

Holy shit!

Was that what the party was all about?

Any calm instituted by the joint evaporated as he weighed the pros and cons of each option. His inbox pinged. Another transcript, dated two days before. A conversation in the chick's cabin.

He opened it up, cursing the delay. At least it was short, inflating his hopes it would be benign.

Adult Male: Pretty gruesome, huh?

*Target Female: Very. I need to show these to my father. Okay.
Let's see what's on that other thing. <Pause> Alright. Here we go.
Let's see what we've got. <Pause> Movies? This definitely isn't
from my camera. Those would be jpgs. It could take videos, but we
never did. We used our phones. I have no idea what this is from.
<Pause> Charlie! This is from the dashcam! I had no idea it had
sound, too. I don't know if I can watch this. Oh, my God.*

Bernie threw up his hands and bellowed an F-bomb that
rattled windows in Upstate New York. Terminator scrambled to
his feet. He reached out instinctively to reassure the dog, then
buried his face in his hands.

Shit! Shit! Shit!

Another equally unpleasant thought struck: Why did it end so
abruptly? Did the listening device fail? Did they find and destroy
it? Or know they were being monitored and leave the premises?

Frustration hissed through clenched teeth as he speed-dialed
Johannsen.

To hell with the party. This couldn't wait.

"Hey, boss. What's up?"

"Monitor Device 4A in the chick's cabin real-time, muster the
team, and gear up. That goddamn Indian found the SD card and
they listened to it two days ago."

"Holy shit."

"Yeah. Any indication they're going public or find the other
data, get your sorry asses over there and stop 'em. And while you're
at it, get that SD card. Confiscate any electronics, too. Computers,
phones, tablets, whatever."

"The usual restrictions?"

Bernie ground his teeth, mind racing. If that information went
public, they'd go down like a turd in the toilet. Didn't matter
whether the chick and her Indian friend were dead or alive.

"Shut this thing down, once and for all. By whatever means
necessary. Do not, I repeat, DO NOT screw this up."

"Roger that."

*Our religion is the traditions of our ancestors, the dreams of our old men, given
them by the Great Spirit, and the visions of our sachems, and is written in the
hearts of our people.*
—Seath'tl "Seattle", 1854

40. PREMONITION

SARA'S CABIN
RURAL FALCON RIDGE
June 15, Friday
4:40 p.m.

Ever since the accident the cabin had been Sara's sanctuary. Now she had something to hide, however, which stole her peace and inflated her paranoia, justified because she was being watched.

Since finding Bryan's Eagle Project the day before she'd done little beside pace the floor, unsure what to do until she could talk to Will.

But how?

She glared at the looming triangular windows framing a postcard view of the Rockies. There were no blinds or curtains, either on the ground floor or their bedroom loft. She had no visible neighbors. She and Bryan made love on that sheepskin rug without a thought to being disturbed, much less watched, day or night.

Now she felt naked and vulnerable, even though it was still light and would remain so for hours. Less than a week from the solstice, dusk lingered until after ten o'clock.

Which gave her plenty of time to get to Denver or even Boulder. Considering the last time, whether that would be safer was debatable.

She and her father discussed whether to change the privacy settings on her phone. The good news was that she fixed it so he knew where she was. The bad news, however, was so would everyone else. If she went anywhere, that needed to be turned off, perhaps even the phone itself, plus remove the battery, to be absolutely sure.

Would that make her safer? Or more vulnerable?

Her thoughts tumbled through tangled loops of indecision. If she texted Will or Charlie, that could be hacked. She had the burner, but once she used it from the house it was no better than her other one.

Dare she leave? No.

Her phone's browser supposedly erased her history. But what about while she was on it? Was that secure? A VPN was supposed to be, but was it? Probably not. Could a key logger be installed on a cell phone? She had no idea. Panic continued to swell, desperation driving her to do something.

But what? An email perhaps?

She got out the laptop and connected it to her phone's hot spot. When she logged into her company email, the first message that caught her eye was from Monster.com, another one right below it. The older one flagged Bryan for a job at EMPI, a management firm. It sounded vaguely familiar, but she couldn't remember why. The newer one, sent that afternoon, was the one she was expecting—an opening for Bryan's old job at the credit union.

Ha. So, the guy quit.

Either he'd found what he was looking for or given up. Interesting information, but didn't make much difference at this point. The short tenure confirmed the likelihood he was some sort of plant.

She started to compose an email to her father, then stopped. Was the firewall secure?

Good grief, when did I become so paranoid?

She knew the answer only too well.

CHARLIE'S CABIN
RURAL FALCON RIDGE
June 15, Friday
5:24 p.m.

Smoke from the second pipe still drifted toward the sky. What Charlie had seen so far rumbled as thunder through his mind. As afternoon waned, he continued to pray.

It started in his stomach.

A queasy wave coupled with chills.

Sure, he was fasting, but that wasn't his usual reaction. Perhaps he hadn't hydrated enough after the sweat.

He shifted his position slightly and focused back on his meditation.

Listened. Quieted his mind. Tuned to the slightest impression.

Another shiver, then a tingling jolt of foreboding. Like the contents of his veins were turning to ice.

He released the pipe from his lips, consumed by unseen dark forces. A whirlwind of hostility assaulted his mind like a slasher movie on fast-forward. Like what he'd felt earlier, watching the accident.

But stronger.

His breathing quickened to compensate for the weight crushing his chest.

Something about it was familiar.

A warning.

Suffocating knowing.

He'd sensed such things before.

The day of the accident.

He drew again on the pipe, pleading with *Maheo* for an explanation as the smoke ascended.

It was something bad.

Deadly.

But what? Who? What was he supposed to do?

More prayers ascended skyward, fervent and desperate.

A lightning-laced maelstrom crackled in his brain. Glimpses teased his mind, unidentifiable shards. Bombardment continued, slamming him with a tsunami of input.

Too many variables struggled for dominance. Gradually, the storm diminished. An F-5 tornado morphing into harmless dust devils oblivious to the wake of destruction left behind.

His heart slowed to heavy, labored beats. Breaths deep and gasping, blood frozen amid a mind-twisting sense of doom.

Another vision formed.

The black Suburban.

Was it a rerun of the accident? Did he miss something?

The vehicle sped past Dead Horse Canyon—

—then made a hard dusty turn, heading for Bryan's cabin.

He winced when a glint of sunlight flared from its windshield.

He opened his eyes. Glanced at the sun's location. The vision was yet to come, perhaps an hour or more away.

A now-familiar voice consumed him as rushing waters.

Your enemy comes with evil intent. Cowardly vehoe *who killed your brother are coming for what Sara has found. Stand with her, do not have fear.* Maheo *is protecting both of you. Grandson, no man is greater than the powers of* Maheo. *Go now and tell her what you have seen and* Maheo's *words.*

SARA'S CABIN
RURAL FALCON RIDGE
June 15, Friday
6:09 p.m.

A knock sounded from the back door. Sara's heart leapt into her throat. There it was again.

Soft.

Unthreatening.

Or so it seemed.

She crept to the edge of a window obstructed by an A-frame crossbeam, hand on the Glock. She peered around it, slowly, cautiously. All she could see was the person's bare back. The hat and braids. Charlie. She opened the door, relieved.

As soon as she saw him her relief evaporated. His face, arms, and bare chest were painted mostly black with different colored symbols. Instead of his usual jeans and boots he wore fringed buckskin and fully beaded moccasins.

Confused by his strange appearance, her anxiety level spiked even higher at the intensity in his dark eyes.

"What's wrong?" she exclaimed.

"They're coming. You're in danger. I'm here to protect you."

"Who's coming?

"The evil men who killed Bryan."

Her hand flew to her mouth. "How do you know that?"

"The grandfather spirits and *Maheo* told me."

Her forehead creased with confusion spiced with worry. It wasn't paranoia. This was real. "Where should we go? What should we do?"

He set his hat on the counter and held his finger to his lips. She gritted her teeth, berating herself for needing a reminder.

"Let's go for a walk," he suggested. "We could use some fresh air."

They strolled up the path as if on a casual hike. She relaxed slightly, grateful he was there. No matter what happened, at least she wasn't alone.

"Why are you covered with paint and dressed like that?" she asked.

He glanced down at his arms and chest. "Oh. It's part of how we fast. I was told to get here immediately and didn't think about it."

"You said they're coming. When? Now?"

"Soon." He glanced up at the Sun, still high over the mountains, then to shadows stretching toward the path. "About an hour."

"Should we leave?"

His expression grew pensive again. "No."

"*No?* Are you kidding? If they're coming, why not?"

"Because *Maheo* said we are safe."

Her jaw dropped. This was not the same Charlie she thought she knew.

"You're troubled. You already sensed danger is coming," he said. "How do you know that?"

By now they were about twenty yards from the house. She huffed out a nervous breath. "I thought I was just being paranoid. I found something. Bryan's Eagle Project. That astronomy website he created. I think that might be where he hid the data."

"That makes sense. I forgot about that. I remember working on it with him years ago. You haven't checked online yet, have you?"

"No. I didn't dare. Dad and Connie are coming out this weekend. I was waiting to ask him how to do it so no one knows. I suppose I could use public Wi-Fi somewhere, but there's nowhere around here, like a library or a Starbucks." Her face distorted with indecision, arms akimbo. "What should we do? Hide it somewhere?"

He gestured to keep walking. "Do you know anyone around here you can trust?"

All that came to mind were the Mah Jongg ladies. In fact, it was Mah Jongg night. Discovering the website left her so distracted she'd forgotten. They'd changed the time and day a while back because Ida wanted to watch some TV show on Thursday nights. They were meeting at Liz's house. The only one she came close to trusting.

"There's one woman I know who I think is okay. She lives about two miles from here. And I'm actually supposed to see her tonight."

"That's perfect. It'll get you away from here and out of danger. Does she have a computer?"

"I think so. Yes! Of course. She's always on *myneighbors.com.*"

He stopped, eyes fixed on the cabin. "Could you tell her yours crashed and ask if you could use hers? To check your email or something?"

Sara blinked. "That's a good idea. I doubt they're tracking everything and everyone. I could download the website to a flash drive. Then we could see what's on it with my computer offline."

"Did you memorize how to get in?"

Sara grimaced. "No. To be honest, I didn't think to. My rote memory isn't very good, anyway. Especially lately. When I found it, I was just excited and couldn't wait to tell you and Dad. I knew it was sensitive, but until about an hour ago I didn't feel so threatened."

"Let's go back and look at what you found. See if he added any notes to the report. Then see what we need to do to get in."

"Sounds good."

Plan in place, they headed back. By the time they reached the deck she didn't like the idea of leaving her house untended. Playing Mah Jongg was about the last thing she felt like doing, anyway. She stopped short of opening the door.

He looked around, startled by her hesitation. "What's wrong?" he whispered.

"I'm not sure I want to leave my house empty," she whispered back. "If anyone's snooping around, it would give them the perfect chance. And if they know everything about me, they know I'll be gone tonight. It's on my calendar. Maybe that's why they're coming, to search the place."

"Makes sense. And if you'd been here, you would have been in danger. It's perfect. You have an excuse to go to her house. You could even take your laptop. And I can stay here, if you like."

"Do you think you'll be safe?"

"Yes. I'll be safe."

His firm tone was confident. She wasn't so sure.

"You do know how to use a gun, right?"

He scrunched up his nose. "Uh, yeah. We got past bows and arrows a few hundred years ago. Why?"

"How about I leave my gun with you?"

"Okay."

As soon as they got inside she went upstairs to retrieve her box of ammo. She set it on the kitchen counter, then unholstered the gun and handed it over.

"Nice! Laser sights and everything."

"Ever use one like this?"

"Yes. I kept a similar one at my ranger station. Mainly if I had to put down injured wildlife or defend myself. Would have required a rather precise shot on a bear. Mine's a smaller caliber, but a Glock's a Glock."

He checked the magazine, then pulled back the slide to chamber a round. She handed him her spare, which he filled with dexterous familiarity.

In the guest room she tossed aside the pillows, and opened the storage bench. Took out the blue plastic box and removed the Eagle Project album. The website coding information was in the back. She slipped it out of the sheet protector.

"Ready?" she asked. He nodded.

They were no sooner back in the kitchen when a huge commotion arose out front. A cacophony of hard-soled boots tromped up the stairs followed by a splintering crash as a team of commandos kicked in the front door.

Six filed inside, decked out in Kevlar accessorized with military rifles, all pointed in their direction.

"Drop the weapon, chief," one of them snarled. "Unless you plan on meeting your buddy in the happy hunting grounds. Looks like you're dressed for the occasion. Nice. You even painted a target on your chest."

Charlie narrowed his eyes as he slowly set the handgun on the counter and stepped away.

The man looked Sara up and down, teeth showcased in a wicked grin. "As for you, Mrs. Reynolds, nice work. Hand it over."

*Day and night cannot dwell together. The red man has ever fled the approach
of the white man, as the changing mists on the mountainside flee before the
blazing morning sun.*
—Seath'tl "Seattle", 1854

41. RAID

SARA'S CABIN
RURAL FALCON RIDGE
June 15, Friday
6:51 p.m.

Tension electrified the room. Sara froze. She knew that voice.
Fury raged, yanking her somewhere between insanity and raw
bravado. She bared her teeth and snarled.

"How dare you! What's the meaning of this? Where's your
warrant?"

He replied with a muzzle sweep. "It's right here, lady."

"Yeah, right. What do you want? You better start explaining.
Right now."

"Or what? You know damn well why we're here. Now hand
it over. *Now.*"

She regarded the paper in her hand with mock innocence.
"This? Fine." She held it out.

He snatched it away, his puzzled look exactly what she was
counting on. "What *is* this?"

"If you don't mind, Rambo, we're working on a website my
husband and his friend here created twenty years ago. We're going
to update it and dedicate it to his memory. Is that a problem? One
that justifies this, this illegal intrusion?"

He swiveled his weapon to the corner. "You and the chief.
Over there. *Move it!*"

She complied, albeit glaring, arms folded in bold defiance. He removed his phone from inside his chest protector and nodded toward his team. "Cover 'em."

The lead guy stepped outside, ensuing conversation unintelligible. Minutes later he was back, his demeanor even more threatening.

"Who are you?" she demanded. "Why are you harassing me? All I'm trying to do is move on with my life after my husband was *murdered*." Her accusatory glower punctuated the sentence.

"I'll tell you who they are, Sara," Charlie said. "Murderers. Murderers and cowards. The same evil that's lurked in these mountains for over a hundred years. They amuse themselves by murdering innocent people at Dead Horse Canyon."

"Shut up! Both of you!"

Another muzzle sweep, then he angled the weapon upward and fired. The blast blared from wooden walls, windows trembling in their frames.

Sara's glare sizzled.

Charlie's eyes narrowed.

The commando matched her heated stare. "Now that it's clear who's in charge, bitch, bring up this website. I mean it. *Now*."

Her eyes drilled into his. "Fine. I need my computer."

He waved one of the others to go with her while he kept an eye on Charlie, whose entire persona reflected the unmitigated scorn of generations.

She picked up the laptop from the coffee table and carried it to the breakfast bar. After connecting to the internet, she brought up a browser, then held out her hand.

"I need that."

He held it up. She typed in the URL, an old Geocities address. She hit *Enter*, hoping with every fiber of her being that Bryan's data stash wouldn't be blatantly obvious.

Sorry, the page you requested was not found. Please check the URL for proper spelling and capitalization. If you're having trouble locating a destination on Yahoo! try visiting the Yahoo! home page or look through a list of Yahoo's online services. Also, you may find what you're looking for if you try searching below.

Her eyes fluttered closed with relief. Wikipedia confirmed Geocities shut down in 2009. She stood up, indignant, hands on her hips.

"It's gone. We'll set up a new one. Is that okay with you, Rambo? Or should I call you Eddie?"

He blinked a few times, then narrowed his eyes. "I don't give a flying fuck what you do, lady. But we're not going anywhere until you hand over every electronic device you got. Your cell phone, computer, tablet, and everything else. That SD card the chief, here, found in the truck, too."

Visceral rage seized her solar plexus in an iron grip.

"How dare you," she hissed. The words crackled like the fuse on a stick of dynamite. *"Get out! Get out of my house NOW or you're a dead man. Do you hear me? DEAD! I mean it. Get out!"*

He leveled the rifle in her direction. "I don't think so, bitch."

"Leave," Charlie ordered, stepping in front of her. "Now. Or you won't like how this turns out."

"Actually, I think I will, chief. Now I can take you both out with a single round." He lifted the weapon's sights to his eye, team members following suit.

Charlie stood tall, heated stare unwavering.

Sara's mind froze. Whatever she felt, it wasn't fear. She stepped over beside Charlie.

"Get out!" she repeated through clenched teeth.

The man's rifle lowered slowly. His icy eyes were rimmed with white as a medley of emotions tripped across his face. He backed up, hands raised.

"Keep going, asshole!" she yelled. "Now! *GET OUT!"*

He retreated as far as the splintered door, reached behind him to pull it open, then waved for his entourage to leave. One tracked wet footprints while the others wore expressions split between wide-eyed and open-mouthed.

"We're just following orders," the leader mumbled, then joined his compadres in a double-time retreat out the door.

Sara's attempt to slam it shut behind them was foiled by sagging hinges. She collapsed in a kitchen chair, hands crossed over her chest. "What just happened?"

Charlie grinned. "Good job, Wonder Woman. Wherever that came from, it worked."

"You know who that jerk was, right?"

"Sure do. The guy in the video. I'd love to get my hands on him in a fair fight."

"To hell with fair!"

A startled cry escaped when her phone rang. She picked it up—Liz.

"H-hello."

"Hi, Sara. Are you coming tonight? Were waiting for you."

"Oh. Uh, yeah. Hi, Liz."

"Are you okay? You sound out of breath."

She swallowed hard, trying to clear her head. "Oh, Liz. I'm so sorry. I can't make it tonight. I'm, uh, right in the middle of something. I can't seem to get used to not meeting on Thursdays." She cringed, hating to lie, but the truth would have blown the woman's mind.

Sorry, Liz. Busy evening. I just threw a band of armed commandos out of my house. . .

"Okay, no problem, dear. See you next time."

"Thanks. Bye, Liz."

She rolled her eyes as she ended the call.

Charlie removed a bottle of Shiraz from the rack over the counter, engaged the nearby cork screw, and yanked it open. He filled a wine glass from beneath the cabinet, and handed it over.

She nodded and sipped, hoping to diminish the aftershock. Gradually her anger dissipated until only a blur of spent adrenaline remained.

"Join me?"

"Thanks, but no. Alcohol is not made for Cheyenne people."

She nodded, vaguely recalling Bryan saying something to that effect.

He sat down across from her, expression hovering between shocked and amused. "So tell me—where did *that* come from?"

Her eyes met his as composure returned. "I have no idea. I've never felt like that before, ever. Something came over me. It didn't even feel like it was me. I've never been so enraged. *Ever.* If I had the gun, I know I would have shot that SOB right between the eyes. To be honest, I felt as if I were a puppet or something. Not myself at all."

"Doesn't matter. It worked."

"For now. But I doubt the issue will go away. It certainly proves conclusively that I'm being watched. How else could they have known?"

"True. But dodging a bullet is always a good thing. Or an arrow. And remind me never to piss you off."

She giggled. "Right." Her hand flew to her mouth.

"I need some fresh air," she said, rolling her eyes at her slip. *What an idiot!*

She holstered the gun and grabbed her wine, then followed him up the path until they reached the usual place.

"The old website being gone works for now, but it only eliminates another place where Bryan may have stashed the evidence," she said. "We're right back where we started. Unless you have any other ideas."

"Possibly." His mien grew thoughtful. "But I think we're on the right track. Since Patrice said you'll find it, I'm sure you will."

"Yes and no. She said you'd be involved, so perhaps you'll lead me to it, literally or otherwise." She sipped her wine as she thought some more. "You know, it still could be in that storage bench. There are several boxes in there, some extremely old, that I haven't checked. His astronomy books are in there, too."

"They must have known somehow that you found that album. First, we need to get rid of any bugs. When your father comes out this weekend he can make sure we got them all. Meanwhile, anything we say inside should sound like we're just setting up that website."

"Agreed. And I need to check that storage bench. As soon as possible. I'm sure they'll be back."

BKSS LLC
ALBUQUERQUE
June 15, Friday
7:20 p.m.

Bernie sat in his efficiency apartment on Coal Avenue nursing a shot of Jim Beam.

Something went wrong.

He could feel it.

Why did the feed die? An electronic fluke? A solar flare? The target set off a bomb?

His cell rang.

"Johannsen?" The man's response sounded like gibberish. "Say again. Slow down, damn it. You're not making sense."

It took several seconds before the heavy breathing ended and words emerged. "Listen, boss. I shit you not. I'm tellin' you the truth. Something weird's going on out there. Something seriously freakin' weird."

"What the hell happened? Did that Indian get you with a poison arrow or something?"

"You know what, boss? I wish it were that simple. *That* I could explain. It wasn't just the Indian, it was the chick. I don't know what the deal was. When that bitch stared me down it felt like she was suckin' the life right outa me."

"Yeah, right. Sounds like projected guilt to me, Johannsen. She saw the dashcam videos, remember? You killed her husband. What did you expect, numbnuts? A kiss on the cheek?"

"Jesus, boss..."

"He's not on your side for this one, Johannsen."

"You weren't there, boss. I don't know how to explain it."

"I watched the feed real-time. From the cameras as well as your bodycam. She was obviously pissed and far from intimidated. That's pretty damn odd for a woman confronted by a half-dozen armed mercenaries. Were you guys in tutus or Kevlar?"

"Then you saw it?"

"Some. Feeds went dead right after you called in. Every one of them. Nothing but static. As if a bomb went off. Major RF interference or something."

"Listen to me, boss. It gave me the willies. The room got real cold. Like we were in some sorta blackhole or something. I don't believe in ghosts or guardian angels or shit like that. But I'm tellin' you, this huge thing. Creature. Something, was there, right behind 'em."

Bernie ground his teeth, blood pressure rising. "C'mon, Johannsen. You expect me to believe that? You just blew another job. We are so fucked. Do you even realize what you've done? What were you guys smoking? A bad batch of crack? Do-it-yourself meth? What have I told you about that shit? Especially when you're on call?"

"No, no. Listen. I swear. All we had was a couple beers. No weed. Or anything else. Nothin'. I swear it on my father's grave. Its eyes were like, well, on fire. It wasn't human. It had this giant beak. Probably ten, eleven feet tall. And wings. I swear, I thought I was dead. That it was gonna eat me right there. The chick and her friend looked like, well hell, I don't know. They looked kinda blurry. Like a force field or something. Like in the movies."

"Yeah, right. Uh, huh. So you're tellin' me tonight's news will announce superheroes are real. Did it introduce itself?" He lowered his voice to subwoofer range and growled out a raspy, *"I'm Bird Man!"* He paused to grind his teeth. "Guess we're out of a job, one way or another, eh, numbnuts?"

"No, boss. I swear. It's true. Every word."

Bernie fumed, still not sure whether to believe him or not. His team lead's claims were a stretch of reality that tried his imagination and patience alike.

Yet, what Johannsen swore he saw was so detailed, the visceral fear in his voice so convincing, it added credence to his wild tale.

He'd heard similar stories before of strange, unexplained occurrences on the battlefield. Often in their favor, though this one clearly wasn't. It was hard to believe some heavenly being wielding powers straight out of science fiction manifested to protect this woman along with her Indian friend.

He put the rest of the team on the phone, one by one, and they all backed the story up. By the time he'd listened to each team member describing the same scene, defying and effectively tromping his natural skepticism, the hair on his arms was standing at attention.

Maybe that crazy woman in Boulder with the flowing white hair was a witch after all.

Whatever happened, their quarry won that battle. So be it. Why was not his problem. He had a job to do. And he doubted the NSA would be impressed with their explanation for why this mission went south.

The only good news was the fact she hadn't found the data. At least not yet. If reports were true she'd be the one to find it, that left one option.

Dead men tell no tales.

Or women, as the case might be.

42. CANOPUS

SARA'S CABIN
RURAL FALCON RIDGE
June 15, Friday
7:50 p.m.

The extension ladder from under the deck leaned against the cedar beam crowning the vaulted ceiling. Sara stood at the bottom stabilizing the base while Charlie checked the fan and light fixture for surveillance devices.

After pointing to two suspicious nubs on the casing, he pried them loose with a putty knife, then tossed down what turned out to be a tiny camera and a microphone. Fortunately, he didn't stop there. Two more clung to the mounting bracket.

They checked everywhere. Electrical outlets, the Danish style furniture, beams, and rocks that comprised the fireplace and chimney. Even the sheepskin rug. The guest room's log walls were particularly challenging.

By the time they finished sweeping the entire cabin, it was apparent the place was crawling with bugs—five cameras and ten listening devices, which now reposed on the kitchen counter.

Sara inspected the insidious collection of privacy violators, teeth clenched with fury. How long had they been there? Recently? Or before Bryan's wreck? At least for now she felt slightly more secure.

"What should we do with them?" she whispered.

His response was a mischievous smirk. "How about something else to spy on?"

"Like what?"

"Wildlife?"

She grinned. "Good idea. I know where the camera from the bedroom should go: Inside the toilet."

"Aimed upstream or down?"

"Down! Shame on you! You're horrible!" she replied, then joined him in a round of stress reducing levity.

All but that one device went outside, far enough from the house not to pick up conversations on the deck and far from their usual rendezvous point.

As they returned to the house, another thought came to mind. "Where'd you put that SD card?" she asked. "We should probably back up those files, too."

He took his hat off the counter and showed her the flap inside. She nodded, catching herself before saying anything more descriptive, just in case.

Her attention shifted to walls of towering glass, open to the landscape beyond. Every tree, every rock, every dip in the terrain loomed with potential hostility. Before long it would be dark, making them sitting ducks.

"We absolutely have to cover the windows," she said. "One of those goons could be on that cell tower with a pair of high-powered binoculars. I have something upstairs that should work."

"A 30.06 would, too."

She agreed, then fetched two sets of king-sized sheets from upstairs. Rummaging through kitchen drawers for something to hang them failed, but the toolbox in the pantry had a small box of finishing nails. With luck, that would be enough.

She held the ladder again while Charlie used them to cover the offending glass, thinking if he ran out of nails she'd scavenge those used for the photos and various paintings.

Which hadn't been checked for bugs.

When he finished, the elegant room looked horribly tacky, the fern-like design on the sheets in firm disagreement with the Southwest style decor. She blew it off, increased privacy well-worth it. At least she wouldn't have to explain it to the Mah Jongg ladies until her next hosting turn, a few weeks away. That gave her time to come up with credible rationale. Or better yet, shutters.

"One more sweep," she said, nodding toward the pictures.

Another mic resided behind the painting over the couch, but that was it. Satisfied, she nonetheless retrieved a notepad and pencil from a kitchen drawer for any highly sensitive communications.

Sara's stomach issued a reminder that it had waited long enough. "I could use something to eat. How about you?" she asked.

"That sounds great. While you do that, would you mind if I took a quick shower? I get the feeling I scare you every time you look at me."

"I'm sorry," she apologized. "You do look rather intimidating. I'm sure it helped get rid of those commandoes."

"If they knew anything about history they'd know messing with a Cheyenne warrior, especially one in touch with the grandfather spirits, is a really bad idea."

"Whatever works," she agreed. "Of course you can take a shower. Let me get some of Bryan's clothes from upstairs. There should be towels in the guest bathroom."

She fixed a quick batch of spaghetti while he took a shower. When he joined her once more in the kitchen he was wearing one of Bryan's polos and a pair of jeans, bringing his appearance back to normal. Whether his strange looks had anything to do with their earlier success she didn't know, but she definitely felt more comfortable when he wasn't all decked out in war paint, even if it was to her advantage.

As soon as they finished eating they parked two kitchen chairs in front of the storage bench and got to work. Since her previous searches hadn't been for listening devices, they took out all the boxes and scrutinized every square inch. No electronic devices, unfriendly or otherwise turned up, likewise any secret compartments.

Another idea to foil her pursuers came to mind.

"How about some music?"

"Great idea."

"Any preference?"

"No. Anything is fine."

She picked through the CDs in the rack next to the fireplace. She grimaced as she flipped past Sarah McLachlan, Josh Grobin, Bryan's favorite, the Jonas Brothers, then Vivaldi, which often accompanied their antics on the sheepskin rug.

"This one called *Nomad* sounds interesting."

She slipped it in the stereo, unsure what to expect. A pleasant montage of native drums blended with chants, whistles, flutes, and animal cries filled the air.

His eyes narrowed to a pensive expression. "I remember Bryan playing that on a boom box, before any of this was built. I think it's from Australia."

She cranked up the volume, then returned to task. Finding Bryan's astronomy books was her first priority. What could be more fertile ground for star-related material? When Bryan stashed anything so remotely without her knowledge still teased her mind.

They hadn't been to the cabin for a couple months prior to their fated trip in April. February, perhaps. How long did he have the data? Did he hide it months before? Or the day they arrived?

Her memory of that time remained entrenched in fog. For all she knew, he'd shown her, but she forgot, along with everything else. Maybe that was why his directions in the truck were so vague. No telling what they talked about the night before the wreck.

She assumed the box in question would be relatively new compared to the others, many of which appeared worn and discolored. Seeing one a few layers down, she handed the top ones to Charlie to set aside, then took it out.

Astronomy blared from its lid, printed in Bryan's flawless hand.

She unfolded the flaps and sorted through the books stacked inside. One about astro-photography, most others related to telescopes or the planets with a few about the myths associated with the constellations. As she flipped through one of the latter, visions of their nights observing the heavens flooded her mind. Happy, innocent times filled with the joy of discovery. She set it aside, determined to avoid another sentimental side trip.

The three-volume hardbound set of *Burnham's Celestial Handbook* caught her eye. Three volumes devoted to the stars— billions of them. She couldn't imagine someone compiling so much information. Her heart leapt, hopeful.

And for some reason, terrified.

A quick look inside revealed they indeed addressed multitudes of stars in considerable detail. The listings were alphabetical by constellation, not specific stars, since most lacked formal names.

Did Bryan have a favorite star? Not that she recalled. She turned toward Charlie. "Any ideas?"

His faraway look accompanied an enigmatic smile. "Canopus. Try Canopus."

The last volume had an index, so she looked it up—*volume one, page 465.*

Maybe they'd find another clue. She caressed its worn dust jacket, the spiral galaxy on its cover staring back like a giant eye. She held her breath and turned to the designated page.

And there it was.

Right in the center, just above the description of Alpha Carina, a.k.a. Canopus. A small compartment cut out with a razor blade. Comprised of just enough pages to contain a tiny, thumbnail-sized USB drive.

Her vision blurred. Charlie's expression mirrored hers as they nodded with wide-eyed enthusiasm.

They returned to the computer on the kitchen table, which she made sure was offline, then turned off her phone to be completely certain.

Her hand trembled as she inserted the tiny device in one of the ports. Three folders came up: *Sara, Charlie*, and *Canopus*. The one with her name contained one document file.

Its date was mid-February—when they'd come out to celebrate an early Valentine's Day. It snowed heavily the entire time, no doubt spoiling any plans Bryan may have had to investigate the site. Weather in March was about the same. Her heart jolted.

No wonder he was so grumpy that trip.

She bit her lip and clicked. A letter. Charlie patted her shoulder and retreated to the living room. One hand rested on her chest as she read.

My dearest Sara,

If you are reading this, I am dead. I've been playing with fire and at considerable risk. This USB drive contains proof of what I uncovered. My intent is to find physical evidence before I go public, because it will be vigorously debunked.

Many high-level government officials and their campaign contributors have colluded with members of Congress to use taxpayer money to fund a project that has no justification. It doesn't relate to national security or legitimate activities with our foreign partners or allies. It's greed, pure and simple, and relates to rewarding those who have funded major political campaigns.

Our current lobbying system has shifted control of our nation from the people to corporations. This has sadly been declared legal by the Supreme Court. Corporations fund candidates who, when elected, introduce legislation that favors the entities that got them there. What I have discovered, however, goes far beyond that.

There are many who believe our world is in jeopardy. Internal and external political forces, foreign relations, and Mother Nature herself are unstable. Some believe an apocalypse is coming. Civil war, a nuclear holocaust, or some natural, worldwide catastrophe, like a solar flare, pandemic, or asteroid strike. Those seeking control may even orchestrate it themselves, to gain power and world dominion.

It's no secret that there are bunkers, deep underground, like Cheyenne Mountain and various others, where military and government officials will retreat given such an event. The mega-rich have their own compounds, built at their own expense.

However, others have demanded that the government provide them with a similar safe-haven, including those who could well afford their own.

These factions are, as you would expect, aware of illegal activities on the part of government officials. These include undeclared and veiled campaign contributions as well as more nefarious activities performed by elected and appointed government representatives. This includes civil servants in various agencies where conflicts of interest are considered business as usual.

It would be a simple matter to blackmail these individuals to provide them with a similar facility. While I never found evidence of coercion, I did find evidence of such a facility, proving blatant collusion.

It's been funded as one of the infamous "Black Projects," most of which relate to the military and national security. These activities are so far beyond Top Secret that even the President is often unaware of what they specifically are.

This is the world of conspiracies where they don't blink at eliminating people like myself who attempt to expose them.

As you have probably guessed, this facility is not far from here. In additional to its clandestine financing, there are also numerous environmental concerns. Its construction is in an area where there is already considerable pollution from abandoned 19th century mines.

Their plan to use geothermal energy for the facility's power source involves fracking, another practice with serious environment issues. The aquifers that provide drinking water for thousands, maybe even millions, flow through this area. There are also fault lines, making it unstable.

This is not some small facility, but one that covers well over a square mile. The disturbances it will cause could have lethal consequences. Its construction alone is irresponsible at best and criminal at worst, even without its scandalous financing.

The files you'll find here comprise the evidence that I've uncovered. If you want to honor my memory, you will find a way to get this information into the hands of someone who can release it to the public.

I don't trust the media, much less federal agencies like the FBI, CIA, and NSA, who are all likely to be involved in some way or another with this massive scheme and cover-up.

For your own safety, this can best be done through an organization like WikiLeaks. They protect their informant's identity.

What I have done is illegal. I have broken numerous federal laws hacking into this data and violated security oaths I took in the Air Force. Some are capital offenses. Security oath violations don't warrant a trial.

Yet, morally, I feel an obligation to reveal these unscrupulous activities on the part of those who have been elected and appointed to look after the best interests of U.S. citizens. NOT their own personal ambitions, to say nothing of further rewarding corporate lobbyists.

The corruption is extensive and real. It needs to be exposed for what it is. It will only be worth losing my life if it is released to the voters to show what our government has become. That is the one final thing you can do for me.

Know that I love you with all my heart and would never do anything to hurt you. I truly hope than my actions have not caused you any harm nor will in the future.

All my love,

Bryan

She stared at it for several seconds, unable to absorb the enormity of what he'd done. The age of the file likewise startled her, that he'd been involved for so long, yet not said a word, until their last fateful trip.

She turned in her chair and saw Charlie pacing the floor between the kitchen and living room. She waved him over, then got up and gestured toward the screen. As he read, his narrowed eyes periodically reversed to arched eyebrows.

When finished, he shook his head and exhaled hard. She exited back to the root directory and pointed to the folder with his name on it.

She pushed the computer his way, reciprocating the privacy he'd afforded her by returning to the storage bench to see what else it might hold.

The Great Spirit made us all—he made my skin red, and yours white; he placed us on this earth, and intended that we should live differently from each other.
—Petalesharo, February 1822

43. DATA

SARA'S CABIN
RURAL FALCON RIDGE
June 15, Friday
9:48 p.m.

Charlie sucked in a soul-bracing breath. He and Bryan were close, but this was unexpected. While he believed they were connected in some way, it was still odd. As if his white brother were reaching out from the grave.

He opened the file and braced for what could be a bumpy ride.

My brother, Charlie,

You have been my most cherished friend in this life. You have taught me so much. I would not be the person I am without your wisdom and guidance. You taught me to see the world through different eyes. I would have never seen it as an integrated whole, with humans, nature, and even the Earth itself tied together in spirit without your insights.

I'll never forget us as teens, gazing at the stars. Your beliefs in the sacred nature of the heavens touched me as nothing else ever has. To see the cosmos as the domain of Maheo instead of through the lens of astrophysics changed me. I never saw astronomy the same again. It opened up the way for me to derive inspiration from the stars. That would have never been possible without your willingness to share your people's most sacred and personal beliefs. Thank you.

If you have not already found it, there's a box with your name on it in the storage bench. I'm sure Sara will help you find it. It contains some of the historical information I found in going through my grandfather's papers.

As you know, I inherited the cabin from him. I didn't realize until recently that he likewise inherited it, that my family's connections with that property go back seven generations to the mid-1800s.

In reading some old letters and journals, I was horrified to discover that my progenitors were among the raiding party responsible for the Dead Horse Canyon massacre.

I feel the need to apologize for what they did. It was so wrong. They stole your land, slaughtered your people, killed off the buffalo for sport and pure greed, then forced you to give up your traditions and way of life.

They claimed to be Christians, yet your lifestyle was more in line with the teachings of Christ than theirs. Then, typical of those guilty of reprehensible behavior, they made you the bad guys for defending yourselves. I'm appalled by their insidious behavior and truly sorry.

There is no excuse for what they did. I'm ashamed to be related to them. That is why I'm exposing the evil deeds of those today who share the same greedy mentality and dark heart as those who exploited your people.

I hope I can atone in some small way for what my ancestors did. It won't compensate for the horrors of the Sand Creek Massacre, the Washita Battle, the Battle of Red Fork, the Fort Robinson Break-out, what happened at Dead Horse Canyon, or the many other injustices, but it's all that I can do.

My life and anything I may have accomplished would not be the same without you. Thank you for putting up with your stupid paleface brother and making me a better person.

I have often thought of your Diné legend of the Hero Twins, who killed the monsters to make the world safe, whatever it took. Likewise, the Coyote Star and his reputation as a meddler who ruins people's plans. I have done what I could to honor them as well.

Forever your spirit twin and brother from another culture,

Bryan

He was reading the letter for the third time when he realized Sara was standing beside him, carrying the box mentioned in the letter.

She held it out and whispered, "This is for you." He stared, too rattled to respond. "It has your name on it."

"Yes. Sorry." He motioned to set it on the table. "I'm still trying to absorb what he said," he whispered back. "You're welcome to read it if you like. It's quite different than yours."

"If it's personal, don't feel you have to."

"It's okay. You need to. I think it'll explain quite a bit."

Her questioning look deepened as she sat down and started to read. While she did so, he released the box's interlocked flaps to investigate its contents.

A small manila envelope held several photographs from some of their hikes and excursions. There were some of their joint projects as well, including when they'd built the canoe. He chuckled at the Cheyenne-style backrests they made from willow branches for sitting around campfires on chilly summer nights.

There was another snapshot of the "sacred pipe" they carved, then used to smoke some local weed to symbolize their bonds of friendship and loyalty. Whatever plant it was made them so sick neither of them ever smoked anything again. At least until he connected with the real thing, his grandfather's sacred red pipe.

The memory evoked a laugh, snagging a questioning look from Sara. He held out the photo and mimed what they'd done. She smiled, then resumed reading.

There were a few pictures of the two of them, probably taken by Bryan's grandfather. Two scrawny teenagers, one red, one white, who each thought he held the world in the palm of his hand. Others showed a blurry campfire and a vain attempt to capture the stars, judging by the smudged moon barely recognizable off to one side.

He placed the photos back in the envelope and picked through the other items. Letters. A few from him when Bryan was away at school or in the Air Force. Old documents, including a diary with pages crumbling with age.

Time evaporated, taking him somewhere in eternity, where all of this made sense. He pondered their time together, whatever meaning it may have had.

Was this how healers and prophets felt?

Ordinary people part of something far bigger?

What was its true message?

He'd never missed his brother so much nor felt him so near. He closed the box. This was something to deal with alone and coupled with prayer and meditation.

Sara's sniffle drew his attention. She turned his way, shaking her head. "I had no idea," she whispered. "This is incredible."

"He never talked of these things?"

"No. Never. I knew you were friends, but I didn't understand how close. My letter told us *what* he did. Yours told us *why*."

Abruptly, she rolled her eyes and slapped her forehead, as if she'd forgotten something important. He jumped, startled, until he saw what she was doing: copying the files to another thumb drive as well as the laptop, after which she replaced the USB drive in its original cache.

Burnham's Celestial Handbook Volume 1 went back in the box with its fellows. She closed the flaps as before and returned it to the storage bench, everything else she'd removed quickly restored to its original position, except Charlie's box.

He pointed to it. "Should we put this back in there, too?"

"No. That's yours. Unless you want to keep it here, which is fine, but maybe not the safest."

"No, that's okay. I'd like to take it home so I can go through it more carefully."

She nodded. "I'm sure that's what Bryan intended."

The storage bench's heavy lid squeaked on rusty hinges as she lowered it, then replaced the pillows, as if to protect what lay within.

"So. What now?" he asked.

"I was going to ask you the same thing."

She opened a Word document and typed: *I guess we should look at this data and see if it's as airtight as he seemed to think. I'd hate to think he died for something that didn't have the potential for considerable impact.*

His keyboard agility was less adept than hers as he responded. *He was smart. He knew what he was doing. I'm sure it's every bit as damning as he said. Why else would they have targeted him?*

I suppose that's true, she wrote. *Let's see what we've got. I sure hope those spooks don't come back.*

His wry laugh originated deep in his chest. *I suspect they got scared away long enough for us to make some real trouble.*

"I certainly hope so," she replied aloud, wearing a wicked smile.

SARA'S CABIN
RURAL FALCON RIDGE
June 15, Friday
10:28 p.m.

Sara opened the folder named *Canopus.* Incriminating was hardly the word. Mostly emails and memoranda that were easily identifiable with black budget items and Congressional Committee minutes. A summary document explained it all, including URLs and other references. It would have taken forever to piece everything together without it, perhaps to the point of never figuring it out.

By just after midnight they'd seen enough, closed the files, then, to make Bryan proud, she copied them to yet another mini-USB drive along with the MP4s from the SD-card. Like before, she hid it in the contact lens case in her makeup bag. She made a similar one for Charlie to keep. After that, she deleted them from her laptop and emptied the trash.

Bryan told her there were ways to recover erased files, unless she reformatted the hard drive. She didn't bother. It wasn't like their adversaries didn't know what it contained or needed the information. Their charge was to destroy it. It was well past the point of hiding, other than as evidence for security violations against her as Bryan's accomplice.

At last they'd found the data. "In the stars" as promised. Now their challenge was to retain it long enough to go public and fulfill his last request.

Charlie came to her place on foot, most likely to do so covertly, and she doubted he felt like making the trek back home. Driving him, then coming back alone had no appeal whatsoever.

"After everything that's happened tonight, I'm rather nervous being here alone. Would you mind staying? You're welcome to stay in the guest room. Those spooks might be back at the butt-crack of dawn," she said, using one of Bryan's euphemisms for early morning.

"No problem. Or I could sleep on the couch. I've done that a few times, when Bryan came up to go hunting."

"No need, use the guest room. Thank you so much for being here. I don't know what I would have done if I'd been alone when those jerks busted in like that."

"I don't know," he said, eyes sparkling with amusement. "I'd say you handled them pretty well."

She shrugged. "I don't think that was me. I've never in my life called someone an asshole before, deserved or not. I suppose what matters is that it worked."

"Indeed, it did."

"Which reminds me. I'll have to ask Dad to bring up tools to fix the door." Surely the least of what she had to tell him. "Goodnight, Charlie."

Their eyes met, something passing between them that hadn't existed before. His look lingered, then he reached over and gave her hands a warm squeeze.

"Goodnight, Sara. I'll see you in the morning. Hopefully not before dawn."

"Amen to that."

Exhausted, but too wound up to sleep, she tossed and turned throughout the night while the past few hours churned inside her head like two storm fronts merging in Tornado Alley.

Even before she had the data she was a target.

She pulled the covers up to her chin, shivering, as the import of Bryan's last request upended every nerve.

What will they do when I release it?

44. GENERATIONS

SARA'S CABIN
RURAL FALCON RIDGE
June 15, Friday
11:53 p.m.

C harlie, likewise, couldn't sleep. The box beckoned, tickling his curiosity. He flattened his palms against its sides as if to assimilate what dwelt within. His people relied on oral tradition, not diaries. What was in that old journal? Whose was it? Was that where Bryan learned his ancestors incited Black Cloud's curse?

Charlie's progenitors were medicine men and women who were practicing healers. All descended from Black Cloud. A strong swelling of truth filled his chest at the implications of what lay ahead.

Since Bryan's accident he'd been repeatedly reminded of his grandfather's teachings. Prior to that, rather than accept his destiny, he'd pushed it away. Whenever Bryan asked about his culture, whether Diné or Cheyenne, he always shared what he knew. He'd been taught well, by his *amasani* and Eaglefeathers.

Ironically, his own commitment to those beliefs was weak. His white brother's interest and reverence for what he shared kept him closer to his roots than he might have otherwise been.

Roots that demanded attention like never before.

A Cheyenne warrior stood up to his principles, even to the point of death, then embraced it when it came. He didn't shy before the point of the arrow.

The point—whether knife, arrow, or spear—pierced the skin. Blood flowed. Death followed. The point likewise pierced the veil that separated mortality from the land of spirits. Accepting death and its pain upon going home to *Maheo* was the way of the warrior. Facing it with courage and honor earned a good place in the hereafter. Cowardice earned the opposite.

Warriors no longer rode ponies to battle. No more warpaths, no more buffalo hunts, no more battles to defend their lands.

They faced other foes.

Not those who wielded bows and arrows or even guns, but those who would steal their heritage as they did their land and hunting grounds. Whoever or however an enemy appeared, a warrior confronted it with courage and dignity.

He pondered his attempt to assimilate the white man's world. Did he betray his people? His heritage? Did obtaining a white man's education, working in his world, and abiding by his rules constitute cowardice?

No.

His grandfather insisted that he pursue an education. To combat the white man required understanding his ways and earning his respect.

His betrayal came when he turned away from the strength he had within. His reluctance to embrace the Cheyenne Way and pursue his destiny.

Medicine men wielded power tied to the land of Spirits. The sacred red pipe took him to that timeless realm. The white man sought to understand nature through science while the red man was integral to it. Their intimate relationship with the Earth constituted a partnership that placed those energies at their command.

Such powers intimidated those who lusted after control.

Thus, they denigrated, even outlawed, ceremonies that enabled such powers. Someone with a direct link with *Maheo* and Earth was not beholden to earthly authority.

Was the chasm separating the races based on fear-driven envy that indigenous people maintained that connection? A connection the white men lost through avarice, greed, and murderous intent?

By aspiring to conquer and exploit nature and their fellow man rather than live in peace and honor the Earth's majesty and power?

His spirit brother, though his skin was white, died rebelling against the very powers that not only exploited, but tried to annihilate indigenous people. Was their friendship the result of some pre-earth covenant to culminate the curse at last? Were they in some mystic way the manifestation of the Diné legend of the Hero Twins?

Energy surged through him, commanding him to cast off what remained of his acquired whiteness and become the full-blooded red man he was intended to be.

Patrice's words echoed confirmation—it was time to embrace his destiny. He'd still be riding two ponies, but this time he knew which one to trust.

He set the box on the storage bench, turned off the light, and felt his way back to bed. He laid down, suddenly exhausted, and in short order fell asleep.

Sometime later, wood smoke teased his senses, then chill mountain air folded around him, alive with singing and the visceral sound of drums. He joined in, singing praises to the Grandfather Spirits for their help and protection. The night sky spanned the heavens above, resplendent with *Yikáísdáhá*, the river of stars known to the white man as The Milky Way.

A tiny spark appeared on the ground, then transformed to a blazing fire. A personage in full ceremonial regalia danced and chanted amid the smoke. His heart leapt with recognition.

Littlebear.

Not as he remembered him, a man defeated by a brutal disease, but a warrior in his prime.

Charlie thought to greet him, then halted when the drumbeat changed abruptly from that of a spring shower to ground-soaking rain.

A second figure emerged.

Again his heart swelled.

Eaglefeathers. Likewise a strong and mighty man.

The cadence increased to that of a summer downpour. Rides the Wind, father of Eaglefeathers, appeared. He took his place, leading the others around the fire.

Torrents of sound like those of a raging storm welcomed yet another. Silver Sky. Beats became that of a pulsing, living force, as Lone Wolf likewise assumed his place in the throng, their dancing frenetic while their collective voices sang the honor song.

Percussions exploded to a thunderous roar. The others stopped. Bowed their heads as yet another joined their ranks.

Black Cloud.

Father of them all.

He assumed his place in the lead, then chanting resumed amid a kaleidoscope of feathers, singing, and celebratory dance.

Charlie stood in awe, each generation familiar within the depths of his soul. Another figure appeared, ghostly and face unseen. He stood before him, beckoning with outstretched hand.

Humbled, yet acutely aware of the strength he had within, Charlie stepped forward.

Destiny's call had never been more clear.

Continued in Book 2
Return to Dead Horse Canyon: Grandfather Spirits

ABOUT THE AUTHORS

Marcha Fox earned a bachelor's degree in physics from Utah State University in 1987, which led to a 20+ year career at NASA's Johnson Space Center in Houston, Texas. Her interests expand far beyond the world of aerospace and hard science, however. The esoteric realm of metaphysics and all things weird and wonderful hold her interest as well.

Forever fascinated by the heavens, when her attempt to debunk astrology backfired, she pursued knowledge in that field as well. She graduated from the International Academy of Astrology's professional development program in 2012 and created ValkyrieAstrology.com. Much of the popular website's informational content can be found in "Whobeda's Guide to Basic Astrology."

Her previous fiction work includes her epic Star Trails Tetralogy series which has been highly acclaimed for its family-oriented plot as well as its palatable and accurate science content. More information can be found on StarTrailsSaga.com.

Born in Peekskill, New York, she has lived in California, Utah, and Texas in the course of raising her family. She has six grown children, numerous grandchildren, and great-grandchildren. Besides writing, she pampers her cats, works with astrology clients from around the world, and tries to keep up with her home, yard, friends, and family.

Pete Risingsun (*Moohtaveanohe* - Blackhawk) is an enrolled member of the Northern Cheyenne Tribe. He is recognized as a Ceremonial Man who is well-versed in his tribe's ceremonies and traditions of the Creator's circle of life. His experience includes serving as a spirit helper to medicine men in ceremonial  sweat lodges, where traditional procedures are meticulously followed. Sweat lodge keepers earn their right to function in that role. After completing his vow to fast four times at *Novavose*, he earns four paints, each of which has important ceremonial significance.

Pete is a proud fifth generation descendant of Chief Iron Shirt, his great-great-grandfather, who was a lodge keeper and powerful medicine man who lived to be 98 years old. At 95, he still rode his white horse to the Busby, Montana fair.

(L to R) Chief Iron Shirt, Philip Risingsun, Pete Risingsun (Author Pete's Grandfather) and Harry Risingsun (Author Pete's uncle). Picture taken c. 1927 by Dr. Thomas B. Marquis.

Pete was born in 1950, the eighth child of ten, and raised on a small ranch east of Busby, Montana, where he became a horseman and hunter at a very young age. When he was twelve, he shot his first deer and also caught a young bald eagle. He and his uncle, David Seminole, raised it in a large cage for three years.

They took four tail feathers for Pete's traditional dancing bustle and then set the eagle free. This uncle taught him traditional dancing as well as how to ride a horse.

After graduating high school in 1968 he attended Montana State University for four years, then was offered a position with Exxon as an employee relations director overseas. He turned it down, instead completing

High School Senior Picture 1968

a three-year apprenticeship in plant operations and working in that capacity for one additional year in Billings, Montana. Working in a refinery a hundred miles from home combined with the discomforts of shift-work made him crave the smell of fresh air as well as getting outside astride a good horse.

Years before, his uncle, Ted Risingsun, told him, "You younger Cheyennes with education need to come home and help your people. Do not forget where you came from." Thus, when he was offered a job as adult education director for the Northern Cheyenne Tribe back home in Lame Deer, he accepted, grateful to see Billings and the refinery fade away in the rear-view mirror.

Upon returning to the reservation, Pete also bred championship American Quarter Horse Association (AQHA) horses, guaranteeing he'd have a good ride available whenever he wanted. He also raised black angus cattle.

His Uncle Ted further encouraged him to follow in his footsteps and become a Tribal Council member. He heeded his advice and served on the Council for six years. In addition, Pete's leadership includes being the first Northern Cheyenne elected as a

Rosebud County Commissioner, a position he held from January 1, 2007 to December 31, 2012.

He's the proud father of one daughter, Echo Raine, who blessed him with two very special grandchildren, Sierra Star and Skyler Seven. He's teaching his grandson about the Cheyenne way of life, which has so far included a sweat lodge and cloth ceremony. Upon graduating from high school, Skyler plans to attend college to earn a degree in a technological field.

Pete is currently retired, but stays busy co-writing the remaining volumes in *The Curse of Dead Horse Canyon* series as well as making and selling sweet grass braids, a sacred plant used in various ceremonies. The profits are shared with Skyler's college fund.

Regarding his experience with this story, he states, "My hope is for the reader to enjoy this book as much as I have enjoyed being the co-author. I write in the spirit of truth based on my spiritual life experiences as a spirit helper to medicine men in the ceremonial sweat lodge. Thank you, Isadore Whitewolf, Cliff Eaglefeathers and Ben Armentrout for your help and friendship."

Pete and his grandson, Skyler, with some of his sweet grass braids.

One of the greatest pieces of wisdom is to know what you do not know.
—John Kenneth Galbraith

ACKNOWLEDGEMENTS

No author can do it all on their own. Credit belongs to so many in the creation of this story, which has only begun. I could not have done so without the help, dedication, knowledge, and imagination of my coauthor, Pete Risingsun. His contribution to this story defies description. Rest assured the two of us are hard at work to complete this trilogy. Charlie and Sara's journey has only barely begun.

The books and media I accessed are too numerous to mention. Most of the quotes at the beginning of each chapter came from "Great Speeches by Native Americans" edited by Bob Blaisdell. I highly recommend it for a candid glimpse of Native American history.

A very special thank you to John Roam at the thedashcamstore.com for brainstorming with me about the capabilities of a dash cam. I'm grateful to my friend, C.C. Reilly, who shares my love and appreciation for Indigenous Americans. She provided vital facts unavailable anywhere else that she obtained from members of the Diné tribe in the Albuquerque area. My friend of many years, John Weintritt, was also key to innumerable elements in this book. His vast experience, intelligence, and insights were invaluable in more areas than I could begin to list.

My beta readers are jewels as well. Many thanks to Jeanne Foguth, Dawn Ireland, Maria Lenartowicz, Lisa Klaes, Scott Skipper, John Reinhard Dizon, and Pat Wardle for your outstanding help slogging through earlier versions of this story. Your input was invaluable for refining and bringing this story to life in the best possible way.

ABOUT ASTROLOGY

While Patrice Renard is a fictitious character, the astrology represented in this story is real. I swear I am not making this up. No one is more astounded than I am. The birthdates of the characters were made up and used with places close to the imaginary ones in the story. How the astrological influences on fictitious characters for the timeframe chosen for the story could tie in perfectly with the plot is beyond my comprehension.

In fact, at times when I wasn't sure what would happen next, all I had to do was refer to the astrological implications of that moment to figure it out. It just so happens I'm also a professional astrologer, so this was easily done. Ironically, this is one of the few times when my dual career with that of an author has been in my favor.

Many times I have been ridiculed and even ostracized as an author because of the prevailing prejudices in modern society against this ancient art. The most avid debunkers tend to hail from religious and scientific circles. Many years ago as a physicist I set out to disprove it myself. Pardon the cliché, but it's not exactly rocket science how that turned out.

If you think astrology is weird, study some of the speculations associated with quantum theory and entanglement which, to any rational person, are even farther out. I'm a physicist and I personally think the concept of parallel dimensions where we exist in all of them is ridiculous, regardless of what the math may say.

Another irony in this technological age is the renewed interest in energy healing and various other ancient techniques long practiced by medicine men and healers among indigenous people

417

worldwide. The Great Spirit is once again revealing them to those with an honest heart and open mind.

Also of interest in the context of this story is the fact that Indigenous Americans have a form of astrology associated with the Medicine Wheel. While it doesn't employ the predictive side like Western, Traditional, or Vedic astrology, it delves even deeper into the psyche and seeking inspiration as needed.

Rather than the familiar zodiac signs such as Aries, Taurus, Gemini, etc., the Medicine Wheel includes animal, plant, and mineral totems along with various other analogies, all closely associated with the seasons and nature. The moons associated with the Medicine Wheel line up exactly with those that define the zodiac signs of western astrology, their meaning essentially the same.

Coincidence?

There's still so much that we do not know.

P.S. One last thing: My mystic name is Whobeda. The quote at the beginning of this section (clearly relevant to Sara) is from my book, *"Whobeda's Guide to Basic Astrology."*